**Also available from
Lindsay McKenna
and Harlequin HQN**

Coming soon

LINDSAY McKENNA

THE LONER

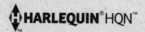

Recycling programs
for this product may
not exist in your area.

ISBN-13: 978-0-373-77772-3

THE LONER

Copyright © 2013 by Nauman Living Trust

This edition published by arrangement with Harlequin Books S.A.

For questions and comments about the quality of this book, please contact us at CustomerService@Harlequin.com.

Printed in U.S.A.

To all the service men and women
who have suffered PTSD during combat.
You are not alone. Nor are you forgotten.
There is help out there. Please know we honor your
courage. And thank you from the bottom of our hearts
for your service and sacrifice to our country.

And to the wonderful, warm and caring staff at
Hotel Opera Roma in Rome, Italy. This dedication was
well earned. Thank you. www.hoteloperaroma.com.

Dear Reader,

Having been in the U.S. Navy and having had Marine Corps friends in combat, I've seen what war does to a person. Post-traumatic stress disorder came into being in the 1980s. Before, it was simply "battle fatigue" or the "thousand-yard stare." Whatever it is/was called, the wounds our men and women in the military get from combat are real. War isn't always in a foreign country. Police, firefighters and EMT/paramedics can suffer from it. PTSD is a global phenomenon and can take decades, even a lifetime, to heal from, if ever.

In *The Loner,* I wanted to bring PTSD to the surface and deal with how it affects the hero, Dakota Carson. A person who has PTSD may well feel like a "loner." This can be overcome with help, love and understanding. When sheriff's deputy Shelby Kincaid meets Dakota, she is drawn powerfully to the angry loner. Shelby feels strongly that everyone should help Dakota instead of throwing him away. They soon realize they share a horribly tragic link, and this creates a meaningful connection between them—and unexpected danger. Can Dakota engage his SEAL-driven experience in order to save her?

Strap in for one hell of a ride.

Lindsay McKenna

CHAPTER ONE

DAKOTA CARSON SENSED danger. A fragile pink dawn lay like a silent ribbon along the eastern horizon. As he exhaled, white clouds congealed for a moment in front of him, telling him it was below freezing on this June first morning. Standing on a small rise at the edge of an oval meadow, he studied a football-field-long swath of willows that ran through the center.

His left arm ached in the cold, reminding him why he'd been discharged from the U.S. Navy and his SEAL team. He'd suffered permanent nerve damage during a firefight. Never mind the post-traumatic stress disorder he coped with 24/7. Now his hyperalertness was telling him something wasn't right. But what was wrong? Eyes narrowing, he scanned the quiet, early morning area. To his right rose the majestic Teton Mountains, their white peaks taking on a pinkish alpine glow.

It was quiet. Too quiet. He'd been a SEAL for ten years and at twenty-eight, he was no stranger to threatening situations. He knew one when he felt it. To his left, he saw a gray movement. It was Storm, a female wolf he'd rescued a year earlier. Thus far, she treated him like her alpha mate, but he was sure she wouldn't hang around as she matured. There was every possibility she'd leave him and join the Snake River wolf pack that ruled this valley in Wyoming. Storm was loping at the edge of the forest, ears twitching back and forth, nose in the air, picking up scents.

Yesterday Dakota had laid five rabbit traps out in these willows. It was one of many places he trapped in order to live outside society and the town of Jackson Hole. Since being released from the hospital and months of painful physical therapy to get his shoulder working, Dakota wanted to hide. He didn't look too closely at why, only that he had to heal up. Ten years spent in the SEALs had been the happiest time of his life, but deployment into Iraq and Afghanistan had taken their toll on his body and emotions.

Sniffing the air, he tried to locate the source of the threat. Grizzlies had their own odor. So did elk. No stranger to studying the land and vegetation, Dakota could spot things few others could. His sniper SEAL training had taught him stealth and tracking.

Storm had disappeared into the tree line again. The months of May and June were prime elk birthing season. It was also the same time when hungry grizzlies came out of hibernation, starving for anything to eat. Elk babies were the number-one food source on their menu. Storm always hunted her own meals. She was looking for smaller prey. One wolf could not take down a baby elk. A pack was needed, instead.

Dakota studied the willows, his hearing keyed, but he heard nothing. Had an elk mother calved a baby in there? What was he sensing? Just because he could sometimes feel a threat didn't mean he knew what the threat was. If a new elk calf was in there, a grizzly could be skulking around, out of his sight, trying to locate it. The bear could have picked up on the scent of the afterbirth before the mother could eat it and destroy the odor. The thick, naked willows reminded Dakota of a porcupine with its back up, the crochetedlike needles raised skyward. The problem was they grew so high and thick, he couldn't see through the grove. There was no movement. No sound.

The air was still. Nothing seemed to move, which was odd because dawn was the busiest time of the day for nocturnal and diurnal animals. The pink along the horizon deepened and the sky above lightened. Dakota could no longer see the myriad stars above his head; they were diluted, having disappeared in the dawn light. It would be a long time before the sun would rise, however. He heard a raven cawing somewhere off in the distance. Other than that, it was as if the earth herself were hold-ing her breath.

For what? He rubbed the back of his neck with his gloved hand, but his old shoulder injury pro-tested with the movement. After allowing his hand to drop to his side, Dakota shouldered a .300 Win Mag Winchester magnum rifle with a sling across his right shoulder. He'd been a sniper in the SEALs and had used this rifle to hunt down the bad guys. Out here in the wilds of Wyoming, where grizzly were the predator, Dakota never tracked or hunted anywhere without a big rifle. Grizzlies, especially this time of year, were hungry, irritable and mean. All they wanted was food and they'd kill anything and anyone to protect their carcass or find.

Dakota wasn't foolhardy. Patience was his best protection. A bear would move eventually, and the willows would tremble and wave back and forth. But if it was an elk calf?

Dakota waited on the rise. He was downwind, something he made sure of because he knew the grizzlies were hunting in earnest. Dakota didn't want his scent to inspire one of those bears to hunt him, thinking he was a posthibernation meal on two legs. His mouth pulled at one corner over that thought. He'd seen enough mayhem and killing.

After his discharge from the navy, his medi-cal issues as fixed as they were going to be, he'd located a cabin high in the Tetons on the Wyo-ming side of the mountains. He'd cleaned it up and started living in the ramshackle, abandoned structure. Never mind that it didn't have electricity or running water. He'd spent the past year in hiding and needed the solitude. There was so much grief and loss in him, he didn't know what to do with it or how to discharge it. Sleep was a luxury. He rarely got two or three broken hours of sleep at night. His heart sank as he considered all that he'd lost since he was seventeen years old and then more losses in the navy. Wounded in a field of fire deep in the Hindu Kush Mountains of Afghanistan, he found his life repeating the nightmare cycle of his teen years.

It's too much pain... Too damned much. Purposefully, Dakota lasered his attention on the willow stand. This was the present. When his mind wandered into the past, it was nothing but a mire of serrating grief, rage and helplessness. He didn't like feeling those turgid emotions. His stomach growled. It had been one day since he'd last eaten. The winter had leaned him down considerably, but he wasn't starving. Dakota set out enough traps to keep meat on his table, but a sudden, unexpected snowstorm yesterday had stopped him from walking his traplines and gathering up the rabbits he'd caught. A cutting, one-cornered smile creased his face. In Afghanistan, his SEAL team endured days without food, water or resupply. So twenty-four hours without food wasn't a tragedy.

He had the traps set up in those willows. Rabbits were plentiful in the wide valley through which the Snake River wound lazily. Had a starving grizzly already found his traps and gobbled up the rabbits? Was that the reason for the sense of danger he felt?

He had to take a chance. Shifting the Win Mag to his left shoulder, he looked down at the P226 SIG Sauer pistol strapped low on his right thigh. The two black Velcro straps around his thick leg held the pistol at just the right angle in case he needed to quickly reach for it. All SEALs were given this particular pistol after they graduated from BUD/S. The .40-caliber pistol was specially made in Germany for them. And it had stopping power. One slug would take a human's life.

The wind had piled up the blizzard snow. Patches of long yellow grass peeked out here and there. As he walked, the grass in the meadow crunched beneath his boots. Each yellowed blade of grass was coated with thick frost. With each step, Dakota tried to stay as silent as possible. The sound could possibly alert the elk mother hidden in the willows. He moved down the gentle slope toward the center of the meadow. Dakota knew from experience an elk mother would defend her calf with her life. And an elk weighed a good thousand pounds, its hooves sharp and dangerous.

Dakota brushed the butt of his SIG Sauer with the palm of his gloved hand. It was an unconscious habit honed in the badlands of the Middle East. He'd unsnapped the retention strap across the pistol so that if he had to reach for it, his palm could fit swiftly around the butt and his fingers could wrap around the trigger. He could draw it up in a single, fluid motion in order to protect himself. He had no wish to shoot an elk. His meat needs were far less than that.

Slowing, the light increasing, Dakota inhaled the scents on the frosty air, his nostrils flaring. He halted and searched for tracks. Some of the grass was clean, shaken free of the frost and snow, about twenty feet south of where he stood. It had to have happened earlier this morning. Craning his neck, Dakota evaluated them. Big print? Little print? Something in between? He had keen eyesight, honed by years of hunting as a teen and, later, as a SEAL. The tracks appeared to be that of an elk.

Dakota stood, debating whether to enter the willows or not. He was used to being afraid but didn't let that rule him or blot out his logical thinking processes. As Dakota turned his head, he could see Storm was trotting the other way along the tree line above him. Her long pink tongue lolled out of the side of her mouth, her gray body blending in to the surrounding shadows. He stared back hard at the willows in front of him. He'd placed the rabbit traps deep within them. Rabbits weren't stupid; they were not going to hop around on the outer perimeter of the willows. Something would quickly spot them from air or ground and they'd be dead in a heartbeat. No, they lived deep within the willows and could thrive.

Just as Dakota took a step forward, the willows exploded in front of him. A cinnamon-colored male grizzly bear roared and crashed through them and launched himself at him. The roaring vibration ripped through him. Dakota took half a step back, seeing the bear's small dark eyes filled with rage. In an instant, Dakota knew the grizzly had been in the willows all along. He'd probably eaten all the rabbits he'd trapped and was snoozing until he heard Dakota approach the stand. Startled and provoked, the bear charged him. The attack was so swift, all Dakota saw was the grizzly's thick rust-colored body hurtling toward him at the speed of a bullet.

Dakota's shock collided with his survival training. It would take too long to pull the rifle off his shoulder and fire off a shot. Without hesitation, as the bear flew toward him like a flying tank, his hand moved smoothly in an unbroken motion for the SIG Sauer on his right thigh.

The bear's spittle, his roar, surrounded Dakota. As he lifted the pistol, he shifted his weight to the right to try to stop the grizzly from fully striking him. If he hadn't moved in a feintlike maneuver, the bear would have slammed him flat on his back, leaned down and ripped his throat out with those bared yellow fangs. At the same moment, Dakota saw the female wolf come out of nowhere. Storm snarled and flung herself directly at the grizzly, her jaws opened, aiming for his sensitive nose. In her own way, Storm was trying to protect him. The valiant wolf was a mere forty pounds against a thousand pounds of angry bruin.

Everything slowed in his line of vision. Whenever Dakota was in danger of losing his life, the frames of reality intensified and then crawled by with excruciating slowness. The grizzly saw him shift, but Storm latched onto the bear's nose. The grizzly roared, swiping at her. The wolf yelped and was flung high into the air. The grizzly tried to make a midcourse correction. As he raised his massive paw, the five curved claws flexed outward, the blow struck Dakota full force.

The SIG Sauer bucked in his hand. Dakota held his intense focus, aiming for the bear's thick, massive skull. The grizzly roared with fury as the first two bullets struck his skull. They ricocheted off! Dakota felt the grizzly's paw strike his left arm. Pain reared up his arm and jammed into his already torn-up shoulder. He grunted as he was struck and tossed up in the air like a puppet. The massive power of a pissed-off thousand-pound grizzly was stunning.

As Dakota tumbled end over end, all of his SEAL training came back by reflex. He landed and rolled, the cold glittering frost exploding around him on impact. He leaped to his feet. The bear roared, landed on all fours, whipped around with amazing agility and charged him again. Only ten feet separated them.

Dakota cooly stood, legs slightly apart for best balance, hands wrapped solidly around the butt of the SIG Sauer. This was not a bear gun, but if he aimed well, he'd strike the charging grizzly in one of his eyes and kill him before he was killed himself. His breath exploded from him as the bear leaped upward, its jaws open, lips peeled away from his dark pink gums to reveal the massive, murderous fangs. Dakota fired three more shots and saw the third one strike into the right eye of the bear.

Too late!

As he threw up his left arm and spun to avoid the grizzly pouncing on him, the bear's massive teeth sank violently into his forearm. There was instant, red-hot pain. The bear grunted, fell downward. Dakota was flipped over and dragged down with the bear, his arm still locked in the animal's massive mouth.

The grizzly landed with a thud, groaning heavily as it sank into the yellow grass. Dakota wrested his forearm out of the bear's teeth. Breathing hard, he staggered to his feet. There were fifteen cartridges in a SIG Sauer.

He held it ready and stumbled backward, stunned

by the ferocity of the attack. He watched the bear breathe once, twice and then slump with a growl, dead.

Dakota gasped for breath, felt the warmth of his own blood trickling down into his left glove. Would the bear move? No, he could see the eye socket blown away by his pistol, the bullet in the animal's brain. The grizzly was dead. Wiping his mouth, Dakota looked around, his breath exploding in ragged gasps into the freezing air. His heart hammered wildly in his chest. The adrenaline kept him tense and he was feeling no pain.

Once he was finally convinced the grizzly wasn't going to get back up and come after him a third time, he created distance between him and the beast. He saw Storm come trotting up to him. She whined, her yellow eyes probing his. She was panting heavily. Dakota looked her over to make sure the grizzly hadn't hurt his wolf. There were some mild scratch marks across her left flank, but that was all.

"We're okay," he rasped to the wolf.

Dakota holstered the pistol and drew up his left arm. He always wore thick cammies. The bear's fangs had easily punctured the heavy canvas material, sunk through the thick green sweater he wore beneath it and chewed up his flesh. There was no pain—yet. But there sure as hell was gonna be.

He sat down and jerked off his gloves. There was

a lot of blood and, chances were, the grizzly had sliced into a major artery in his left arm. He went into combat medic mode, one of his SEAL specialties. This meant he never left on a hunt without his H-gear, a harness he wore around his waist that had fifteen canvas pockets. Dakota jerked open his camo jacket. His hand shook as he dug into one pocket, which contained a tourniquet. Quickly, he slipped the tourniquet just below his elbow and jerked it tight. Pain reared up his upper arm, but the bleeding slowed a lot at the bite site. Tying it off, Dakota dug in another pocket, which contained a roll of duct tape. From another, he pulled out a pair of surgical scissors, sharper than hell. He straightened out his right leg out in front of him, then dug into the deep cargo pocket above his knee. In there, he grabbed a battle dressing.

He had to get to the hospital in Jackson Hole. *Sooner. Not later.* Dakota hated going into town. Hated being around people, but this grizzly had chewed up a helluva lot of his arm in one bite. He quickly placed the battle dressing across the wound, then wrapped it firmly with duct tape. Not exactly medically sound, but duct tape saved many a SEAL from more injury or bleeding to death over the years. After cutting the duct tape with the scissors, Dakota jammed all of the items back into his H-gear.

He was in shock. Familiar with these symptoms, Dakota picked up his rifle and signaled Storm to follow. She instantly leaped to her feet and loped to his side. Looking up, the sky lightening even more, Dakota knew he had a one-mile trek back to where his pickup was parked. Mouth thinning, he shouldered the rifle and moved swiftly through the thick grass. When the adrenaline wore off, he'd be in terrible pain. The shock would make him drive poorly and he could make some very bad decisions behind the wheel. It was a race of ten miles between here and the hospital to get emergency room help.

Cursing softly, he began to trot. It was a labored stride, the grass slick with frost, but he pushed himself. His breath came out in explosive jets, and he drew in as much air as he could into his lungs. Anchoring his wounded arm against his torso, he moved quickly up the slope and onto a flat plain.

Dakota could feel the continued loss of blood. Arteries, when sliced, usually closed up on their own within two minutes of being severed. However, the only time they wouldn't was when they weren't sliced at an angle. Then he knew he was in deep shit. A major artery could bleed out in two to three minutes. His heart would cavitate, like the pump it was, and then he'd die of cardiac arrest. Fortunately, the tourniquet was doing its job. It bought him time, but not much.

As he lumbered steadily toward the parking lot at the end of a dirt road in the Tetons, he thought it would be a fitting end if he did bleed out and die here. Some poor tourist hiker would find what was left of his body days or even weeks from now. The grizzlies in the area or the Snake River wolf pack might find him first. The shocked hiker would find only bones, no skin or flesh left on his sorry-assed carcass.

Mind spinning, Dakota continued to slip and slide through grass and drifts of knee-deep snow. Soon, the sun would bridge the horizon. It was a beautiful day, the sky a pale blue and cloudless, unlike yesterday. The snow from the blizzard was knee-deep in places. Several times, Dakota stumbled, fell, rolled and forced himself back up to his feet. As he ran, he discovered something: he wanted to *live.*

Why now? his soggy brain screamed. *All you wanted to do before was crawl away like a hurt animal into the mountains, disappear from civilization and live out the rest of your life. Why now?*

Dakota had no answer. He'd hidden for a year. And he'd healed up to a point. He wanted nothing to do with people because they couldn't understand what he'd been through. No one would get that that was a life sentence—to spend the rest of his days on the fringes of society.

His heart pumped hard in his chest. Ahead, he could see his beat-up green-and-white rusted Ford truck. *Only a little bit farther to go.* Gasps tore out of his mouth, his eyes narrowing on the truck. With no idea where this sudden, surprising will to live came from, Dakota reached his truck. Storm halted, ready to jump in. He staggered, caught himself and then jerked the driver's door open. The wolf was used to riding with him since he'd found her as a pup.

Dizziness assailed Dakota as Storm jumped in. He shook off the need to collapse, and glanced down at his arm. The battle dressing was a bright red, blood dripping down his hand and off his curved fingers. The cold was numbing, so he felt nothing, not even the warmth of his own blood. Struggling, he climbed into the truck. Dakota knew it would be a race to reach the hospital in time. The tourniquet stood between him and death right now. That gave him relief as he put the truck into gear and drove slowly down the wet, muddy road.

Storm whined. She thumped her tail once, catching Dakota's darkened eyes.

"It will be all right," he growled, wrestling the truck around, pain now pulsing rhythmically through his bite site.

But would it? Wasn't that what he always told his SEAL friends who were shot and bleeding out? Sure to die, no matter what he did to try to stop the bleeding? *It will be all right. Sure.* Dakota jammed all those terrifying moments from the past out of his thoughts. He had to concentrate. He had to reach the emergency room of the hospital or die trying....

CHAPTER TWO

SHERIFF'S DEPUTY SHELBY Kincaid was walking toward the emergency room entrance to the Jackson Hole Hospital. She had paperwork on a prisoner that had to be updated by Dr. Jordana McPherson. The cool morning air made her glad she had her brown nylon jacket, although her blond hair lay abandoned around her shoulders. Something unusual caught her eye. Slowing, Shelby hesitated near the E.R. entrance. Was the guy pulling into the parking lot drunk? It was only 6:00 a.m., but she knew from plenty of experience that drunk drivers didn't care what time it was.

The rusted-out Ford pickup crawled to a stop across two empty parking lanes. Shelby frowned and watched as the driver's-side door creaked open with protest. She was less than a hundred feet away from the truck. The driver soon emerged. She didn't recognize him as a local. He wore a two-day beard on his face. Something was wrong. Maybe it was her sixth sense, but Shelby stuffed the papers into the pocket of her jacket and quickly walked toward the man.

She spotted a gray dog in the front seat but kept her focus on the man in camo gear. He was tall, broad-shouldered and reminded her of a hunter she'd see in the fall around Jackson Hole. But this was spring and no hunting was allowed. This man was clearly in pain. His hair was black and military short, face square with high cheekbones. She'd never seen this dude before and she felt a sudden urgency that he was in trouble. The stride of her walk accelerated.

As he lurched drunkenly out of the seat, his large hand caught the edge of the door or he'd have fallen out. It was then Shelby noticed the strapped pistol on his right thigh. She tensed inwardly. Her blue eyes widened for a moment as he spun around, losing his grip on the door, barely able to keep his feet beneath him. That was when she saw his bloody arm pressed against his torso.

As she approached the truck, the dog whined. It was a sound of worry.

"Can I help you?" she called out. "I'm Deputy Kincaid."

The man bent over, as if willing himself not to fall down. A dark red trail of blood ran down his left pant leg. He'd obviously lost a lot of blood. Automatically, she pressed the radio on the epaulet of her jacket located on her left shoulder.

"Annie, this is Shelby Kincaid. I'm out here I the parking lot of your E.R. Kindly get me a gurney and two orderlies? I've got a man out here a hundred feet from your door with an arm wound. He's lost a lot of blood." She clicked off the radio just as he raised his head toward her.

For a moment, Shelby felt her heart plunge. His face was drawn in pain, his lips thinned, the corners of his mouth drawn in, his pain evident. There was nothing tame about this guy. He was well built, powerful, yet the look in his light gold-brown eyes was marred with vulnerability. As he tried to straighten his left arm, he managed to rasp through gritted teeth, "Get me to the E.R."

THE WOMAN REACHED OUT, her hand wrapping quickly around his right arm. "Lean on me," she told him. "I've called for help and they're on the way. I won't let you fall."

The world began to gray out around Dakota as the tall, statuesque blonde in a sheriff's deputy uniform firmly gripped his upper arm. He was surprised at the cool authority in her unruffled voice, the strength of her hand around his arm. She looked like a Barbie doll, one who easily brought him into a standing position and guided his arm across her shoulders. For a Barbie doll, she was in damn good shape.

"Bullet wound?" she asked, taking his full weight.

"Bear bite," he managed to rasp out, closing his eyes. "I'm going to faint. Too much blood loss…"

Instantly, Shelby placed her feet apart for better balance. She felt him go limp. *Damn!* She might be five foot eleven, but this guy was taller and bigger than she was. Glancing upward, she saw the gurney flying toward them with two men in green scrubs pushing it as fast as it would go.

Within moments, the two young men arrived. Together, the three of them wrestled the unconscious hunter up and on the gurney.

"Get him inside," Shelby ordered, her voice tight with tension. She trotted at his side as the orderlies pushed the gurney full speed toward the doors. Gripping his good shoulder, Shelby didn't want him to be knocked off while the gurney slipped and slid on the ice and snow across the asphalt. She glanced down at him. In that moment, the hunter looked vulnerable. But just barely. The duct tape around his bleeding left arm made her frown. *Duct tape?* Helluva way to stop a wound from bleeding out. Who was this guy?

Inside, Shelby spotted Dr. Jordana McPherson, head of E.R., running to meet them as they came inside the warm entrance.

"Shelby?" Jordana called, running up.

"Hunter, I guess. Said he was attacked by a bear

and had lost a lot of blood," she told the doctor. She stepped aside as they pushed the gurney into a blue-curtained cubicle. Shelby watched as Jordana quickly took a pair of scissors and cut through the silver duct tape on the hunter's bloodied left arm.

"Okay, good to know. Who is he? Do we have any identification on him?"

Instantly, two other nurses appeared in the cubicle to help the doctor. They locked the wheels on the gurney.

Shelby moved next to the hunter. His face looked like chalk beneath his dark stubble. She sensed danger around this man for no specific reason. Quickly patting down his camo pants, she felt something in the right pocket on his thigh. She slid her fingers down into the deep pocket.

"God, he has everything in here but the kitchen sink," she muttered, pulling articles out and laying them beside him. Finally, she discovered a wallet and stepped back as the nurses covered him with a blanket and started an IV.

She opened up the wallet. "His name is Dakota Carson." Shelby looked over at Jordana. "Ring any bells, Doc?"

"Yes," Jordana said, pulling the entire duct tape assembly away from his arm. Wrinkling her nose, she said, "I thought I recognized him. He's an ex-SEAL, just got a medical discharge from the U.S. Navy. I saw him once, a month ago. He was supposed to come here for follow-up physical therapy on his left shoulder."

Nodding, Shelby placed the wallet on a tray where the nurse had placed all the other items. "Never seen him before."

"Mr. Carson is a loner." Jordana's mouth tightened as she surveyed his chewed-up lower arm. "This bear has done some major damage to him...." Jordana looked to her red-haired nurse. "Alanna, get me an O.R. ready. And call in the ortho surgeon, Dr. Jamison. Get me his blood type." Taking out her stethoscope, she pulled back the camo jacket and placed it over his heart.

Shelby felt the urgency and saw it in Jordana's face. She'd come to like the E.R. doctor who was good at what she did. "How bad?"

"Bad," she muttered, throwing the stethoscope around her neck. "He's right, he's lost a lot of blood."

Just then, Dakota's eyes slowly opened. "He's coming around," Shelby warned the E.R. doc.

"Amazing."

Shelby placed her hand gently on his right shoulder. "Mr. Carson? You're here in the E.R. at the hospital. You're in good hands." She looked into his murky-looking brown eyes, which were full of confusion. He opened his mouth to speak, but only a groan issued forth. Shelby tightened her hand on his shoulder. The man was in incredible shape. *A former Navy SEAL.* She knew enough about SEALs to understand he was a warrior, the toughest of the tough. His eyes wandered for a moment, but then they stopped and focused on Shelby.

Sucking in a breath, Shelby felt the full measure of his intense gaze. Those eyes were hunter's eyes. Huge black pupils on a field of golden-brown color. Surprise flared in his expression, and then, something else she couldn't interpret.

She gave him a slight smile. "You're in good hands. Dr. McPherson is here. You're going to be all right."

Jordana came around and Shelby released him and stood aside.

"Mr. Carson, I'm Dr. McPherson. Can you hear me?"

Dakota managed a sloppy grin, only half his mouth working because of the surging pain. "Yeah, Doc. I remember you. I missed a bunch of appointments. I'm blood type A. I'm gonna need transfusions. Bear cut an artery in my left arm…."

"That's what I needed to hear," Jordana said quietly, patting his shoulder in a motherly way. "I'm leaving the tourniquet in place until we can get you into surgery and stabilized." She lifted her head, called to the second nurse, "Joy, get me two pints of type A ready in the O.R."

"Right away, Doctor."

"You're gonna need one and a half pints to put in

what I've lost," he grunted. His gaze moved from the worried-looking doctor to the woman standing behind her. *Barbie Doll.* Damn, but she was beautiful with her sandy-blond hair falling around her shoulders. Her blue eyes were wide and curious. What didn't make any sense was her sheriff's uniform, all dark brown slacks that hid her long legs and a nylon jacket showing her name and badge on it. Shelby Kincaid. Funny, for a moment, he thought he recognized her. But from where? His mind wouldn't work. He memorized her name.

"We'll see," Jordana said. "You're going to need more than stitches on that bear bite, Dakota."

He smiled a little as the nurse came and stuck a syringe of morphine into the IV tube to drip into his vein. "I figured as much. Just wanted to make it here so you could work your magic, Doc."

Patting his arm, Jordana said, "I'll see you in a few minutes, Dakota. I've got to go scrub up."

Dakota felt the pressure of the nurse putting a clean dressing on his wound. At first, it hurt like hell, but then, as the morphine began to flow through his veins, the pain eased considerably. All the time, he held the gaze of the beautiful deputy sheriff standing nearby. Who was she? Looking at her oval face, those blue eyes that reminded him of the turquoise beaches of Costa Rica, that set of full lips, he just didn't think she fit the image of a

deputy sheriff. There was concern in her eyes—
for him.

"Mr. Carson," Shelby said, keeping her voice
low as she approached him, "who do you want me
to notify? Your wife? Parents? Someone needs to
be contacted. I can let them know." Automatically,
Shelby reached out, her fingers resting gently on his
broad shoulder. This time, the muscles beneath her
fingertips responded. An unexpected heat surged
through her. Shocked, Shelby tried to ignore her reaction. This man was half dead from loss of blood,
yet the warrior energy around him beckoned to
some primal part of herself.

Dakota tried to focus. The Barbie doll sheriff's
deputy had a nice, husky voice. It felt like warm
honey drizzled across him, easing his pain even
more. Her face was inches from his. Her blond
hair had darker strands mingled with lighter ones.
Some reminded him of gold sunlight, others, of
dark honey. His gaze drifted back to her eyes. God,
what beautiful eyes she had. He could dive into
them and feel her heart beating. Wildly aware of
her long fingers against his shoulder, he muttered,
"I've got a wolf out in my truck. Her name is Storm.
She's bonded to me. Don't take her to a dog pound.
Keep her…keep her with you… I'll get out of surgery and take her home with me, please.…"

He wasn't making sense, but Shelby knew the
nurse had given him a dose of morphine to stop

the pain. People said funny things when drifting in a morphine cloud. His focus began to fade. "Mr. Carson, who can I call? I need to tell your family where you are."

The husky urgency in her voice felt like a warm, sensual blanket. Dakota was feeling no pain now, thank God. Instead, he could focus on this incredibly arresting woman, her face so close he could rise, capture that sinner's mouth of hers and make it his own. She looked familiar. But from where? A broken laugh rumbled out of his chest. "I have no one, Barbie. Just me and my wolf. And she doesn't answer my cell phone."

"Where do you live? I can take your wolf back to your home," Shelby asked, trying to remain cool and professional. Again, she saw that devil-may-care grin cut across his tense, chiseled face. He was darkly tanned for this time of year, which told her this ex-SEAL was outside a helluva lot. She didn't want to admit how much she liked touching this man. And she saw something else in his lion-gold eyes—desire. It was the morphine, she was sure.

"You'll never find it. No address. Just a shack in the woods. Just keep my wolf with you." He struggled to sit up. "This repair on my arm isn't gonna take long. If you can take care of her until I get released, I'll appreciate it."

Hearing the sudden, emotional urgency in his gruff tone, Shelby straightened. She gently pushed him back down on the gurney. The pleading expression on his face startled her. In that moment, Dakota Carson looked like a scared little boy watching his world self-destruct. There was something magical, a heated connection, burning between them. "Yes, I'll take care of her for you, Mr. Carson."

Instantly, the man seemed to relax, a ragged sigh escaping from his tightened lips. He closed his eyes. What she didn't expect was his right hand to reach out and grab hers. She felt the strength of his fingers as they wrapped around her wrist.

"Th-thank you...." he rasped.

His fingers loosened and fell open. The nurse had put another syringe into the IV, the drug rendering him unconscious in preparation for surgery. Shelby gently picked up his arm hanging over the gurney and placed it at his side.

"He's out," Alanna told her.

"Good. How long will the surgery be, you think?"

Shrugging, Alanna motioned for the two orderlies to come in and transport the patient to the E.R. "I don't know, Shelby. Maybe an hour if all goes well. Could be nerve damage. We'll see...."

"Okay, I'll drop back in an hour. I've got some paperwork for the heard nurse to fill out at the nurses' station before I leave."

"Great. Want me to call you on the radio when Mr. Carson comes out of E.R?"

"Yes, could you?"

Alanna nodded and smiled. "Can do."

Shelby watched the two orderlies wheel the unconscious ex-SEAL off to surgery. Standing there for a moment, she digested all the unsettled emotions the stranger had stirred up in her. He was dangerous, risky to her heart. Frowning, Shelby shook her head. She looked down at the blood smeared across her jacket. *His blood.*

This was the first time she'd seen a bear-attack victim, and it wasn't pretty. Her fingers still tingled when he'd suddenly reached out and gripped her. Strong fingers, but he monitored the strength of his grip around her wrist, she realized, even in a morphine state. Definitely a special kind of soldier.

She knew little about SEALs. They were black ops. Secret. Defenders of this country. And heroes in her opinion. The look in his eyes guaranteed all of that. The man had shaken her, but not in a bad way, just an unexpected way. He'd somehow gotten to her womanly core. She'd been responding to him man-to-woman. Blowing out a breath of air in frustration, Shelby turned on her booted heel and forced herself to get the paperwork finished. First things first. She'd leave the papers with the nurses' desk and then go out and make sure the gray wolf was all right.

As Shelby approached the desk, an older nurse

with steel-gray hair beckoned to her. Shelby recognized nurse Patty Fielding.

"Hey, Shelby, do you know about that guy?" Patty whispered, coming up to her at the desk.

"No. Why?" Shelby handed her the papers that needed to be filled out.

"He's known as The Loner around here. He got here a year ago and was supposed to see Dr. McPherson about his shoulder injury once a week. He never came back for subsequent appointments after the first one."

Shelby's heart went out to Dakota Carson. "He's a military vet," she whispered, feeling sorry for him.

"Oh, honey," Patty said, taking the papers, "he's also a SEAL. Those guys rock in my world. They're on the front lines around the world fighting for us. They're in harm's way every time they take a mission." Patty shook her head. "Such a shame. He's an incredibly valiant vet. He's got a lot of problems, physical and mental."

"And was he seeing Dr. McPherson for his arm injury?"

"Technically, yes, for nerve damage. But she's our PTSD expert here at the hospital, too."

Standing there, Shelby asked, "Is that why he lives alone? Out in the middle of nowhere?" She recalled the Vietnam vets who had PTSD. At that time, it wasn't diagnosed except to call it "battle fatigue."

Patty filled out the forms and signed them with a flourish. "Yes, and those guys got no help at all. It broke my heart. Oh, and no address on Mr. Carson."

"What about family?"

Patty sighed and said, "His parents died in a crash when he was eighteen. Froze to death during the blizzard. They found their car two days later and it was too late."

Shelby's heart plummeted. "That's so sad."

"Yeah, this guy has had a very rough life. You don't know the half of it." Patty smiled and handed her the papers. "Gotta go!"

"I'll be back in an hour."

"Take care of that wolf of his," she said, lifting her hand in farewell. "She's a sweet girl."

Shelby smiled a little and thanked the nurse for the information. As she headed out the doors of the E.R., the sun just crested the eastern horizon. What was it about this ex-SEAL that grabbed her heart? Grabbed all of her attention? Somehow the name Carson was one she knew. Stymied, Shelby walked carefully over the slick areas of black ice and circumvented the patches of snow. Out in the parking lot, she could see Carson's beat-up truck. It looked a lot like him, Shelby thought sadly. There was something in his eyes that shouted incredible loss. Loss of what?

CHAPTER THREE

SHELBY HAD THE FEMALE gray wolf and she rode quietly in the backseat of her Tahoe cruiser. She just dropped off the papers to the courthouse when she received a call from Alanna.

Picking up the radio, Shelby continued to drive slowly through Jackson Hole traffic, on her way out to the hospital. The hour was almost up. "Go ahead, Alanna," she said.

"Shelby, Dr. McPherson said for you to drop by at 9:00 a.m. Can you do it?"

"Sure," she said, glancing at the clock on the dashboard. "I thought I was supposed to come back in about twenty minutes."

"No, Dr. McPherson said the surgery on Mr. Carson's arm is going to be longer than she anticipated."

"Roger that."

"Thanks, out."

Placing the radio back in the bracket, Shelby grimaced. If the surgery was taking longer, it meant Dakota Carson's bear bite was a lot worse than anyone had thought. Her shift ended shortly, but she'd told the commander at the sheriff's office what had happened. Steve McCall was humored to see a gray wolf in the backseat of her cruiser. Lucky for her, Steve, who had been her father's replacement as Tetons County sheriff, accepted her sometimes quirky days. But all deputies had unusual days every once in a while.

As she drove, Shelby couldn't shake the intense look in Dakota Carson's eyes. What was his story? She had more questions than answers. Maybe, if she got lucky, she'd intersect with Jordana and find out. As the head of E.R. for the hospital, Jordana McPherson knew just about everything and everyone. Another good source was Gwen Garner, who owned the quilt shop on the plaza.

A call came in, an accident on a side street, and Shelby figured she had time to take the call before showing up at the hospital. Even though she was focused on the accident, her heart was centered on the mystery of Dakota Carson. What the hell was he doing out at dawn killing a grizzly bear? That was against the law. And the Tetons National Park ranger supervisor, Charley, wasn't going to be happy about it, either. The ex-SEAL was in deep trouble whether he knew it or not.

DAKOTA CARSON WAS IN recovery when he slowly came out from beneath the anesthesia. As he opened his eyes, he saw two women standing side by side. Dr. McPherson smiled a silent hello. But his gaze lingered on the sheriff's deputy. In his hazy in-between state, Dakota was mesmerized by the strands of bright color in her hair.

"Dakota? Good news," Jordana said. "We were able to fix your arm." Her lips twitched. "And it's got a nice, new dressing on it without the duct tape."

Dakota liked and trusted the woman doctor. One corner of his mouth hitched upward. "Good to hear, Doc. Thanks for patching me up."

"Do me a favor? Move your fingers on your left hand for me. One at a time."

He moved them. "All five work," he said, feeling woozy and slightly nauseated. Carson knew it was the anesthesia. The nausea would pass.

Jordana slid her hand beneath his. She gently turned his heavily bandaged arm over so that his palm faced up. "Do you feel this?" She pricked each of his fingers with a slender instrument, including his thumb.

"Yeah, it hurts like hell. They're all responding," he assured her.

"Good," Jordana said, moving his arm so that it rested naturally at his side.

Dakota looked around. "When can I leave?"

"You need to spend the night here, Dakota."

"No way," he grunted, trying to sit up. Head spinning, he flopped back down on the pillow. The deputy was frowning, but even then she looked beautiful. She no longer wore her big, puffy brown nylon jacket. It hung over her left arm. Shelby was tall, maybe a few inches shorter than he was. Her shoulders were drawn back with natural pride. The look in her blue eyes, however, was one of somber seriousness. He had a feeling she wanted to question him about the dead grizzly. There would be hell to pay for killing a bear out of season.

"Way," Jordana said, placing her hand on his white-gowned shoulder. "You're still in shock, Dakota. You know what that does to a person? You're no stranger to it."

He scowled. Dr. McPherson was a PTSD expert. When he'd come back to Jackson Hole, the navy had ordered him to see her once a week for his symptoms. Of course, he saw her only once. He looked up at the physician. "Doc, I just want the hell out of here. You know why. Just sign me out, okay? I'll be fine."

Jordana patted his shoulder. "I can't do it, Dakota. You're a combat medic. Would you let your wounded SEAL buddy who had your injury and experience walk out of here?"

Dakota grunted. "SEALs suffer a lot worse out in the field, Doc. We're used to pain. Suffering is optional. You know that." He pinned her with a challenging glare.

Shelby was startled by the acerbic exchange.

Carson didn't seem to like anyone. But he was in pain and coming out from beneath anesthesia. Both could make a person feisty.

Jordana glanced over at Shelby. "You have a spare bedroom?"

Shelby blinked. "Why…yes." What was the doctor up to? She felt suddenly uneasy.

"You have Dakota's wolf with you?"

"She's out in my cruiser and doing fine." Shelby frowned and dug into Jordana's gaze, confused.

"I've got a deal for you, Dakota," Jordana said, her voice suddenly firm and brooking no argument. "If Deputy Kincaid will consent to drive you to her house, which isn't far from the hospital, and let you stay overnight, I'll release you. I know how you hate hospitals and closed-in spaces. Deal?"

The look of shock on Barbie doll's face told Dakota she wasn't prepared to have him as a visitor. "No way, Doc. As soon as I'm able to wear off this damned anesthesia, I'm outta here and you know it whether you sign a release on me or not."

Jordana's beeper went off. She pulled it out of her white coat pocket. Frowning, she said, "I've got to go." Looking over at Shelby, she said, "Talk some sense into him, will you? Because I refuse to sign him out of here unless he goes home with you."

Surprised, Shelby found herself alone with a man who exuded danger to her heart. His face was washed out, but now there was a flush in his cheeks, at least. "Mr. Carson, are you staying in this hospital?"

Dakota studied her beneath his spiky lashes. He felt and heard the authority in her tone. She wore no makeup, but God, she didn't have to. He liked what he saw way too much. He'd been without a woman for too long. And she had a great body beneath that uniform.

"How's my wolf?" he demanded, ignoring her question.

"Storm is fine. I gave her a bowl of water just before I came in here." Shelby met his belligerent glare. "Are you in pain?"

"No more than usual."

"I see."

"You don't, but that's all right."

Testy bastard, she thought. "Look, I need some answers on why you killed that grizzly this morning."

Okay, she was going to play tough. "Because it charged me," he growled. "I know it's illegal to shoot a bear in a national park, Deputy Barbie Doll." He really didn't dislike her, but his mood was blacker than hell. The drugs were loosening his normally reined-in irritability.

"My name is Shelby Kincaid."

He smiled a little. It was a tight, one-cornered smile. Did Dakota dare tell her she was a feast for his hungry gaze? The anesthesia was wearing off fast now, and he felt some returning strength. "Okay, Deputy Kincaid. I was out to pick up my trapline in a stand of willows when the bear came out of nowhere and charged me." He stared up at her. "What was I supposed to do? Let the bastard kill me because it was out of season?"

Her mouth twitched. "No," she said. Pulling a small notebook from her pocket, she wrote down his explanation. "Why are you out trapping animals?"

"Because I choose to. That's not against the law."

"No, it's not. Where do you live? I need an address."

"Third mountain to the north in the Tetons. Where I live, there is no address."

"Try me. I was raised here. I think I know just about every dirt road in this county."

"Do you know how beautiful you are when you're pissed?"

Shelby leaked a grin. This ex-SEAL took no prisoners. Neither did she. "Thanks, but let's stick to the investigation?"

Shrugging, Dakota actually found himself enjoying her spirited conversation. In some ways, Shelby reminded him of his late sister, Ellie. Both had a lot of spunk and spirit. A sudden sadness descended upon him and he scowled. "The bear charged me. I shot the bear. End of story." Her blue eyes narrowed. Still, he savored her husky voice. It reminded him of honey, sweet and dark. He looked at her left hand. No wedding ring. He assumed she was in a relationship. A woman this damned good-looking would have men hanging around her.

"Tell me where you live."

Dakota sighed. "I'll give you GPS coordinates if you know how to use them. It's on a no-name dirt road. It doesn't even have a forest service designation number to it."

"Which mountain?"

"Mount Owen," he growled. "Now do you know where it's at?"

Shelby stood her ground with the ex-SEAL. She reminded herself that he was still coming out of shock and surgery. "I do. When I was a teen, I was up tracking in that area many times with my dad."

"Tracking?" Dakota certainly didn't expect that answer. He was a damned good SEAL tracker. He'd spent years tracking Taliban and al Qaeda in the Hindu Kush Mountains.

"Why so surprised?" Shelby grinned at him. If Dakota wasn't so testy and sour, she'd like his company. If he didn't have that two-day growth of beard, he'd be a cover model for *GQ*. He was in top, athletic shape and she liked the way his thickly corded neck and shoulders moved.

"Tracking isn't exactly what I expected to hear coming out of your mouth."

"Surprises abound, Mr. Carson. There's an old

miner's shack up at eight thousand feet on a narrow dirt road. It was pretty well in ruin the last time I was in that area. There's an old sluice box next to the creek. That shack sits about fifteen feet from the creek. At one time, gold was found in the Tetons, but the miners exhausted it." She studied him. "Now, is that the cabin where you live?"

Amazed, he simply uttered, "Yeah, that's it." How the hell did Deputy Barbie Doll figure out his hiding place? Dakota found himself readjusting his attitude. There was more to her than he thought. And it triggered a curiosity in him he rarely felt. Most women he'd been with in the far past were interested in getting married, having kids and settling down. As a SEAL, he was in a two-year cycle, with six months of it being deployed into the badlands of Afghanistan. It didn't leave much time to cultivate an honest-to-God relationship with a woman, which was why all of his entanglements crashed and burned.

"So, you were heading for your trapline when the bear charged you?"

"Yes, it's that simple."

"Do you have a phone?"

He managed a sour laugh. "Up there? You know there's no phone or electric lines up to that shack." Dakota saw her face go dark for a moment. She obviously didn't like being reminded about the obvious.

"Cell phone," Shelby amended in a firm tone. What was it about this guy? He was positively bristling and his hackles rose in a heartbeat. It was like flipping a switch off and on with him. Yet when his mouth relaxed and his eyes lost that glitter of defensiveness, she saw another man beneath that grouchy exterior. She liked that man and found herself wanting to know him better. Much better.

"Yeah," he muttered. "I got one." He gave her the number and added, "Of course, I get, maybe, one or two bars, depending on the storms up there at that elevation."

"I know," she said, writing the info down on her pad.

"How would you know?"

She felt the gauntlet thrown at her feet once more. His eyes were dark with distrust. "Because," she answered in an unruffled tone, "I was tracking a lost child up in that same area a year ago. I found the lost boy I'd been tracking. When I tried to call in on my cell, I couldn't get a signal."

Surprise flowed through Dakota. "You tracked a lost boy?" This blew his mind. Women did not know how to track.

"Yes." Shelby kind of resented his genuine surprise. He wasn't the only one with skills. Then the sudden relaxation came to his face. Interest glimmered in those gold-brown eyes of his. She felt a shiver of yearning move through her as the look he gave her was primal, sexual. What was happening here? Stunned by her own reaction toward this snarly ex-SEAL, Shelby said, "Let's stick to the facts, Mr. Carson."

Dakota opened his mouth and then closed it. He regarded her with a little more deference. "The only thing women can track is a sale price of clothing at a department store."

Shelby couldn't contain her laughter. "What are you? A Neanderthal? I can track as well as any man. Better."

"Who are you?"

Her entire body reacted to his growling question. Now the wolf was circling the prey—her. "We don't have time for that, Mr. Carson. I need to get the location of where you shot the bear in order to notify the Tetons Forest supervisor. They'll want to find the bear, get it out of there and bring it back to their headquarters for autopsy."

All business. Still, Dakota's mind reeled over the fact that she was a tracker, of all things. And he knew this area like the back of his hand. It was serious, rugged, backcountry mountainous area. Even a skilled hunter could get lost and disoriented. And she hadn't. As he gazed up into her sparkling blue eyes, he saw banked humor in them. He gave her the directions to the meadow where he had killed the bear.

"Great, thanks," Shelby said. She walked away, pressed the button on the radio on her left epaulet.

Watching her, Dakota liked what he saw. She was definitely a throwback to the Victorian age with the proverbial hourglass figure. Her breasts were hidden by the Kevlar vest, but he could tell they were full. Her hips were flared and she had long, long legs. Damn, she was a good-looking woman. He warned himself that she was in a relationship, lay back and closed his eyes. He had to get out of this place. There was no friggin' way he was staying overnight.

"How are you feeling?" Shelby asked when she came back over to his gurney. "Better?"

Opening his eyes, he said, "Yeah. Better."

"We have two forest rangers going out to find your bear."

"Am I going to be charged?"

"I doubt it. I'll talk to Charley over at Tetons HQ tomorrow. It sounds like self-defense to me."

His mouth curled into a slight grin. "Oh, it was, Deputy. It was. You should have been there."

"No, thanks. I've had enough grizzly interruptus too many times when I'm tracking. I like to stay away from them. They're big and they're fast."

He held up his bandaged arm. "Tell me about it."

She liked his black humor. "You were lucky."

"No luck at all. I had the situation under control." Well, almost. If not for Storm charging the grizzly and biting the bear's nose, he wouldn't have gotten the second shots to kill the charging beast.

"Yeah, right." Her mouth twitched. "I'll see you tomorrow."

"No, you won't."

Shelby frowned. "You have to stay here for the night, Mr. Carson. Or go home with me."

He sat up, his head clear. The nausea was ebbing. "Bull. I'm leaving…." He threw off the blankets and gave her a look that warned her not to stop him.

CHAPTER FOUR

SHELBY WATCHED DAKOTA Carson get up, unsteadily at first. His calves were knotted, which told her what good a shape he was in. He calmly removed the IV because he knew how to do it and dropped the needle and tube back on the gurney.

"Your clothes are kept in that locker room," she said, pointing to a door on the left. "Probably got your last name on one of the lockers so you can find them."

He stopped and studied her. Something about Shelby intrigued him. "You're smart."

"I'm field smart, Mr. Carson."

His mouth twitched. Yeah, she was damned smart for not getting in his way. "If you were a man, you'd rear up on your balls and try to stop me."

"I have a titanium set, but I choose my battles very carefully."

His mouth drew into a sour smile. "You ever been in the military?"

"No."

"Shoulda been." He turned and walked slowly but surely toward the door.

Shelby wasn't sure if it was a compliment or an insult. She waited until he was gone and called Jordana McPherson. By the time she arrived, looking upset, Dakota Carson was coming out the door, fully clothed. When he saw Jordana, he glanced over at Shelby.

"I called her," Shelby said.

"Yeah, I remember. You pick your battles."

Smiling, Shelby nodded.

"Dakota?" Jordana called.

"No sense in trying to talk me out of leaving this place, Doc. You know I can't handle closed-in spaces. I'll just be on my way."

Jordana shoved her hands in the pockets of her white lab coat, giving him a pleading look. "There's a high probability of infection after a bite like this, Dakota. I've written you a prescription for antibiotics, but I'm worried. Usually, if there is infection, it's going to hit you in the first twenty-four hours after the operation. That's why I wanted you to stay overnight for observation. If you could agree to stay at Shelby's, her house is only a block from this hospital, I wouldn't worry so much. Please…"

Halting, Dakota studied the deputy. Oh, he'd like to go home with her, all right. For all the wrong damn reasons. "No."

Jordana reached out, her fingers wrapping around

his right arm. "Dakota, you have to! That's a bad wound. You're a combat medic and you know the drill. If you could just stay overnight and let me give you an antibiotic IV drip? One night, and drop by and see me tomorrow morning to check it. I'll feel better."

"Sorry, Doc, but I gotta go…." He shook off her hand. Glancing at the deputy, he growled, "Now?" Dakota expected the deputy to try to stop him.

Shelby stepped aside. "Timing's everything."

Walking slowly by her, Dakota got his bearings and moved toward the elevator. Neither woman made an attempt to stop him.

The elevator doors whooshed closed. Jordana gave Shelby a desperate look. "He shouldn't leave."

"I know," she muttered. "Give me his prescription and I'll get it filled and make sure he has it before he drives off. I'll follow him at a safe distance."

"Can't you talk some sense into him?" Jordana handed her the prescription.

With a sour laugh, Shelby said, "He calls me Deputy Barbie Doll. Do you really think I have any sway over him?"

"Hardly." Scratching her head, Jordana groused, "Unbelievable."

"Is that SEAL behavior?" Shelby asked, walking with her to the elevator.

"No. It's his PTSD, Shelby. He's got a very bad case of it. Closed-in places throw him into deep anxiety. He prowls around like a caged lion if he can't escape." Jordana added, "I feel so bad for him. He's a decorated vet, with the silver star and two purple hearts. But he just won't come in for weekly therapy."

The elevator doors opened and they stepped in. "I'll see what I can do," Shelby said. "But no promises."

"He's been out on that mountain for a year, Shelby," Jordana said in a softer voice. "Alone. And he's unable to socialize, to fit back into society. It's as if he's still in combat mode and he can't do anything about it."

"I saw him struggling earlier," Shelby murmured. The doors opened to the main floor of the hospital. Walking out, she turned to the right. "There he is."

"Get those antibiotics for him and follow him," Jordana said, touching her shoulder. "He's a vet. He's earned our help even if he doesn't want it."

Mouth quirking, Shelby shrugged into her coat. "He fights everyone. All the time, whether he should or not."

"Good luck."

She'd need it. Shelby watched him walk gingerly down the hall toward the main exit sliding glass doors. He didn't look over his shoulder, although she watched him operating like a predator on the hunt. Dakota Carson missed nothing, his gaze swiveling one way and then the other. He might have just come out of anesthesia, but the man was alert. Jordana was right: he was operating in combat mode. He might be in the U.S., but his mind and emotions were still in Afghanistan.

Dakota made it to his truck. He fished the keys out of his pocket. Two parking spaces down was the Tetons sheriff's cruiser. Storm was looking out the window at him, wagging her big, fluffy gray tail. He smiled and felt a sense of safety. When he looked up, he saw the blond deputy crossing the street to where he was. She stopped and handed him an orange prescription bottle.

"The doctor wanted you to take this antibiotic," she said. Their fingers touched momentarily. An unexpected warmth moved up his arm, which aggravated him. He stuffed the bottle into his pocket.

"I need my wolf," he told her, getting into the cab. He shoved the key into the ignition and turned it.

Nothing. Just a clicking sound.

Cursing to himself, Dakota turned the key again.

"Battery's dead," Shelby said matter-of-factly. "Cold weather can suck the life out of one real fast."

Dakota sat back and glared at her. "Sure you didn't do something to my truck so I couldn't get home?"

Shelby shrugged. "No, but if you don't believe me, lift the hood and check it out yourself."

He did just that. In cold weather, batteries

drained quickly. He saw some rust corrosion around the terminals, but that wouldn't stop the battery from turning over the engine. *Son of a bitch.* Dropping the hood, Dakota straightened. The woman stood right where she was the last time he saw her, a concerned look on her oval face. He met her shadowed blue eyes and felt as if he could fall into them. What was it about this woman that gave him that sense of safety? Dakota pushed the feeling away.

"I imagine you're feeling pretty good about this?"

"Not at all, Mr. Carson. I want to help you, not make your life any more miserable than it already is." Shelby didn't like their sparring exchanges, but he was terse and defensive. Given his PTSD, she could forgive him and just try to make life a little easier on him.

Dakota studied her in the tense silence. Her husky voice riffled across his flesh. He felt her genuine care. He'd been without a woman for so damn long, it scared him. But a lot of things scared the hell out of him. The morning sky was clear after the blizzard from the day before. The strong sunlight warmed him. "Can I get you to drive me and my wolf back to my cabin?"

Her heart contracted with pain for him. The anger in his eyes died as he must have realized the hopelessness of his situation. He swallowed his considerable pride and asked her for help. She

ached for him. "Yes, I can do that. When I get back,
I'll take your battery over to the service station
and get it charged. You need to come back here tomorrow morning to see Dr. McPherson, anyway.
We can pick it up then and you'll have your truck
again."

"You do choose your battles."

"I don't see you as a battle, Mr. Carson. I see you
as someone who needs a helping hand right now."

Shaking his head, he slid out of the truck. "Okay.
Wheels up. Let's rock it out."

Shelby didn't expect a thank you. She wasn't
familiar with the military slang he used, either.
His face was pale, and she knew he was fighting
to appear confident. He didn't fool her at all, but
she said nothing, walking over to her cruiser and
unlocking the system.

When Dakota climbed in, his wolf whined and
wagged her tail in welcome. He grinned and stuck
his fingers through the wire wall between the front
and backseats. The look in Shelby's eyes startled
him as she climbed in. For a moment, he thought
he saw tears in them. Her blue eyes were wide
with happiness. An unexpected heat surged through
him. He turned around, pulled on the seat belt and
closed the door. Shelby didn't behave like most
women he knew. She was different. Very different.

On the way out of the town, Shelby asked, "Do

you have enough food and water up there? We can always stop at a grocery store."

"I'm fine," he managed. As he leaned his head back against the seat rest, exhaustion finally caught up with him. In moments, he was asleep.

Shelby headed out of town, up the long hill that would put them on the road toward Grand Tetons National Park. She knew exactly where Dakota Carson was holed up. The radio chatter broke the silence, but her mind and heart focused on the injured vet sleeping in her cruiser. Once, she looked at his profile. His nose reminded her that he might have some Native American heritage in his blood. And his skin, although washed out, looked more tan than white. In that moment, he seemed vulnerable. It twisted her heart to think of the terror he must have undergone and survived. She quirked her mouth. She had a few symptoms of PTSD herself, but so did everyone who worked in law enforcement. It just wasn't as bad as for a military person.

When the cruiser stopped, Dakota snapped awake. Wide awake. Looking to the left, he saw his cabin. "You found it."

Shelby grinned. "I told you I knew where it was." She turned and studied him. "How do you feel?"

He lifted his bandaged arm. "Better."

"Good. You needed the sleep." He needed some care. And she found herself wanting to do just that for this gruff, injured vet. Why? Something tugged at her heart. And triggered her needs as a woman for him as a man. She had no idea why. Shelby opened the door and climbed out.

Dakota couldn't figure this woman out. No one knew where this road was. But she did. After getting out, he opened the back door and Storm leaped out.

The first thing Shelby did was go to the shack. Carson had done a lot of work over time to fix it up. Once, it had been a log cabin with white plaster between the thick logs. Over the years, all of the plaster had cracked and fallen out, leaving huge gaps between the logs. Now mud and moss stuck in between them, to ward off the cold. Up here, snow was still about three feet deep in shaded spots. Trees were thick, and only the happy gurgle of a nearby creek broke the muted silence. Turning, she saw Dakota making his way toward his home.

"You've fixed it up," she noted, gesturing toward it. "New roof. It needed one. And you've repaired the spaces between the logs." At least he wasn't lazy. Shelby noted the entire area was picked up, clean and organized. He cared, she realized. In his own way, the man was trying to make life a little better for himself, even if it was in the middle of nowhere.

"I've had a year to make it less windy inside."

Shelby watched the wolf bound happily up to the

door. The animal sat, panting and wagging her tail, as she waited for Carson to walk up. He pushed the grayish wood door open with his foot.

"Not locked?"

"No need. I have a wolf alarm."

Grinning, Shelby said, "Point taken. You're good to go?"

Dakota hesitated at the door. "Yeah."

Shelby stepped forward, pulling a business card from her shirt pocket. "Here's my business card." She took a pen and circled her number. "This is my private cell phone. If you need anything, call me. Day or night, it doesn't matter." His eyes narrowed as he took the crisp white business card. Her fingers tingled briefly when they met his. "Dr. McPherson is really worried about infection. I want you to have a lifeline, all right?"

The silence fell between them. Dakota regarded her from beneath his straight black brows. "You do this for everyone?" he demanded, his voice suddenly gruff. He tried to stop the warm feelings flowing through his chest because she cared.

"Anyone," she assured him quietly. Just the raw, anguished look in his eyes hit her in the chest like a fist. There was such need in Carson, but he was so broken that it brought tears. She turned so he wouldn't see them. Shelby's voice was roughened. "Meet you here at 0700 tomorrow?"

He nodded, watching her turn away from him.

She seemed so out of place. Her blond hair was like sunlight in the dark, muted shadows of the woods surrounding the area. She was like a ray of sunshine in his own darkness. "Yeah."

Nodding, Shelby headed back toward the cruiser.

"Hey...thanks..." he called.

Turning on her boot, she flashed him a tender smile. "Anytime. Take care...."

"Are you sure you weren't in the military?"

Shelby forced tears away and met his confused gaze. "No. My dad, though, was in the Marine Corps. He served in the military police for ten years before getting out." She gestured toward Jackson Hole. "We ended up here and he became a sheriff's deputy. Later, he became commander. He just retired two years ago to fish the trout streams."

Mouth compressed, Dakota said, "That's good to know."

"Why?"

"Because you're behaving like a SEAL. You take care of your teammates."

Shelby didn't know what that meant, but it was important to him. "I'm just glad to be of help, Mr. Carson."

"Call me Dakota."

"Will do..."

For a moment, all Shelby wanted to do was turn around, walk straight up to him and throw her arms around his shoulders. That was what he needed: a little TLC. Yet the exhaustion in his eyes and face, that gruff exterior, warned her off. She'd been a deputy for years and could read body language and facial expressions pretty well. That ability had saved her life in the past, but Shelby didn't feel threatened by this ex-SEAL. If anything, her heart reached out for him, wanted to help him even though he pushed all her efforts away.

She watched him disappear into the claptrap cabin. Frowning, Shelby walked back to her cruiser. She was sure that Cade Garner, who was now second in command at the sheriff's department, and her boss, would be happy to hear she was off duty. She climbed into the cruiser. Cade would understand because of the unusual circumstances. So often, even as law enforcement officers, they dealt in humanitarian ways with the citizens of their county. It wasn't always about handing out a speeding ticket. She was raised in the giant shadow of her father, who had taught her that she should always look to help others who needed it. Shelby looked up to him and was inspired to go into law enforcement as a result. It was a good choice, one she had never regretted.

As she turned the cruiser around, worry ate at her. She wasn't a paramedic, although she had advanced first-aid training. Jordana's worry was real. Over the past two years, she'd become friends with the doctor and knew she didn't show her worry often.

Shelby drove slowly down the steep, muddy road, heading back toward Jackson Hole. Something gnawed at her. Taking a deep breath, Shelby tried to shrug it off. Dakota was a man in his element up here in the raw, untamed Tetons. Apparently his SEAL training had given him the ability to survive in the harshest of environments.

As she drove down the narrow, twisting road, she figured out she'd do a Google search of SEALs and educate herself. Her father had been a military police officer in the marines. As a child of a military family, she recalled her moving from one base to another every two years. She lost good friends she made, never to see them again. It had been emotionally hard on Shelby, but her father was good at what he did. And she was proud of him, as was her mother. But she'd never heard him mention SEALs. Once her shift was over, Shelby would drop by for a visit to her parents' home on the other side of town. Maybe her father would know more about this special breed of military men.

CHAPTER FIVE

THE NIGHTMARE BEGAN as it always did. Dakota was following his LT, Lieutenant Sean Vincent, up a slippery scree slope in the Hindu Kush Mountains of Afghanistan. It was black. So black he couldn't see a foot in front of him without his NVGs, night-vision goggles, in place over his eyes. Everything became a grainy green. The only problem was there was no depth of perception when using them, and the four-man SEAL team slipped, fell, got up and kept moving.

They were hunting an HTV, high-value-target, Taliban warlord who was hiding out in the cave systems of the Hindu Kush Mountains. The wind was cold and cutting, the Kevlar vest and winter gear keeping him warm. A terrible feeling crawled through Dakota. They called him "woo-woo man," because he had a sixth sense about danger and coming attacks. After three tours in the Sand Box with his platoon, everyone listened to him.

They were ready to crest a ridge at twelve thousand feet. Their breath was coming in explosive inhales and exhales. The climb of four thousand feet at midnight to catch the warlord by surprise, would be worth it. Or would it?

Dakota was ready to throw up his hand in a fist to signal *stop,* to warn the other SEAL operatives.

Too late! Just as the LT breasted the ridge, all hell broke loose. Enemy AK-47s fired. Red tracer bullets danced around the LT. Dakota saw him struck, once, twice, three times. The impact flung the SEAL officer off his feet, sent him flying backward, the M-4 rifle cartwheeling out of his hands.

Dakota grunted, crouched and leaped upward, catching the two-hundred-pound SEAL before he crashed into the sharp, cutting rocks. Slammed backward, Dakota took the full brunt of his LT's weight. He landed with an "oofff," on his back, the rocks bruising and biting into his Kevlar vest plates. He heard the two other operatives scramble upward, in a diamond pattern, to protect him and the LT as they skidded out of control down the steep grade of the mountain.

A hail of bullets, screams of Taliban charging their position, filled the night air. The SEAL team held their position up above, firing systematically, picking off the men as they launched themselves at them. Head shots, every one.

Dakota came to an abrupt halt, a huge boulder stopping their downward slide. His flesh was torn up beneath both his legs, his elbow raw and bleeding. "LT!" He dragged the unconscious officer around the boulder for protection. Dakota was their combat medic on the team. It was his job to save the lives of his team, his family. Glancing around the boulder, he saw Mac and Gordy on their bellies, firing upward, taking out every Taliban who surged over the mountain at them.

Hands shaking, he carefully turned the officer over. He'd worked with Sean for five years. They'd grown up together in the platoon. He was twenty-eight and had just married Isabel before going out on this rotation, their first child on the way. Blood gleamed dark along the LT's throat. Dakota saw where two of the three bullets had struck the LT in the chest. The Kevlar had stopped them from killing him outright.

A loud RPG explosion occurred. Automatically, Dakota threw himself over his LT, a rain of rocks hailing down all around them. He heard Mac yell. The next moment, a grenade was fired by the SEAL. More explosions lit the night on that cold ridge. Rolling off the officer, Dakota heard the throaty fire of the M-4s. Both his teammates were fighting back with fury. He heard their comms man, Mac, call for air support. They needed it.

As he pulled away Sean's collar in his quick examination, Dakota noticed the terrible wound the third bullet had created as it sped through the side of his neck. Gulping, tears blurring his vision for a second, Dakota forced down his emotions. Rapidly, he applied a battle dressing with pressure to the side of Sean's neck. He could feel the warmth of the SEAL's blood as it leaked quickly out of the white dressing and through his fingers. He was going to bleed out, his carotid artery cut in half by the bullet. *Oh, God, no, no, don't let this be!* Bullets whined around Dakota. He heard a roar of the Taliban to his right. Jerking his head up, he saw at least ten Taliban rush around the slope from another direction, firing at him.

Dakota had to return fire. In doing so, he had to lift his hand and stop the artery from bleeding out. It was a terrible choice....

Groaning, Dakota awakened in a heavy sweat. His chest was rapidly rising and falling, his mouth opened in a silent scream. Flailing around on his bed, the springs creaking, he tried to run from the rest of the nightmare that dogged him. His heart pounded so hard he felt as if it would tear out of his chest. Throwing off the wool blankets, burning up, he pulled himself upright. The moment his bare feet hit the cold surface of the floor, he opened his eyes. Perspiration ran down his temples. He could taste the sweat at the corners of his mouth. Tears were running out of his eyes and no matter what he did, Dakota couldn't stop them.

Oh God, no...no.... Sean died right there. Right behind that friggin' rock in the middle of nowhere.

He jammed his palms against his closed eyes, trembling. His muscles bunched and knotted. If only... if only he'd have died instead of Sean. He left his beautiful, pregnant wife behind. Somehow, they got off that ridge before being decimated. The Night Stalkers sent in an MH-47 Chinook accompanied by two army Apache combat helicopters. Making a heroic landing, one of the four wheels on the mountain, the others in thin air, Dakota carried his dead LT and himself on board. Then the other two SEALs jumped off the ridge, slid down the rocky scree and leaped into the awaiting helo. As the Chinook powered up and left the ridge, the Apaches lit it up like the Fourth of July, cremating every one of those bastards, sending them straight to hell.

The shaking wouldn't stop. Dakota rubbed his eyes savagely, trying to force the tears to stop. Sean was like the brother he'd never had. Sean's platoon was his family. *Burning up.* He was burning up. At this time of year, it was below freezing at night, but barely. Why wouldn't his body cool down? His mind felt spongy. Dakota realized he wasn't thinking clearly. The nightmare still had its claws into him. *Still...*

Forcing himself to his feet, Dakota staggered. Dizziness assailed him and he found himself falling backward onto the bed. He hit it with force, one metal leg bending and snapping. The jolt of the bed falling on one side shocked him. Breathing hard, his heart refusing to stop pounding as if he were in the middle of a heart attack, Dakota forced himself to focus. It was something SEALs did well. He placed two fingers on his pulse. It was leaping and bounding as if it were about to tear out of his skin. By now his body should be calming down, cooling down. But it wasn't. His flesh felt scalded beneath his fingertips. *What the hell?* And then it hit him: he had a fever. *Shit.* Doc McPherson was right: infection had set in after the surgery.

Lifting his head, his eyes narrowed, sweat running and following the course of his hard jaw, Dakota tried to think. As he tried to get up, the dizziness felled him. The bed sagged and tipped to one side where the leg had been broken off. His left arm throbbed like a son of a bitch. He looked at it. The arm had swollen so much that the skin on either end of the tape bulged outward. When he touched it, his arm was hard and hot. Bad news.

Help. I've got to get help or I'm gonna die. I've gone septic...

Moonlight shifted through the small glass windows, which were smudged with dust and dirt. A flash of white on the wood table caught his wandering attention. Dakota knew he'd never get to his truck, much less drive it down the mountain to get help.

Barbie Doll...need to call her... Said she'd help...

The cell phone lay next to her white business

card on the table. Could he reach it? Dakota forced himself up, staggering those five feet to the table. He sat down in the chair before he fell down. With shaking fingers, his mind hallucinating from high fever, he slowly punched in the numbers. Would Barbie Doll answer? Did she really mean what she said? She'd help him if he needed her, or was it just lip service? Dakota had never felt so goddamned useless. He'd been a SEAL. He knew how to survive. And yet a high fever was raging through him, had dismantled him in record time. If that blond-haired angel didn't answer her cell phone, he knew without a doubt she'd find him dead on the floor when she dropped by at 0700.

His senses began to spin. Dakota tried to focus on the phone ringing and ringing and ringing.... Blackness began to assail him. He fought the fever. Fought the darkness encroaching upon him. He couldn't see anymore. Everything was turning black. *Oh God, I'm going to die....* The grizzly bear had gotten its revenge....

Soft, beeping noises slowly brought Dakota out of the darkness. He heard women's voices. Far off. Too far to understand, but he tried to listen anyway. He had that familiar sensation, as if he was drowning and swimming toward the surface. It reminded him of being a SEAL frogman. He'd had his LAR V Draeger rebreathing system malfunction at fifty feet in the warm waters of the Arabian Sea during a night mission. Holding his breath, Dakota swam strongly, pushing his flippers hard toward the surface. It was barely dawn, but he could see the light above him through his mask. His chest swelled, he felt the pressure, felt the reflex to breathe. But he couldn't! If he did, he'd inhale a lungful of water and drown. Struggling, fighting, kicking, he willed himself to hold his breath just as he'd done back in BUD/S in that pool. Was he going to make it?

And then a gentle hand touched his sweaty lower arm. Instantly, it broke the hold darkness had on him. Dakota inhaled audibly, gulping in a huge, deep breath. The fingers tightened a little, as if to steady him, help him to reorient. Yes, the hand was cool, fingers long. He could feel their softness against the dark hair and sweat rolling off his arm.

Dragging his eyes open to slits, Dakota saw nothing but blurred green walls. The hand. That cool, soft hand. He forced himself to close his eyes and concentrate. Between heaven and hell, Dakota fought to move toward the light. Toward that hand that was like an anchor promising him life, not death. His mind churned, hallucinated and then like a tide, flowed out, leaving him lucid for a few moments.

"It's all right, Dakota," a voice whispered near his ear. "You're going to be all right. You're safe...."

Her breath was warm, a hint of cinnamon on it, maybe. Dakota absorbed her husky, breathy tone, the warm moisture caressing his ear and cheek. He felt her fingers tighten just a little, as if to convince him to believe her. Most of all, he was safe. He felt safe even though he swam in a mix of hallucinations and God knew what else. Where was he?

Shelby kept her hand on Dakota's arm. Jordana McPherson stood on the other side of the bed, watching him. Lifting her gaze, she met Jordana's. "He's coming around…."

"Yes," the doctor murmured, checking the IV drip that was slugging his body with antibiotics and fighting the massive infection within him. "Finally. He's past crisis. He's going to make it."

THE AFTERNOON SUN SLANTED through the window near the hospital bed. "It was a close call," Shelby said in a low tone. She watched Dakota struggling to regain consciousness.

Snorting, Jordana rolled her eyes. She watched the monitors for a moment. "No need to tell you. You're the one who found him at two o'clock this morning." She frowned. "If you hadn't responded to his call, he'd have died. He went septic. I was so afraid of that."

Shelby noticed the red streaks—a sign of sepsis—running up his left arm. His biceps were sculpted and hard. If a streak had reached his heart, it would have killed him. Now the red streaks were receding. Even in his semiconscious state, with a high fever, there was nothing but pure masculinity about Dakota Carson. The man was in top shape. He wasn't heavily muscled, just lean and honed like a fine knife blade.

"Okay, monitors are looking better. His heart rate and pulse are finally lowering." Jordana sighed. "His fever's coming down and now at one hundred three. And his oxygen concentration is okay, considering what he just went through. Stay with him until he gets conscious, okay? I don't want him waking up and being thrown into instant anxiety because he doesn't know where he is. He's going to be woozy for a while."

"I'll stay with him."

"Thanks. Are you off duty?"

"Yeah, for the next three days."

"Don't you love shift work?" Jordana grinned.

"I do." Shelby gazed down at Dakota, who was still struggling. "It came in handy this time."

"Tell me about it. If you need me, buzz." Jordana waved and disappeared out the door of the private room.

Quiet descended on the small room. Shelby shifted a little, keeping her hand on Dakota's good arm. She wanted to touch this man, this warrior. Her talk with her father yesterday had shed a ton of light on SEALs. And truly, Dakota Carson was a genuine hero. A real warrior. As she gazed down at his pale features, the darkness of the beard making his cheeks look even more gaunt from the ravages of the fever, her heart expanded. She moved her fingers gently up and down his arm. She felt even more drawn to this enigmatic man. This loner who held so much pain deep in his heart. How much darkness held him prisoner? Shelby wondered.

His eyes slowly opened. Leaning down, Shelby smiled, catching his wandering gaze. "Dakota? It's Shelby. You're back in the Jackson Hole Hospital."

His eyes moved slowly back to hers. Shelby felt his neediness in that moment. Her breath hitched. There was anxiety and fear in his expression, turning them a muddy brown color. Without thinking, she reached out and threaded her fingers through his damp, sweat-soaked black hair. "It's okay. You're okay. You had a close call with an infection, but you're going to be all right."

Shelby sounded like an angel whispering to him, calling him out of the darkness that still wanted to drag him back down into hell. As her fingers touched his burning scalp, the coolness soothed his agitation, stopped the panic deep in his chest. The look of calm on her face touched him. In seconds, he relaxed. Watching her, Dakota was sure he'd died and gone to heaven.

His voice was raw. In a barely heard, ragged whisper, he managed, "Angel…"

Shelby withdrew her fingers from his hair. "Not me." She laughed softly. "I'm no angel."

A sense of warmth, of coming home, stole through Dakota. That half smile of hers, that humored look dancing impishly in her eyes, gave him a sense of peace he'd never felt before. What was going on? He didn't care. All he could do was absorb her grazing touch across his forearm. It was Shelby, he decided. His mind shorted out, wandered and then came back to sharper focus.

"Wh-what…"

Shelby leaned near, her lips inches from his ear. Quietly, she repeated the information to him, watching to see if his eyes would focus. As she spoke, he seemed to relax. She saw the evidence in the monitors on the other side of his bed. His pulse became normal. His breathing settled. She understood a soft voice could tame a person in shock at an accident site. Knowing this from her own experience, she repeated once again the information slowly.

His gaze followed hers as she slowly straightened, continuing to keep her hand on his arm. His pupils grew larger, as if grappling with comprehension. What kind of anguish was he experiencing right now? What was he seeing?

When she lifted her hand away, he groaned. The monitors chattered. His blood pressure rose, his pulse skyrocketed and his heart started to pound.

Shelby automatically placed her hand back on his right shoulder. The blue cotton gown hid the hard muscles beneath, but she could feel them leap and respond to her touch. Amazed, Shelby watched the monitors stop beeping so loudly. All his functions lowered back to normal. *Touch.* That was it. A thread of joy coursed through her, sweet and unexpected. Tilting her chin, she gazed at Dakota's lashes resting against his pasty cheeks. His mouth, once pursed with pain, was now relaxed.

What would it be like to kiss this man? His mouth was beautifully shaped, the lower lip slightly fuller than the upper. If given the chance, he'd probably be one hell of a kisser. Absently, she moved her hand across his shoulder. His chest rose and fell slowly, no longer swift or moving with anxiety.

She was shaken and emotionally moved by the unexpected experience. Even watching him fall into a deep sleep affected her. He'd been trapped within some unknown nightmare, fueled by the high fever. When she looked once again at the monitor, she was stunned. His temperature had been a hundred and three. Now it had reduced to a hundred and one! How was that possible? Shelby wished she knew more about medicine. She'd asked Jordana later.

Hooking the chair with her foot, she slowly pulled it over to Dakota's bedside. Because her touch was a powerful healing agent, the least she could do was stay. And allow her touch to give him some peace. As Shelby sat down, she slid her hand across his gowned shoulder to his lower right arm and remembered her dad's words of warning.

"He's a man carrying so much grief and pain he doesn't know where to put it all, Shelby. He's seen too much. He's survived things we can't imagine. He's a wounded warrior and the past runs his life."

Shelby felt close to tears. Tears for him, for the horror he still carried within him. Dakota was perilous to her heart. And yet she felt driven to be near him. Most shocking of all, she wanted to care for him. Somehow, Shelby knew love was the key to this man who now slept. Shaking her head, Shelby told herself she was crazy. A man like this would be like a black hole, sucking the life out of everything he ever touched, destroying it.

Or would he?

Shelby heard her dad's warning words. "Be careful, Shelby. You care about this vet too much. You have no experience with his kind. If you get close to him, he'll emotionally destroy you. He's got a severe disorder and he doesn't know how to handle himself, much less a woman who's trying to help him. Stay out of his way, Shelby. Don't get involved."

CHAPTER SIX

DAKOTA AWOKE SLOWLY to the sound of a robin singing nearby. Dragging open his eyes, he was met by
brilliant sunlight coming through frilly white lace
curtains. The light hit the pale blue wall opposite
of where he lay. His brows drew down. Where the
hell was he? What had happened?

The door quietly opened. His eyes widened
when he recognized Shelby. She was dressed in a
simple orange T-shirt, body-hugging jeans and a
pair of well-worn moccasins. Her hair gleamed like
gold as she walked through the slats of sunlight.
When she saw he was awake, she smiled.

"Welcome back to the land of the living. You're
at my home."

Dakota pushed himself up into a sitting position. He found himself a helluva lot weaker than
he wanted to be. Looking down, he noticed he was
wearing a set of blue pajamas. A clean white waterproof bandage covered his left arm. His flesh appeared normal, no longer swollen, bluish or oozing
pus. He was no longer feverish, his skin cool and

dry to his touch. He looked up as Shelby poured some water from a pitcher.

"Thirsty?"

"Yeah," he managed, his voice hoarse. He took the glass.

"You've been out for two solid days," she said, watching him gulp the water. Jordana had warned her he'd be thirstier than a camel when he came out of his fevered state.

Wiping his mouth with the back of his hand, he handed her the glass. "More?" And then he added, "Please?"

Shelby poured him another glass. "You had us all worried there for a while," she said. His hair was spiky and stiff with sweat. He definitely needed a bath. Still, she thrilled to the fact that his eyes were once more clear and he was fully present.

The water satiated him. "I thought the grizzly was going to get even with me."

Her mouth quirked. "Almost did. Dr. McPherson flooded you with antibiotics through an IV. It was touch-and-go for a while because you had sepsis, blood poisoning."

"Karma's a bitch," he said, his voice stronger. "How did I get here?"

Shelby sat on the edge of the bed, near his feet, facing him. "Dr. McPherson had you brought over here by ambulance a couple hours ago." She saw his brows raise. "She didn't want you waking up in

a hospital. She said you didn't like small rooms. I
volunteered my place. It's close enough to the hospital in case you relapse."

Looking around, Dakota felt comfortable in the
queen-size bed in the large room. He lifted his chin
and met her gaze. "Why are you doing this?"

"Because I've seen your cabin and frankly, it
sucks. I wouldn't put a sick dog up there to get
well." She wanted to add that vets deserved the
best, not the worst, when they were injured.

Her lips twitched, merriment gleaming in her
blue eyes.

"You should have seen it before I got there. It
was a dump," he said.

"Oh," she said as she laughed, "I did. Remember? I've been to it many times before you home-
steaded it."

His mind wasn't functioning fully yet. Frowning, Dakota finally remembered. He moved his
hand across his jaw. "I need to shave. And I stink."

"Wouldn't disagree."

Smart mouth. Beautiful lips. Dakota appreciated her dry sense of humor. And he was feeling
remarkably calm. Almost always, he had anxiety
upon awakening. But it was gone. Completely gone,
which confused him. "Give me a little while to get
my bearings."

"Take as long as you need. By the way, I've
checked on Storm daily. She seems happy to stay

outside the cabin. I couldn't find any dog food for her."

"She hunts for her food. And she'd rather be outdoors than in." He was grateful for her care of the wolf. It told Dakota she cared a lot more than most people did. "Tell me what happened. The last thing I remember was trying to call you."

"You did."

"I don't remember your answering. I think I blacked out after punching in the numbers."

"My phone rang and I picked it up. There was nothing at the other end, but I could hear Storm whining in the background. I hung up and checked the callback number and I put it together."

"And you drove up there?"

"Yes. When I entered the cabin, you were out cold on the floor. You were burning up, your dressing was oozing pus and smelled foul. Storm was whining and sitting near you. I called the fire station and told them to meet me with an ambulance at the bottom of the mountain. No one would ever know how to get up to your cabin."

Nodding, he studied her beneath his lashes. "You can't be strong enough to haul my ass off that floor by yourself."

Her mouth drew into a wicked grin. "I did." Wasn't easy, but Shelby did it because the other choice was leaving him to die on that cold floor.

"You aren't a Barbie doll after all. I owe you a full apology."

Thrusting out her hand, she said, "Apology accepted. Call me Shelby, will you?" When his hand swallowed hers up, Shelby felt his animal warmth, his strength, and yet he monitored how much pressure he put around her fingers. This was the second time he'd touched her. Really touched her. There was incredible masculinity and power around Dakota. It called her and she felt almost helpless not to respond to it—to him.

"Shelby...yes, I'm sorry I called you Barbie Doll. I guess—" he reluctantly released her long, beautiful hand "—my prejudice about women with blond hair is showing?"

"Dumb blonde prejudice?"

"Yeah."

Shelby didn't want him feeling any worse than he already did. There was a sincere apology in his eyes. "Don't worry about it. Are you hungry, Dakota?" She liked the way his name rolled off her lips. Right now he looked fully relaxed. When would that change? What would cause his anxiety to return? Jason, her older brother, had the same kind of symptoms after three tours in Iraq. And no one had been able to save him. Not even her. Shelby tried to remember her dad's words of warnings when she'd filled him in on Dakota's military background. Yet when she met and drowned in

Dakota's gold-and-brown eyes, she felt her heart opening so wide it made her momentarily breathless. Did he realize the effect he had on her? She didn't think so.

Rubbing his stomach, he said, "Yeah, a little. But look, I don't want you going out of your way—"

"I'll let you know when you're a burden, okay?" Shelby said it half in jest and half with seriousness. Standing up, she asked, "What would you like? I'm a good cook."

He gazed up at her. She was tall, her shoulders thrown back with natural confidence. Without her uniform on and with that orange T-shirt outlining her upper body to show every curve, he lost his train of thought for a moment. "I…uh… Eggs and bacon sound good."

"Toast? Jam?"

He nodded. "If it's not too much trouble?"

"Coffee?"

He groaned. "God, that sounds good. Really good."

"Cream? Sugar?"

"No, black."

"Anything else?"

"You? For dessert?"

Shocked by his response, Shelby was fully aware of the sudden glint in his eyes, that predatory look a man gives to a woman. Heat surged up her neck and into her face. "Let's stick to the eggs and bacon, shall we?" Shelby turned to leave and said teasingly, "I think that's about all you can handle right now."

He had the good grace to give her a sheepish smile. "I think you're right." He watched her leave as soundlessly as she'd arrived. What the hell was wrong with him? Dakota sat up, pushing the covers aside. Shelby was beautiful, playful, intelligent and smart-mouthed. It all conspired to make him brazen.

Looking down, he realized he was aroused. *Damn.* He jerked the covers over the lower half of his body and tried to piece together what had happened to him two days earlier. He couldn't get Shelby's body out of his mind. She had nice, wide hips, the kind a man liked to slide his large hands around to hold and guide her. Her breasts were full and he wondered what it would be like to cup them. Shaking his head, he cursed softly. Horny as hell, Dakota didn't like the fact that his body was acting like some love-starved teen's.

Shelby deserved better. When she came back about twenty minutes later with a tray of food, the first thing he said was, "I'm a lousy houseguest. I'm sorry for what I said earlier. You didn't deserve it."

She set the wooden tray across his lap and noticed the bulge beneath the covers. She tried to keep her face carefully arranged. "Apology accepted. You nearly died a couple of days ago. You're still coming out of it. After almost dying, everyone feels emotionally up and down. In my experience, people say a lot of things in that state."

He took the pink napkin and laid it absently across his broad chest. The eggs looked perfect, several slices of thick bacon and whole-wheat toast on the plate. His stomach growled. "You give a person an amazing amount of rope to hang himself on," he told her wryly, picking up the fork.

Shelby sat down, facing him. "Being a deputy, you find people teach you a lot along the way. I've handled a lot of situations where there's shock and trauma going on." There was something satisfying and even healing to her as she watched him hungrily eat.

He stuffed the eggs into his mouth. Closing his eyes, Dakota simply absorbed their warmth and taste. How long had it been since someone made him a home-cooked meal? For a moment, he felt overwhelmed. He opened his eyes. Shelby sat with one leg tucked beneath her, relaxed, her expression calm. "I imagine you're a pretty cool dude in a gunfight."

"Is that SEAL talk?"

"Being a gunslinger? Yeah, I guess it is."

He ate, starved now. Dakota could tell he'd probably dropped ten pounds, and his stomach was reminding him of that loss in spades. He could feel the food taking hold, reviving his body, replacing his lost strength.

"Do you miss it? I mean, being a SEAL?" Jason seemed to miss his platoon, always wanting to return and go back to Iraq to be with them, not stick around here to visit their parents or her. The military was a powerful draw, but she couldn't grasp why.

Her voice had gone soft and it was as if she had whispered against his skin. Did Shelby know how her husky voice affected him? Dakota shrugged. "Yeah, I miss it." More than she would ever realize.

"Do you have family around here?"

"I did. My parents died in a snowstorm after their truck slid off on a back road and got stuck in a ditch."

"I'm so sorry. When did it happen?" Shelby knew of other people who had died of hypothermia during the long, brutal winter across Wyoming.

Pain filtered through Dakota and he stopped eating. He could tell she wasn't asking to create social conversation. She cared. "I was eighteen." As dark rage and grief stirred deep within him, he quickly tried to shut down all feelings. "It was a long time ago," he said more gruffly than he'd intended.

Shelby sensed a shift in Dakota. She saw devastation in his eyes and then he quickly dipped his head, breaking contact with her. Moistening her lips, she asked softly, "Do you stay in touch with your SEAL teammates?"

"Yes, with a few of the guys."

"They're like your family?" He had none of his own, so she could see Dakota regarding the guys he worked with as family.

"Yes, they are. How'd you get so wise for someone so young?"

Shelby shrugged, a ribbon of sadness flowing wide and slow through her. "Ever since I found out you were a SEAL, I've been trying to understand and learn about them. Because Jason, my brother, was an Army Ranger, never spoke about his life or what he did in the military. When he came home on leave, he never talked about what he did over in Iraq. Not ever." Shelby felt shut out and disconnected from her brother, whom she loved so much. Every time Jason came home on leave, there was a thick wall standing between him, her parents and herself. No matter what she tried to do to reach him, she failed.

"Why?"

"Because you're a big question mark in my world." *Because you remind me of Jason. I couldn't save him. Maybe I can save you?* The words were nearly torn out of Shelby. Stunned by the powerful, invisible connection Dakota had wielded with her, she was unable to deny it or stop it from happening.

A rush of desire coursed through Dakota. There

was such an openness to her, as if she trusted the world. How could she? There were bad guys everywhere. It was a world covered in camouflage as far as he was concerned. A powerful sense of protection toward her welled up within him. Okay, she was a law enforcement officer and knew how to take care of herself. But here, in her home, in this room, there was a terrible vulnerability that suddenly shone in her expression, especially her eyes. Something had happened to her. That much he knew. It was his sixth sense working. It always did when there was danger or threat.

Dakota tried to probe beyond her expression. Shelby was good at hiding, he discovered, but she couldn't stop it from showing in her eyes. If he sensed correctly, something tragic had happened recently to her. But what? He couldn't ask now. *Maybe later.* He managed a one-cornered smile, wanting to lift her out of the darkness only she knew about. "Don't be too curious about me. I'm a dead end."

She sighed and wrapped her arms around her drawn-up knee. Dakota was trying to tease her, but right now her gut was a knot. Her heart was squeezing with fresh grief, which wouldn't stop flowing outward and making her want to cry. "Interested, not curious. There's a difference."

He smiled thinly and picked up the mug of steaming coffee. "Interested why?"

She took his challenge and tried to deflect the real truth. "I like to learn about people. I see them as my teachers." Jason had been a hard teacher, nearly breaking her. She'd loved her brother with a fierceness that couldn't ever be controlled or stopped. They had been so close growing up. So many happy memories until…

"So, I'm a bug under your microscope of life?" he teased, a grin edging his mouth.

"I wouldn't say a bug," Shelby protested. Jason and Dakota were so much alike, it scared her. The PTSD was their shared, dark connection. Struggling, Shelby forced herself out of her own personal mire and focused on the man in her bed. How handsome Dakota was when he was relaxed. It was a remarkable change from meeting him out in the hospital parking lot. And where had his PTSD symptoms gone? She wondered if he was peaceful because she was here with him. Did one person make that big of a difference to someone like Dakota? Did she really have that much influence over him?

Shelby had never had that kind of effect on Jason. He grew irritated and irrational when she tried to talk with him. But Dakota was different, or at least, for the time being. The terrible, unanswered questions ate at her. Had she pushed Jason too far? All she wanted was that closeness they'd shared before he'd joined the military.

"What, then?" Dakota challenged, relishing the fresh coffee.

Shelby fumbled, avoiding his sharpened gaze. There was nothing weak about Dakota, the beard making him all the more male and therefore dangerous to her emotions.

"Out of words for once? Or are you carefully choosing our battles?"

Upon hearing the growl of his teasing, she lifted her chin. Her smile faded. The grief from her past stained the happiness she felt being around him. "I…sensed something about you, Dakota. I couldn't put my finger on it. I felt your desperation, your need." Shelby gave him a helpless look. "I knew someone once, who was a lot like you." She choked back the rest of the admission. It was too painful to say. Too painful and shaming to admit. Finally, her voice husky with emotion, she admitted, "There's just something about you that draws me."

Her softly spoken honesty rattled him as nothing else ever could. Seeing the flush across her cheeks, the sudden, unexpected grief shadowing her expression, Dakota felt like the proverbial bull in a china shop. Before he could think of something to say, Shelby looked as if she was going to cry.

She quickly uncurled from the bed and picked up the tray from his lap. "I brought some of your clothes down from the cabin the other day and washed them. You'll find fresh Levi's, a T-shirt and socks in the bathroom across the hall." She turned and left the room without another word.

Well hell! That went well, didn't it, Carson? Shelby had been generous with him. And he'd acted like a total jerk. Something deeper, more visceral was going on between them. Dakota threw off the covers in frustration. He had to get out of here or he'd do something really stupid. He felt protective toward Shelby. He wanted to hunt her down, pull her into his arms and love her until they both died of pleasure. Snorting to himself, Dakota knew he was no prize. He was a horse's ass, if anything. Looking around, he felt more like his old self before the infection damn near snuffed out his life. He was strong and solid again. He spotted a towel, washcloth and soap on the dresser, and walked over to pick them up.

Opening the door, he padded out into the highly polished oak hall and spotted the bathroom. Dakota heard the pleasant clink of dishes and running water out in the kitchen. The sounds were familiar and soothing to him, reminding him of his happy childhood. It sent a pang through him, reminding him of how much he'd lost. Scowling, he sauntered into the bathroom and shut the door. He had to get the hell out of here.

CHAPTER SEVEN

DAKOTA CAME OUT OF THE bathroom in bare feet, a pair of gray socks dangling between his fingers. He rubbed his recently shaved jaw. Something was different, but he couldn't name what it was as he ambled up toward the kitchen to find Shelby. Was it the long, hot shower washing off three days of crud? Getting rid of the high-fever sweat? Or was it her? As he'd lathered up with the pine-scented soap, he felt his heart opening. It was the damnedest sensation, one he'd never felt before. The soap bubbles and rivulets of hot water mixed with steam had cleansed him. His old strength flowed quietly back into him.

His focus, his being, centered on Shelby. She didn't have to take him in. Dakota sensed there was a reason behind her doing so. And he had to know. Now. Shelby stood at the sink, hands on the counter, gazing out the window. She didn't hear him coming. He'd been taught how to walk quietly during SEAL training, and that skill was with him to this day.

Shelby was lost in a morass of emotions, mostly grief and guilt, when she realized Dakota was standing a few feet away from her. Looking up, she saw his hair was mussed and damp. His eyes, clear and intense, unsettled her. The dark green T-shirt stretched across his broad shoulders and powerful chest. There was nothing weak about this man. *Nothing.* He was standing in a pair of Levi's, his feet bare. A number of white scars ran across both feet.

"Look at me," Dakota ordered softly, placing his finger beneath her stubborn chin.

A wild tingle fled through her over his unexpected touch. Lifting her lashes, she met and fearlessly held his gaze. Her breath hitched as his finger moved, slowly tracing the line of her jaw.

"There's something you haven't told me, Shel… Why would a woman let a stranger, someone she didn't know, into her house?"

He called her Shel. The endearment came out tender and coaxing from between his lips. His roughened finger lingered at her neck. Heat radiated off his athletic body, male heat. Her entire lower body went soft and hot. He'd barely touched her and she was melting inwardly, starving for his touch. Shelby started to speak, but grief unexpectedly flooded her.

Shifting his hand, he cupped her cheek with his roughened palm. "Shel?"

The callused palm against her cheek shattered a door she'd kept locked for almost nine months. Shelby swore she wouldn't go there. Would never... Oh God, she was crying! Hot tears winded down her cheeks. Dakota's gaze held hers. This wasn't a stare-down. Somehow, he'd sensed her grief. Her loss. And when tears slipped from her eyes, his face went tender with concern.

She whispered brokenly, "I—I lost my older brother, Jason, less than a year ago." She closed her eyes, the shame too much to bear. "H-he was an Army Ranger. He'd come home on leave after his third tour in Afghanistan." Sniffing, Shelby felt her heart being torn in two with all the grief she'd managed to wall up and hide from. She blinked, everything blurring because the tears continued to fall.

"Tell me," he urged, moving closer, their bodies inches from each other. Her pain was driving him crazy. Whatever it was, Shelby was devastated, her mouth contorted, the tears falling faster and faster. Sliding his long fingers around the slender nape of her neck, burying them in the softness of her hair, he angled her chin just enough to catch her tearful gaze. "You helped me. Now let me help you."

A fist of pain and gutting grief raced up through her. She could barely breathe the words. "Oh God, I'm so ashamed, so ashamed, Dakota. Jason committed suicide once he left us and went back to Afghanistan." There, it was out. Unwilling sobs rolled out of her. Blindly, Shelby sought refuge from it and took a step forward—into Dakota's arms.

His gray socks dropped to the tile floor. A groan issued from deep within Dakota as she fearlessly came to him. Her knees began to buckle, and he swept her up hard against him, holding her as she sobbed. The sounds were wild, harsh, and her grief nearly overwhelmed him. Nestling his jaw against her hair, the strands tickling his cheek, he held and gently rocked her. Her brother had been in the army. His mind whirled with the implications and information. Worst of all, he'd killed himself. Without thinking, simply responding, Dakota caressed her mussed hair with his lips. He kissed her fragrant skin where the hairline met near her ear.

Because of how much pain she'd been carrying, she must have seen her brother, Jason, in him. Dakota reined in his sexual hunger for her. God knew, he was aching and he wanted her, but this wasn't the right time or place. Instead, he focused on caring for Shelby the way she'd already cared for him. He moved his hand downward, rubbing her back as he tried to ease her pain. Shelby's weeping grew deeper. *Hold her. Just hold her,* he told himself.

Dakota didn't know how long they stood melded together in the kitchen. Slowly, Shelby's sobs lessened and finally ceased. Her fingers were pressed against his chest and he felt her warmth, her woman's strength even though the storm had passed. Lifting his chin, he leaned down, his lips brushing her ear. "Tears are never wasted, Shel…."

Shelby felt his moist breath, his tenderness. The strength of his arms gave her a sense of safety. As wounded as Dakota was, somehow he had the heart, the soul, to give back to her when she needed it the most. With the slow thud of his heart where her cheek rested against his chest, Shelby felt the backlog of pain dissolving.

Dakota continued to hold her. Right now she felt like a newborn, completely incapable of doing anything on her own. Shelby had never felt weak or unable to do anything she set her mind to. The grief and shame of Jason's suicide had wrecked her in ways she was unprepared for. And Dakota was here, holding her safe, absorbing her pain, her loss. Somewhere in the haze of her sorrow, she could see just how mentally tough Dakota really was. He was a deeply wounded warrior, and yet, in her hour of need, he rose to help her.

Shelby slid her arm beneath his, her fingers moving against his narrow waist. "I—don't know what happened. I didn't mean—"

"Shh," he rasped against her ear, content to feel her smooth, soft skin against his cheek. "No I'm-sorrys. Okay? You loved your brother. I know what it's like to lose…"

She felt him hesitate and then clear his throat. His arms tightened around her for a moment.

"You've been sitting on a lot of grief for a long, long time," Dakota told her. "I think my being here brought it all up. He was a Ranger and he did work similar to what the SEALs do. That's a lot of stress on a man, Shelby. Constant, sometimes nonstop stress for a solid year. It's hell on everyone."

Barely opening her eyes, she hiccuped. "I—I should have known he was in trouble, Dakota. I should have…"

"Why? You aren't trained to see pain a man wants to hide from you. Hell, I fooled a ton of shrinks for years so I could go back and be deployed with my platoon." *My family.*

She felt and heard his dark chuckle. The vibration riffled through her, soothed her torn emotional state. "There was never a sign…never. My poor parents, they're still devastated by it. We're all hurting so much…."

"I know, Shel, it's not easy to get over." Hell, he still hadn't gotten over the loss of his sister, Ellie, but now was not the time to bring that up. Dakota wanted to focus on Shelby's needs. Her warm, soft body molded against his. Her breasts were full, and he swore he could feel the nipples through that orange T-shirt she wore. Her breathing was softening, becoming normal now. The hiccups disappeared. Lifting his hand, he moved his fingers against her flushed cheek, removing the last of her tears.

"Things like this have their own time and way

with us. I'm sure your brother, Jason, was pretty burned out from constant danger, constant threat of dying. He probably lost some of his best friends over there. It all accumulates over time, Shel. It takes a toll on us. Some guys know how to defuse the grief. Some don't. Those are the ones who drown in it. Some turn to drugs. Some to drinking. And—" he lowered his tone "—some kill themselves because the pain is just too much for them to bear."

He gently brushed his fingers against Shelby's skin. How incredibly tender he was compared to his warrior self, moved through her thoughts. Her flesh tingled and Shelby found herself never wanting him to let go of her. "My dad was in the Marine Corps, a military policeman. Jason and I were military brats. Jason so badly wanted Dad to be proud of him."

"The Rangers, like the SEALs, demand a certain kind of mental toughness that damn few men will ever have," Dakota told her in a gruff tone, drying her cheek. Shelby's eyes were closed, a few small beads of tears clinging to her blond lashes. *Fragile.* She was fragile. Desperately, Dakota searched for the right damn words. But what were they? Hell, he was no philosopher. Not a poet. He was a SEAL in his heart and soul. "Shel, you can't blame yourself for what Jason did. You can't control anyone but yourself." Somehow Dakota wanted to ease her pain. But how?

Sighing heavily, Shelby nodded ever so slightly. She soaked up his male warmth, the strength he was feeding her. "I just don't know how to get over it. Neither do my parents. Every time I see them, there's this sorrow in their eyes. They're hurting so much. I want to help them, but I don't know how."

"Time will heal all of you, Shel." Dakota said the words but didn't believe them himself. Ellie's murder was like a hard lump of coal burning out his heart, slowly destroying his soul. His rage toward her rapists and killers was never far away from his memory. If he could get his hands on those two slimy sexual predators who had stolen her life, he'd kill them without remorse.

Slowly, Shelby eased away from Dakota. She didn't want to, but she knew she must—or else. Fully aware of his arousal, she understood he was there to somehow, in his own way, help her. Heal her. Yes, Dakota's touch was many things: healing, sexual, sensual and oh, how badly she ached to take him into her bed and lie with him. Looking up, she saw a golden glitter in the depths of his eyes, that of a man wanting his woman. The grief had subsided and seemed to have dissolved.

Surprised and relieved, Shelby knew she was an emotional mess right now. He released her from his embrace. He wanted her as much as she wanted him, but now was the wrong time.

Shelby leaned her hips against the kitchen counter, moving her fingers through her mussed hair, trying to tame the damp strands that had soaked up some of her tears. As she looked over at Dakota, she saw the dark blotches on his T-shirt where she'd cried so hard. Where she'd sobbed out her pain. Lifting her hand, her long fingers grazed the damp material. "I owe you another T-shirt."

Dakota caught her hand, brought it up to his lips and brushed a kiss on the back of it. The scent of her as a woman intoxicated him, his nostrils flaring as he inhaled her as deeply as he could into his aching body. "You were there for me. Remember?" He managed a lopsided smile as he released her hand. "I still don't know how the hell you got me off that floor and into your cruiser."

Tucking her hands in front of her, Shelby whispered, "Because I couldn't stand to see you die… and I knew you were dying."

"I was another Jason?"

Compressing her lips, she hung her head. "Y-yes, I guess you were."

"Only, I wasn't committing suicide, Shel."

Lifting her head, she managed a weak shrug. "No…no, you weren't. But inside me…" She touched her heart with her fingers. "I didn't want you to die. Jason took his life out in the bush. He had no one, Dakota. And neither did you." Her heart stirred with anguish. "Jason talked to no one about how he felt. The guys in his platoon never knew why he'd taken his life. They were just as shocked by it as we were."

"Your brother was a hero, Shel. I don't care what anyone tells you or what you think you know." He saw her eyes go dark with agony and he stepped up to her, slid his hand beneath her jaw and held her gaze. "Jason was a warrior. And you need to honor him for that, not how his life was taken. He's a hero in my eyes. So many times out there, you see too much. And some guys can't handle the amount of emotional hits they take over time, they can't process it...."

"Jason never talked about the missions. They were top secret. I—I tried to draw him out, because I could see how much he was suffering." Shelby closed her eyes, wanting his closeness. He gently moved his hand across her hair and allowed it to come to rest on her slumped shoulder. "I failed."

"No," Dakota rasped, his voice stronger. "You did not fail him. You felt he was in trouble, but you're no mind reader, Shel. None of us are."

She absorbed the warmth of his roughened hand on her shoulder. Did Dakota realize he was steadying her? "Then how did you realize I was hurting?"

His mouth pulled into a pained line. "At first, I

didn't. But then, as I showered, it all fell into place. I saw I'd somehow upset you in the bedroom."

"I was just thinking about you in that bed... knowing you'd almost died, but we were able to get you to the hospital in time...." Shelby admitted.

He heard the weariness in her voice, the ache of loss. "And no one was able to reach Jason in time?"

Nodding, Shelby lifted her hand and rubbed her face. "Right."

"And that's when you started feeling the grief you've been sitting on. I watched you close down."

"Yes, I was thinking about Jason. It wasn't your fault," she said, searching his hooded gaze. "Please, believe me. It wasn't you, Dakota. I guess these past couple of days have torn off the scab I was keeping over all the emotions I was running from since Jason died."

Moving his fingers in a gentle motion, he followed the line of her shoulder, slid his fingers up across her neck until he cupped her jaw. Moving forward until he could feel the female heat coming off her body, he leaned down. His mouth hovered inches from her own. "Sometimes," he whispered, "when two people are in pain, the best thing they can do is help each other. Shel, I want to kiss you, but I won't unless you tell me it's all right."

Her lashes moved upward and he drowned in the blue of her gaze. Her pupils were huge, black and shining with life once again. In that second,

Dakota knew he'd helped Shelby, even if just a little bit. Their breaths quickened, mingled moisture flowing against each other's faces.

His mouth hovered above hers. His body screamed for release, wanting her in every way possible. Her eyes held a touch of fearlessness, black against that gleaming background of turquoise.

He felt the rush of her breath against his mouth, saw her lashes shutter against her flushed cheeks. He heard her whisper the word, "Yes." In moments, he curved his mouth against hers, and Dakota knew his life was about to change forever.

CHAPTER EIGHT

A SMALL MOAN ROSE IN Shelby as Dakota took her mouth, his arms wrapping around her, drawing her close, into himself. She moved her arms upward, sliding around his broad shoulders, which felt like granite beneath her fingertips. Oh God, this was exactly what she needed! In some distant part of her barely functioning brain, she could feel his mouth cherishing hers, his arms holding her as if she were fragile and might break at a moment's notice. His breath was short, sharp as he slowly tasted her mouth for the first time. Reveling in the sense of safety and protection he automatically gave her, Shelby returned his deep, searching kiss. Nothing had ever felt so right. Nothing...

Her cell phone rang.

At first, it startled Shelby. She clung to his male mouth, tasting him, absorbing him as a man, as a warrior. Yet she felt him tense when the phone went off, too. Sadness mixed with the raging need buried deep in her belly. She wanted Dakota. All of him. In every way imaginable.

The phone continued to ring.

"Damn phone," Shelby muttered against his mouth. "I've got to get it, Dakota… I'm sorry." She reluctantly pulled out of his arms.

Throbbing heat soared through Dakota as he released Shelby so she could walk quickly to the table where her cell was. His mouth tingled wildly. He could taste her on his lips. Her scent teased his nostrils. She was flushed, her eyes drowsy, filled with arousal—for him. Having felt so beaten down by the past year, Dakota felt strong and good once again. Shelby's lips had been sweet, woman-strong, and she was meeting him without reserve. God, how he wanted her in his bed, beneath his hands, wanting to take her…

Grabbing the cell, Shelby opened it. This was the sheriff's cell phone and she knew it would be about business. "Shelby."

"Cade here."

Closing her eyes for a moment, she turned and stared longingly toward Dakota. His face was hard, eyes intent upon her. He wanted her. She wanted him. Damn the phone call. "What's going on?"

Dakota stood relaxed near the kitchen counter listening closely to Shelby's breathy voice. The flush in her cheeks slowly left. His gaze locked on her mouth. He could feel her kissing him eagerly, with abandon, once again. Knowing he could have healed some of her raw pain and loss, he wondered if there would ever be another time. Seeing her brow wrinkle, her voice suddenly go low, he sensed something very bad had just occurred.

Leaning down, he picked up the socks, ambled over to the table, pulled out a chair and sat down. He tugged them on each of his feet, and listened to the conversation. Their moment together was gone. He grieved over the loss. Shelby straightened, her body going tense, her voice strained. What the hell was happening? Did Cade Garner call her at home like this often? She was supposed to be on her off day. Disgruntled, Dakota felt his state of arousal ebb away. Whatever the conversation, it was deeply affecting Shelby. The soft, drowsy look he'd seen as he kissed her was replaced with sudden intensity coupled with anxiety. And if he read her right, it was fear.

Shelby listened closely to Cade.

"Is Dakota there? I'd called over at the hospital and Jordana said she'd had him moved to your place."

"Yes…he's here. Do you want to talk with him?" Shelby stared across the table at Dakota. He looked grim now, the desire doused in his eyes. Regretting losing the heated moment, she said, "Okay, hold on." She reached across the table and handed the cell to him. "It's Cade Garner. He needs to speak to you."

Surprised, Dakota took the phone. Their fingers met and he hungrily absorbed her fleeting touch. Her eyes were anxious-looking and he saw her chew on her lower lip for a moment. "Dakota here," he rumbled, putting the cell to his ear.

Shelby turned, wrapping her arms tightly about herself as she walked to the kitchen counter. God, her world had suddenly been turned inside out. Her mind raced. Yet she kept one ear on Dakota's reaction to what Cade was going to ask of him. Rubbing her brow, she felt a slight headache coming on. Oh God, they escaped! And now her life wouldn't be her own until they were caught—again.

She turned, desperate to hold on to the beautiful, healing moments before with Dakota. His face had gone tense, eyes flashing with what she interpreted as anger. His mouth, those lips that had moved commandingly against hers, had stolen her breath, taken her on a wild, hot ride into near oblivion, were now pursed. Thinned to a single, hard line. Shelby could feel his powerful reaction to what Cade was filling him in on. Wincing internally, Shelby watched as if a bomb had gone off near Dakota. He slowly rose out of the chair, his mouth taut, his fingers curling slowly into a thick fist. What was going on? She didn't understand, feeling the tension suddenly swirl through the room as if a tornado had just struck.

"We'll be there in about thirty minutes," Dakota growled. He flipped the phone closed, set it on the table and lifted his head. His gaze locked onto Shelby's. For a moment, she looked fragile. He recalled that wild, hot kiss that held such promise of things to come. Drenched with rage, with shock, he held her frowning gaze, those beautiful lips compressed.

"We need to talk," he said, gesturing for her to come and sit down at the table. "Cade wants us at the sheriff's office in thirty minutes."

Hearing the low growl in his tone, Shelby nodded. She allowed her arms to drop to her sides and then sat down opposite Dakota. "Two convicts escaped. He wanted to ask you if you would track with me to find them."

Dakota rubbed his recently shaven jaw. "Yeah. Only," he said as he sighed roughly, "there's more to it you don't know, Shel." He reached out, gripping her hands folded in front of her on the table. "Damn, I didn't want to discuss this with you yet."

She tilted her head. "Do you not want to track with me?" She remembered his initial reaction to a woman being able to track. His hand was rough on her soft skin, but it felt comforting to her.

Shaking his head, Dakota released her hand, reared back on two legs of the chair, looking up to the ceiling, fighting his violent emotions. "No... no, it has nothing to do with that, Shel." He took in a ragged breath, looked at the ceiling for a long moment and then back to her. "I was hoping not to have this conversation with you for a long time. You're hurting right now. Damn. I'm sorry. So sorry…"

Shelby could hear the undisguised anguish in his tone. "I don't understand, Dakota. What is it? You look really upset." Her first reaction was to get up, throw her arms around him and hold him. The raw, gritty look in his eyes startled her. Made her afraid. What was he hiding?

"Cade told you that two death row convicts, Vance Welton and Oren Hartley, just escaped. That they're heading for Yellowstone National Park to disappear into the forests so the authorities can't find them." His eyes shuttered closed for a second. His mouth became a hard line, as if he was fighting back a barrage of unknown emotions.

"Dakota? What is going on? Do you know these two criminals?"

His heart twisted hard in his chest. For a moment, Dakota wasn't sure he could handle it. It took every ounce of SEAL control over his feelings to stop it from happening. The wariness on the edge of Shelby's voice helped him. Gulping hard, he shoved everything—everything—back down deep inside himself. Opening his eyes, he stared down at the table for a moment. "This is coming at the wrong damned time," he breathed, his voice sounding like a rasp against metal.

Shelby reached out. She wanted to touch him.

Her fingers slid over his tightly balled hands. "Dakota? What's wrong? Let me help?" She tipped her head to catch his downcast gaze.

How could he feel so goddamned miserable? Dakota couldn't recall any firefight feeling as dangerous and life-threatening as how he felt right now. He opened his hands, needed Shelby's warm, firm touch. Studying her long fingers, he turned them over gently in his palms. He struggled to find the words he needed to speak.

He lifted his head. If it had been anyone but her, Dakota wouldn't have said what he was going to say. The words, each one, tore out of him, a razor slicing into his tightened throat, bleeding him out, bleeding him dry until he thought he was going to die as Ellie had died.

"When I saw you out in the parking lot of the hospital, I thought I knew you, Shelby. I was in too much shock to pursue it. And talking to Cade just now, I realize where I saw you—in the Cody, Wyoming, courthouse nine years ago."

Shelby kept staring at him. Her mind wrenched back to that time and place. It became clearer. She shook her head. "Your last name…Carson…I thought I knew the name, but so much was going on at the E.R., I just couldn't remember."

"I know these two bastards, Shelby. My sister, Ellie Carson, was nineteen when those two jumped her when she was leaving Cody University one evening. She—she was taking classes to become a registered nurse. I was seventeen at the time. They hauled her into an abandoned house nearby and…" His voice dropped. Tears jammed into Dakota's eyes and he was helpless to stop them from forming. Shelby's hands tightened around his and her face suddenly went pale. The rest had to be said, like cutting into a very old, festering wound to release the toxins eating away at his soul. "They tortured her, raped her repeatedly and finally slit her throat and killed her."

Without thinking, Shelby stood up and quietly moved around the table. Dakota had pushed his hands across his face, trying to hide the tears coming down his drawn cheeks. She pulled up a chair, sitting facing him. Slipping her arms around his tense, bunched shoulders, she nestled her head against his clenched jaw. "I'm so sorry, so very sorry, Dakota. My God, I didn't know…." She held him with her woman's strength.

The past struck Shelby full force. She'd had one day in court to testify and she remembered seeing the Carson family, the grief on their collective faces. Vaguely, she recalled the teen boy with the parents. That had been Dakota. Time had changed him markedly from a tall, slender boy into the man he was today.

A new feeling flowed through her as she held him. They were both frozen in time over a horrific event that clearly connected them today. Dakota was still held prisoner by it. A shudder worked through him, and Shelby sensed his internal strength to control the violence of his grief. He was strong in ways she would never be. Kissing his cheek, Shelby inhaled his male scent. She continued to place small, tender kisses against his brow, cheek and jaw. Little by little, she felt him begin to relax, to trust himself to her caring arms.

Gradually, Dakota stuffed all the rage and horror down into a hole he never wanted to open again. Shelby's arms were strong and he greedily absorbed her silent care. Her lips were soft and healing against his flesh, and God, how badly he needed her. An IED going off under him would have thrown him into the same kind of shock he was experiencing right now with the news Cade Garner had just given him.

He eased Shelby away from him and held her hand, a lifeline for him as he stared into her eyes filled with compassion. "Thanks," he managed, voice rough with unshed tears.

She continued to hold his hand. "I remember you in the courtroom now, Dakota. And your parents. I was there for only one day to testify in capturing them. I wasn't there for the whole trial, although I had been briefed on it by the prosecutor's office." She swallowed against a forming lump. "That's why you looked familiar to me and vice versa."

Shaking her head, she muttered, "At times like this, we all need someone. You were there for me. Now I'm here for you. Did you tell Cade you'd track with me?"

Nodding, he studied her soft, long fingers. "Yeah, I did."

"There's more to this story, Dakota."

What else could there be? He frowned. "What are you talking about?"

"I was just coming on the sheriff's force as a deputy, my first week, and my father was still the commander here. I'd graduated from high school at sixteen. I was one of those bright kids who skipped grades." She managed a disconcerted smile. "I went to a law enforcement academy and graduated at eighteen. We got word of the terrible murder of your sister. Law enforcement was able to prove those two escaped into Yellowstone. My father had been teaching me to track since I was five years old. He knew I was good at what I did. He ordered me to go with a multi–law enforcement team of other trackers and dogs to try to find those two."

Looking deep into her eyes, feeling as if he could fall into them, be lost forever and never look back, Dakota nodded. "Cade didn't tell me that."

Shelby moved her fingers across his hand, a hand with so many scars on the front and back of it. Each white slice was pain he'd experienced. Softly, she wanted to give him respite from a life that was obviously filled with nothing but suffering. "I left the team once we were inside the park. I had a hunch, and it played out to be correct. I found the car they'd stolen near Norris Basin. I called it in and followed them on foot into the woods."

His skin crawled as he realized she had been in absolute jeopardy with Welton and Hartley. Eyes widening, Dakota knew if they'd ever found her, they'd have raped and murdered her just as they had Ellie. His throat closed off. "You must have found them first?" He saw a tight grin pull at her lips.

"Better believe it. They were like two bulls. Broken brush, bent limbs they'd stepped on. You know how hard it is to track on a pine needle floor, but they left plenty of other clues for me to follow."

In utter disbelief, he demanded, "Did you corner them?"

"Yes." She rolled her shoulders to relieve the tension of that moment when she'd suddenly come upon the two murderers. "I was fresh out of law enforcement training. The only time I'd ever fired my pistol was at practice targets. I found them resting by a group of boulders, pulled my pistol and told them to freeze. I called on my radio for backup."

Disbelief soared through Dakota. He remembered first seeing Shelby in that courtroom. Even though she wore a sheriff's uniform, to him she didn't look more than a mere slip of a young girl. "What did they do?"

"Cursed at me," she said wryly.

"They didn't think you were going to really shoot them?"

"Oh, they got it," she answered, her voice hardening. "They were sexual predators of the worst sort. I'm prejudiced against that kind of man, anyway."

"Welton was the ringleader. Didn't he challenge you?"

Shaking her head, her eyes taking on a dark look, she said, "I told them to make my day."

Dakota remembered the famous line spoken by Clint Eastwood in *Dirty Harry*. A grin edged his mouth. "They believed you."

"It's a side of me you haven't seen yet, Dakota. I hated them. I'd never felt hate before, but standing there, my pistol in my hands, aimed at them, I hated. I told them to just give me one excuse to blow their heads off their shoulders."

Dakota saw the spark of anger deep in her blue eyes. There was nothing cute or fuzzy about Shelby right now. He was seeing her strength, an internal kind that he was well acquainted with. It was shocking to see she possessed it, too. But why not? Women were strong, he knew. "They sat there?"

"Yes. I had them lie on their bellies, hands behind their necks. The rest of my team arrived and they cuffed them, read them their rights and hauled their asses back to Cody, Wyoming."

"Unbelievable." He gave her an assessing look. "You must be one hell of a tracker, then."

"I am. My dad taught me well."

"Wasn't he worried for your safety? He knew Welton and Hartley had already killed my sister."

"Yes, he was. But he also knew he'd taught me how to track and use a rifle ever since I could remember. I knew Yellowstone like the back of my hand, Dakota. What my dad didn't want me doing was peeling off from the main team, which I did." Her laugher was throaty. "When I got back to the office to write up my report, he chewed my ass royally. He told me never to leave my tracking partner again."

"At least someone had some common sense."

Shrugging, Shelby sighed and released his hand. "I was young and green. I've got nine years in with the sheriff's department and I'm a lot more seasoned now. And smart," she added, seeing the look of respect come to his face. It made her feel good because earlier, Dakota had treated her like a helpless, brainless doll.

"I sat through the entire trial. My parents were shattered by the loss of Ellie. I sat there hating them, wanting to wrap my hands around each one of their throats and slowly killing them, like they'd killed my sister."

She sighed. "You were only seventeen. It must

have been so hard on you," she murmured, "and on your poor parents."

Nodding, Dakota wiped his face harshly with his hand. The past was staring him in the face. Again. "I wanted to even the scales. So many times, I tried to imagine the terror, the pain that Ellie felt. It nearly drove me insane. I finally had to get away and I escaped and went into the navy. I couldn't handle all the feelings ripping through me. My parents were depressed. I couldn't help them."

"I'm sure I'd feel exactly the same way." Shelby watched him struggled with his emotions. "Are you sure you want to track with me? Will you be able to control your emotions, clear your head to track?" Instantly, there came a feral change in his gold-brown eyes, that of powerful focus. She actually felt an energy shift around him. The change was startling. Was this his SEAL training coming out, the warrior side taking over? Because if it was, Shelby had no question that Dakota would not only track with her; he'd find them. And he'd want to kill them.

"You only know a small part of me." He said the words in grate. "I'm a SEAL. I'm no longer in the navy, but the training will always be with me. I have my reflexes. My knowledge gained by six months of deployment every two years into Iraq and Afghanistan. I have the control I need to hunt down these sick bastards."

"Okay," she said, standing up, "then we need to saddle up. Cade is expecting us shortly."

His gut clenched and he stared at her. "You let me do the tracking." He wanted those two bastards so bad he could taste it. Find them and kill them.

Her brows rose. "Excuse me?" She saw his face grow cold.

"You don't need to go along," he grated.

She scowled. "There's no way I'm staying off this case."

Gut churning, Dakota felt a desperation similar to when Ellie was announced as missing. He'd intuitively picked up that she was in trouble. That same feeling washed over him again. Shelby stood there, looking so damned confident. And his heart lurched with new terror. What if they got ahold of Shelby this time? What if he wasn't there to protect her? She'd gotten lucky the first time she'd caught those two. He rubbed his chin, holding her stubborn stare. "You can't go along with me."

Shelby held on to her mounting anger. Instead, she tried to understand what was going on in his mind. Was he worried about her? Shelby considered his reactions carefully, her instincts telling her that Dakota's past was bleeding into the present. He might not even see her right now. He might see Ellie. And if he did, Dakota would want her safe, not on the trail tracking with him. She opened her hands, a plea in her husky tone. "Look, I know a lot's gotten dumped on you, Dakota. I can take care of myself out there."

His heart lurched with other emotions he thought he'd never experience. And just as abruptly, he buried them. The tender expression in Shelby's eyes touched him. All he could do was shake his head. There was no way he could get involved with her on a personal level. His rage was always there, lurking. Dakota was sorry he'd kissed her. Sorry to his soul because she didn't need a wounded, broken man in her life. He wanted to protect her from himself, as well. She deserved something a helluva lot better than him.

"We'll see…" he growled, finally. He would talk to Cade Garner and convince him to keep Shelby safe and he'd do the tracking by himself. Alone, as he had been for so many years already.

"Okay," she murmured, wanting to defuse the tension. "We'll talk about it later."

Rising, the sound of the chair scraping back across the tiled surface, Dakota muttered softly, "Wheels up." He walked over to her, cupping her elbow, looking down into her uplifted gaze. "We're going Down Range."

"What does that mean?"

"Going into combat." He was. She wasn't.

The warrior emerged in him. No longer did she see grief or unbridled emotions in his flat, hard eyes. His entire demeanor had shifted. Dakota was not open or vulnerable anymore. Just the opposite, hard as titanium with a ruthless, calculated expression. He meant business. He was going to extract the revenge he'd always wanted against these two convicts.

The realization left her throat dry. If she hadn't seen and experienced the softer side of him as a man, she would have been deeply shaken by his countenance right now. Was this how Jason was on a mission as a Ranger? Did he change faces? Put on this warrior mask to do his work?

Mouth dry, she whispered, "Yes, we're going Down Range…together."

CHAPTER NINE

VANCE WELTON SMILED. They'd just stolen their third car within Yellowstone Park and were five miles away from the south entrance to the national park. Driving the speed limit, Vance told Oren, "We did some serious planning. The cops have *no* idea where we are."

Oren Hartley, twenty-nine, black hair and blue eyes, stretched out his long legs. "Well, we did this once before. We ought to get it right the second time around, don't you think?" He absently chewed on a toothpick lodged in the corner of his mouth.

Snorting, Oren said, "Dude, you got that right." His short, thick hands moved firmly on the steering wheel of the stolen Toyota Camry. They'd stopped at Grant Village at a gas station and restaurant inside the park. Looking for a nondescript car had been their objective. The dark blue Camry filled the bill. It had been easy to steal it from the corner of the busy parking lot.

Oren pushed his fingers through his short hair.

"They're gonna think we're hiding in Yellowstone again."

Oren's thin brows drew down. "Yeah, well, we aren't making that mistake again."

"Hiding out in the Tetons and goin' after that bitch, Shelby Kincaid, was a good idea," Oren drawled. He shifted the dark sunglasses on his nose. He'd found the pair in the glove box of the car. Not only that, a suitcase in the trunk was full of men's summer hiking clothes they could wear. Best of all, whoever the owner of the Camry was, he was about their height of five feet ten inches. Making sure they changed clothes and cars every few hours had been a major part of their plan in order to evade law enforcement. Even though the dude who owned this car would eventually walk out to find it gone, the reporting on it would take time.

Hands tightening on the wheel, Welton snarled, "She tracked us down and put us in prison." Thin mouth moving into a hard line, he added softly, "First things first. We'll take one of the many dirt roads in the Tetons park, find a cabin somewhere on a slope, hide for a few days and get settled in."

"Goodbye, Yellowstone," Oren sang out, lifting his hand as they drove out of the national park. He chuckled. "Dadgum, but this is easy."

"Don't get too cocky, hillbilly."

Oren sighed. "I figure we'll stop halfway between here and the Tetons and swap out cars. Colter Bay Village is our next stop."

"Yes." They wore latex gloves to ensure that their prints would not connect them with the car theft. Vance knew law enforcement because he'd had battles with them since he was twelve years old. He'd shot a dog, and the neighbor had seen him do it. He liked to see how a bullet would kill an animal, but he really got pissed when he was thrown into the juvenile court system. It was just a stupid dog! That was all right, he got even with the neighbor who reported him to the police. At fourteen, he'd sneaked out of the house in the early morning hours and set fire to the guy's house. And too bad, the family had died in the fire.

Chuckling to himself, Welton felt proud that no one ever pinned that house fire on him. At an early age, he found out he liked sex, too. Never mind his father liked to play with his genitals since he could remember. Vance liked hunting down innocent little girls and sticking it to them. Of course, that came to a roaring halt when a mother discovered him with her seven-year-old daughter. At fifteen, he was once again thrown in a juvenile detention facility. Good thing his records were sealed when he turned eighteen.

"Hey, I can hardly wait to start tracking the bitch myself." Oren rubbed his hands together, a grin coming to his round face. He wore a blue baseball cap. They knew they had to disguise themselves in order to stay under the radar of cops and the public. "But, man, I got needs, Vance. You sure we can't take some time out, get our rocks off and then go hunt Kincaid down?"

Vance snarled. "Hell no! Keep it in your pants, you dumb hillbilly. I've been planning this for a long time and I'm damn well not diverting from it so you can screw around."

Oren sighed dramatically and pulled the bill of the cap lower over his eyes. "You're no fun, part-ner."

"Kincaid caught us." His voice lowered to a growl. "We're sticking to my plan. That bitch, once we find her, is gonna be so friggin' sorry she ever tracked us down in the first place." He had nightly dreams about tying her to a bed, torturing her and then raping her. He was going to watch the fear come to her eyes, listen to her scream, watch her bleed. Oh, he'd keep her alive for a couple of weeks, torturing her daily, enjoying her pain, paying her back for what she did to them.

Oren dug into the glove box, looking for some-thing to eat. "I'm with you all the way, good buddy. You sure you have a place that's hidden away so no one will ever find us?"

A chuckle erupted from Vance. The forest was on either side of the two-lane highway, the sky a powdery-blue midafternoon. "I do. Remember? We lived in this area before we got caught? I'm going straight to Curt Downing in Jackson Hole first. We ran drugs for him. Now maybe he can help us out a little. We need a truck that isn't stolen. He owns a trucking company. He'll have plenty of trucks around we can use."

Gleefully, Oren located a couple of protein bars in the glove box and drew them out. He tossed one in Vance's lap and tore off the wrapping on the second one. "I never trusted Downing. He's too full of himself," he murmured, chewing the honey-sweetened grains. "You never know what he's thinking. And my hillbilly instincts tell me he's not gonna be happy to see us show up."

"Too bad. He owes us. He just has to be reminded of it, is all. Downing can supply us with money and a truck."

"He's a slick bastard, Vance. I don't think he's gonna willingly do anything for us."

"Well, we'll have a little chat," he said, smiling smugly. A sheriff's cruiser passed them. They'd seen a number of law enforcement vehicles throughout the park—all looking for them. Although Vance had a bald head, he was going to let the hair and beard grow so that he wouldn't be so easily identified.

"There goes another deputy dawg," Oren drawled, hooking his thumb over his shoulder.

"They all think we're hidden in Yellowstone. The dumb assholes."

"What's first on our list?"

"Get another car, get inside the Tetons National Park and then find us a cabin."

"Then go seek out Downing?"

"In that order," Vance said, looking in his rearview mirror to make sure that black Tahoe sheriff's cruiser was still heading into Yellowstone. It was. Glee filled him. All the years of careful planning were finally going to pay off.

"THIS IS A FUBAR," Dakota said quietly to Shelby as they stood near the rear of a multi–law enforcement meeting in Yellowstone. His eyes flashed with frustration as he watched the FBI, the U.S. Forest Service rangers and the sheriff's deputies from two other surrounding counties standing around a huge table filled with maps of the park.

Shelby stood next to him remembering their kiss. They had driven up on orders of Commander McCall. Leaning close, an excuse to touch him, she whispered, "Cade Garner is the only one who might be able to break this logjam. He'll be here shortly."

Instinctively, Dakota inhaled her fragrance. After they'd gotten the call, their intimate time with each had come to an abrupt, jarring halt. His gaze dropped to her mouth. Instantly, his body went hot. "The right hand doesn't know what the left hand's doing here." They'd stood in this room for two hours, watching reports come in on a number of stolen cars. A forest ranger had a large map hanging up on one wall and was putting red pins in it where the vehicles had been stolen. It was simple math in Dakota's mind: the escaped convicts were stealing them, swapping out the cars, throwing law enforcement off their trail and heading south, out of the park.

Grimacing, Shelby couldn't disagree. Cade Garner finally entered the large, crowded room. He wore a serious expression on his face and he went directly to the FBI agent, Collin Woods, who was running the show.

"We've got a new report of a Toyota Camry being stolen near the south gate of the park," he told Woods, handing him the paperwork.

Wood, who was in his mid-forties, short and lean, studied the report. He handed it to the forest ranger who was pushing red pins on the wall map. "Put it up," he ordered.

Cade studied the map. "These guys aren't staying in Yellowstone," he warned everyone. Going to the map, he traced his finger across the eastern gate highway. There were two red pins. At the main intersection, where the highway went south, there were now three red pins.

Woods scowled. "Vance Welton and Oren Hartley hid for two weeks near Norris Basin in this park. They aren't going to change their *modus operandi.*"

Shelby moved her head, a silent gesture to tell Dakota to follow her. She was the only woman present. He gave her a bare nod in return and they moved around the group huddled around the table. Garner's face went dark with anger. His eyes flashed. He was a good sheriff's deputy, now number-two man in the Tetons County department.

"No?" Cade Garner jammed his index finger into the third red pin area. "That stolen car is only twenty-two miles from the south entrance to the park."

"You're assuming it's them," Woods said, impatient.

"Damn right I am," Garner breathed, holding his anger in tight check. He turned to Shelby. "You tracked these sick bastards before. Does this look like their M.O.?" he asked.

Shelby noticed the dismissive look Woods gave her. He was an arrogant little man in a black suit, white shirt and dark blue tie. She moved her finger along the highway at the east gate entrance. "Yes, it does, Cade. Look here." She brought her finger to Norris Basin, in the northwestern area of the park. "When I was tracking them, they had already turned south and were heading in the direction of the south gate entrance on foot."

"You can't be sure of that," Woods spouted. "You can't read their minds."

Dakota stepped around Shelby, glaring into Wood's arrogant face. "Listen, she's a tracker. In order to successfully track a target, you have to get inside the head of the escapee. She knows what the hell she's talking about." He loomed over the agent, who cowered beneath each of his carefully enunciated words. Woods took a step back, scowling up at Carson.

"And just who are you?" Woods challenged.

Dakota was the only man in civilian clothes, dressed in jeans, a red polo shirt and hiking boots in the room. He stood out like a sore thumb.

"Agent Woods," Shelby spoke up, her voice strong and brooking no argument, "this is Dakota Carson. Our commander requested his aid. He was a U.S. Navy SEAL, a tracker and sniper in his platoon."

Woods shrugged. "Whatever…we're not over in Afghanistan."

Cade Garner moved a step closer toward the FBI agent. "Agent Woods, you obviously don't appreciate what SEALs do. Mr. Carson has a lot of experience tracking in some of the worst places in the world, and successfully tracking down the enemy. We need him on this hunt for a thousand good reasons."

Quirking his thin mouth, Woods said, "Great. This is just what I need."

Dakota's right hand curled slowly into a fist. The little bastard. He had respect for all law enforcement but they'd been cursed with one bad apple. He gave Cade a warning look. This agent didn't know squat.

Most of the men were restless, wanting to do something other than standing for hours in this room trying to figure out the location of Welton and Hartley.

"Mr. Woods, with all due respect, Deputy Kincaid tracked these two sexual predators and murderers for two weeks here in Yellowstone. The dogs lost their trail a number of times, but she never did. Your presumptions about my team are baseless," Cade Garner said.

Shelby felt Dakota tense behind her. He came and stood at her shoulder. Automatically, she moved her hand back, warning him to remain silent. This was a turf war between Garner and Woods.

Woods shrugged. "The FBI has trackers, too," he flung out defensively to the group.

"They didn't find these two the last time," Garner reminded him acidly. "It was Shelby Kincaid, a sheriff's deputy. She was born here and she knows the land like the back of her hand," he said in a low voice.

"I wasn't on that case. I'm on this one and it will be different."

Shelby almost laughed. She placed her hand against her mouth so Woods wouldn't catch her smiling.

Garner drew himself up, his eyes slits as he surveyed the tense room. "Gentlemen, we've got two of the worst sexual predators in our county loose." His voice dropped to a warning rasp. "And I'll be damned if anyone is going to get caught up in the fact that our best tracker is a woman and damned good at what she does."

Garner turned, jamming a finger at the map. "My instincts are screaming at me that these two are already out of the park and heading south. I'm calling my commander, alerting him to just that and seeing if another car gets stolen between here and Jackson Hole. These guys have a plan, Agent Woods. And I'm not wasting one more minute of my time here in this damned room. We must follow the string of stolen cars. It's our only choice."

Dakota felt himself imploding with rage. He wanted to jerk Woods up by his expensive black suit lapels and pin his scrawny ass on that wall map. Ellie had been tortured and raped and had died at the hands of these two convicts. He felt Shelby's cool fingers pulling his fist apart, lacing them between his own. It broke the circuit of his building anger. She looked up, met his gaze, and barely shook her head. How did she know he was ready to kill the little weasel?

"Well, you go right ahead and call your commander," Woods said. "This is our command post."

Cade gestured to Shelby and Dakota to follow him. "Fine. You call me when you think you know what the hell you're doing. The evidence that Welton and Hartley are heading south toward Jackson Hole is as plain as those red tacks on the map."

Shelby kept her mouth fixed to stop her smile. Woods smirked, lifted his chin at an imperious angle as Cade spun on his heel and strode toward the door.

She turned and followed him. So did Dakota.

Once outside the building, Cade turned to them. He glanced at his watch. "Okay, there's nothing you two can do right now. If we can't find these two, you can't track them."

Dakota liked the way the deputy thought. "Why would they not hide in the park again? They managed to evade everyone for two weeks."

Cade's expression became grim. His gaze moved to Shelby. "I didn't want to say anything in there, Shelby, but my gut's screaming something else at me. It would explain why they're not trying to hole up in Yellowstone."

She frowned. "What?" Rarely had she seen her boss this worried. Or tense.

"Don't you see, Shelby? Those convicts are coming after you."

Shocked, she stared up at Cade. Her mouth dropped open for a second, considering the possibility. "I—never thought about that."

"I'm worried for you. You're the one who put them away. Vance Welton is well-known to get even, to take revenge on anyone who crosses him. You have his file, you know his background. It can't be lost on you that if he ever escaped, he'd want to finish business with you first."

For a moment, Shelby stood and allowed the idea to sink in. Dakota's hand on her shoulder felt stabilizing. "I wasn't thinking in that direction," she choked out. It made perfect sense.

Cade looked around the busy parking lot filled with tourists. Keeping his voice down, he took a step toward them. "Look, I hope like hell I'm wrong, Shelby."

"You're not," Dakota growled. "I came to the same conclusion a while ago."

Cade nodded, grim. "You're good at this, Dakota. You might not be in law enforcement, but you have one hell of a wolf nose on you. We have two things we must do. First, see if another tourist reports a stolen car on the south highway out of Yellowstone. That would be the Colby Bay Village area. Second—" his gaze burrowed into hers "—we need to get you to a safe house, Shelby. If

Welton and Hartley are around, they're going to watch and wait for the right moment to grab you out of your home."

Shelby automatically wrapped her arms across her chest. Vance Welton was a sexual predator from seven years old onward. There were two cold cases involving other young women in Cody, Wyoming. They had been kidnapped, tortured for weeks, raped innumerable times before their throats were slit. Law enforcement was sure this was Welton and Hartley's work. It was their M.O. Unfortunately, the law couldn't get enough evidence to prove it. And neither of the two would admit doing it during interrogation for Ellie Carson's murder.

Shelby had attended the trial for the murder of Ellie Carson for only one day, but it was one she'd never forget. Shelby shut her eyes, remembering the event. Remembering how the body of beautiful Ellie Carson flashed across a screen to show the jury just exactly what Hartley and Welton had done to her. A tremor passed through Shelby, the horrifying color photos never forgotten.

Dakota placed his hand on her shoulder. He saw the shock registering in her eyes and wanted to protect her. These two murderers would never get near her. "She's got a safe house, Cade."

"What?" Shelby twisted a look up at his hard, unreadable face. The man she knew was no longer present. This was the SEAL warrior and she could feel the tension radiating around him like a thunderstorm about to unleash its destructive power.

Cade looked at her and then over at Dakota. "Your cabin?"

"That's right. It's damn near impregnable. One way in and one way out. Most people can't even locate the road." He dug into Shelby's widening eyes as she realized what they were talking about. "You'll stay with me, Shelby. Those two gomers won't be able to find you. They might find out where you live, but you aren't going to be there. Not until we can apprehend these bastards."

Shelby stood mute for a moment, considering all the ramifications. She felt Dakota's fingers dig a little more firmly into her shoulder, as if to keep her from protesting.

What would it be like to live with him? Their connection was already fiery. Where was this going? Could she handle him and still be alert for Welton and Hartley? The fact that they might be tracking her shook her as little else ever had. "I just never thought…"

"That you'd become their target?" Dakota asked, holding her shaken gaze.

"I don't know if you remember his outburst because you weren't there for the entire trial," Cade said to Dakota. "After Shelby left the stand, Welton screamed at Shelby. He promised he'd get out and hunt her down. And he'd kill her just like he killed Ellie Carson."

Dakota felt an invisible KA-BAR knife slitting him from groin to neck, opening up everything between those two points. The serrated blade was used by SEALs precisely because it gutted and killed swiftly. Nothing was left alive after a slice or jab from this military knife blade. His heart contracted and he felt a new, different pain as he regarded Shelby. He'd forgotten that outburst in court, so mired in his own grieving at the time. His mind spun with anxiety—for her. Welton's threat in court did nothing but confirmed his intuition.

"I remember that…now…" His voice dropped to a rasp.

She couldn't hold on to the terror moving through her. "Y-yes. He said all those things." Opening her eyes, she gave Dakota a helpless look. "It didn't occur to me after Welton escaped that he was coming after me."

"Well, he's going to have to come through me first," Dakota said.

CHAPTER TEN

"ANOTHER CAR HAS BEEN stolen at Colby Bay," Cade informed Shelby and Dakota. They had arrived at the sheriff's department only minutes earlier, when a dispatcher gave him the news.

Shelby stood, hands on hips, her mind churning over the situation. "Okay, that confirms it's probably them. Is the car going to be checked for fingerprints?"

Cade sat at his desk, moving paperwork around. "Yes, as soon as I can get a forensics tech up there."

Dakota moved restively around the small room. He hated enclosed spaces like this. "What about the other cars stolen? Who's checked them for prints?"

Cade grimaced. "Agent Woods had his other FBI agent out doing it."

"Great," Shelby said, frowning, "we'll get those results when hell freezes over."

"Now, now," Cade murmured, grinning sourly, "we can't speak ill of our FBI cohorts. Woods is just not the ideal agent for this case. I'm sure they'll get their results to us. It's just a question of when."

Snorting, Dakota stopped pacing and growled, "Things would be done a helluva lot differently if a SEAL team were put on this op."

"I'm sure," Cade said. His gaze moved to Shelby. "We need to sit down and plan what's happening with you until we can apprehend these two."

Shelby held up her hands. "Whoa. What does that mean, Cade? I've already agreed to stay up at Dakota's cabin. Isn't that enough?"

"I'm inclined to take you off the duty roster, Shelby. I want you out of sight. Completely. Welton and Hartley know you work here. I wouldn't put it past them to watch this place."

"Oh, hell, Cade, I'm not going to stop doing my job! I'm not scared of those bastards! I know how they operate. Leave me on the job, because I don't think they'll try to grab me."

"Like hell they won't," Dakota snapped. He saw the stubbornness on her face. His heart lurched with fear for her safety. "You need to disappear, Shel." Dammit, she had to be protected! He knew those two criminals. His heart shrank in terror of them ever laying a hand on Shelby.

Every time he whispered her name like an endearment, her skin tingled as if he'd stroked her with one of his callused hands. She met and held his hooded stare. There was no question Dakota was the biggest, baddest guard dog she'd ever run into. "Look," she pleaded to him, "I will go stir-crazy up in that cabin of yours. I need to work! I have a very low tolerance for boredom."

Dakota shook his head, holding her glittering blue gaze. "I have to keep you safe, Shel. The only way to do it is stay at the cabin." He wanted to shake some sense into that head of hers. He didn't want to admit he was attracted to her, wanted her, but the end of the story was brutal. He was afraid he'd end up hurting her because the extent of his PTSD symptoms were severe.

Cade nodded. "He's right, Shelby. Until we can find out where these two are, you're in danger. I'm not risking your life. I know you'll hate being taken off the roster, but this is for your own good."

"Damn. This isn't fair."

"It isn't fair that those two gomers want to kill you, either."

Glaring over at Dakota, Shelby pushed her fingers through her hair in an irritated motion. "How long do I have to hide?" she demanded tightly of Cade.

"I hope only a few days," Cade said soothingly. "I'm sorry, Shelby, but you need to go with Dakota over to your house. Pack a few bags. He'll guard you. He knows how to watch out for bad guys. I'll breathe a lot easier once you get the hell out of Jackson Hole. A cabin off the grid and up in the Tetons is your best bet."

"Damn," she muttered, turning and jerking open

the door. She headed down the hall and pushed
through the glass doors into the reception area.
Outside, the day was sunny and bright. Anger
moved through her as she went to the parking lot.
Dakota was on her heels. She could feel him, not
hear him. He walked like that wolf of his, unde-
tected.

At her cruiser, she retrieved her assigned rifle
and tracking gear and removed them. After lock-
ing it back up, she saw Dakota looking around the
area. The sheriff's headquarters was opposite the
courthouse, both on the same side of the street. She,
too, was more alert than usual.

"Okay," she called to him, "come on." The idea
of staying with Dakota was making her go shaky
inside. Shelby felt as if she were suspended above
a fire. Either way, she could get burned by this
situation.

Dakota followed Shelby. He had memorized
Welton's and Hartley's sick faces a long time ago.
Seeing them older helped, too. Revenge flowed
strong and palpable through him as he walked
Shelby to her green Toyota Land Cruiser. She was
angry and upset. She'd settle down once they got
out of here. Right now she was a target. Were those
bastards already here in town? Dakota wasn't going
to take any chances. He wore his SIG Sauer pistol
in a drop holster low on his right thigh, and it felt
good to have it handy. He wished he had an M-4,

the rifle SEALs carried out on missions. A pistol was a secondary weapon in the SEAL arsenal. A last-ditch stand between him and the bad guys. The M-4 would blow those bastards away with one shot each. His rifle was up at his cabin, and from now on, he'd be carrying it with him. He savored that possibility because he wanted nothing more than to avenge his sister's death at their sick, murderous hands.

"Coming?" Shelby called, sliding into the driver's seat. How different Dakota behaved. He was on guard and alert. The look in his eyes would have scared her if she hadn't been kissed by this man earlier.

Dakota climbed in. "They probably don't know what kind of vehicle you're driving yet. So let's take a slow ride around the block where you live. See if you notice any strange cars you don't recognize."

Shelby put the car in gear and drove it out of the parking lot. "That's a good idea," she admitted, the anger bleeding out of her voice. Glancing over at his set profile, she added, "You'd make a damn good cop, Dakota. You have the instincts of one."

His mouth barely twitched. "SEAL training, Shel. The training you get, the experience you accrue, always comes in handy."

She gripped the wheel a little tighter. The traffic was normal for this time of day as she headed in the direction of the hospital. "I don't mean to be a petulant child about this."

"But you are." He slid her an unwilling grin. She was frowning and he could see she was worried. "It's okay. I wouldn't like to be yanked off my job, either. But it's for the best."

"Yeah," she muttered, "I know."

"You made the right decision to come to the cabin."

"No, you and Cade made it for me." Shelby said nothing else, shuttling between anger and desire. Her body responded to his gruff voice and she felt an acute ache. How the hell was she going to live in that cabin with him? He only had a twin bed in there. The rest of her mind was focused on the escaped convicts. Her skin crawled as she recalled those stomach-turning photos of Ellie. *My God.* If they were really going to seek her out, treat her the same way, Shelby was relieved that Dakota was with her. The man was truly the right person to help protect her.

They drove slowly around the block. Shelby's house was a one-story, two-bedroom home with a white picket fence and a small yard. "I don't see anything out of place," she told Dakota after they'd swung around the block.

"Okay, let's go pick up whatever you need. But first, I'll check around the house before I give you the signal it's all clear."

RELIEF WAS SHORT-LIVED as Shelby drove her Land Cruiser up the steep, muddy road toward Dakota's cabin. She still wore her sheriff's uniform, and her radio on her shoulder came to life. Pressing the button, she heard Cade's voice.

"Shelby, all the stolen cars have been checked for prints. All that was found was the owner's prints. Nothing else."

"Roger that. Keep us in the loop?"

"Roger. Out."

"They're using gloves," she muttered to Dakota, paying attention to the curve that would take them up to eight thousand feet and his cabin.

"That's what I was thinking." He heard the concern in her tone. "How are you doing?"

Shrugging, Shelby said, "Scared. Angry. Wanting to find those two. Wanting my life back."

Dakota couldn't help himself and stared at her profile. His gaze just naturally fell to her mouth. He'd kissed those lips, felt the heat of her mouth bloom beneath his, felt her return his hunger in equal measure. His lower body tightened, reminding him just how long he'd been without a woman. He fought his need to protect Shelby from himself. How he wished he could kill the tendrils of need growing daily inside him.

"How's your arm doing?" Shelby asked, gesturing to his bear bite.

"Okay."

"No heat? Swelling?"

"None." And then he added drolly, "I'm being a good boy. I'm taking my antibiotics, Doc."

Giving a throaty chuckle, Shelby pulled into the driveway. "We need to pick up your truck."

"Tomorrow." Dakota saw Storm come trotting around the cabin, her yellow gaze pinned on the Toyota.

"She's beautiful." Shelby sighed, turning off the engine and opening the door.

"Yeah, she's all wolf," he agreed, climbing out.

Storm trotted up to Dakota and whined, rolled on her back, exposing her belly. The greeting was that of a subordinate wolf to the alpha male wolf. He leaned down and rubbed her belly, which she loved.

Shelby stood and watched them, a soft feeling moving through her. Dakota might have PTSD, but he was gentle with her and with the wolf. Storm leaped to her feet, tongue hanging out, the expression on her gray face one of unfettered joy that Dakota had returned home.

Looking around, Shelby studied where the cabin sat from the perspective of safety. The small clearing was surrounded by thick forest. The brook behind the cabin gurgled happily. She felt safe up here. Maybe it was the thick stands of fir. She glanced toward Dakota, who was rubbing Storm's broad, flat head, a smile tugging at the corners of her mouth. Maybe it was him.

Dakota pushed the door of the cabin open with his foot. He made a mental note to fix the lock. Before, it hadn't mattered. Now it did. He helped carry in one of Shelby's two suitcases. Throwing it on the unmade bed, he said, "You get the rack."

"What about you? Where are you going to sleep?" She looked around the chilly cabin. It hadn't been cleaned up since she'd arrived that early morning to get Dakota to the hospital. She picked up the chair and slid it beneath the table. The place was simple, the furniture spare.

"On the floor," he said. He noticed her concerned look. "The six months I was out with my SEAL platoon, we slept on the ground when out on missions. A wood floor is the Ritz." He allowed a hint of a smile.

"Not my idea of the Ritz," Shelby muttered. Looking around, she saw his dresser. There was no electricity. No water. It hurt her to think he'd remained up here for a year, alone. This was no way for a human to live.

He brought over a large steel bowl and set it on the dresser. He pulled out a towel and cloth and set them down. "Sorry, but the only bathing facilities are either climbing buck naked into that cold stream or washing up in here."

"I feel like I've regressed to pioneer days."

Dakota chuckled. "Believe me when I tell you, this is luxury compared to what I was used to having."

"It's hard to picture." She opened one suitcase and pulled out a set of jeans, a short-sleeved T-shirt and socks. It was time to get out of her sheriff's uniform and go civilian. Turning, she saw him filling a rusted pot with water from a nearby jug. The kitchen, if it could be called that, was a counter with one aluminum sink. The plumbing beneath went through a hole drilled through a log, to dump the water outside the cabin. "You making coffee?"

"Yes. Want some?"

It was all one room. No bathroom, either. "Yes, please." And then she smiled at him. "Hey, if I can have my coffee in the morning, I'm in heaven."

Dakota felt his heart expand in his chest over her husky laughter. He lit a magnesium tab on a metal hot plate and set the pot over it on a wire grate. This tab would create instant heat, enough to perk coffee. It also wouldn't create smoke that might alert Welton and Hartley if they were in the area. He doubted they were, but he was taking no chances by firing up the woodstove. They'd follow the white smoke and find Shelby.

"I'm going to change."

"Go ahead."

She sat down on the bed, unlacing her black boots. Dakota's back was turned to her. The white-

hot magnesium tab was hard to look at directly because it glowed like a sun. The smell was terrible
and she was glad he'd opened the window above the
sink to let the noxious odor waft out of the cabin.
She stood and shimmied out of her trousers. Un-
buttoning the shirt, Shelby placed them aside. Her
skin goose-bumped in the coolness. She reached
for her green T-shirt and pulled it over her head.
Would Dakota turn around and stare? No, she could
see him deliberately dawdling at the counter.

"Are SEALs gentlemen?" she wondered, pulling on her Levi's.

"We're warriors with an ethos," he said, wiping down the counter with a damp rag. "We have
a strict code of conduct."

"Sort of like the samurai warriors?"

He forced himself to look out the window, not
turn around and watch her dress. "Something like
that."

Thoughtful, Shelby said, "I didn't know that
about the SEALs."

"We conduct ourselves to a higher bar of training."

"Unlike Welton and Hartley, who have no honor
at all."

"They're scum," he muttered, steel lining his
voice. He stopped wiping off the counter, his fist
clenching the damp cloth.

"I won't disagree with you, Dakota. I'm dressed now. You can turn around."

He turned. Shelby looked damn good in those Levi's that clearly revealed and celebrated her long legs. The green T-shirt outlined her breasts and flat stomach. He watched like a starved wolf as she released her ponytail, her golden hair cascading softly about her shoulders. He had to turn away or he was going to do something he'd regret. "I need to fix the bed. I fell on it when I went septic with high fever. I broke one of its legs."

"I can help." Shelby held up her hands. "I'm good with tools, too."

"Why am I not surprised?"

She heard the teasing in his tone and saw the respect in his eyes. His left arm had to be tender and sore, even though he never complained about it. She had a hunch SEALs didn't whine about much of anything. Dakota was a poster child for them. They just sucked it up and kept on going no matter how much pain they were in. Like he said, pain was inevitable, but suffering was optional.

She pulled the bed out and noticed the bent leg. Feeling edgy because of herself, not him, Shelby tried to contain her feminine yearnings for Dakota. This was the wrong time and place to get caught making love, with Welton and Hartley looking for her.

Dakota dropped the damp cloth on the counter

and walked over to a corner where his toolbox was. There was anguish in his eyes. Was he remembering Ellie? Taking in a deep, ragged breath, Shelby wanted to help him in some way, to ease his grief from the past. But how? His kiss had been so damned healing for her. And yet, as Dakota walked toward her with the toolbox in hand, Shelby knew they needed to remain safe and undiscovered from the convicts who were at large. Personal needs had no place here.

CHAPTER ELEVEN

"WHAT WAS ELLIE LIKE?" Shelby asked as they worked together to repair the broken leg on the bed.

On his knees, Dakota glanced up toward her. Shelby was at his shoulder, holding up the bed so he could remove the broken leg. He could smell her, his nostrils inhaling her sweet scent.

"She was an incredible person," he began, his voice low with feeling. Taking a screwdriver, he began to methodically remove the screws that held the bent metal leg to the bed frame. "We were born and lived over in Cody, Wyoming. My dad was a farrier, a damned good one, always in high demand by ranchers outside the city. Ellie was two years older than I was."

Shelby watched him work. When she gently asked about his sister, his eyes grew light with fond memories. Good memories. His mouth relaxed as he worked. "Your dad shoed horses? What did your mom do?"

Dakota wanted to tell her everything. The care burning in her blue eyes made him open up more than he ever had to anyone else. "She was a full-blood Cheyenne Indian. She met my father and they fell in love."

Shelby knew how important it was to talk about family. "It sounds like it was a happy time in your life?"

Nodding, Dakota placed the fallen screw on a cloth beside him. He went to work on the second one. "My dad taught me how to hunt deer, fish, track and find my way through the mountains from the time I can remember. My mother stayed at home, cooked, cleaned and sewed. She made beautiful leather beaded purses and pouches." He sat up, hands resting on his long, thick thighs. "My dad had been in the U.S. Navy and he's the one who got me to thinking about trying to become a SEAL."

"And Ellie? How did she fit into your life?"

Momentary pain flitted through Dakota's heart. He looked down at his hands. "Ellie was an extrovert like my dad. I took after my mother, the strong, silent type." A slight smile tipped one corner of his mouth. "Ellie was incredibly beautiful. She had my mother's dark brown eyes. Ellie was outgoing and the most popular girl at her high school. She was kind, Shelby. She worked in the soup kitchens of Cody almost every weekend. She was an assistant kindergarten teacher at a women's shelter. She believed in helping those who had less than we did."

Reaching out, Shelby touched his slumped shoulder. The pain in his voice was almost unbearable.

"I'm sorry, I didn't mean to make you feel like this. I just wanted to understand you better, your family, was all."

An unexpected heat flowed through him. Did Shelby know how much her voice affected him? Made him want something he couldn't have? He set the tool on the floor. Against his better judgment he took her hand and cradled it within his larger one. "I'm finding I'm an open book around you." He met and held her gaze. Were there tears in her eyes? And he saw something else…desire. Instantly, he rejected the thought. He moved his fingers across her open palm, felt the softness of her flesh but also saw the small calluses across it, too. Shelby was a strong, confident woman.

"You remind me a lot of my mother. She was tough, strong and self-reliant. There wasn't anything she couldn't do." He reluctantly released Shelby's hand. What the hell was the matter with him? Wanting something he could never have.

"I thought you had some Native American blood in you," she said.

He snorted and touched his nose. "Yeah, my beak." He picked up the tool and focused on the bed once more. Because if he didn't, he was going to do something that could never happen between them.

"I like your profile. It's strong. Unwavering."

"That's my mother's genetic doing," he muttered. He leaned down as Shelby got to her knees and positioned herself so he could take out the last screw on the bent leg.

"There," he growled, triumphant. The four screws were finally removed. Sitting up, he looked over at Shelby. He felt care radiating off her. "You can let the bed down. I'm going to find a piece of wood the same length as the leg, and fix it so you have a bed tonight."

Shelby set the bed down. Dakota offered her a hand to get up. Reaching out, she curved her fingers into his. He drew her to her feet as if she were a feather. The muscles in his right arm tightened and she felt his monitored strength as she stood. It took effort to let go of his hand.

"How's your left arm feeling?" she asked, pointing to the dressing around it.

Dakota stepped aside, picked up the toolbox and set it on the table. "It's okay."

"No pain? Swelling?"

"There's no infection," he assured her.

Shelby sat down at the table, watching him put the tools back into the beat-up metal toolbox. "You've had a hard life," she offered in a low tone.

"Who hasn't?" Dakota saw the shadow in her eyes, her face set. He ached to touch her golden hair that fell in a soft curve around her face and shoulders. How could he have thought she was one-dimensional? One couldn't always trust first impressions. The realization that she was like his mother sent warmth through the cold grief he still held over her passing. His mother had been incredibly strong. When the family fell apart over Ellie's murder, it was she who had gathered all of them within her unwavering embrace.

Shelby picked up the mug and saw there was still some coffee left. She sipped it. "I think I understand why you're so protective. When I first met you, you were really tough and hard."

Closing the toolbox, Dakota walked it over to the corner and set it down. "I still am." He sat down in a chair opposite Shelby and picked up his cooling coffee. "I always will be."

Looking over the cup she held between her hands, she said, "Because you're a SEAL?"

"Yes."

Shelby saw Storm lying near the door. The wolf's ears twitched as they spoke in low voices. She realized the female wolf was listening in her own way. "Tell me about Storm." Shelby wanted to stop digging into his old wounds regarding his family. His light brown eyes softened as he turned and looked over at the wolf.

"I was out laying my line of rabbit traps last April when I ran up on a grizzly who was digging into a wolf den. She'd already killed the mother, a black wolf, who was trying to defend her newly born pups. The grizzly had just come out of hibernation and was starving. She probably picked up

the scent of the newborn pups, followed it and discovered the den."

Shelby said nothing, her hands around the mug.
The grief had left his eyes. "She killed all the pups,
too?"

"All but one. When I unexpectedly came upon
her, I startled her and she took off. I went over
to see if anything was left alive. The mother was
part of the Snake River wolf pack. I'd seen her and
the pack from time to time, running their territory
across the valley. The mother had given her life to
protect her pups. I heard a whine and got down on
my hands and knees to search the torn-up den. I
found a little runt of a gray pup buried in a lot of
dirt at the end of the den tunnel. Drew it out and
there she was." He hitched a thumb over his shoulder toward Storm and smiled.

"What happened next?"

"I checked the pup and she was dirty but unhurt.
I tucked her into my jacket and brought her back
to the cabin. I'd just gotten some groceries from
town and had some cow's milk. She was so tiny
her eyes weren't even open yet. I had an eyedrop-
per and warmed up the milk, put some sugar and
salt in it and started to feed her." He smiled fondly.
"She was one hungry pup."

Shelby drowned in Dakota's gold-brown eyes.
When he was happy, she saw the gold tones in

them. Her heart lifted as she held his gaze. "And you didn't call Game and Fish?"

"Is that the deputy sheriff questioning me?"

"No, not really. Your secret's safe with me," she said. He should have handed the pup over to the state to be cared for. Knowing how alone Dakota was, she understood why he hadn't; even he needed company. The company of a wolf. He'd lost everything else: his sister, his parents. He'd lost being in his SEAL platoon, something that gave him a sense of family. "I'm glad you happened upon the situation. Storm looks happy to be with you."

"She saved my life in that grizzly fight the other day," he said, drinking the rest of his coffee. "She's a year old now, and I think she's going to be missing her own kind pretty soon. I expect her to disappear some day. She goes out and finds food for herself and sometimes she's gone for days at a time. I don't know whether she's looking for her pack or she's just hunting."

"Storm never liked dog food, huh?" Shelby grinned.

He grudgingly returned her smile. "Couldn't get her to eat it. She refused. I finally figured out she needed raw, red meat. I'd just skinned a rabbit and cut some of it up for her. She gobbled it down and that's when I realized I'd be hunting for two of us until she got old enough to hunt on her own."

The rumble of his laughter moved through Shelby as if he was touching her physically. The lightness in his brown eyes made her feel good, made her want him all over again. "Storm seems like a wonderful companion." Looking around the cabin, she murmured, "I couldn't live out here alone."

Dakota moved the cup between his large, square hands. "Shock and trauma leave scars, Shel. I'm like that wolf—happy to be free to roam in the woods. I feel calmer when I'm out here." And then a corner of his mouth drew inward. "I don't expect you or anyone to understand." Yet his fingers positively itched to release the mug and, instead, frame her face, slide his fingers through those golden strands and kiss her senseless. The memory of that kiss in her kitchen burned through him. Dakota wanted more. He wanted Shelby. All of her.

"I know they do," she said in a quiet tone. "Dr. McPherson wants you to come back to the clinic. She says she can help you."

Dakota snorted. "How? By medicating me up to my friggin' eyeballs so I don't know my name? Therapy?" He straightened. "Sorry, but that's not my gig. Talk isn't my thing. And I'll never use drugs."

Tilting her head, she asked softy, "Do you feel better talking to me about your past? Your family?"

"Hell, you're different. You're no shrink poking and prodding into my brain like an elephant." He met her smile with one of his own, absorbing her dancing blue gaze. Shelby was so clean, less touched by life. He was battle-scarred in comparison to her. His life had gone from happy to a war at age seventeen when Ellie was murdered. When she died, he lost a piece of himself. And joining the SEALs and going to war only reinforced the war elements that ran as a continued theme throughout his life.

"Jordana McPherson will not poke or prod you, Dakota. Nor will she necessarily prescribe drugs. She just wants to give you a saliva test to check your cortisol levels. There's new research available that shows high cortisol is found in people with PTSD. It's just a test...."

"I'll think about it," he growled, none too excited about the prospect.

"She was right, you know," Shelby said, reaching out and sliding her hand over his. "You went from one war into another."

Dakota nodded, picked up her hand and held it. "Yeah, there's always a war going on inside me, Shel." And that was why, no matter how damn badly he wanted her, he could never have her. "And with Welton and Hartley on the loose and in the area, you'd better believe I'm on war footing. I'm going to find those two and put an end to their lives."

A small shiver moved up her spine as she witnessed the sudden hatred and animal-like focus come to Dakota's eyes. She couldn't blame him. Shelby had no other siblings in her family now, and she tried to imagine how she'd feel if the situation was reversed. If Jason was murdered instead of Ellie by those convicts. How would she feel then?

"I hope someone identifies or sees them," she whispered, her voice off-key.

"They'll make a mistake," Dakota promised her. He studied each of Shelby's fingers, the nails clipped short on her no-nonsense hands. "Where did you get all these calluses?" He grazed them with his index finger. There was such hidden pleasure in touching her.

"My parents have a home on the outskirts of town. I help my dad cut and chop wood for the winter." Her skin tingled hotly as he traced each of the calluses across her palm. Throat going dry, Shelby wanted to explore Dakota in the same way he was exploring her. The kiss had never left her and even now, as she licked her lower lip, she wanted to taste him again.

"Your dad taught you to track, hunt and chop wood?" He forced himself to release her hand. "Did he want a son?"

"Fair question," Shelby said, reclaiming her hand. Her flesh still had wild, heated shocks moving through them afterward. "The answer is no. My dad wanted me to be able to handle any situation that came up. He never believed women were weak, just the opposite. I loved going out hunting with him. I didn't like killing things, so I was happy learning to track and identify the different animal tracks, instead."

"And he's a tracker?"

"He was. When he retired as commander of the sheriff's department, he had arthritis of the spine. It really hampers his movements now." Sadness tinged her tone. "He can't hunt or fish very much. Or chop wood anymore. I really feel badly for him. Arthritis runs in his side of the family."

Nodding, Dakota forced his hands around the coffee mug. "Your dad should be proud of you. You're smart, educated and you don't take grief from anyone." His mouth curved ruefully. "Even me and I know I'm a handful."

Meeting his warm gaze, Shelby felt her insides turn weak with need. "You are, but you're not mean. You're wounded, Dakota." Her voice dropped to a whisper. "There's a huge difference."

He hadn't thought of himself in that particular light. She didn't know how dangerous he could become when his PTSD got out from beneath his steel control. Looking around the cabin, he said, "We've got a lot to do to make this place work for two people." As he rose to his feet, Dakota wondered how the hell he was going to sleep with Shelby only a few feet away from him. Oh, he didn't mind sleeping on a wood floor. Hell, that was good digs compared to sleeping out in the rocky, freezing mountains of Afghanistan. Now, that was a bitch.

What really ate at him was how close Shelby would be to him. He'd be able to reach out a long arm and touch her. His lower body grew hot with longing just thinking about it. Yet, as he put the cup in the sink, Dakota knew it wasn't right. Yes, they'd kissed. But would it have led to something else? To bed? He wasn't sure and he wasn't going to use this situation to trap Shelby and force her into a corner. Dakota was smart enough to respect her. Plus, he had to remain alert and protect her, not get distracted. Distraction got a person killed damned fast.

Still, as he moved around the cabin, he chafed. So often, he'd wake up at night screaming, caught in the throes of a nightmare from a SEAL mission. He wasn't sure what he'd do if that happened tonight. The nightmares released all his carefully closeted emotions, grief and rage. He knew from being in the hospital, wounded, that nurses were careful around him precisely because of what he'd endured. If he was asleep, they would pinch his toe to awaken him. He'd automatically come up swinging. They knew his hands were lethal weapons, and that he could kill with one blow if they got too close to him.

Worried, his mouth quirking, Dakota wasn't sure what to do. Should he warn Shelby about his nightmares? She was the last person he wanted to accidentally hurt. The last one.

CHAPTER TWELVE

Curt Downing was in his office at Ace Trucking when the door opened. It was dark outside and he was rushing to finish off some paperwork. His stomach grumbled; it was 9:00 p.m. and he still hadn't eaten dinner. His back to the door, he twisted around. His eyes grew to slits. The door closed, two men were standing and looking at him. "What the hell are you two doing here?"

Vance Welton grinned, glad that the blinds were closed. The small office was ensconced deep within the main trucking bay. "Hey, boss, long time, no see." He gestured to his partner. "You remember Oren Hartley?" His yellowed teeth were revealed when he smiled. "We worked for you at one time. We need some help."

Turning in his chair, Curt stared disbelievingly at them. "You stupid bastards! The whole damned state is looking for you two!"

"Yeah," Vance said, shoving his hands in the pockets of his jeans, "we know." His smile became broader. "Been stealing cars to keep the cops and

FBI off our asses. We need a set of wheels that's legal. Figure you can loan us a truck for a while?"

Scowling, Curt sat there feeling the danger surrounding the two escaped convicts. Both looked grim. Pistols were stuck into the waist of their jeans, hidden by shirts that were too big for them. Curt always kept a Glock pistol in his drawer. Now he wished he had it sitting on his desk. "Yeah, you worked for me. But I don't owe you anything, Welton. You were a lousy truck driver anyway."

Vance's brown eyes grew thoughtful. "Well, boss, considering I was trucking your heroin, marijuana and cocaine all over the West, you don't have much room to talk."

"Just what the hell does that mean?" he snarled, hands curving into fists.

Welton shrugged and looked around the small, warm office. "Read between the lines if you want. We need a set of wheels that won't come up stolen."

"And you're leaving town?"

"Sort of," Welton said, then glanced over at Hartley. "We got some unfinished business here in Jackson Hole to attend to first and then we'll move on. Don't worry, you won't be implicated. If the cops see your truck, they'll think we're some of the hired drivers from your company."

"And if I don't agree to this?" Curt snarled, tensing.

Vance fingered the handle of the pistol in his

waistband. "Well, now, it would be a shame for your men to discover you dead in your office tomorrow morning. Wouldn't it?" He added a feral smile to go with his threat.

Inwardly Curt was enraged. In his business as a regional drug lord, he dealt with scum like this all the time. His mind flicked over the possibilities. "You have business here?" He jabbed his finger down at the floor.

"We do."

"Mind telling me what it involves?"

"Can't."

"Won't?" Curt growled.

Vance moved his hand over his triangular-shaped chin. He felt the stubble of hair growing out on his face. "The less you know, the better off you'll be."

"But if you're caught in one of my trucks—"

"We're not gonna get caught. And we intend to change our looks. It will be hard for anyone to identify us."

Nostrils flaring, Curt felt evil around Vance. His small, close-set eyes never left him. He was a sexual predator, a murderer and a sociopath. "How long are you going to be hanging around here?"

"As long as it takes. Need to do a little hunting…"

Curt shook his head. "You're putting me in a helluva spot, Welton. If I give you a truck and you get caught, those damned sheriff's deputies and the FBI are going to climb down my ass." He jerked a hand in a gesture toward the truck bay. "I've got too much to lose and you know it."

"I always liked seeing you sweat," Vance said, continuing to smile. "If you don't give us a truck and five thousand dollars, all in twenties, I'll make an anonymous call to the sheriff's department I'll tell them how you smuggle drugs all over the West." His brows moved upward. "You think they'd like to hear from me?"

Rage tunneled through Curt. "You son of a bitch!"

"Thank you. Now fork over the keys to one of your many trucks that are parked out there." Vance thrust out his hand. "And the money, too. We need some operating funds."

Getting up, mouth set, Curt knew better than to push Vance. He knew his prison record. His hand rested over the butt of the pistol in his waist. Walking to the Peg-Board hanging on one wall, Curt jerked off a set of keys. He turned and tossed them at Oren Hartley, who caught them.

"There's a dark green Chevy truck at the end of the first row. Take that one."

"No company sign on the door?" Vance demanded. "We want to blend in, not stand out."

"No, that's why I'm giving it to you. All my

other trucks have *Ace Trucking* painted on both doors."

Going to his desk, Curt pulled open a drawer on the right-hand side. "This is it, Welton. You can't ever come back here and ask me for anything else again."

"We'll see," Vance murmured.

Curt pulled out the cashbox, set it on his desk and opened it with a set of keys.

"Look at all that cash," Oren said, gawking into the box. "Hooooeeee, that's a chunk of green-backs."

Curt counted out five thousand dollars in small denominations. He shoved the bills to the edge of the desk.

"Thanks, boss," Vance said, picking them up. He took half and gave Oren the other half. "Stuff it into your pockets," he ordered.

"Now get the hell out of my life," Curt snarled.

"Gladly," Vance said, opening the door. "Later, gator."

Curt sat down, fuming after they'd left. The door was still open and he stood and slammed it shut. *Dammit!* Pushing his fingers through his sandy red hair, he got up and angrily paced the office. What the hell could he do? If he went to the sheriff's, he could tell them Welton and Hartley held him up, stole money and a truck. The downside, and it was a steep cliff, was Welton, who had driven for him for a year, would turn him in. He'd take a plea bargain and turn state's evidence against him and his drug operation. It was rare that Curt felt so damned helpless.

As he finished up his paperwork, Curt could only hope those two bastards wouldn't get caught in his truck. And what the hell was this about some business in Jackson Hole? They had no ties to this place! Cursing softly, he jerked open the left drawer and dropped in the receipt bag that would go to the bank tomorrow morning. What were those two up to? It would be smarter for them to hightail it out of Wyoming and disappear.

"WHAT ARE YOU DOING?" Shelby asked, having just put the sheets and covers on the bed. Dakota had his sleeping bag tucked beneath his arm, heading for the door. It was 10:00 p.m.

"Going to sleep outside."

"What?" She stared at him, uncomprehending. "It's below freezing out there at night, Dakota." Part of her deflated. She wanted him close.

"I want to keep you safe," he growled, hand resting on the doorknob.

"You're guarding me from the outside?" She studied his darkening eyes. What was going on here? All evening, she'd seen Dakota close up, un-available, as he worked to make the cabin hospitable for her. He'd dusted, cleaned the floors and swept down the cobwebs from the corners.

"You ever been around a combat soldier?" He hated bringing up her dead brother, Jason, but he had to.

"Only Jason." Brows drawing down, she said, "What's he got to do with this?"

"When Jason stayed with your parents, did he ever wake them up at night?"

Shelby thought for a moment. "Well...yes... sometimes." Tilting her head, he stared hard at him. "What's this got to do with us?"

"Your brother had PTSD. The dark is when the nightmares stalk us." He tried to soften the growl in his tone because he saw her distressed by the fact that he was going to leave the cabin. "I had a good friend over in Afghanistan, a Green Beret. He was a top soldier, but he'd seen four rotations of combat in that country. The last time he came home after his tour, he had nightmares." His mouth tightened. "His wife tried to wake him up one night when he was in the middle of one. He kept a pistol under his pillow." His voice lowered. "He shot and killed her, mistaking her for an enemy who was attacking him in the nightmare."

Gasping, Shelby's eyes widened. "Oh my God...."

"It wasn't pretty. He got tried for manslaughter and spent five years in prison. When I heard about it, I remember the firefight that probably pushed him over the edge. The Taliban had come over the hill. There were seventy of them and ten Green Berets. It ended up in hand-to-hand combat. He was the only survivor in that skirmish and it scarred him."

Shelby stood quiet, feeling terrible for the soldier and his wife. "You think you're going to have a nightmare tonight? And you're afraid you'll hurt me during it? That's it, isn't it?" Her heart pounded.

The shadows deepened in his eyes and he nodded.

"Okay, if you wake up, I promise I will not come out of this bed to help you. That way, you can stay in here."

Shaking his head, Dakota rasped, "You don't understand, Shel. Sometimes I wake up and I sleepwalk. I'm fighting my own ghosts from my Afghan tours." He held up one of his hands. "I can easily kill with one of these." He hated that tears flooded her eyes. Just as swiftly, they disappeared. "I don't want to hurt you. You're the last person on this earth I'd want to harm. Do you understand?" Dammit, she was waging a good campaign of reason against him. If he stayed in the cabin, he'd take her. He'd take her and love her until neither of them could move afterward, so completely exhausted. He'd been so damn long without a woman. And most women didn't appeal to him anyway, but she did.

A lump formed in Shelby's throat. "Okay..." Taking a step forward, she whispered, "You have to see Dr. McPherson. I've heard of her working with other vets who have had similar issues. She's been able to help them, Dakota." Swallowing hard, Shelby felt the heat of tears pushing into her eyes. God help her, all she wanted to do was take those few steps and throw her arms around Dakota and hold him. Hold him against the night terrors that she clearly saw in his gaze. For a moment, he looked sad, but quickly covered it up.

"Yeah, I think I will see her. But not right now." He moved his shoulders to get rid of the accumulated tension in them. "The woodshed is near the creek. Storm and I will be out there."

"What if it snows?"

He held up his down sleeping bag. "This is specially made for SEALs in cold climates. It looks pretty ratty, but it keeps me plenty warm."

"Damn, Dakota, I didn't mean to force you out of your own cabin," Shelby muttered, frustrated. She put her hands on her hips. "Maybe I should stay at my parents' home."

"No."

The swift response stunned her. "What? You think Welton will try to find me there? He doesn't know my parents live here."

"Welton is a sociopath," Dakota began heavily, "and you can't ever assume he's stupid. Most of them are damned brilliant, Shel. I worry about your parents, too. I called Cade Garner a few hours ago and asked him to warn them. It's up to your dad to decide what he wants to do. Frankly—" he rubbed his jaw "—I told Cade to ask them to leave town until we can verify if these convicts are in the vicinity or not."

Her throat tightened. "I didn't even think in that direction. Do you know what Cade found out? Are they going to leave?"

He nodded. "I talked to him earlier this evening on my cell. Your dad wanted you to come with them, but Cade told them you wouldn't do that."

"He's right about that," Shelby muttered. "I want to track those two and land their asses back in federal prison like I did before."

Dakota respected her decision. "I'm having a helluva time looking at you and grasping the fact you tracked them down." Giving her an uneven grin, Dakota added, "That's a backhanded compliment, Shel. Old dogs like me have to learn new tricks. Tracking isn't a gender skill. I'm just too used to working with the men of my SEAL team. It just never occurred to me a woman could do it, too."

Her shoulders slumped, the tension bleeding out of her. "Tomorrow, we need to start sniffing around, Dakota. I want to find them. My gut tells me they're going to hole up in the Tetons."

Nodding, he said, "Bingo. Welton hid in the mountains of Yellowstone. The last stolen car has put him in our vicinity. We'll go see Cade tomorrow and start creating a mission plan to locate them."

"Are you really going to sleep outside every night?"

"Yes. It's better this way." *For you. For me.* He struggled and said, "I don't like it, but I couldn't live with myself if I harmed you, Shel." He held her steady gaze. She was upset and concerned. Not for herself, but for him.

"Well," she groused, trying to lighten the tension, "I'll miss you."

"Yeah?" It made him feel good for the first time in such a long while. She had the capacity to reach him in a place he thought had died when he was seventeen.

A slow, heated male smile touched the corners of his mouth. Shelby recalled the scalding desire he'd sparked within her before and she responded powerfully to that glittering look in his eyes. Now he was the wolf stalking her. It excited her, made her want to beg him to stay. It was a selfish and foolish thought, not worthy of herself. Or him. He was putting his life on the line to protect her.

"You realize when we pick up their trail, Dakota, we'll be out in the woods for maybe days on end."

He saw the challenging light in her eyes. "Yes, that occurred to me."

"Unless we're humping two tents, we'll be sharing one. Together." She set her jaw, hands on her hips.

He studied her, the silence intensifying between them. "That thought didn't escape me."

"And you aren't going to sleep outside the damned tent, Dakota. I won't let you."

"No?" The heat in her eyes made him feel good about himself as a man.

"No. It will be just you and me. I'm not afraid of you. I'm a law enforcement officer. I can take care of myself."

As he met her steady, challenging gaze, his mouth curved faintly. "Let's cross that bridge when we get to it." He twisted the doorknob. "Remember, if you hear me yelling, do not come out and rescue me."

"Okay, but I won't like it, Dakota. I'm not a weakling. You think you're so dangerous that no one on this earth can help you."

"Talk to the nurses at Landstuhl Medical Center in Germany. I sent one flying across the room one time. She was new to the hospital and they failed to warn her not to come running to my bedside if they heard me screaming at night." He shook his head. "I broke her arm. I felt really bad about it after I woke up."

Shaken, Shelby said, "If you scream and you wake me up, I won't guarantee you anything, Dakota. How do I know if Welton and Hartley aren't holding you prisoner? You could be in real trouble and need my help."

Grimly, he rasped, "Those two would never get within a hundred feet of me. They'd be dead in a heartbeat. You stay inside this cabin and do not go out that door until morning. Understand?"

CHAPTER THIRTEEN

SHELBY JERKED AWAKE when her cell phone began ringing near her head. She'd placed the iPhone near her pillow, in case the sheriff's department or her parents called. Blinking, she sat up, the covers falling away from her pink flannel, long-sleeved nightgown. She focused her drowsy attention on the iPhone. As she picked it up, she saw it was dawn.

"Shelby here," she whispered, rubbing her eyes.

"Shelby, it's Cade. Sorry to wake you up so early, but we need your help."

"You got a line on Welton?" she mumbled, rubbing her face.

"No. Not yet. We just got a call from Yellowstone Forest Rangers HQ. They've got a camper who is missing. Apparently his wife brought her husband, who has Alzheimer's, to the park because he loved being in the woods. When she awoke this morning, he was gone. She has no idea where and there are thousands of acres of woods surrounding them."

Shelby sat up, her feet touching the cool wood

floor. She heard a knock at the door. "Hold on, Cade…" She pulled the cell away. "Come in," she called.

Dakota entered the cabin, concern written on his features. Storm squeezed by him, wagging her tail.

Shelby said, "It's Cade. They've got a missing man up in Yellowstone."

Nodding, Dakota put the rifle in the corner after shutting the door. He focused on the phone conversation as he lit a magnesium tab, opened the window and got the coffee going.

After finishing the call, Shelby got out of the bed, the pink nightgown falling to her slender ankles. Dakota felt his body respond. The gown was old-fashioned, with ruffles across the bodice. It was pink with tiny white roses across the material. There was grayness in the cabin, but even in low light, he saw the wheat and gold colors of Shelby's hair tumble around her shoulders.

Shelby was hotly aware of Dakota's gaze upon her as she went to the table and pulled a notebook from the pocket of her shirt. Once she wrote down the information on the missing man, she glanced up to meet his hooded gaze. There it was again, that connection between them. He was dressed like the night before. Had he slept in his clothes?

She gave Dakota the intel on the missing man. Moving over to the bed, she pulled on a clean pair of thick socks for hiking. It was cold in the cabin and she wanted to get warm.

"And Cade wants me to go along?" he asked, placing two mugs out on the counter as the coffee percolated on the heating grate.

"Yes. Will you?" She lifted her head after putting on the thick socks.

"You're going nowhere without me until we find those two gomers," he said.

"Turn around. I need to get dressed."

"I'd rather watch."

"Another time and place, Dakota."

"I'll hold you to that, Shel." He turned, facing the window.

Shelby grabbed civilian clothes. She never tracked in her sheriff's uniform. Even though it was early June, it was cold in the area. Taking a dark brown cable-knit sweater, she pulled it over her head. A set of heavy corduroy trousers of the same color completed her uniform. She pushed her fingers through her mussed hair. "Okay, you can look now."

Dakota did. The dark sweater brought out the color of her hair. His fingers itched to investigate those shining strands as she pulled out a brush and comb from the opened suitcase on the floor. The chocolate-colored trousers did nothing but remind him how long and beautifully sculpted her legs were. Scowling, he turned and poured hot coffee into the awaiting mugs.

"Here, breakfast."

Taking the cup, she thanked him. "Did you get any sleep?" she asked.

Dakota sat down at the table, coffee between his large hands. "Some."

"Why do I not believe you?" She pulled her hiking boots from the suitcase. "You look like death warmed over."

"And I never thought this cabin would look so good as when you were in it." He sipped his coffee, watching her reaction over the rim of the mug.

Grinning, Shelby pulled on one boot and then another. She met his dark, assessing eyes. "I slept like a baby. Probably because I knew you and your wolf were keeping me safe from the bad guys."

"Close to the truth," Dakota murmured. When she stood up and smoothed the corduroy down across her thighs, his body reacted. "Come and get some coffee in your veins. We'll talk tracking strategy."

Groaning, Shelby nodded, pulled out the chair opposite him. Storm came and sat next to her, resting her head in her lap.

"Does Storm like me?" she wondered, sitting down and gently patting her head.

"She's taken a shine to you."

"Is that unusual?"

"She's a female alpha wolf. She may see you as a female beta wolf."

Picking up her coffee, Shelby chuckled. "Is she worried I'm going to take her mate?"

His brows moved upward for a moment. "Could be."

"Do I have to roll over on my back and expose my belly to her to convince her that you're safe with me?" A warmth exuded from Dakota. It enveloped her. His light brown eyes gleamed with unspoken desire. For a moment, her gaze fell to his well-shaped mouth. A mouth she was already familiar with—and wanted to taste again. Only longer and more deeply.

"Let's get back to business," he growled. "Have law enforcement or the rangers started a search for this guy?"

"They're just starting because they need light." Shelby glanced toward the window. "I feel sorry for the wife. She and her husband used to come to Yellowstone every year for two weeks and camp. He was a birder. It gave him such joy to be in the woods."

There was real concern and sadness in her blue eyes. "Why are you so touched by this situation?"

"I try to put myself in the wife's place. How would I feel? They've been married for thirty-five years. That's a long time. And I can't imagine her terror when she woke up this morning and he wasn't at her side. That's hard on the heart, Dakota."

"Anyone ever tell you that you're a softy beneath that sheriff's uniform?"

Shelby took his gruff teasing in stride. "I think that if you turned this around and it was one of the men in your SEAL platoon lost, you'd have a similar emotional response. Don't you?"

Her intelligence was wide and deep. He liked her ability to help him understand in ways he never had before. "Okay, I see your point."

"So, I'm not some 'softy' as you put it. We're going to have to deal with the wife. She's going to be upset and anxious."

"Guilty feeling, too, I'm sure."

"Yes. See? You're not as hard-hearted as you'd like the world to think."

"Maybe not." Dakota gave her a soft grin.

"If one of your men was lost, you'd do everything in your power to find him."

"I'd go to hell to find him if I had to, no question."

"Right." She finished off her coffee and set the mug aside. "Let's get saddled up. We can stop inside the south entrance at Grant Village and grab some food. This could be an all-day, all-night kind of track."

Dakota rose. "We'll leave Storm here. I don't like her around groups of people. They'll think she's a wild wolf and start getting weird about it."

"Can she track?"

"If I give her a piece of fabric the person wore, yes. She's good at finding a trail. Cuts my tracking time down."

She smiled at the gray wolf. "We could use her today."

"I don't like running into Fish and Game types with a wild wolf trotting at my side. They'd want to take her away from me."

Shelby grabbed her knapsack and pulled on her thick, warm dark green coat. "No kidding. You'd get fined up to your butt and back, too."

"Duly noted," Dakota said drily, pulling his rucksack out of the closet. He reached inside and pulled his H-harness off a hook.

Shelby stopped packing her knapsack and watched Dakota. The odd-looking piece of gear settled around his shoulders and fastened it around his narrow waist. "That's a nifty-looking piece of equipment. How many pockets have you got in that thing?"

"It's my H-gear. All SEALs wear it. We call it second-line gear." He pulled open a drawer at the counter. "I got fifteen pockets in this thing and I can carry ammunition, protein bars, a tourniquet and anything else I might need on this hike."

Impressed, she saw him filling each one. "That's a lot of weight if you're stowing mags of ammunition in it, isn't it?"

"It's not unusual if I'm wearing my first, second and third line of gear to be carrying sixty-five pounds on my body, and that includes my rucksack."

"Phew, that's a lot." But then, she was coming to realize SEALs were not the typical American male at all. Dakota was strong, tall and powerful, but he wasn't muscle-bound. He was a finely honed athlete who was in amazing shape.

"Normal weight for us to hump on a multiday mission," he assured her. He took a sheathed knife from his ruck and strapped it around his left thigh. On the other thigh, he already wore his SIG Sauer.

"I feel like we're going to war," Shelby said, locating her gloves in the suitcase.

"Don't kid yourself. We are. There's nothing to say Welton and Hartley aren't snooping around up there, either," he warned her.

Mouth quirking, Shelby said, "Yeah, I already thought in that direction."

He picked up his rifle, a modified M-4 that he routinely carried on SEAL missions. This was a civilian model of the military weapon he used to have. The only downside was that he couldn't slap a grenade launcher below the barrel. Grenades were frowned upon out here in the civilian world, but they could come in damn handy if he had to use them.

"How's your arm doing this morning?" she asked. "Do you need the dressing changed?"

"No, it's fine. It's healing well. You can help me change it tomorrow or whenever we get off this track."

"Just remember to take your antibiotics with you. I don't know how long we're going to be out there looking for this guy."

"Are you always such a mother hen?"

"Nah, just special for you, Carson." She pulled the knapsack over her shoulder. There was a shadowy grin on his unshaven face.

Pulling on his camouflage jacket of green, dark brown and tan, he met her smile. "Let's go Down Range."

Shelby pulled the door open. Dawn was coming, light infusing the area. Storm bounded out the door and disappeared into the surrounding woods. She opened the rear of the sheriff's cruiser and stowed her gear. So did Dakota.

"Is Storm off hunting?"

"Yeah, every morning and night."

Shelby retrieved the keys from her jacket pocket. "What will she do if we're still tracking tonight and don't get back here?"

Dakota placed his H-gear next to his rucksack. "Nothing. She comes and goes as she pleases. She always comes back at some point."

After climbing into the driver's seat, she started the vehicle and then called the sheriff's department to let them know they were on their way to the campground in Yellowstone. Dakota climbed in and closed the door. She appreciated him being along.

Shelby pulled out and turned around near the cabin. "I'm looking forward to working with you. First time I've ever tracked with a SEAL. I'm sure I'll learn a lot from you."

"It's a little different from how you track."

"How so?" Shelby asked, driving down the long, narrow, winding road toward the valley. The sky was lightening, a pink color following the shadow of the night.

"We're tracking gomers. It's kill or be killed."

"Do you think Welton and Hartley have anything to do with this missing guy?"

"No. My gut tells me they're in the Tetons. I don't think they're stupid enough to hide in Yellowstone again. They got caught by you the last time. Welton won't make the same mistake twice."

Her skin crawled with momentary fear. They were probably hunting her right now. "I just hope we can find this guy alive. The nights are below freezing up at that altitude."

Dakota could hear the worry in her voice. "Alzheimer's is a bitch. We'll find out more from his wife." He noticed Shelby's thin brows knit and the worry in her profile as she turned onto the main highway that would eventually lead them into Yellowstone. Across the road was a small herd of buffalo, their breath like misting shots from their nostrils as they hungrily grazed on the early grass coming up from the long winter. Their shaggy brown coats kept them warm in any type of weather.

"Did you get any sleep last night?"

He turned his attention to her. "Not much. I got it in snatches."

"Nightmares wake you?"

"Always."

"You're probably so sleep-deprived you're used to it." It hurt Shelby to realize he suffered all the time. Jordana often talked about PTSD symptoms, that insomnia was a major component. Over time, it added another horrific layer of stress upon the person.

Dakota managed a dark chuckle. "Stop worrying. When my SEAL team was deployed over to Afghanistan for six months, no one got much sleep. We'd be operational around the clock on some missions. You learn to gut through it. The thought of being killed keeps you alert and awake."

"For a day or two?"

"Sometimes longer."

Shaking her head, she muttered, "I think I'm deciding that you guys who join the SEALs are supermen. You'd have to be."

"There's a six-month course everyone goes through," he told her. "It's called BUD/S. And it's hell on earth. It weeds out the wannabes from the rest of us who want it bad enough to work through any kind of pain and training they throw at us."

She shook her head. "Then what drives you SEALs, Dakota?"

"Heart. Teamwork. Family, I guess." He looked around the empty highway. "We're looking to belong to something bigger than ourselves. To be a part of something that's important."

Hearing the wistful note in his voice, she glanced over quickly to see his face soften for a moment. "Maybe the P.C. response would be that you're patriots? But really, underneath, you want to belong?"

"Yes," he said, "and our patriotism is strong. The bottom line is we know we can protect America and her people."

"You lost your entire family," she said. "Did the SEALs become your family instead?"

He felt his way through her deep insight. Taking in a breath, he released it and said, "Looking at it from that perspective, yeah, I got my family back. But it's more than that, Shelby. We're warriors. We want our gun in the fight. We believe in what we're doing—getting rid of the gomers on this planet. We like combat. We're never more alive than when we're in a life-and-death dance with the bad guys. We feel as a platoon, no one is better than we are. We're training eighteen months of every two-year cycle. Then we're deployed overseas to hunt and make a difference in the war effort for six months."

She brushed a strand of loose hair over her shoulder as she considered his quiet, impassioned words. "I couldn't possibly do what the SEALs do." She met his glance. "Truly, Dakota, you are a hero in my eyes."

CHAPTER FOURTEEN

SHELBY WAS EAGER TO get on with the track. They'd
arrived, talked to the distraught wife about her husband, Tony Banyon, who had wandered off sometime during the night. A number of other people,
volunteers, were looking for him, too. Dakota got
them on the same page with a plan. Every group
would work in a grid pattern for maximum cov-
erage.

The sun was just rising as Dakota picked up a
trail outside the camp. No one else was a trained
tracker, so the officials allowed them to follow what
they found. The rest of the groups would begin
searching other grid-assigned areas. Their breath
was white, the temperature in the twenties. Shelby
let Dakota take the lead, his gaze fixed and moving in front of him. The woods were thick and the
light bad because of the forest canopy above them.

The pine-needle floor was brown and soft. It
had snowed two days earlier, melted and Shelby
felt it was a good time to track. A man's footprint
would leave a minuscule depression even in the

soft, spongy brown needles. She could see Dakota was quickly following the slight depressions as it led deeper into the woods.

They had tracked for an hour, up and over a small hill, when he held up his fist. She halted beside him, breathing hard. "Is that a signal you just gave me?"

He turned, looking over at her. Shelby's cheeks were a bright pink from the exertion of the climb. "Sorry. Yes."

"Is that nonverbal SEAL talk?" she ventured, appreciating his nearness. Dakota looked almost invisible in the camouflage gear. He blended in almost to the point where he couldn't be seen. Only his face made him stand out against the mottled light and dark of the woods.

"It is. Don't you deputies have hand signals?"

"No. What does it mean when you raise your forearm in a fist?"

"Stop."

"I did. I'm pretty good at this." Shelby gave him an evil grin.

Heat flowed through his sweaty body as he saw Shelby's teasing smile. He almost leaned down to kiss her. Almost… Turning, Dakota pointed down the hill. "This guy, from what I can tell, probably left about two o'clock yesterday morning. He seems to know where he's going. He's not wandering around in circles. People who are really lost walk around in circles."

"It looks like he stops and rests for a bit, and then moves on," she agreed.

"Poor bastard," he breathed, shaking his head.

"At least he took his coat, hat and gloves."

"You can still freeze to death from hypothermia in this stuff, Shel. Real damn fast. It takes no prisoners."

"You were in the mountains of Afghanistan. You would know."

"Yeah, and we were operating at twelve thousand feet, twenty below Fahrenheit and the wind blowing like a banshee." He touched his gear. "I'm wearing five layers of specially designed cold-weather gear. That poor guy doesn't have anything near that to survive in."

"I don't think we'll find him alive, Dakota," Shelby said softly.

"I don't, either. Helluva way to die."

"I wonder if he did this on purpose."

"What? Walk away knowing he'd freeze to death out here?"

"Yeah. Maybe he had enough of his mind left to know how much of a burden he was becoming to his wife. Maybe he couldn't stand seeing her suffering and working so hard to keep him safe. I've seen other suicides like this."

Dakota could see the raw concern in her blue

eyes. He was losing control. And God, that was the last thing he needed right now. Control to keep his hands, his mouth, off Shelby. Her trembling words, the grief on her face, did something internally to him. He couldn't name what it was, only that it happened. Taking off his glove, he said roughly, "Come here…." He slid his hand along her clean jaw. Tilting her head up slightly, he moved close. "You have the softest heart, Shel…" He leaned down, curving his mouth across her parting lips. He'd seen the look of surprise and then heat and desire enter her eyes as he'd shifted, captured her and kissed her.

Shelby had been aching to continue the first interrupted kiss they'd shared days ago. Momentarily startled by his unexpected move, she stepped forward, sliding her arms around his broad shoulders, drawing him against herself as she met and moved her lips against his plundering, commanding mouth.

His breath was punctuated against her nose and cheek, his callused hand feeling raspy, fingers sliding down her jawline and curving around her nape, drawing her hard against him. She felt the full force of his hunger and she responded, matching his desire with her own. There was something incredibly haunting and vulnerable about Dakota; she felt it, couldn't put it in words. Yet, as their lips moved together, she felt him quiver. He rocked her lips open and they tasted each other. She pulled him as close as they could get with all the gear on between them. His beard was harsh against her cheek, but she didn't care.

The heat built explosively between them. She glided her tongue boldly against his. Instantly, he groaned, his fingers capturing the base of her skull, holding her so he could plunder her more deeply. There was such need erupting between them, Shelby realized. She ached to somehow get closer to him, to his flesh. Never had she had a kiss like this. It was rough, unbridled and primal. But so was she.

Gradually, Dakota came out of the lust haze and need for Shelby. He realized he had probably bruised her soft lips. She wasn't afraid of him. No, she was just as assertive as he'd been. Easing the pressure of his mouth against hers, inhaling her feminine scent, a mix of sweetness and pine, he reluctantly broke contact.

He barely opened his eyes, but instead drowned in the blue luster of her glistening eyes. Dakota brushed her wet mouth, wanting to ease any pain he might have caused her. He hadn't intended to hurt her. Hell, he hadn't intended to kiss her at all! He was shattered in another way, unable to control his needs for her. His body trembled inwardly, the ache increasing between his legs. There was no disguising his feelings for her. Her flared hips rested against his. He knew Shelby could feel his hunger in real time. Placing small, gentle kisses against her cheek, brow and finally, upon her mouth once more, he rasped, "I wanted to finish that kiss we started at your house." That wasn't a lie. Hell, he was thinking about kissing her every friggin' minute of the day. He felt like a drug addict. He felt trapped, his heart and body screaming for her and his mind imprisoned in PTSD screaming he had to stop—or else.

Her mouth curved softly into a smile. "I did, too."

"I'm sorry if I hurt you." He touched her lower lip with his thumb, moving it gently across the swollen, glistening surface.

Shelby shook her head, tried to struggle out of the all-consuming kiss. "No...you didn't hurt me." As she looked up at his scalding gaze, her body exploded with a need that shocked her. "It was mutual, Dakota. I wanted you as much as you wanted me."

Though he didn't want to let her go, Dakota knew he had to. Their five minutes of rest were over. Releasing her, he stepped back. Studying her in the silence, a few birds calling somewhere beyond them, Dakota memorized her oval face, those fierce blue eyes that shone with desire for him alone. Somehow he had to keep his hands off her. Somehow... "We need to keep going."

Nodding, Shelby said, "I'll take over the tracking."

"I could use a break." Tracking took every ounce of a person's concentration. His body clamored for more of Shelby's kiss and he struggled to establish control over his body. She was like a missing key to his heart and soul. How could he stop her effect on him when she'd already melted his control with just one damn kiss? Shelby had opened him up in ways that rocked his dark, wounded world. There was nothing shy or reclusive about her kiss—or her.

As she moved past him to pick up the trail, Dakota's mouth twisted with pain and frustration. Whatever they shared, whatever it was, made him feel whole. And that was a joke, because he was broken in so many ways. Shelby appeared in his life, and his goddamn heart thought that she could transform him. His mind knew otherwise, that the effects of trauma didn't just disappear.

Dakota kept his attention on the surrounding area. Everything seemed quiet, the woods always making him feel embraced by nature. He took the radio from his belt and checked-in to Ranger HQ, giving them an update as well as their current GPS position. Because the woods were so thick, the cover impossible to penetrate, it would do no good to use a helicopter to find the poor gent. Ground tracking was the only way to find Banyon.

After signing off, Dakota watched Shelby track.

She was good. Every once in a while, she'd kneel down, study a depression, look around before moving on. That was the only way to find out if the lost man might be somewhere ahead. Tracking was not done quickly. Sometimes it was, depending upon the spore or print. Here, Dakota knew pine needles, especially if dry, were hell to track in, slowing everything down to a near crawl.

Shelby moved silently, the woods making the area dim and dark. There were rocks here and there, fallen logs, but for the most part, Tony Banyon seemed to have a destination in mind. She felt bad for him. She half expected to find him huddled by a tree. But that didn't happen. The man seemed to be in good physical condition because his stride was even, not choppy or unbalanced. She tried to keep her mind on her work, but her body was like a starved animal, her lower area between her thighs wanting to be satisfied. Dakota's kiss had forced her to acknowledge she missed having a man in her life. He reminded her fully that she was a woman with healthy needs. Up until now, she could ignore them. Dakota was like a match striking against her, flaring her dormant body back to explosive life. And she'd felt his arousal earlier, wanted him in every way.

At the end of the slope of the hill, an hour later, Shelby stopped. Dakota came soundlessly up behind her. It felt like a warm wave embracing her from behind. She looked to her right, amazed at how silently he could move. His face was set, gaze scanning the area down below them. "This guy is moving out. And he knows where he's going. He's got an objective in mind."

"Yeah," Dakota growled, "but where? The wife said he did a lot of birding in this area and knew it well." He gestured to the steep slope that led down into an even thicker area of woodlands. Taking out his map, he had her hold two edges of it. "About ten miles ahead, there's a meadow. I'm hoping we can find him alive. If we do, we can get him to that meadow where a helo could come in and pick us up."

Shelby was no stranger to reading a topographical map. "Our GPS is putting us in a northern trek with Tony." She shook her head. "I'd swear he knows where he is."

"Maybe. Remember, the wife said he'd walk ten or fifteen miles a day with his camera and binos, binoculars, because he was a birder."

Shelby absorbed Dakota's overwhelming male nearness. She tried to ignore the desire banked in his brown eyes that seem to burn right through her heart and lower body. When he'd kissed her earlier, she'd seen gold in the depths of them, too. Her mouth continued to tingle off and on from his hungry kiss. "It's 11:00 a.m.," she muttered. "And if his track continues toward that meadow, it's a long way from here to there."

Tracking was an art coupled with a lot of patience. Dakota nodded. "We can't just assume he's heading there, though." He gestured to the darkening woods in front of them. "This area has heavy woods. We're going to have to be careful and watch to see if his tracks don't suddenly peel off in another direction."

"Yeah, the depressions are getting more and more shallow. It will be easy to miss a print."

"That's because the needles are drying out."

"Damn." Shelby sighed, studying the map one more time. It was hard, slow work if pine needles completely dried out. They would be forced to slow down even more and start looking for one or two pine needles being turned the wrong way to indicate someone had stepped on them. "This isn't good."

"Not for him, it isn't."

Shelby glanced up. "I wish like hell we didn't have this kind of tree cover. I wish we had a military helo available with thermal imaging on board to detect his body heat. I just feel like he's going to die."

He reached out and slid his hand across her shoulders. "I know. But that kind of helo isn't available."

Shelby folded the map and handed it back to Dakota. They'd already made six miles into the forest following him. There were patches of snow on the ground along with only a few open areas. Early June weather meant a mix of rain, sleet, snow and sunshine. A few slats of light made their way down to the ground, bright yellow spots in the gloom of the forest. "Can you track for a while?"

"Yes." He took the lead. It was going to be a long, hard day as spring storm clouds continued to gather around them. The rangers had warned the volunteer group this morning that a swift moving cold front would sweep through the area at sunset. And that was bad news for Tony Banyon.

DUSK WAS FALLING and the storm chased them. Shelby couldn't hide her frustration that they still hadn't found Tony. All afternoon, they'd called out his name about every quarter mile. They would stop, hoping to hear a reply. Nothing. The sky was a gunmetal gray, the winds blowing hard and sharp. Spits of sleet already began to cover the area. Dakota called a halt to their search because it was getting too dark to track. Shelby reluctantly agreed.

They were a mile from the meadow. Dakota had already picked out an area of heavy brush that would give them protection against the growing gusts of wind. She helped by clearing the space with a long, fallen branch, smoothing it out for their tent. Her stomach growled with hunger.

Dakota finished off the radio transmission with HQ, giving them their GPS coordinates. They would stay and ride out the storm. He turned and saw that Shelby had chosen a good place for their tent.

"This is a fast-moving storm," he warned her. "Weather guy just said it will hit this area right now."

Shelby straightened. "It's already starting."

"He said the storm should clear off by tomorrow morning," Dakota growled. "The snow is going to cover Tony's tracks. We'll make a best guess tomorrow morning and then head toward the direction of the meadow as soon as we get enough light." His mouth turned grim. "I hope we run into him." It would be too late, but he didn't say it. He could see the truth on Shelby's face.

"Yes, first light," she whispered. "It's the best anyone can do under the circumstances."

Opening the ruck, Dakota pulled out the desert camouflage tent. He wished he could somehow ease her worry. Shelby was the type of person who cared deeply about everything and everyone. His job right now was to get her mind off the man who was lost somewhere out beyond them. He tossed her some of the stakes that would keep the tent from flying away in the gusts of wind.

For the next ten minutes, they worked quickly and without speaking. Darkness was falling rapidly now. Shelby straightened, studying the tent. "This is military issue?"

"Yeah. SEAL stuff. What? You're looking at it like it's not very protective?"

She saw the shadows on his face as he knelt at the front and opened the Velcro flaps. "No," she said slowly, "I'm thinking that it's cramped. How do you get two people in there?" Her heart started a slight pound as she considered his closeness in such a confined space. Until this moment, her mind and heart had been on Tony and his situation.

"You do," he said. "This is cold winter gear. SEALs sleep two to a tent because body warmth will keep them from freezing to death." Looking up, he pointed toward the tops of the trees around them. "We're going to get hammered tonight with heavy, wet snow. The temperature will drop below zero." Her brows moved down as she stared with a question in her eyes.

"Are you going to have nightmares tonight? Turn over and think I'm the enemy?"

It was a fair question. Dakota pulled over his rucksack. He took out two MREs. Opening his jacket, he pulled two magnesium tablets from one of the pockets of his H-gear. "You have a choice," he told her quietly, gesturing for her to come over and sit down with him and eat beneath the protection of the overhanging tree limbs.

Shelby brought her pack over and sat down

cross-legged on the pine needles. It was almost dark. Their breaths turned to white vapor as the temperature fell rapidly. Dakota expertly set the MREs on two small metal grates and lit the magnesium tablets beneath them. He'd already cleared the area so no fire could start as a result. Rubbing her gloved hands together, she said, "What are my choices?"

Hitching a thumb toward the tent, Dakota rasped, "If you're worried I'll try to kill you in there during the throes of a nightmare, I'll sleep over there." He pointed to a group of bushes that would provide protection against the wind and snow. How he hoped she wouldn't ask him to leave. He understood her wariness but he'd never wanted a woman more than Shelby. He could feel his body turning traitor on him, his massive control dissolving in the heat of his need to feel her warm, firm body against his flesh. His mind just wouldn't stop. Nightmares be damned. Shelby had fractured the massive wall he'd hidden behind. Dakota had no answer for why or how she did. Only that she did. It left him starved for her, shaky, needy and his control slipping by the minute as they sat together. He prayed she'd take the first choice. She had to.

Shelby could barely see the outline of heavy bushes near the tent. The magnesium tabs were so bright, it was like sudden sunlight piercing the dark, ruining her night vision. She stared into his hooded eyes. Her body responded with aching need to that heated look. "What's my other choice?"

"Let me lie with you, love you and we'll spend the night in each other's arms. I promise, we won't be cold…."

The words, barely above a whisper, flowed hotly through her. She stared at him. His eyes were hard and intelligent, his mouth pursed. The beard had deepened and accentuated his high cheekbones, strong nose and full mouth. "You're serious?" she asked.

A slight twitch pulled at the left corner of his mouth. "Never more serious."

Her eyes widened momentarily. *Just say yes, Shel.* He'd willingly sleep outside in his specially made sleeping bag and survive nicely out in the coming snowstorm. And he didn't want her to decide based on worry he'd freeze to death. He knew her well enough to know because she cared so deeply, she'd make a poor choice. He was hoping his bluntness would scare her enough to make the right decision.

"Wouldn't you freeze out here?" She gestured toward the brush.

"No, Shelby. I took winter training up at Kodiak Island, off Alaska. We were out in the rain, snow and cold for three weeks. Trust me, I can survive any kind of storm conditions." He watched her consider the situation. There was no question he wanted her. The real question was: did she want him?

"I'll think about it," she muttered. "Are those MREs hot enough to eat? I'm starving to death."

CHAPTER FIFTEEN

COLD SLEET BEGAN to pummel the area as they quickly finished eating their MREs. Shelby stared through the near darkness at Dakota. "You know I don't want you out in this miserable weather," she said.

"Don't worry about me tonight, I'm tired." It was the truth. But right then his body caught a sudden burst of energy. Desperate energy. Why hadn't Shelby taken the first choice? He surrendered inwardly. Maybe it was a year's worth of being alone and lonely that snapped his control where she was concerned. Maybe…just one night… just one and he'd get her out of his blood. "I figured you'd choose door number two. You have such a soft heart, Shel. You feel sorry for any poor son of a bitch. Even me." It was more truth than teasing. No one needed a broken, scarred vet in her life. He'd only make it more miserable.

Shelby muttered defiantly, mouth quirking, "You're such a bastard, Carson."

He came over and smiled down at her. All

around them the sleet continued to thicken, the sound like tiny pebbles striking the limbs and pine branches. "It worked, didn't it?"

She could see the fatigue in his eyes. "Yes. And you're getting your ass into that tent. I refuse to lie awake worrying about you out in this crappy weather."

Without hesitation, he got down on his knees, opened his sleeping bag and pushed it inside the cramped quarters. "You're such a marshmallow, Shel."

His shoulders were broad and she could literally feel the heat rolling off his body as she knelt beside him and pushed her sleeping bag into the tight space. "Yes, I am," she said. "But so are you."

He barely twisted a humored look in her direction. The chips of ice had stuck to strands of her hair. "No, not me. Somehow, soft and SEAL aren't synonymous. No one has ever called us marshmallows, either."

Laughing, Shelby turned around, leaned back on her heels as she opened her pack to locate food. "They both start with an *s,* smart guy. You put on this fierce, tough front, but in the end, you have a big heart, Dakota."

His eyes narrowed intently upon her. Instantly, she felt that stalking energy around him. The night was nearly complete. "For example," she went on conversationally, pulling out two protein bars, "you saved Storm. You could have let that grizzly finish the job, but you put yourself in jeopardy by standing your ground. The bear would have known Storm was hiding in that burrow."

"Get inside," he growled, gesturing to the opening in the tent. "We don't need to chat out here and get wet if we don't have to."

Shelby grinned as she moved into the tent. She caught the glint of acknowledgment in his eyes regarding her argument. The two bags were right next to each other, the tent high enough to sit up in, but that was all. Dakota dragged in their packs and stowed them at the door after he squeezed his bulk into the tent. The Velcro on the openings were quickly closed. The pelting of the ice crystals continued. She handed him a protein bar after he sat cross-legged on top of his bag.

"Dessert?"

She was dessert, but he didn't say it. "Thanks," he said instead, taking the bar. As they touched fingers, he relished their brief contact.

Just then, Shelby's radio went off. She pulled it out of her pocket and answered it.

Dakota listened to the conversation, his brow dipping over the news. When she placed the radio above her head and near the sleeping bag, Dakota saw the concerned look on her face. She pushed the hood back, her hair mussed. "So, someone identified Vance Welton?"

The tent became warm very quickly, and Shelby unzipped her coat and shrugged out of it. She would use it as a pillow later. "Yes. Good thing Cade had photos of those guys put on television. It worked."

He could barely see Shelby, but he could feel her. Unconsciously, he inhaled her feminine scent. "How are you feeling about this development?"

"Considering it was my neighbor who saw him walking by my house, shaken," she admitted, unhappy. Shelby busied herself by untying the laces to her boots and shoving them off her feet. Getting on her hands and knees, she placed them at the end of the tent, near the entrance. She sat cross-legged once more, facing Dakota. "It bothers me a lot. I'm just glad my mom and dad decided to leave town until this is over." A cold shiver made its way up her spine.

Hearing the edge in her voice, he added, "Shel, we're going to find them and we're going to put them back behind bars where they belong."

"Count on it," she said. "I'm more worried about the women in town, Dakota. These guys are rapists and murderers. They're loose, like wild animals."

"Tomorrow," he assured her, "at first light, we'll start working our way toward the meadow and hope we run into Tony." It would snow all night and there was no way they could find him in the dark as a snarling storm whipped around them. They could get lost and die of hypothermia themselves. Under any other conditions, Dakota would have pushed on through the night trying to find the man.

"I wish we could do more to help Tony, but I know we can't. It's depressing." She finished off her power bar and located her canteen by touch. Opening it, Shelby drank deeply. The cold water soothed her anxiety about the radio call. "I can hear the worry in Cade's voice. He's thinking what we're talking about. No woman is safe with them prowling around," she said.

Dakota savagely pushed down his grief over his sister's death. "And we need to assume that Hartley is around, too. They worked as a team last time. It would be stupid to think Welton is working alone."

Capping her canteen, Shelby shoved it in a corner. "Where are they staying? That's what we need to find out."

"A better question is, did they steal another vehicle? Is someone missing a car or truck in Jackson Hole?"

"It's the right question to ask," she agreed. "It could give us a lead, a place where they might be hiding." The heat in the tent amazed her. She shed her sweater, down to a silk camisole. Modesty no longer an issue, Shelby shed her jeans and stuffed them down at the entrance along with her boots. With thick socks on her feet, her silk briefs and camisole, she pulled open her down sleeping bag, slid down inside it and faced him. She was glad Dakota was with her. Shelby felt fearful even though she knew the convicts were fifty miles away. Tomorrow, they had to return to Jackson Hole after, hopefully, finding Tony. Shelby knew she'd be anxious and alert going back home.

After finishing his protein bar, Dakota shrugged out of his winter gear and stripped down to his boxer shorts. He rolled the coat into a makeshift pillow. Wildly aware of Shelby's nearness, he reined in his desire for her. Right now she was worried and she had a right to be because Welton and Hartley were trying to find her. He could hear the veiled nervousness in her husky voice. She was struggling not to be affected by the news, but hell, she was human. And she'd already seen the carnage these two convicts caused up front and close before.

"Comfy?" he asked her.

"Yes. It's incredibly warm in here. This is an amazing SEAL tent you have!"

"The SEALs get the best of everything," he told her. "This sleeping bag is a product of the best minds around the world creating it for us so we could survive minus forty below if we had to." He opened it and slid in, using the Velcro to close it up to retain his body heat. After punching the jacket into a pillow, he lay down, facing Shelby. He could smell her damp hair and could hear her soft breathing. *So close.* Shelby was inches away from him.

"You guys deserve the best," she told him.

He reached out, his fingers making contact with her naked shoulder. He felt the warmth of her flesh beneath his callused fingertips, and it sent a keening ache through him. "Listen, stop worrying, Shel. We're going to find these gomers." He grazed her damp hair. Nostrils flaring, he inhaled her scent, honey mixed with pine. The combination was like an aphrodisiac to him, sending a sheet of fire burning through his hardening lower body. Her brow was wrinkled beneath his exploring thumb and he gently smoothed out the lines. "Go to sleep. I'm here…."

She closed her eyes. Dakota filled the tent with his size. She felt his protection like a warm blanket, erasing her fears and worry. Exhaustion came over her and the anxiety loosened its grip as she focused on his fingers stroking the curve of her neck and sliding across her shoulder. "Thanks, Dakota. It means a lot."

Dakota waited until he was sure Shelby was asleep. As tired as he was, he couldn't sleep. His mind was focused on the fact that Welton had been identified just outside her home. Lying on his back, hands tucked behind his head, he listened to the sleet finally go away to be replaced with soft, huge white snowflakes plopping gently on the sides of their tent. The wind was picking up and he could hear the gusts singing through the Douglas fir. That sound was like a lullaby to him. Despite his hunger for her, in moments, his lashes dropped and he fell into a deep, dreamless sleep. In the end, the strain upon their physical bodies won out.

SHELBY AWOKE WITH a scream. She launched into a sitting position, caught in a nightmare where Welton had her by her throat and was choking her.

Instantly, Dakota jerked awake. Fully awake. Without thinking, he sat up, reached out and found her in the darkness. "Shel…it's okay," he rasped, dragging her into his arms. "It's just a nightmare. You're safe…."

She gave a cry of relief. She didn't resist him, but instead collapsed in his arms, her head coming to rest against his shoulder.

"Oh…God…" A low moan tore out of her throat, her hand pressed against her neck. "Welton was choking me."

"Shh, it's just a bad dream," he whispered, pulling her next to him. He smoothed her mussed hair, his fingers threading slowly between the dry, silky strands. "He can't hurt you, Shel. I won't ever let that happen. You're okay, you're safe."

His moist, heated breath flowed across her cheek and ear. The trembling that had held her captive began to dissolve as his lips lightly grazed her cheek, her brow and hair. "I never have nightmares, Dakota. Not ever."

"Don't worry. The nightmares don't kill you. I

have them every night. I don't know what I'd do if I didn't have them."

"You're sick," she mumbled, smiling a little as his teasing short-circuited her terror. Shelby burrowed her face into his shoulder. His male scent ate away at the edges of her bad dream. She heard his rolling chuckle. The sound surrounded her and she slipped her arm around his slab-hard belly. Sometime during the night, he'd opened his bag and the material was bunched up around his waist.

"No, just being honest," he rumbled, smiling a little into the darkness. He savored the feel of her body against his, the curve of her waist as he slid his hand across the swell of her hip. Automatically, as if he were soothing a fractious, frightened horse, he trailed his fingers from her shoulder down the length of her spine to her hips. The camisole was a thin barrier and he fought to ignore the silky motion beneath his fingertips. When she burrowed closer to him, her hips nuzzling against his, he knew she was silently asking him to love her. Dakota grew hard. Wanting her, knowing it wasn't the right time, he forced himself to keep his ministrations light, not intimate. Perspiration popped out on his brow and across his shoulders as he wrestled control over his own body. At the same time, another part of him screamed its need to make her his.

Shelby ran her hand up across his naked back, feeling a number of long scars beneath her fingertips. Had to be war wounds. How much pain had Dakota endured? Wherever she traced, his flesh tensed. The nightmare had been so violent, so real. Shelby wanted to do something to make it disappear. Without thinking, more out of instinct, she lifted her chin, rose on her elbow, sought and found Dakota's mouth in the darkness.

When her lips touched his, he was startled. Her mouth was soft and searching, cajoling him to respond. He placed massive control over his body, but he was like a primal animal, wanting to take her hard and fast, stamping his maleness into her. His other side wanted to make her a partner, not something to be used. He gritted his teeth, lifted his hand, found her left shoulder. He eased Shelby onto her back, her body against his.

"Shel, is this what you really want?" His voice was husky with concern. He saw the fear banked in her drowsy eyes. Was she running away from the nightmare or running toward him? When a person thought she was going to die, there was an equal, violent will to prove she was alive. Having sex was one helluva way to confirm life over death.

"Yes, I want you," she breathed, feeling his hand around her back, drawing her up on her right side. "Now. And to answer your question, yes, I'm protected. No more questions." She eased out of his sheltering embrace, pulling off the camisole and quickly dispensing with her silk panties and socks.

Dakota pulled open his sleeping bag to allow her next to him. Her hips touched and then pressed against his. She had to know how much he wanted her. And when her hand ranged down to his waist, fingers easing beneath the waistband of his boxers, smoldering heat built rapidly within him. She pulled and tugged the rest of his clothes off his body.

Shelby felt the hard strength of his erection pressing insistently into her soft, rounded belly, her own body flexing, aching for him. Dakota slid his arm beneath her neck, drawing her fully up against him. His hard length sent wild shocks rippling down into her womb. Her core grew hot and moist instantly as the beat of his heart thundered against her breasts. Yes, this was what she'd been wanting. Him. All of him. And it had never seemed so right as it did right now.

"Kiss me," she breathed against the hardened line of his mouth.

His massive control began to crack as her soft lips waged a sweet campaign against him. She sought and found his mouth. Her fingers tangled in his short hair, trailing around the nape of his neck, pulling him down upon her. There was nothing shy or hesitant about Shelby, and Dakota curved his mouth hotly against hers, feeling the returning pressure of her lips, feeling her womanly smile beneath his. She was warm, responsive and when she pressed her hips against his, a groan broke free from deep inside him.

The moment Dakota lifted his hand, his roughened fingers cupping around the curve of her breast, Shelby lost the real world. Her flesh tingled, shards of electricity racing across her skin as those fingers caressed and explored her tightening flesh. The hunger of his mouth plundering hers, his thumb and index finger teasing the nipple into a hardened, needy peak, broke the nightmare and her whole world burned around her. His hips ground into hers, pushing her onto her back, his weight coming down upon her.

Everywhere she moved her fingers, his flesh tensed his muscles leaped beneath her as she mapped out his body, memorizing it and him. It filled her with satisfaction as a woman knowing her feminine power could physically affect him so powerfully. Her fingers grazed across his powerful chest, touching the dark strip of hair and following it down the center of his body that disappeared into his groin. His entire body tensed. There was an urgency to mate with this scarred warrior, this man who held her carefully, as if she were fragile china that might shatter in his embrace. His arms around her, his lips burned a trail of fire from her jaw, neck and down to her breasts. Her world exploded and she became mindless as his mouth settled upon the first nipple, his tongue lavishing it, suckling her, sending her deeper into a need she'd never felt so intensely before. Her body tightened and nearly convulsed as the shocks flew wildly down to her core.

Hips restless, Shelby moaned as his mouth captured the second nipple, his hand brushing her rib cage and easing toward her waist. His fingers sought and found the apex of her thighs, and a softened cry of pleasure tore out of her throat. His large palm flattened out over the area, his fingers moving downward. Somewhere in her cartwheeling mind, she understood Dakota wanted to please her. This wasn't a man taking sex from a woman for selfish gratification. No, this was a man wanting to awaken her body fully, then meet as equals. As his fingers tangled in the heat and wetness of her, she moaned his name, pleading for more of him. Heart racing, her breath coming in ragged gasps, she pushed against his hand, wanting more. Wanting him.

Dakota felt her silkiness, her slick warmth, telling him she was ready. In one moment, he pulled her over him as he settled on his back, her curved, damp thighs straddling his narrow hips. He could hear her gasping for breath, trembling violently as he brought her hips forward. A little cry tore from her as he moved against her heat, slowly entering her, giving her time to adjust. Gritting his teeth, he wrapped his large hands around her hips as she flowed down onto him, hot and slick. The last of his control disintegrated as she moved with him, her fingers digging convulsively into his chest as he established a wild rhythm between them. Dakota arched his hips against hers and heard her cry of pleasure tremor through her throat. He captured her hips fully against him, bringing more pressure to bear within her, pleasuring her, driving her to the edge of rapture and into his arms.

His hands were relentless, and he thrust deeply into her. He drove Shelby to the edge of mindlessness, her body quivering, spasming as he felt her begin to clench around him. An explosion occurred deep within her body and Shelby gave a hoarse cry, her back arching, head thrown back. The rivulets of fire raced outward like circles on a pond, each one more intense, more pleasurable, than the last within her quivering, taut body. And when he leaned upward, his lips capturing her hardened nipples, more explosions released wildly within her.

Lost in the darkness, the heat and feel of her body dissolved. Dakota eased her off him and moved her onto her back. His weight felt wonderful against her body and he nudged her thighs open to receive him again. Waves of glittering sensations blossomed hotly within her core as he moved powerfully within her. He took her swiftly, thrusting deep, stamping her with his maleness, claiming her in the only way a man can claim a woman. Shelby lifted her hips, knowing it would send him over the edge of pleasure. Dakota suddenly tensed. His hands curved into fists on either side of Shelby's head, his back flexing, violently trembling. A low animal growl rolled out of his chest, the delicious sound reverberating through every cell of her body. She wrapped her long legs around his narrow hips, her face pressed against his neck, their breathing chaotic, sweat slick between them. He released powerfully into her body. More scalding explosions occurred within Shelby, and all she could do was cry out hoarsely and cling to Dakota, who held her a willing prisoner within his arms and against his body. She tasted the sweat across his temple, her mouth searching and finding his. Their mouths clung together, sharing joy, sharing the fire continuing to erupt between them. The coolness of the below-freezing temperature did nothing but make her keenly aware of the sleekness of their burning bodies moving in primal unison with each other.

Collapsing against him, Shelby sobbed for air. Dakota slowly eased off her and brought her against him. Their bodies glowed against each other, their hips fused, their legs entangled. She nestled her head against his shoulder, her fingers moving against his sandpapery cheek, sliding across his damp, short hair. She kissed his corded neck, feeling his powerful pulse beneath her lips. Shelby smiled weakly, leaning up, drawing Dakota's head toward her so she could kiss him one more time.

His mouth ravished hers, but then became tender and coaxing. Her body was satiated as never before, Shelby curved her hand against the hard line of his jaw. This time, she moved her lips softly against his. His hands skimmed slowly down the breadth of her body and she could feel him memorizing her, gentling her with his touch alone. Shelby discovered a new level of emotion opening up her thundering heart. Fierce feeling flowed through her, taking her to another level of happiness she'd never experienced before.

Once Dakota eased out of her, Shelby nestled against his chest, he drew the sleeping bag over them. He made sure she was completely covered, his large hand coming to rest, finger splaying outward against her hip. It was a claim of possession. A man taking his woman, protecting her, loving her.

She closed her eyes and whispered, "I never want this to end." And then she fell asleep, utterly spent and cocooned within Dakota's arms.

CHAPTER SIXTEEN

THE NEXT MORNING, A quarter mile away from the meadow, they discovered Tony Banyon. He'd curled up, knees to chest, next to a Douglas fir and died of hypothermia. Shelby's heart broke as she took off her glove and held it to the man's neck, looking for the pulse she knew she wouldn't find. His skin was faintly bluish-gray. No pulse.

"He died at least four to five hours ago," Shelby whispered, straightening. At the height of the storm. There was no possible way to have found him in time. She saw something gripped in his gloved hand and gently eased it out from between his frozen fingers. As she read the scrawled note, her heart broke even more.

"It's a suicide note," she whispered, handing it to Dakota. Tears came to her eyes. "We were right. He knew what he was doing all along. He didn't want to be a burden to his wife any longer." Her voice broke and she stared down at the man. "This is so sad...."

Dakota read it, his mouth pursing. He handed

the note back to her and shrugged out of his rucksack. He pulled out a dark green blanket and gently
placed it over the older man's body. "He didn't have
a chance out here and he knew it," he muttered
darkly. Dakota honored his courage to look into
death's face and surrender to it. Not many men
could do that.

"That's a special kind of bravery," Shelby
agreed, her voice raspy with tears. She pulled out
her radio, cleared her throat and called HQ, giving
them the information. The head ranger would pass
on the contents of the note to the wife. Shelby was
glad she didn't have to give the wife the contents
of the note. She wasn't sure she could remain de-
tached. A helicopter would meet them in an hour
in the meadow. She looked over to see the mask
on Dakota's face, his eyes dark with suffering for
the man and his wife.

"At least this guy died in a place he loved," he
muttered.

"Yes…" Shelby managed, her voice a bit stran-
gled. Emotionally, she was thinking of the wife,
their long marriage and to have it all come to a sad
end like this. She stuffed the radio back on her belt.
"We need to transport him toward the meadow."

"I'll do it. Can you carry my ruck?"

Nodding, she hefted his heavy rucksack strap
over her left shoulder. They had a good amount
of distance to the meadow with knee-deep snow

slowing their pace. It was nearly 7:00 a.m., the sky a light blue with scattered clouds left in the wake of the swift-moving storm from last night. She watched Dakota as he gently brought the man's body into a fireman's carry across his broad, capable shoulders.

"Let's go," Dakota said, barely turning his head to catch her gaze. There were tears glistening in Shelby's eyes. He was touched deeply, too, but forced his reaction away, the way he always did. The man was small, weighing only about a hundred and thirty pounds. Dakota could easily carry him through the forest. They arrived at the oval, and the helicopter flew in ten minutes later.

Shelby sat with Dakota in the helicopter, holding his gloved hand. Dakota wished he could take away the anguish he saw in her eyes. Shelby was easily touched by human suffering. And he loved her even more than before. Dakota wasn't looking forward to driving back to Jackson Hole. They would get dumped into another kind of brutal storm, one that promised either life or death.

"ANYTHING NEW ON WELTON?" Shelby asked Cade Garner as they arrived at the sheriff's department. They had returned midday from Yellowstone after filling out a lot of paperwork on Tony's death at Ranger headquarters. Dakota stood relaxed at her side.

Cade was at his desk, papers strewn around it. "No. Your neighbor, Cat Edwin, who works at the fire department, spotted him."

Frowning, Shelby sat down in front of his desk. "She didn't see a strange or unknown car?"

"Nothing." Cade grimaced. "We're running their photos on local television with the evening news and we'll continue to do it every day. We're going to have to catch a break."

Dakota took a chair and sat down. "We know Welton is focused on Shelby. And he was caught in front of her home."

"Which was stupid of him, but lucky for us," Shelby said almost choking on her growing fear. Being stalked wasn't something she would ever get used to.

"But it shows he's that cocksure he isn't going to be recognized," Cade warned her.

"That's what you want," Dakota said, "because that kind of brazen behavior will eventually get him caught."

Shelby pushed her damp palms against her jeans. "I'm more worried that Welton and Hartley are going to kidnap another unsuspecting woman, Cade. That's what has me going. I feel like I can take care of myself where those two are concerned, but what about all the innocent women who live here in Jackson Hole?"

Cade nodded and became somber. "I'm worried

about it, too. I don't have unlimited manpower to devote a couple of deputies to find these two. We talked about strategies yesterday after Welton was spotted. If I had extra people, we could go to the local banks and grocery stores to look at video to see if we can spot them that way. They have to eat."

"Let me volunteer for that duty, then," Dakota said, giving Shelby a glance. "It's easy enough for me to sit and watch videos to try to spot them."

"I can deputize you," Cade said, liking the idea.

"But you'll have to be interfacing with a lot of people," Shelby warned, worried about his PTSD symptoms.

Dakota shrugged. "I lived with PTSD symptoms for years out in Afghanistan. I'll deal with it here." His eyes locked onto hers. "Your life is on the line. And these two are wolves walking among sheep. Ellie died because they were loose. I don't ever want another woman caught in her position. Not ever."

The low growl in his voice convinced her. There was pure hatred in his eyes for the two convicts. She glanced at Cade, who gave him a nod of approval. "If Cade can make it happen, that's fine with me." She stood up. "I'm going to get back on the rotation schedule, Cade. I can't sit up at Dakota's cabin twiddling my thumbs. I need to be out on the beat."

"Go get cleaned up and then come back in this

afternoon after lunch. I'll put you back on the duty roster."

"Welton and Hartley know she works here. Aren't you worried about that?" Dakota asked.

"Yes, but look, Shelby is a seasoned deputy. She has a cruiser, she knows the lay of the land around here and she's going to remain alert," Cade said.

Shelby reached out and touched Dakota's shoulder. "I'll be okay."

Mouth quirking, Dakota stood. He wasn't so sure, but that conversation would be in the cruiser on the way to his cabin.

"See you later," Cade called as they left his office.

The midday sun was warm with a breeze that made Shelby keep the knit cap on her head. She noticed Dakota scowling as he walked with her. He was scanning the area. But so was she. Climbing into the black Tahoe sheriff's cruiser, she waited until he got inside before starting the vehicle. Her body still glowed from their lovemaking last night.

"I can't sit and wait," she told him, backing the SUV out of the parking slot.

"They're actively looking for you."

"So?" she said, putting the cruiser in Drive and guiding it out of the parking lot. "Where else can they find me other than at my house?"

"They're hunters, Shel," he said, worry in his tone. Dakota ran his hands through his short hair.

"You can't get complacent. I worked with sniper teams in the SEAL platoon from time to time and they never relaxed or took downtime when on an op. For them, the enemy was out there 24/7. To assume the enemy slept wasn't something they took for granted, either. When they were out hunting, one man slept and the other stayed awake. They never both slept at the same time for fear of being caught by surprise."

The streets of Jackson Hole were wet with melting snow from the storm that had roared through the area last night. The same storm that had caught them. It was impossible not to be affected by Dakota—every part of him. Her body still felt his hands moving across her, remembering her, pleasuring her. He fulfilled a hunger in her that no man ever had. Shelby glanced over at him, his profile set, mouth thinned, telling her he was worried for her.

"I promise you, I won't get caught flat-footed. You keep forgetting I was the one who found their trail and tracked them for three days before I caught up with them at Norris Basin."

Reaching out, Dakota slid his hand down the curve of her thigh. He remembered her strong legs straddling his hips. Even though he wanted her all over again, he knew he had to get a handle on his desire and remain alert. "You've already proven yourself," he said. "You're the hunted now. This is a different mind-set, Shel. An involuted game turned upside down and you're the target. If I had my way about it, you'd stay at the cabin and not be seen anywhere near this town."

She lifted her hand and placed it over his. "I think you're seeing me through the eyes of a man who isn't used to working with women who are as good at what they do as you are."

His brows rose a little as they sped through a long curve of four-lane traffic through the center of town. "You're good all right." His lower body throbbed with need for her. She was a fierce, assertive lover, and that was when he realized just how confident Shelby really was. It was a surprise, but one of the best he'd had in a long time.

Laughing softly, Shelby gave him a tender look before returning her attention to her driving. "What are we going to do, Dakota?"

"About us?"

"Yes."

He stared at her full lower lip, hotly recalling her mouth skimming his chest, her kisses burning his flesh with such intense pleasure. "You and I aren't going to like my answer. Until Welton and Hartley are caught, nothing changes up at the cabin."

"What? You're going to sleep outside?"

"Yes. I'm the lightest sleeper in the world, thanks to my experience. And if those convicts get lucky and find where you're staying, I'm your first line of defense."

Scowling, Shelby muttered defiantly, "I knew you were going to say that."

He patted her thigh. "This is the kind of war my platoon fought over in Afghanistan. While the terrain changes, the enemy's mind-set doesn't. They want you, Shelby. And if Welton is ballsy enough to be caught out in broad daylight in front of your house, that tells me he's arrogant and on the hunt."

"A war," she said, unhappy. They crawled through the central plaza area, rife with tourists from around the world drawn to the famous Western town.

"It's a mind-set you have to embrace and understand. I worry that maybe you're overconfident, Shel. Yes, you tracked those two down, you hunted and captured them, but the tables are turned now. You can't afford to rest on yesterday."

As she sped out of town, up a long, easy hill with the elk refuge fence and land on the right and a huge black, rocky hill rising thousands of feet into the sky on the left, Shelby knew he was right. "Look, I'm scared. Okay? But I can't let fear run me, Dakota. If I allow it, I'll freeze and I'll get distracted. Both those things can put me in their crosshairs, and we know it."

Though he wanted to stop the car and hold her safe, he said nothing. Shelby was highly intelligent and she was a good law enforcement officer. "I wish," Dakota groused, "I could somehow transfer my years of experience over in Afghanistan into your head. Welton and Hartley remind me of the Taliban. They are damn good hunters. They knew the lay of the land and we didn't. They'd grown up in those mountains and knew them far better than we ever did. And those were all advantages they had over us. We lost some good SEALs because of it."

They crested the hill, the Tetons shining with a new coat of overnight snow on their slopes to the left. She never got tired of seeing them, their gray-blue granite flanks gleaming in the bright, overhead sunlight. "I wish I could do a Vulcan mind meld with you, too." She gave him a soft smile. The look in his eyes was one of raw concern. His sister had died at their hands. And after making love with this warrior last night, Shelby felt his fierce, unrelenting protectiveness around her.

Shaking his head, Dakota said in a low voice, "Dammit. I can feel them around, Shelby. I can feel them hunting you."

"THAT BITCH ISN'T AT her house," Vance griped to Hartley. He'd just returned from getting food from the local supermarket in Jackson Hole. Hartley was continuing to put up plastic across the three windows in the broken-down cabin to stop the cold drafts. The hammer, nails and large roll of plastic lay on the yellowed kitchen counter.

Oren stopped what he was doing and came over to help unload the bags of groceries. "Were you able to get near the sheriff's HQ?"

Opening the refrigerator, Vance said, "No. I checked it out. The sheriff's department is about a hundred feet from the courthouse and they're on the same side of the street. On the other side is nothing but row upon row of houses. And they're all pretty close together with individual fences up between each one. I can't walk between them." He scratched his short hair growing back on his head. "As soon as I'm done here, I'm going over to the address of someone with her last name. I think it's her parents."

"Two for one?" Oren asked, taking the cans and stacking them on an open shelf to the left of the kitchen sinks.

"Maybe. Maybe she's holed up with them."

"Then what?"

"I want her. If we're stupid enough to blow the brains of her parents out, the cops will know it was us. And I want to keep a low profile and hunt her down. I don't need cops swarming all over this place because we shot them."

"But if you can't get her?"

Smiling a little, he said, "Then we'll go back

and target her parents. It's just another form of payback."

"And then we'll hightail it out of here?"

"Damn straight." He had sexual dreams every night that gave him an erection without fail. He took care of it on his own, but not as he wanted. Remembering Ellie Carson, how soft and young she was, he itched to be inside another woman. But not just any woman. Shelby Kincaid was going to be tied up on that bed in the corner, splayed out, naked, and he was going to make her bleed. Just as Ellie had. He could still remember her whimpers, her begging him to stop hurting her. For now he had to bide his time. He finished putting the groceries away.

"You keep gettin' this place cleaned up. It's damned cold up here at night. I'm gonna slip back into town. There's a gun dealer outside the town, and we need a couple of good pistols and two rifles," Welton said.

Oren Hartley returned to cutting out large, rectangular pieces of thick plastic for the next window that needed to be fixed. "Be careful. You know they do background checks."

"That's okay." He patted the back pocket of his jeans. "Our new IDs are in place. That dude with the Garcia drug cartel did a nice job on our new license and social security cards. Worth the two thousand it cost." Welton smiled a little, feeling good about their steps toward throwing the cops off their trail. He rubbed his jaw. The prickly growth had given his triangular face a fuller look. As he pulled on a dark blue baseball cap, his camouflage was in place. Few would be able to identify him as a convict on the run.

"Be careful out there," Hartley drawled.

"Always," Welton called over his shoulder. He shut the door to the cabin and looked around. A rutted dirt road led up to the cabin. He could see one of the Tetons shining with a coat of overnight snow through the tall Douglas fir that surrounded them. They had happened upon the broken-down cabin by accident. The road had been hidden by overgrown brush. Luckily, Welton sensed it was a good path up the slope.

As he walked across the muddy ground to the truck, Vance congratulated himself. They'd successfully evaded law enforcement. Even Shelby Kincaid wouldn't be able to pick up their trail. Snickering, he climbed into the truck and shut the door. The cabin was an unexpected gift because it was clear to him whoever had owned it hadn't been back to it in a decade or more. The log walls were splintered, peeling and hadn't gotten a coat of shellac to protect the outer logs from the long, hard winters in the area. The windows all had caulking that had frozen, dried and fallen out, leaving wind whistling through the cracks. There was electricity to the place. The refrigerator was at least fifteen or so years old, but it still worked. A new tank of propane fired up the stove so they could cook their meals.

As he backed out and turned around, the wheels spinning in the mud, Welton drove down the steep slope. Moose Lake was far below, a popular hiking destination for tourists. Between the thick forest, he could catch occasional glimpses of the smooth blue surface of the small lake.

There was a spiderweb of dirt roads all across the eastern slopes of the Tetons. He'd scoured them relentlessly since finding the cabin, wanting to know what the odds were of a stupid tourist finding them by accident. The good news was there were no hiking trails above or below their cabin. The slope was steep, littered thickly with pine needles and thousands of Douglas fir standing guard to hide them.

As he slowly crawled around the curve, there was a window, a break between the firs. He could see down where the slope met the valley floor. Moose Lake was off to his left and he saw a gravel road leading from it to the main highway through the national park. Braking, Welton got out and stood observing the traffic. He was always interested in who was up and moving about. He picked up a pair of binoculars and scanned the main highway. His heart began to beat harder as he locked on to a black Tahoe SUV, a sheriff's cruiser, coming north.

Eyes squinted, Welton watched the cruiser drawing closer. He was too far away to see who was in it, except the outline of two people. Was this part of the ongoing attempt to find them? What got his attention was that it slowed down, took the Moose Lake turnoff and headed toward him. Fear trickled through him. Had the cops identified him? Seen him in the truck? Mouth dry, Welton watched intently, wishing like hell he had weapons on him.

To his surprise, the cruiser slowed and made a turn onto another less-used gravel road that led north of Moose Lake. The sunlight was overhead and for a split second, he thought he saw a glint of blond hair on the driver. What the hell? He remembered the color of that hair. Damned if it wasn't Shelby Kincaid! Hands tight around the glasses, Vance felt excitement mix with fear. The cruiser disappeared beneath the cover of the fir, gone from sight.

Welton stood there, his mind whirling with questions. Had Kincaid found them? *No, impossible.* He'd been damned careful to be in his cap and dark glasses. His beard had grown enough to hide his pointed chin. Rubbing his mouth, Welton looked at the area where the cruiser had disappeared. There was a narrow road there, he knew. He got into his truck, opened the glove box and jerked out a map of the Tetons. Opening it, he hunted for the red X he'd put on it, indicating their cabin. Once he found it, he moved his finger down. There were several capillary-like dirt roads north of Moose Lake. He hadn't had time to explore the northern area beyond their cabin.

As he lifted his head, the sun slanting into the window of the truck, he thought for a moment. So, what was Kincaid doing in this neck of the woods? He knew she was a damn good tracker. The last thing he needed was her snooping around. Maybe she was heading up to Lake Jackson to get a latte? Maybe that's all it was.

Slowly continuing down the steep incline, Welton felt glee over his discovery. There was nothing more exciting to him than stalking a woman. And now he was going to check out those minor dirt roads that crisscrossed the slopes of the Tetons, just to make damn sure Kincaid hadn't found them. He fantasized about capturing the bitch and grew hard. He could almost see the expression on her face when she realized he'd gotten to her.

CHAPTER SEVENTEEN

"SHELBY, GOT A MINUTE?" Cade crooked his finger as she walked by the open door to his office.

She'd just gotten into uniform and came back to the department when he called her in. "Sure. Got my schedule ready?"

"I'm working on it." He handed her a piece of paper. "Check this out. I've been ratting through every file known on Welton and Hartley, and look what popped up."

Frowning, Shelby stood near his desk, reading the information. "They worked here? For Curt Downing?"

"Yeah," Cade growled. "Our homegrown regional drug lord is connected to them. Small world, eh?"

She read the rest of the information. "Yes, but that was nearly a decade ago. Downing hired them as truck drivers for his newly established trucking company here in Jackson Hole."

"Hey, it's a lead. I'm going to put an undercover agent over there to keep watch," Cade said.

"I didn't think we had the manpower to do something like that."

Cade smiled a little. "I got a call from the FBI earlier. They have a hand in wanting these two bastards taken down as swiftly as possible, too. They're assigning four FBI agents to me. They'll be here by this evening."

A little relief trickled through Shelby. "That's good news."

"And more good news. I'm getting volunteer deputies from surrounding counties coming in to start searching for these two. I can't have civilians doing it, because they're armed and they'll kill."

Nodding, Shelby handed the paper back to him. "How many men?"

"Ten. It's a good number. I'm going to meet with them and the FBI agents tomorrow morning in the conference room. I'd like you and Carson to be present. You and he know the trails and roads of the Tetons like few do."

"Dakota knows the Tetons better than most," she agreed, thinking out loud. "He's been hunting, fishing and trapping on their slopes. If anyone knows the back roads, the old, broken-down cabins, it's him."

"Which is why I want him here. These deputies coming in will go undercover, appear to be tourist hikers in the Tetons. It's good timing, because this

is when the tourists come in, after the snow melts."
He smiled and looked up at Shelby.

"How are you doing? This has to be damned
stressful on you."

"It is but I'm not going to whine. I feel better
being on the job. I'll be looking for those two as I
work the town and surrounding highways."

"Let Dakota know we'll be convening at nine
tomorrow morning," he said.

"I will," Shelby said. "Am I on duty right now?"

Grinning, Cade said, "Sure are. We've got an
extra cruiser out there. Why don't you just keep
your eyes and ears open here in town? We've got
the photos of those two on TV. I'd like you to go
over to the supermarket and talk to the store manager. Dakota said he'd go over and watch the store
videos once he got his dressing changed over at the
hospital on his bear bite. Those two have to eat and
I'm hoping someone's seen them."

"I'll start with grocery stores and then check at
the gas stations. I'm assuming they have a set of
wheels."

"Good plan. Let me know if you get anything."

"You'll be the first to know," Shelby promised.
She would head to her locker, pick up her weapon
and belt. She felt a tad better that she was allowed
to go back to work, but then her mind turned to
Dakota. On the way to his cabin earlier, she'd convinced him to see Dr. Jordana McPherson. It was

time for him to get his bear bite looked at by the physician. Shelby also persuaded him to see her about his PTSD symptoms. Would he? Damn, he was one stubborn man. Her steps slowed to the locker room. She couldn't stop thinking of their night together. They had been starving for each other. Was it just about sex? She had no answers. At least, not yet. For now she had to focus her mind on Welton and Hartley.

"YOU HEAL UP FAST," Jordana McPherson congratu-lated Dakota. He sat on a gurney as she cleansed the bear bite wounds and gave him a fresh, clean waterproof dressing to cover the forearm.

"Good, because I need to use that arm."

"You were lucky the bear missed a major nerve." She pressed her latex-gloved index finger near one of the puncture wounds. "If that had happened, you'd have lost complete use of your hand."

"Don't even want to go there, Doc," he rumbled. Dakota sat in a cubicle in the E.R. There were very few emergencies under way from what he could see. Jordana's touch was quick and professional. The red-haired nurse at her side handed her the new dressing.

"There, you're good to go for another five days," Jordana said, smiling.

Dakota waited until the nurse left. He slid off

the gurney and rolled down his shirt. "Doc, you got a minute?"

She was pulling off the gloves and dropping them into a receptacle. "Yes, it's quiet as a mouse around here."

"Can we talk in private? Go to your office?" He knew as head of the E.R., Jordana would have an office that afforded privacy. "Sure, follow me."

They left the cubicle and went down a hall.

In her office, Dakota closed the door behind him. Jordana's desk was clean and efficient, like her. He sat down once she took a seat. "You said you could help my PTSD symptoms?"

Nodding, Jordana said, "Yes. We've got more research available, Dakota."

She opened a drawer and handed him a small box. "This is a saliva test. If you'll follow directions and send it in to the company, they'll send me the test results. Basically, it's checking your cortisol levels four times in one day. It gives me a baseline to see what's going on with that hormone in your body."

He frowned at the box. "I'm sure my cortisol is through the roof."

"More than likely," she said, her voice soft with compassion. "By any chance, are you doing this because Shelby pushed you?"

Dakota met her gaze and saw merriment in her eyes. "Is it that obvious?"

The doctor chuckled. "I've been trying to get you to come in and take this test ever since I met you a year ago."

"Guilty as charged, Doc." He held the box in his hand, resting it on his thigh. "Shelby doesn't take no for an answer."

"I think you've met your match. I don't know which of you is more bullheaded."

"She is."

Nodding, Jordana gestured to the box. "Look, there is an adaptogen created by a pharmaceutical company that can lower cortisol levels back to normal. That's good news for people with PTSD. It's a one-month cycle of taking the adaptogen and then you stop. We retest you after three months to find out where your cortisol level is."

"So," Dakota said, looking at the nondescript cardboard box in his large hand, "you can make my PTSD symptoms go away?"

"Some of the symptoms, in most cases. That, or dialing them down tremendously so you don't suffer from them 24/7." Tilting her head, Jordana held his gaze. "Would you like to sleep at night, Dakota? Get rid of insomnia? Anxiety? Not jump at your shadow?"

"Sure I would."

"We can do that with this adaptogen treatment. Once you follow the protocol, which is twenty-four hours in length, send in the kit and I get the information back from the company, I'll have one of my nurses call you for an appointment. Then you'll come in and we'll get you on that adaptogen and change your life for the better. How does that sound?"

"Like a miracle," Dakota admitted. "I've had PTSD for a long, long time, Doc. And I won't get drugged up to my eyeballs to dull the symptoms. I may only have half a life, but it's all I got. I'm not going to let a drug take what's left."

"I understand," she murmured, giving him a sad look. "Shelby did the right thing in goading you to get tested."

Dakota felt his heart open just thinking about her. "When I first met her, I thought she was a Barbie doll."

Laughing lightly, Jordana stood and pulled her white lab coat on. "Shelby is deceiving in that way. She's beautiful and I've seen more than one guy project that image on her. Just because she has blond hair doesn't mean she's one-dimensional."

"Far from it," he agreed, standing.

"You two must get along." She walked around her desk, placing two pens in the breast pocket of the lab coat and picking up her stethoscope.

Of all the people he'd met in the year since he'd come home, Jordana was someone Dakota always trusted. There was compassion in her eyes, in her touch and proof of her care of others. Much like Shelby, he realized. "Yes, she's one of a kind," he admitted.

"I think she's good for you. Matter of fact, I think you're good for Shelby, too." Jordana halted at the door and looked up at the craggy vet.

"She's special, Doc."

Smiling, Jordana reached out and squeezed his upper arm. "Take care of her, okay? Cade Garner called me earlier today to let me know what was going on in trying to find those two convicts. I worry for Shelby. I know she can take care of herself, but she's potentially got two murderers hunting for her, wanting revenge."

"I've got her back, Doc. Don't worry."

Jordana opened the door. "Good. If nothing else, Dakota, you're the biggest, baddest guard dog she can have."

"SEAL power."

Jordana knew of his military background. She let her hand drop from his arm. "Exactly. Use it to the hilt, Dakota, because until these dudes are captured, Shelby is in danger." She frowned. "And so is every other woman around here...."

"I know, Doc. I'm sure Cade will keep you updated."

"Yes, he's been good about that. We've already warned our women employees to be careful and be much more alert. We have male security guards escorting our nurses to their cars at night now. We can't be too careful."

DAKOTA HEARD A VEHICLE coming up the road. So did Storm. The wolf went to the door, ears up, alert. The sun was beginning to set in the west. He glanced at his watch and saw it was 7:00 p.m. Shelby got off duty about this time, and it had to be her. Opening the door, he walked out into the shadowed woods that surrounded the area.

Shelby drove up in her green Toyota Land Cruiser. She parked and climbed out, no longer in uniform. Storm raced up to her, wagging her tail.

Laughing, Shelby turned and met Dakota's hooded eyes. "How did your day go?" She fondly petted the wolf's broad head.

"Okay," he said. "I found a videotape of Welton going in and leaving the supermarket. So that's good news. Cade has sent a deputy over to work with the manager and get the grocery clerks up to speed. If he was there once, he'll be back."

"Yes, Cade told me about it before I left after my shift was over." She smiled. "It's a step in the right direction."

Dakota nodded. "What's in there?"

"I brought us dinner." She reached in and brought out two sacks. "Chinese," she said, handing him one of the two sacks.

"Smells good," he told her.

"Better than eating a can of cold beans," she said, wrinkling her nose and drowning in his slow, heated smile. Just touching his fingers, remembering them grazing her flesh, giving her such pleasure, made her go weak for a moment.

"Let's get inside," he said, looking around. It was as normal as breathing for Dakota to scan the area, listen to the sounds or see if anything looked out of place. Satisfied it was safe for the moment, he followed Shelby into the cabin.

As she set her sack on the counter, Shelby asked, "How is your arm? Did you talk to Jordana?"

Dakota shut the door and locked it. "Yes to all the above. My arm is healing up fine."

The cabin was grayish-looking inside. Dakota didn't want a lantern turned on because it would make the cabin a target to anyone trying to locate her. He took no chances.

"Good. And you're going to take the cortisol test?" She pulled out several cartons and set them in a line on the counter. Just looking at him, Shelby felt her body hotly respond to that predatory gaze of his. There was no question, Dakota was a hunter.

He set his sack on the counter. "Come here," he rasped, pulling her into his arms. "I've missed the hell out of you today." He leaned down, curving his mouth over her lips.

Moaning as his mouth slid and rocked her lips

open, she felt his hands splay against her soft pink angora shell. She moved her hips against his, wanting him in every way. She drowned in the hunger that exploded between them.

Her arms slid around his shoulders. She tasted sweet, a hint of chocolate. Smiling to himself, his hand raking through her loose blond hair, capturing her, he tilted her head just enough to kiss her thoroughly. Her breath was rapid, moist against his unshaven cheek. Her moan was caught in his mouth and he absorbed the sound, her breasts pressing against the wall of his chest. He wanted to take her here. Now. It would be so easy to pull her to the bed, undress her and love her. God, how he wanted to do just that. In the back of his melting mind, he knew it wasn't wise. Danger lay somewhere out there. Someone was hunting Shelby and wanted to not only hurt her, but kill her.

Reluctantly, he tore his mouth from hers. Opening his eyes, Dakota saw her blue eyes filled with desire. He'd seen that look in her eyes before. Last night. He held her, his thumb moving across her wet lower lip. "Damn, you make me feel like a starved wolf, Shel." He leaned down, grazed her lips, felt her smile beneath his mouth. Her slender fingers moved up the hard line of his jaw and framed his face. But he forced himself to pull away from her mouth.

"I'm starved for you all the time," she whispered, giving him a wicked look.

"As much as I want to drag you to the bed and make love with you all night long, we can't."

Nodding, Shelby lost her smile. "I know...."

Dakota reluctantly released her, cursing the circumstances. The ache in his lower body was painful. Damn, how he wanted to bury himself in her, love her, fly with her. It was a shattered dream. At least, for right now.

"I keep thinking we could go to a hotel room somewhere in town," she said huskily, touching the side of his temple, seeing a small white scar across the area. It hurt her to think how he'd gotten it. In battle, for sure. She looked up and fearlessly met his slitted eyes, felt his heat even standing inches away from his powerful, tense body. "Want to?"

"You're a damned tease."

"I know. You've turned me into one. Can I help it if you're the best lover I've ever had?"

"You're the wild woman, not me. Do you know that?"

She grinned. "Only with you, Dakota. It's you. You make me lose every inhibition I ever had."

Lifting his hand, he slid his fingers across the crown of her golden hair, taming some of the strands back into place. "As much as I want to go to that hotel, we can't. We could be seen, Shel. You know that."

"It's hell being trained in law enforcement," she griped good-naturedly. She stepped back, putting enough distance between them so she wouldn't be tempted to continue touching him, learning his body, feeling him react and pleasuring him. "I'll be a good girl for now. Come on, let's eat while the food is still hot."

"The only food I want is you. And you'll never get cold."

"Damn, Dakota, you're making this tough." Shelby saw a slight grin leak into the line of his sensual mouth. A mouth she wanted to kiss, explore and have tease and tantalize her forever.

"We're good together, Shel."

"Too good." Taking a deep breath, she picked up a container and pressed it against his chest. "Food. Let's eat."

"Can I have you for dessert then?"

CHAPTER EIGHTEEN

SHE WAS LATE. After a quick glance at her watch, Shelby left the sheriff's office. The sun was behind the hills in the west. All day, law enforcement and the FBI agents had been arriving and gearing up to find Welton and Hartley. She'd been in meetings off and on, her head aching from giving info to the men who would begin combing the Tetons. Rubbing her brow, she headed toward where she'd parked, in an auxiliary parking lot behind the courthouse. What a long day.

Shelby hurried down the sidewalk, the area that now looked like a used-car lot because of the extra activities. She had called Dakota and he'd suggested they meet at Mo's Ice Cream Parlor at the main plaza for dinner. As she walked past the three-story gray-brick courthouse, she smiled softly. Ordinarily, she knew he would never eat in a restaurant; the noise was too much for him. Yet Dakota was putting himself outside his comfort zone for her. There were few options for a good hot meal at his cabin, so he'd opted for Mo's.

Turning into the asphalt parking lot, Shelby hesitated. Where had she put her Land Cruiser? The place was packed. The lights in the lot had not come on yet, making it harder to spot it. Her mind was still on the presentations she'd been giving to different groups. And she wasn't in her normal parking spot, which contributed to her confusion.

She remembered she'd parked the Toyota near the gray-brick wall in the sixth row of seven. She quickly threaded between the aisles. Fruit trees had been planted near the wall, taking away the urban look. Approaching her vehicle, she pulled out the key. Shelby slowed, as she always did, and focused on the interior of her Land Cruiser. It wasn't impossible that one of the convicts could be hiding in there and waiting to jump her. She inspected the inside closely, finding nothing out of place.

Satisfied, Shelby opened the car door to climb in.

A hand suddenly clamped her mouth, yanking her backward off her feet.

Shelby hit the asphalt hard. Nostrils flaring, she tried to scream, the hand pressing hard against her mouth and nose. Pain shot through her head as she violently struck the pavement. Eyes wide, she saw it was Oren Hartley. His blue eyes were slits as he maneuvered around her, his fist cocked.

Shock rolled through her. He held her down on her back, his knee pushed into her chest. A scream drowned beneath his hand as he cocked his arm, fist coming straight for her head.

Her face exploded with pain. A cracking sound went off through her head as his fist connected solidly with her cheek and nose. She was stunned, partly conscious from the strike. Adrenaline surged through her. Somewhere in her graying senses, Shelby realized no one would see the act. The Land Cruiser was parked next to the other tall SUVs. She was in trouble.

Gasping, she saw Hartley grin. His teeth were yellow. Grabbing her by the collar of her uniform, he got off her. She sobbed for breath, warm blood spreading across her lips and chin. Shelby wasn't even aware her nose had been broken, but she had a feeling it might be. As soon as Hartley removed his knee, she instinctively kicked out. Her boot connected with his groin.

Grunting, Hartley released her, his hands flying to his crotch. He leaned over, his mouth open in a silent scream of agony, eyes wide with surprise.

Shelby scrambled to her knees and got one last look at the murderous expression in the convict's eyes. He limped backward one pace, gasping, unable to straighten.

It gave her the split second she needed. As she scrambled to her knees, her ears ringing with sounds, pain reared up through her face. Shelby snapped off the restraining strap holding her pistol. In one motion, she whipped the pistol up and aimed it at the staggering convict.

"Freeze!" she yelled, both hands around the butt of her pistol.

"You bitch!" Hartley snarled, trying to make a lunge for her.

Shelby fired.

Hartley crumpled with a scream, grabbing for his left calf.

As she shoved herself to her feet, dizziness struck her. Shelby kept the pistol trained on the convict now writhing on the ground with a leg wound. Pressing the button on her shoulder radio, she called for backup, giving her location. She'd shot Hartley in the calf and she'd done it on purpose. The bastard wasn't walking away this time. Worse, she knew he probably wasn't alone.

Shelby warily looked around, gasping for breath, her pulse pounding with fear. Was Welton close by? She saw no one else. And help was on the way. Never once did she remove her focus on Hartley, who was moaning and cursing, his hands wrapped around his bleeding calf. He wasn't going anywhere.

As soon as help arrived, Shelby sat down in the opened Land Cruiser door and pulled out her cell phone. As she called Dakota with trembling fingers, she watched as Hartley's hands were cuffed behind him. An ambulance arrived, its lights flashing.

"Hello?"

Gulping, wiping the blood from her nose, Shelby rasped, "I'm in the courthouse parking lot. Hartley tried to take me down. Everything's all right. He's in custody. Can you get over here?"

"Stay there, Shel. I'm on my way...."

Nodding, she felt the shaking begin in earnest. One of the sheriff's deputies, Tom Langley, walked over to her.

"You need to be patched up, Shelby. Are you able to get to the ambulance or do you want some help?"

She managed a grimace toward the forty-year-old deputy. "I—I'm okay, Tom. Dakota's on his way. Just get that bastard over to the hospital."

Langley nodded grimly. He reached out, his hand on her shoulder. "You're looking pretty roughed up, Shelby. You want me to stay until he gets here?" He looked around. "I'm worried that Welton could be hiding nearby."

"You're right," she muttered, wiping her nose, looking at her hand that was now red with her blood. "Yeah, stay. I can use your help."

Dakota found Shelby sitting in the driver's side of her Land Cruiser, the door open, the deputy standing vigilant guard. Night had fallen, and he was alarmed at how bad she looked under the sulfur lights. He nodded to Tom, thanked him and eased his bulk between the opened door and Shelby. His eyes slitted as he saw her nose was puffy, bleeding and her cheek swollen. It broke his heart in two.

Dakota reached out. "Let's get you to the E.R. You've got a broken nose."

Shelby looked into his deeply shadowed face. There was rage banked in his eyes. "Hartley jumped me. He must have been hiding on the other side of my SUV."

Sliding his hand around her arm, he gently pulled her out of the vehicle. "Don't talk, Shel. You're looking pale. Can you stand?"

Nodding, she stood and had never felt safer as when Dakota's arm went around her shoulders. She leaned against him, feeling her knees grow mushy as the adrenaline began to leave her. She was glad he was strong and tall. He locked the SUV up with the key.

"I screwed up," she muttered as he led her to his pickup truck. "I should have gone around the Land Cruiser, looked—"

"Stop talking, Shel. Conserve your energy." He opened the door of the pickup and helped her inside. He worried as her eyes went cloudy. She was in shock. After buckling her in, Dakota closed the door. As he searched the parking lot, now crawling with deputies, a white-hot rage tunneled through him. Where was Welton? Had the bastard slipped away when their attack failed?

Shelby lay back, eyes closed, while he drove the short distance to the hospital. On the way over, she told him what had happened. The quiet anger swirled around Dakota. He didn't talk at all, but his mind seemed to operate at warp speed. Was this the SEAL reaction? The man who had survived years in hostile environments? Her nose and face ached so much Shelby couldn't think very far beyond that.

"Stay here," Dakota growled, opening the door. He'd parked the SUV at the doors of the E.R. "I'll get a gurney. Stay put."

The warning in his voice reverberated through Shelby. Not to worry, she didn't want to go anywhere. Her head hurt. Her nose ached like hell. Tipping her head back, Shelby closed her eyes as some of the fear and realization that she'd almost been kidnapped seeped like a poison through her. She tasted fear and had never felt as vulnerable as she did right now. The only thing between her and those two convicts willing to capture her was Dakota.

"She's going to be okay," Jordana reassured Shelby and Dakota. Standing in an E.R. cubicle, she'd finished looking at the X-rays.

Shelby sat up on the gurney. "That's good," she muttered, barely touching her nose. The swelling had begun in earnest. At least the bleeding had stopped.

Jordana nodded. "I use homeopathic remedies to stop the swelling." She placed some white pellets in Shelby's hand. "Take these, let them melt in your mouth. Hopefully, it will stop you from looking like a raccoon by tomorrow morning."

Grinning lopsidedly, Shelby did as she instructed. "Thanks, Jordana. So, my nose is fractured?"

"Yes, hairline. No surgery needed. It will be sensitive for a month, but you'll heal up fine." She checked the swelling on her left cheek and quickly cleaned it up. "You've been roughed up, but you got off a lot better than Hartley."

"I wanted to blow his head off," she admitted, giving the doctor a quick look.

"I understand," she soothed, adding some antibiotic ointment to the scratches on her cheek. "Dr. Collins is taking care of him. You shot him in a good spot. No major damage, but he's not going anywhere fast. You clipped his wings." Her lips twitched and she held Shelby's dark stare. "Right now they're taking him over to another wing of the hospital, up on the sixth floor, with two deputies guarding him. I heard Cade Garner just got here and he's going to interrogate him."

"Hopefully to find out where Welton is holed up," she muttered. "Thanks, my cheek feels better."

"You're welcome. I'll send a nurse to get you a

prescription for any residual pain you have with your broken nose. I'd try a couple of aspirin first, however."

Shelby nodded and then looked up at Dakota. She continued to feel the harnessed rage vibrating around him. He'd said little, and it was starting to worry her. Reaching out, she covered his hand with hers. His was so scarred-looking compared to hers. "How are you doing?"

Dakota looked down at Shelby. Her face was bruised. He could see purple shadows beneath her eyes, all thanks to Hartley breaking her nose. Lifting his hand, he gently eased some gold strands away from her cheek. "Okay. I'm more concerned about you."

"I'm coming down from the attack. I feel like so much jelly held together by skin at this point, if you want the truth."

Dakota allowed his hand to come to rest on her slumped shoulder. "You handled the situation fine."

Seeing the pride in his darkened eyes, she couldn't help but protest. "I should have checked out around my Land Cruiser. I checked inside, but not around it. It was a rookie's mistake. My head was still wrapped around all those briefings I gave the law enforcement guys today. I was distracted. I should have been focused."

He heard the censure in her husky voice. All he wanted to do was hold Shelby. Hold her and keep her safe. But she wasn't safe and Dakota knew it. "Listen, why don't you lie here on the gurney and rest for a while? I need to go talk to Cade. I have a plan, but I need his help on it. Okay?"

Though she gave him a quizzical look, Shelby did as ordered and lay back down on the gurney, the pillow feeling good behind her aching head. "What plan?"

Dakota watched her with that enigmatic expression. He had his own agenda. Trying to ease the worry in her eyes, he leaned down and tenderly caressed her lips. He eased away. "I'll tell you more, later."

CADE GARNER HAD JUST come out of Hartley's hospital room when he saw Dakota come striding down the hall. Nodding to the two armed deputies at the door, he went to meet him.

"How's Shelby doing?" he asked, putting his notebook in his pocket.

"She's okay," Dakota said, looking beyond the deputy to the room where Hartley was kept under guard. "You get anything from Hartley?"

Cade shook his head. "He's not talking. Smart-assed bastard. He lawyered up. Now I have to give him his call to get an attorney tomorrow morning."

"Let me talk to him," Dakota said, drawing him aside.

"I can't do that. I want to, but it's against the law."

Hand slowly curling, Dakota stood glaring at the door where Hartley was inside. He wanted the son of a bitch dead. "Okay," he rasped. "I need to get Shelby somewhere safe. I know your family ranch has a number of cabins on it you rent out every summer to tourists?"

"Yes, my parents have rentals." He quirked his mouth. "You're worried that Welton knows where your cabin is?"

"It could be compromised, and until I know for sure, I need Shelby somewhere safe."

"Well, maybe safer," Cade said, frowning. "It would be better if both of you were at our ranch. She's going to need a full-time bodyguard."

Dakota silently promised she was going nowhere without him from now on. "She's going to want to go back to work."

"I need her, Dakota. She's the one who tracked Welton and Hartley in the first place. Everything's in motion now. I can't take her out of the equation, and you know that."

He didn't want to hear it, but agreed. "Okay, but I'm in the mix."

"I want you with her," Cade said. Looking at his watch, he said, "I'll call my parents and find out which cabin you can have. Let me get back to you later tonight by cell? It won't take too long."

"I appreciate it," Dakota said, meaning it. He knew the deputy was up to his ass in alligators with the search moving forward plus trying to squeeze intel out of Hartley as to Welton's whereabouts. The deputy turned and walked down the hall toward a set of elevators.

Dakota stood for a moment, checked out the area. The room was at the end of a hall. The nurses' station was around the corner. There wasn't much activity on this floor; plus, it had been cordoned off to keep reporters and nosy people away from it. He studied the two deputies and knew both of them.

Looking at his clock, he decided to get down to the E.R. and keep Shelby company. It was where he wanted to be. As the rage moved lethally through him, Dakota stared at the door one moment where Hartley was, memorizing it. He was going to get to that son of a bitch and, one way or another, get the information on Welton's whereabouts. His mouth hardened, and he kept going down the hall.

DAKOTA HAD MADE SURE Shelby was comfortable in the cabin on the Garner family ranch. It was near 10:00 p.m. A wrangler kept guard outside the cabin. Dakota drove back to the hospital. Everything was quiet. It was time.

Only one deputy was at Hartley's door when Dakota arrived on the sixth floor. He checked out the nurses' station. One woman was hard at work on the computer, entering info. Turning, he headed down the tiled hall. Deputy Gary Epson raised his head.

"Hey, Gary, how's it going?" Dakota asked. The man was twenty-one, fresh from law enforcement training.

"Hey, Dakota, fine. How's Shelby doing?"

"Fractured nose, roughed up, but she's going to be all right."

"That's good news." Epson looked around, a worried look on his face. "Hey, I gotta get to the bathroom. Can you stand here for a few minutes? My partner is down at the cafeteria grabbing a bite to eat. I'm not supposed to leave, but nature is calling. Would you? Hartley's cuffed to the bed, so he isn't going anywhere."

Dakota nodded. "Sure, go ahead. Your secret's safe with me."

He waited until the deputy disappeared around the corner. He knew the restrooms were near the nurses' station. Turning on his heel, he entered the room swiftly and silently.

Hartley was sitting up, wearing a blue gown, his one leg wrapped in a white dressing. He looked like a skinny jaybird. Dakota quietly shut the door and closed the distance on the convict. He didn't have much time and he was going to make the most of it.

CHAPTER NINETEEN

"HEY!" HARTLEY YELLED. "Who the hell are you?" He saw the tall, dark-haired man with eyes like slits heading straight for him. It was his posture, his shoulders hunched, head leading his body, his hand curled into a fist at his side that scared the hell out of him. Fear shot through him. He had no way to escape the stranger.

Without a word, Dakota's fist shot out like a striking snake. It connected solidly with Hartley's fear-etched face.

The blow sent the convict slamming into his bed, jerked sideways by the cuff holding his left wrist to the railing. He cried out once, slumped to the floor, his nose bleeding profusely.

Without a word, Dakota leaned down, grabbed the guy by his shoulders and hauled his ass up on the bed. He pushed him down.

Eyes wide with fear, Hartley cringed away from the man. "Who are you?" he shrieked, trying to get away from him.

"Your worst nightmare," Dakota hissed. He

yanked Hartley back, slamming his head into the pillow, his long, greasy hair between his fingers. Savage pleasure hummed through Dakota as he saw he'd broken the man's nose. It was crooked and bleeding heavily. He put his face inches from Hartley's and snarled in a low growl, "I'm Ellie Carson's brother. Ring a bell?" He tightened his grip on the man's hair.

Hartley gasped, the name hitting home. His eyes widened even more, his mouth opening. "Oh God…"

"I want to know where Welton is. I'll give you one chance to answer me or I'll kill you. Got it?"

Hartley saw murder in the man's narrowed eyes, the way violence surrounded him. His nose was bleeding heavily, the blood spilling down his lips, chin and splattering onto the blue gown across his chest. Hartley knew the man would carry out his threat. "He's in a cabin off a dirt road. Th-there's no road name."

"It has a number, asshole. All forest service roads have a number. What is it?" he snarled, his breath puncturing across Hartley's frightened features.

"I—uh…uh…"

There wasn't much time. Dakota knew the deputy would be back very shortly. He raised his right hand and slowly curled it into a fist. "I can kill a man with one strike."

Welton made a mewing sound, trying to move, but Dakota had him pinned. Escape was impossible. "Y-yes…the number is 420."

Dakota smiled. "Smart move. I broke your nose because you broke my woman's nose earlier this evening."

Hartley blinked once. He'd hidden a shiv that the deputies had not found, beneath the bed, just in case. His hand reached out, feeling for it, found it with shaking fingers. Hartley knew he was a dead man. His fingers wrapped around the four-inch shiv. With a grunt, he wrenched up his right arm, aiming to sink the shiv into the man's chest.

Dakota saw the flash come up in Hartley's hand. His reaction was automatic. In blinding seconds, he bunched his fist, striking Hartley in the temple, sending broken bone splinters into the man's brain. He never even felt the shiv penetrate his lower arm.

Hartley slumped suddenly, dead in his hands.

Son of a bitch! Breathing hard, Dakota held the little bastard's limp body. Remorse flowed through him. He didn't need this. Although Hartley sure as hell deserved to die, Dakota knew this would be a messy detail. *Dammit!* The bloody shiv lay nearby. Blood was dripping from his left forearm, near where he'd received the grizzly bite. The drops congealed on the floor near Hartley. Mouth tightening, Dakota turned and knew he had to do the right thing. Cade Garner would have to be notified. He'd just killed a man in self-defense, and the weapon and his wound would prove his story. Still, Dakota hated the complexity that this would cause. Right now all he wanted to do was go find Welton. But that wasn't going to happen. He'd have to wait.

As he walked out of the room, Gary, the deputy, was returning. It was going to be a long night. He pulled out his phone to tell Shelby what had happened. She wasn't going to be happy, either. No one would be.

WAS HE IN TIME? Dakota stood quietly as he stalked Welton's cabin. Would Welton know Hartley was dead? Cade Garner was keeping the information off the airwaves in hopes that he could nail Welton at the address Hartley had given him. He moved like a shadow near the road leading up to the cabin where Welton was supposed to be. He wore dark clothes, a black bandana around his head, dark green and black face paint, his eyes adjusted to the thin wash of moonlight through the forest. Without a sound, he trotted up the curve.

Ahead, Dakota saw the silhouette of a cabin. He halted and knelt down behind some brush, waited and watched. His breath came sharp and fast, mouth open so no one could hear him breathing. In his left hand he held his M-4. He had a Nightforce scope on it and he could see through the dark with it. His SIG Sauer was strapped low on his right thigh, the restraining strap released so he could smoothly pull it out and use it if he had to.

Dakota heard and saw nothing. There was no vehicle around, either. Was Welton here? Had he somehow realized he was being hunted? Unsure, Dakota moved like the shadows around him, soundlessly, as he checked out around the ramshackle cabin.

Nothing.

His senses were on high alert. He drew close to the house. The porch was grayed by weather, several boards sticking up that needed to be nailed down. Moving silently, Dakota made it to the door. Gloves on so no one could lift fingerprints on him, he tested the knob. It moved. It wasn't locked. He slowly looked around, his ears keyed to the sounds of the night. Nothing seemed out of place.

In an instant, Dakota slipped through the door, M-4 jammed against his shoulder, the barrel pointed toward anything that moved. After swiftly entering the cabin, he cleared it. The place was empty.

Dakota continued to look around and made sure the only door had nothing behind it. Everything was quiet. Welton was not here. Turning, he began a quiet search of some clothes strewn across the empty bed. It took him ten minutes to search through everything. Welton was either out on the prowl or had been nearby when Hartley had jumped Shelby and then disappeared.

And then it struck him. Dakota realized that Welton might have tracked Shelby back to his cabin after that incident. *Damn!* With a soft hiss, he turned on his heel, leaving the cabin and hurrying down the narrow road toward his well hidden truck far below.

BY THE TIME DAKOTA HAD driven up to his cabin, it was 2:00 a.m. The moon was low on the western horizon. Not taking any chances, he parked his truck near brush at the base of the road. He ran silently full tilt up the road, M-4 in hand. If Welton was up there, he'd know shortly. His breath came in quiet gasps, and as he neared the cabin, Dakota spotted no vehicle. And no one seemed to be around.

Moving into the shadows, the trees and brush hiding him, Dakota kept his M-4 up and ready to fire. He used the Nightforce scope to detect any thermal heat movement of a human being hidden nearby. *Nothing.*

As he moved parallel to the front door, he saw it was ajar. He never kept the door open. Kneeling, he waited and watched. The crickets were chirping. They always stopped singing if they were disturbed by human activity. His instincts screamed that Welton had already been here, not found Shelby and had left. *Damn!* Quickly moving, Dakota checked out around the cabin before entering it. When he did, he found the place tossed. Everything was on the floor, the mattress torn apart. His mouth turned into a snarl as he surveyed the mess. Welton had followed Shelby!

There was a whine at the door.

Head snapping up, Dakota saw Storm quietly enter the opened door.

Relief flowed through him as the wolf came over, licked his gloved hand, tail wagging. Dakota petted her head, so glad Welton hadn't found her. The convict would have killed Storm without a second thought.

"Good girl," he murmured, running his hand over her back.

He took off his clothes and put them and the gloves into a bag. After washing his hands and face, he drew out a new set of clean clothes.

Once dressed, Dakota went outside and noticed a half-eaten rabbit on the ground near the porch. Storm hunted every night. In this case, hunting had saved her life. He paced soundlessly across the porch. The road was powder-dry dirt. There could be footprints from Welton imprinted in the soil. A new kind of satisfaction thrummed through Dakota as he carefully retraced his own footsteps. He'd come up here tomorrow morning and find what kind of shoe or boot Welton was wearing. It was one step closer to finding the murderer.

SHELBY AWOKE SLOWLY. Her headache was gone. And her nose wasn't aching. She turned over in the luxury of a queen-size bed. Reaching out, she felt a warm spot where Dakota had lain earlier. Sunlight lanced around the edges of the window where the dark burgundy drapes were drawn. Pulling herself up, she felt achy and sore. The door was open and she could hear the clink of pots and pans out in the kitchen.

She pushed her hair out of her face and forced herself to sit up. Her bare feet touched the pine floor, grounding her. The smell of coffee laced the air and she lifted her nose, inhaling deeply. It smelled good. She was surprised she could smell anything at all with a broken nose. Sitting there, she felt her heart move powerfully with love for Dakota.

"You're up...."

Dakota stood in the doorway, dressed in body-hugging Levi's and a black T-shirt. She gave him a drowsy smile. "How did you know I was smelling the coffee you were making?"

His heart wrenched as he looked into her cloudy blue eyes. There was still swelling on the left side of her nose and a crescent of purple beneath her left eye two days after the attack.

"I felt you wake up," he said, walking over and handing her the bright yellow mug with steaming coffee.

"Thanks," she murmured, meeting his hooded gaze. He had shaved, his hair gleaming from a recent shower. "You look good," she said, sipping the coffee. "How long have you been up?"

"Not long." Dakota sat down on the bed next to her, careful not to slosh the coffee out of the cup in her hands. "You awake enough to hear some news?" he asked. Her blond hair was badly mussed and needed brushing. Lifting his hand, he slid the strands gently across her shoulders. The pink flannel gown she wore was soft-feeling beneath his fingertips. She closed her eyes for a moment, enjoying his touch, absorbing it into her bruised body. He kept his rage over her attack on a leash. Right now his focus was on her.

Shelby knew yesterday evening when Dakota had come back to the cabin that he'd accidentally killed Hartley. And she'd persuaded him to have the puncture wound looked at. A clean white dressing was on his forearm. Dakota had regretted killing Hartley. He'd wanted to see the bastard go to death row and suffer a very long time before they pumped him full of chemicals to finally take his miserable life.

Shelby glanced at the clock on the bed stand. It was 9:00 a.m. This was two days in a row she'd slept in late, and she knew it was because of the shock and trauma she'd endured.

He moved his fingers around her nape, her skin

warm, the silk of her hair tangling between them. "Cade's talked to the county prosecutor about what happened with Hartley. And he's not pressing charges against me." He heard Shelby gasp. Her head snapped up, her eyes widening as she stared over at him.

"Thank God," she whispered, pressing her hand against her pounding heart.

Dakota explained the judgment by the prosecutor. It would be seen as defending himself. He wouldn't go on trial and he wouldn't go to prison, a relief to him. As he continued to touch her, he felt the tension dissolve in her shoulders.

He'd left their bed at one o'clock this morning, looking to find Welton. And then Dakota had driven to his cabin to find it had been ransacked. By 3:00 a.m. he'd returned here to sleep with Shelby at his side. He hadn't slept much, his mind churning over what Welton might try next. At 5:00 a.m., he'd awakened and allowed Shelby to sleep as long as she wanted.

"After I drove up to our cabin last night, I found the door standing open." His voice deepened. He knew this would upset her. "Welton knew where we were."

Setting the mug down on the bed stand, Shelby could sense the anger in his voice and in his eyes. She turned, her knees pressed against his right thigh. "But…how…?"

"I suspect he followed you. He might have been hiding nearby when Hartley jumped you. Or he might have seen your cruiser on the highway below my cabin by chance. I just don't know." Dakota tenderly leaned over and kissed her wrinkled brow. "Don't worry, we're safe here, Shel. By the time I got up to my cabin, he was gone."

Shelby smelled warm and sweet. Dakota wanted to continue to kiss her, but the timing was all wrong. "I woke up at five this morning and I decided to drive back up to my cabin. It was too dark to search for tire tracks or footprints. The good news is that I found his footprints this morning. Cade sent up a forensics team and they made impressions. That will help in tracking him."

"Things are moving fast," Shelby said more to herself than him. As his hand moved gently across her shoulders, she sighed.

"You look upset," Dakota said, kissing her temple. "What's going on in your head?"

"I sat here after I got up thinking I could have died out in that parking lot. I guess it's shock hitting me."

The tremble in her softly spoken words tore at him. "Come here." He brought Shelby into his arms, gently holding her. She came and nestled her head against his shoulder, her brow against his jaw. When her arms went around his waist, Dakota drew in a deep, ragged breath. He wanted to love her, tenderly, erase the fear he knew was lingering within her about her own brush with death. Pressing a chaste kiss to her hair, he said in a low tone, "You defended yourself. You saved your own life, Shel. You're a well-trained law enforcement officer and you got the upper hand."

She released a ragged sigh and closed her eyes. "I was so shocked by the attack. So…scared…" Shelby opened her eyes and eased back just enough to meet his gaze. There was turbulence—and desire—in his light brown eyes. "Do you know what made me fight back with everything I had?"

"No. What?"

"When Hartley slammed me to the ground and I was semiconscious, I realized that I loved you, Dakota." She smiled softly and slid her fingers across his sandpapery cheek. "I don't know when it happened or how it happened, but lying there with his knee crushing my chest, seeing the look of murder in his eyes, I knew I loved you…."

Whispering her name as if it were a prayer against her lips, Dakota took her with all the tenderness he possessed. He curved his mouth against her parting lips, wanting to somehow infuse her with his strength and love. He knew he could love her, heal her and help reclaim her life once again. But not right now.

Welton was on the prowl and Dakota could feel the convict, feel his murderous intent toward

Shelby. If he admitted his feelings, he couldn't go back. He couldn't survive losing Shelby. For now, all he could do was drown in the returning splendor of her kiss, the heat between them. As he sat on the bed with this fierce, independent woman who had fought to live, he knew without a doubt, he loved her, too.

CHAPTER TWENTY

"SHELBY, I NEED YOUR help," Cade Garner called on the phone. "We've got a tourist in Tetons National Park whose three-year-old boy walked away. He's lost. I need some good trackers. Are you available?"

After two weeks of being holed up at Cade's parents' ranch, Shelby was more than ready. "Yes. Have you contacted Dakota?"

"I have. Drive on in. I'm putting you back on the roster and you'll be a deputy again."

"Thank God," she muttered. After hanging up, she quickly traded her shoes for a good pair of hiking boots. Going into the bush to hunt for a missing child would require some different clothing. The sun was streaming across the valley as she climbed into her Land Cruiser and took off. The day was bright, cloudless and warm.

For two weeks, Shelby had stayed on the ranch, a relatively safe place. Dakota had been hunting for Welton every day in the Tetons. He'd found the convict's tracks, but it was a dead end. No one knew what kind of a vehicle he had. Forensics had taken impressions of the tires of a vehicle down at the end the road, but they were a variety that a good half of Jackson Hole residents had on their vehicles. There was no way to find him in that avenue of investigation.

Touching her cheek, she noticed that the scratches she'd acquired were gone. The swelling around her nose had disappeared. In a mirror, Shelby looked normal, no hint of the violence done against her. But she could still feel its effects. Frowning, she drove at the maximum speed limit, wanting to get back to work.

"HEY, GOOD TO SEE YOU," Cade called as Shelby entered his office.

Dakota was with him looking at a wall map of the Tetons.

"Nice to be here. Thanks for letting me go back to work. I was slowly going crazy out there." She grinned. Her gaze moved to Dakota, and she saw the worry banked in his brown eyes. Probably for her. He wanted her off this case for good, but Cade had refused to release her. Her body responded to Dakota's hooded, smoldering look. This morning, before he left for work, they had made long, tender love. As much of a warrior he was, she'd discovered over the past two weeks how gentle he could be with her. Her love for him grew daily.

"What do you have?" Shelby asked, moving to where Dakota stood.

"Three-year-old boy, Bobby Parker, walked away from his parents' campsite this morning. The mother was watching him, went into the tent for two minutes, came out and he was gone."

"Poor Mom," Shelby murmured. "Kids at that age are so fast."

"I'm more worried about a grizzly finding the kid," Dakota muttered. He punched the wall map with his index finger above where the camp was situated. "I was over in that area two days ago. I ran into two male grizzlies. One was a cinnamon color and the other was a dark brown. One had a collar on it for tracking purposes and the other did not. I reported both to the rangers and gave them photos. What's bad about this is that brown grizzly is a newcomer. No one knows its behavior or its pattern of where it's going to go to find food. He's a wild card in this track."

Mouth compressed, Shelby said, "That's not good news."

"Bears at this time of year are starving," Cade said, scowling. "I have Charlie, the Tetons Forest Service supervisor, on this. He's assigned three rangers to try to locate the whereabouts of this new bear. He's worried the grizzly might mistake the child for a baby elk and kill it."

A cold shiver ran down Shelby's spine. "It's not a good situation."

"So you two are going in with major weapons in hand," Cade warned them. "Carry your rifles and a pistol."

"I'm staying in my civilian gear," she told Cade.

"Good. Just show your identification to the parents once you arrive. I'm gathering another group of searchers and volunteers right now, but I need you on this now."

Dakota nodded and walked around Cade. "We'll get over there now."

Shelby said, "I'll pick up a radio for Dakota at the desk."

"Good. Test them out before you start tracking with our dispatcher. Make sure they have fresh batteries in them."

"We're good to go," Shelby said, walking out with Dakota.

In the hall, Dakota looked over at her. She wore a bright red long-sleeved blouse beneath her dark green jacket. "You sure you're ready for this?"

She could hear the veiled worry in his deep voice. "I am." Shelby reached out, caught his fingers for a moment and squeezed them. "I have to get back to work, Dakota. I'm fine. I'm healed up."

"If I had my way, you'd be chained to the bed." A hint of a smile lightened his dark expression.

"I know you're worried for me, but you can't

hide me away in a castle. I need to work. I can't let what Hartley did stop me from living. You know that."

"Yeah," he groused, giving her a frown. "You're hell-bent to get back to your deputy work."

"Look, this is a lost child. We'll be tracking together. And we have radios. I really don't think this kid disappearing is Welton's work. It's an accident. And we should be able to find him pretty quickly. I hope." She had tracked lost children before in the Tetons, and each time she found them alive and well.

Dakota halted at the dispatcher's desk, where the woman handed him a radio. He thanked her and they walked toward the front door.

SHELBY CALMED BOBBY's frantic parents at the campground. While she took the information for a report, Dakota had already identified the child's tennis shoe tread and was following it into some brush located at one end of the large campground. By the time she reached him, he waited to show her the track.

"There's no reason why this kid would plunge into this kind of brush," Dakota growled, pointing at the broken small twigs and branches.

Shelby knelt nearby, studying the scene. "Is it possible the child heard a sound in the brush? If he did, he might have gone through it to investigate."

Scowling, Dakota saw the trail of tiny branches and torn green leaves in the wake of the child's exploration into the brush. "Good call."

"Or maybe there was a baby elk on the other side of these willows?" Shelby stood up and craned her neck, but she couldn't see over or through the thick brush.

"Let's go on the other side of this area and see."

The warmth of the morning climbed. Shelby shrugged out of her green jacket and tied it to the pack she wore. The pine needles were dry and cracked beneath the soles of their boots as they made it to the opposite side of the willow stand. She watched Dakota slow to a stop. He searched the area. Moving quietly to his side, she saw what he was looking at. There were some disturbed pine needles near the exit point in the brush. Moving forward, she leaned down, studying more closely.

"The problem with pine needles is that they destroy the track on the sole of a shoe," she muttered. She turned to glance up at him. "What do you think?"

"I think the depression is a little too deep for a three-year-old kid," he said. Kneeling down on one knee, he examined it intently for a moment.

Shelby looked around. "But there are no other prints anywhere else."

Rubbing the back of his neck, he growled, "I know."

"Maybe the boy was running?" She pointed to the heel area of the depression. It was deeper than the toe area.

"Running toward what?" he said, unhappy. Dakota had a bad feeling about this. He was jumpy anyway because of worry about Shelby.

Slowly rising, Shelby walked parallel to the footprint and searched for other depressions. The problem was there were a lot of rocks up the face of the mountain along with dry pine needles scattered and thinning out across the area. "I'm spreading out to look for bear spore…." She hated even saying it. A grizzly could have been sniffing around this side of the willows, the child could have heard the bear and gone through the brush to investigate. A quick, cold shiver raced through her. Automatically, she prayed that the grizzly did not find the child.

Dakota took steps in the opposite direction, carefully looking near the edge of the brush for any sign of bear spore. *Nothing.*

"Dakota?" Shelby called. She knelt and waited for him to come over to her. His face was hard and unreadable.

"Look, scat."

He leaned over, hands on his knees, next to her. "Yeah, but that's old bear scat. At least two days."

"I know," she said, disappointed. "But what it does prove is there is grizzly in this area." Her voice trailed off and she stood up.

Dakota reached out, pushing a few gold strands away from her healed left cheek. "Don't go there," he said. "Not yet…"

Her skin tingled in the wake of his grazing touch. Despite how hard he looked, the lethal power that swirled around him, she reacted to his tender look and his finger trailing down the line of her jaw. "You think it's a grizzly?"

Shrugging, he studied the steep, rocky hill above them. "It's a lead, Shel. That's all."

She rested her hand on his broad chest, the heat of his skin emanating from beneath the dark brown shirt. There was a change in his eyes, and the line of his mouth softened. "We need to find this boy…."

Leaning down, he curved his mouth across hers. Shelby's response was heated and filled with promise. He slid his hand against her jaw, tilting her head slightly, and deepened their kiss. He inhaled the sweet scent of her as a woman, tasting her, absorbing her. Reluctantly, Dakota eased away, her eyes drowsy and filled with desire. "Let's keep going. We got good daylight. Kids are fast but they tire out, too. We'll probably find him within a mile of the camp."

Mouth tingling, Shelby yearned for another time and place with Dakota. She could never get enough of this warrior whose scarred hands were tender, sending her into realms she'd never gone before.

"Okay," she said, her voice softer than normal. "We have to find the boy before it's too late...."

"Let's hold out hope for him, then." He wrestled inwardly with his feelings for Shelby. Dakota was plagued with worry over his PTSD and, some night, hurting her. He felt as if he had one foot in heaven and one in hell. And with no quick, easy answers to fix it or fix himself. *Damn.*

Shelby moved away from Dakota, feeling heat, the power exuding from around him, the invisible rippling effect making her dizzy with need. Dakota could look at her a certain way and she would feel her body blossom in anticipation of his touch or kiss. Getting hold of her emotions, she turned and pointed to the edge of the hill. "I think the boy might have tried to find an easier way up this hill. What do you think?"

"Don't know. You take that side of it and look. I'm going to go up the rocks."

Shelby nodded. Trying to find the trace of a footprint on rock was nearly impossible. Yet she saw Dakota shift gears to the black lava rock face scattered with brown pine needles. She had the rifle over her shoulder as she went nearly a tenth of a mile to the right of where he was tracking.

Dakota would look up every once in a while to check on Shelby's location. There was no brush on the hill, just Douglas fir, like soldiers standing at attention. He'd then shift back to looking for a few pine needles out of place among the millions that were not. It was tedious, intense work to try to find those three or four needles.

Shelby followed the curve of the hill. To her left, Dakota was about halfway up the rocky face. She was finding no depressions in the floor of the forest. Disheartened, she was leaned over, moving slowly, head down, gaze fixed and moving from right to left.

She felt more than heard movement to her right. *What?* Lifting her head, she twisted and looked. A brown grizzly male, nearly seven hundred pounds, was less than a hundred feet away from her. Fear shot through Shelby. The bear whuffed—a warning.

Without hesitating, she jerked the rifle off her shoulder. It was instinctive to flip off the safety. She knew from long experience to keep a bullet in the chamber at all times.

The bear charged, roaring.

Dakota jerked upright, hearing the roaring sound. Suddenly, to his horror, he saw the brown grizzly hurtling toward Shelby. Without thinking, he pulled his pistol out in one smooth motion. Shelby stood her ground, jamming the butt of the rifle into her shoulder, aiming and firing.

The bear was hit in the shoulder with the first shot.

In seconds, it would be on top of her.

Dakota leaped to one side, hands on the SIG, firing one, two, three, four shots into the angry, charging bear. He didn't miss.

Shelby fired a second shot, not even hearing Dakota firing his pistol to the right of her. The bear leaped, its long curved claws aimed right at her head. She twisted her body, pushed herself to the left, firing the rifle as she fell toward the ground.

The grizzly swiped at her, roaring, his mouth open, teeth bared. Shelby landed hard. Rolling, she tried to get away from the bear. It landed with a heavy thud next to her. Eyes wide with terror, she saw it lift its paw, blood running out of its one eye. She gasped and dug the toes of her boots into the floor of the forest, lunging away from the grizzly.

She was breathing hard, the strap of the rifle tangled around her left arm. Dakota raced up, his pistol aimed at the dying bear. His face was a mask of intensity. He lifted the pistol and fired a cartridge at point-blank range into the bear's thick skull. The round went in and the bear groaned, slumped and then lay still.

Dakota released the emptied magazine from the pistol, pulled out another magazine from his gear and slammed it into the SIG. He then turned on his heel, holstered the pistol and quickly moved to Shelby's side. Her face was pale, her eyes wide with terror.

"It's all right," he soothed, picking her up. He

untangled the leather strap from around her left arm. "Are you okay?"

Shelby's knees were weak. She reached out and grabbed for his arm. "I never expected this...." she rasped hoarsely, gazing at the dead bear less than ten feet away from her. Shaken, she heard her voice trembling. "I must be under some kind of dark cloud. God, that was close." She felt his arm slide around her shoulders, drawing her up against him.

"Too damned close," Dakota rasped, pulling her hard against him, his gaze never leaving the bear. Grizzlies were known to look dead, but rise and attack again.

Closing her eyes for a moment, Shelby leaned heavily against him. "The bears have it out for us." She remembered Dakota being attacked earlier in June.

"They're nothing to mess with at this time of year. They're hungry and they're willing to defend their territory. That bear was here before. It's his territory." He pressed a kiss to her mussed hair. "You were in his territory and that's why he charged you."

Shelby slid her arms around his lean waist, breathing raggedly from her brush with death. "Thanks...thanks for being there. Why did you use your pistol and not the rifle?"

He moved his hand across her back, feeling her

trembling in earnest now. Dakota recognized it as the adrenaline surging through her body. "Couldn't get it off my shoulder fast enough, Shel. When you're in a situation like this, you go for the second line of defense, the pistol."

Shaking in earnest, Shelby nodded. "Thank God you were there. I hit the bear in the shoulder the first time. My second shot bounced off its skull. I couldn't believe it!"

"You were caught flat-footed," Dakota said, his voice low with feeling. "You did the best you could. Bear skulls are the thickest in the world." He knew if he hadn't been with her, the bear would have killed her. Inwardly, his gut clenched. To lose Shelby after he'd found her would be like tearing his heart out of his chest. He'd never felt this way about any woman. Holding her tight, he pressed small kisses along her hairline and cheek. "It's okay, Shel. It's okay."

As he held her, Dakota began to realize how much Shelby was helping him to heal. It wasn't anything she did consciously; it was just her. He squeezed her gently and released her, checking her expression. Dakota was always stunned that his touch could soothe her so quickly. Was that love? A part of him didn't want to go there, but his pounding heart did. As he drowned in her blue gaze, he felt an incredibly powerful ribbon of blinding emotions explode through him. The sensations heated, healing and lifting the darkness that always haunted him. How could a man like himself, filled with demons, ever learn to love? Somehow he had.

CHAPTER TWENTY-ONE

DAKOTA HEARD A SMALL cry. It was the child! *Where?* He twisted his head toward the sound. It was coming from over the hill where the grizzly had attacked Shelby.

"Did you hear that?" Shelby whispered, giving him a look of disbelief.

"Yeah, stay here." He left her standing there, running across the rocky, slippery area toward the sound in the distance. Dakota trotted past the dead grizzly and broached the hill. His sharpened gaze caught the three-year-old boy near a stand of willows, a small limb in his hand. He was frightened, tears making paths through the dirt and scratches on his face.

Relief sizzled through Dakota as he slowed and walked up to the boy. Kneeling down, he said, "Bobby?"

The boy sniffed and scrubbed his eyes. "Y-yes. I want my mommy...."

"I'm going to take you to her. My name is Dakota. Are you hurt at all?" He saw the boy's eyes were red-rimmed. He was dirty from crawling through the willow stand.

"N-no, but that bear was following me." He lifted his hand and pointed at the dead grizzly up on the hill. His squeaky voice became stronger as he lifted the stick to show Dakota. "But I picked this up. I was going to hit him and scare him off with it."

Smiling a little, Dakota took the stick and set it aside. "You're a very brave boy, Bobby. Are you thirsty?" He pulled the canteen from his belt, opened it and handed it to him.

Without a word, Bobby put the canteen to his lips and drank.

Dakota watched water dribbling from the sides of the child's mouth as he slugged down the liquid. Finally, when he'd had enough, Bobby shyly handed the canteen back to him. Capping it, Dakota said, "Ready to go?"

"Yes, but I can walk."

Straightening to his full height, Dakota grinned at the plucky child. He held out his hand. "Okay, ready? My partner is on the other side of the hill. We're going to pick her up and then take you home. Your parents are very worried for you."

"Okay," Bobby said, slipping his small hand into his large one. "I'm hungry."

"I bet you are. Let's go find Shelby and then we'll see if I've got a protein bar you can have."

Bobby brightened. "I like protein bars!"

Smiling to himself, Dakota checked his stride to match the child's steps. He took the radio from his belt and called in to Cade Garner, reporting they'd found Bobby Parker. Dakota could hear the relief in the deputy's voice. Cade would then have one of the deputies staying with the parents at the campground give them the good news.

Shelby's eyes widened as Dakota reappeared at the hill with Bobby walking at his side. She grinned, sliding the leather strap of the rifle over her left shoulder. Bobby waved to her, as if he were on some kind of exciting grand outing. Shelby waved back and met them halfway. She knelt down and introduced herself to the child. Touched by Dakota's gentleness with the three-year-old, she smiled up into his eyes. There was a softness in them she'd not seen before. Clearly, Bobby liked holding on to his large, scarred hand.

"Let's take Bobby home."

Shelby stood and walked to the other side of Bobby. She gently held the boy's other hand, feeling a rush of relief that the child had not been killed by the grizzly.

"THAT GRIZZLY WAS STALKING the kid," Dakota told Shelby later as they drove back to the Garner Ranch.

"I got that."

"He was stalking Bobby when you happened

upon them. The grizzly saw you as a threat to his forthcoming dinner." Dakota slid a quick glance toward her. She looked shaken and pale from her run-in with the bear. Anyone would be. When an animal of that speed and weight attacks, there are seconds between surviving and dying.

"It scared the hell out of me." Shelby pushed her fingers through her dirty hair, wishing for a hot shower.

"You reacted right away," he said, complimenting her.

"Yeah, but I couldn't shoot worth a damn."

One corner of his mouth crooked. "Listen, you did what you could under the circumstances."

"You were cool as a cucumber. I hit the ground and saw you running and firing at the grizzly. Every shot hit that bear. You didn't miss."

"I had to hit him."

She heard the low growl in Dakota's tone, saw the look of anxiety in his gaze as he caught hers. "You moved so swiftly. You were completely focused on that grizzly. I've never seen someone move and shoot like you did."

"SEAL training," he said, reaching out and capturing her hand. There were several scratches across her fingers where she'd hit the sharp volcanic rocks.

"You shot the bear in the eye. That's damn good

shooting." She remembered he'd shot the other bear that had bitten him in the arm with an eye shot, too.

Dakota swelled with some pride. He felt good beneath her praise. "Thanks. I was a sniper, so I'm not half bad at hitting a target. The grizzly was moving so quickly I fired six shots into him before I got his eye and brain."

"I couldn't hit the broad side of a barn in that battle," she muttered, shaking her head.

"Stop being hard on yourself. You were startled, the grizzly was too close. You were lucky you got that rifle off your shoulder to shoot at all." He squeezed Shelby's fingers gently and saw some of the self-indictment leave her blue eyes. "Let's get you home. I think a shower is in your future." He caught her lips pulling into a wry smile.

LATER, AFTER A SHOWER and clean clothes, Shelby combed her damp hair. Her hands were scratched and bruised. She got off lucky. She could smell bacon frying out in the kitchen. Dakota was making them a late lunch of his favorite food, breakfast. Resting her hands on the sink, she stared into the foggy mirror. She loved this ex-SEAL. He'd just saved her life. Never would she forget the swift, blurred movement of his hand as it went for the pistol slung low on his right thigh. Or how quickly Dakota had moved, that pistol always level as he ran, firing into the grizzly. And yet, when it was all over, he was solicitous, caring for her. Later, he was incredibly gentle with little Bobby Parker. He was a man of depth and he intrigued her. The whole situation hadn't rattled him at all. Never mind that he'd already captured her heart.

Setting the comb aside, Shelby left the bathroom and padded down the hall to the kitchen. The smell of bacon frying and pancakes in another large skillet filled the air. "It all smells so good," she said, inhaling.

Dakota turned over the pancakes and looked over his shoulder. Shelby was dressed in a simple pink T-shirt, jeans and moccasins. Her damp blond hair hung in straight strands around her shoulders. "Go sit down. I'll serve you." He quickly flipped the pancakes onto a large platter, lifted the bacon out of the skillet and turned off the stove. Worried, he saw darkness in her eyes. Leftover shock, he was sure. Shelby had had two near misses with death. First with Hartley and now this. How was she really holding up emotionally? Dakota would tread carefully and continue to silently assess her well-being.

"Looks great," Shelby said, meaning it as he placed the plate in front of her.

"Figured some good breakfast food would go down easy," he said, watching her rally and pick up her knife and fork. Would she eat? Dakota wasn't sure, but he sat down with his own plate and dug hungrily into four stacked pancakes slathered with melting butter and Vermont maple syrup.

Shelby pushed the pancake around, chewed on some bacon, but discovered she really wasn't hungry. The day was bright, the sunshine slanting through the kitchen window. Sighing, she muttered, "You went to all this trouble and I just can't eat, Dakota…." She set the flatware aside. Instead, she picked up the coffee and sipped it.

He rested his hands on either side of his plate, gauging her reaction. "I've seen this kind of reaction before," he told her quietly.

"What do you mean?"

With a one-shoulder shrug, Dakota said, "When my platoon was Down Range in Afghanistan, we were always out in bad-guy country. Sometimes things would go wrong. The squad I was with had two of their shooters wounded in a helluva gun battle with an HVT, a Taliban opium drug warlord." He held her dark gaze. "SEALs are more than a team, Shel. They're family. You train, live, eat, breathe with these guys for years. They're my brothers. My family."

She could feel the intensity of his words, the passion behind them. "I'm glad you're letting me into your other life, your world. It had to rock you when those guys were wounded."

"It did. It shook every one of us. We're trained to be combat medics, and believe me, our skills saved their lives." He hesitated, choosing his words carefully. "When we got a medevac in there to take out our wounded, we then were lifted out later. Our team was in shock. Our men being wounded was like being wounded ourselves. We didn't know if they'd live or die at that point. We were caught up in so many conflicting emotions." Dakota pushed the empty plate aside and folded his hands, holding her gaze. "There is no manual, no training on earth, Shel, that teaches you how to react, how to handle your emotions for these moments. When we got back to our base, our officer in charge took us out of combat for a week to decompress."

"Why?"

"Because we were too emotionally rattled to be a hundred percent focused out in the field. He recognized the symptoms. And no matter how hard we tried to sit on our emotions, our anxiety, grief and rage, it didn't work. We're human. In the end, our AOIC, Jake Ramsey, had us stand down and it was the right call." Dakota reached out and slid his fingers across her bruised right hand. "Shel, you're in the same position I was over there. You don't recognize how compromised you are after a traumatic event. You think you're a hundred percent, that you've got a gun in the fight and you're confident in yourself and your abilities."

His fingers tightened imperceptibly on her hand as he watched moisture collect in her eyes. Shelby was fighting back a lot of emotions, trying to control them. It wouldn't work and Dakota knew it. "I wish…I wish I'd had someone like you to just hold me, talk me down, listen to me over there when it happened."

The heat of his hand permeated her cooler one. His words struck her heart and gut. "Okay, so I'm where you were?"

"Something like that."

Closing her eyes, Shelby sat back in the chair, a rush of emotions starting to erupt within her. The terror clawed at her chest, struggling to leap into her throat and fly out her mouth. "Okay," she whispered, her voice unsteady. "I hear you. I get it."

"I know you don't like staying here at the cabin and you want to get back to work, but it's not the right time, Shel. I know you're bored out of your skull. So were we. We had to take our guns out of the fight. We wanted back at that Taliban warlord and take his ass permanently out of the fight. Our OIC knew we weren't ready to climb back into the saddle."

Shelby wiped her eyes with trembling fingers. "I feel so damned helpless, Dakota." She'd spoken the words softly, the pain sandwiched in between the words. His hand moved gently across her forearm, soothing her. His eyes were so old-looking with far too much combat experience beyond them. He saw what was going on with her even though she didn't. More tears rolled down her cheeks. Shelby pulled her hand from his, reached into her pocket and found a tissue.

"So what do I need to do? I have to recover, Dakota. Welton is still out there hunting me. Damn, I feel like a raw target of opportunity." Her voice grew angry. "I want that son of a bitch! I want him so bad I can taste it. He's out there prowling around. I'm so afraid he's going to capture some unsuspecting woman and—" Her voice cracked. "Your sister paid a horrible price. I don't want any other woman to go through what she did."

"That makes two of us," Dakota agreed. With his finger he eased the damp strands of hair behind her delicate ear. "Listen to me, Shel. Decompress for a week. I'm out there, I'm hunting that bastard for both of us. I have a score to settle with him and I'm going to find him."

The words were spoken with controlled hatred. There was such raw rage he held inside himself. And just as quickly, the look of a committed warrior to his sworn enemy disappeared. Her ear tingled where he'd grazed it with his finger. "I believe you. I just worry for you," she said.

"Don't worry about me. I've had years to handle my feelings toward Welton where Ellie was concerned. I'm not coming off a hot firefight having two of my friends wounded. I'm very focused and calm about hunting Welton down. My emotions aren't going to get in the way of me finding and eliminating him. They're going to help me find him."

Shelby knew without a doubt that if Dakota found Welton, the convict was dead. Maybe Cade Garner and the rest of the sheriff's department didn't realize it, but she did. She felt that steel coldness within him, knew it was lethal and knew Welton's last look at the world would be this warrior's face.

"So you want me to just hang around the cabin? I can't even go on another lost child request?"

He shook his head. "I think it would be best if you just rested for a while, Shel. You've had two near-death brushes in two weeks."

"I feel like I've got a black cloud above my head," she griped.

He smiled sourly. "It seems that way. Third time's the charm and, frankly, I don't want you testing that one out to see if it works or not. Okay?"

Nodding, she stuffed the tissue back into her pocket. As she held his gaze, she felt her heart swell with such love for him. There was no question she was falling in love with him. Reaching out, she slid her hand over his.

"There's just something about you that touches my soul, Dakota. I have trouble even putting it into words. I like it. I want it and I want you."

He gently turned her hand over, brushing her

soft palm with his work-worn fingers. "You own my soul, Shel, whether you know it or not." His voice dropped to a rasp. "You're an incredibly strong, good woman. I don't know how I got so damned lucky in finding you, but I'm grateful." He picked up her palm and pressed a kiss to the center of it.

Absorbing his lips upon her flesh, the wild tingles racing up her arm, touching her pounding heart and making her feel safe, she managed a trembling smile. "I don't want to lose you, Dakota."

A silent joy filled his chest. He closed his hand around hers and leaned close. "You won't lose me. If I can survive three deployments in Afghanistan, I'll survive anything the civilian world wants to throw at me." Dakota's brows moved down and in an urgent tone, he added, "But I can't protect you as much as I wish I could, Shel. That's why you have to work with me, stay here and stay safe."

"Nowhere is really safe, Dakota. You and I both know that."

"You're right. But plenty of cowhands here on the Garner Ranch are watching out for you when they can. Just stay here for another week. Let me go find Welton."

Her stomach went queasy on her. Though she was beginning to understand how capable Dakota was as a warrior and a hunter of men, she still worried about him. Welton wasn't as stupid as Hartley had been. He was still around, still waiting, tracking her and timing when he'd reappear in her life. It was a gut knowing. Not one she wanted to share with Dakota. He was fiercely attuned to finding Welton. But who would find her first?

CHAPTER TWENTY-TWO

"Here's your gun and badge back, Shelby."

"Thank God," she said, taking them. When she shot Hartley, it was mandatory the deputy go on paid administrative leave until an investigation surrounding the death was completed. She slid the gun in the holster at her side and pinned her badge on her uniform. "This is good luck," she told Cade. "My weeks of incarceration are up, too."

Cade nodded and smiled a little. "You've had one hell of a month so far, Shelby. I think Dakota was right in asking you to stand down for two weeks. Did it hurt you?"

She grinned sourly. "Not really. He was right." Turning, she said, "Where is he?" He had left her bed early last night, continuing to track and trying to find Welton.

"He's more SEAL than ex-SEAL," Cade warned her. "Night is their specialty, so he's out walking a grid pattern in hopes of finding Welton."

She sighed. "He has reasons to do it."

"I know. If I were in his shoes, I'd be out there hunting Welton, too."

"Well, we have other fish to fry," he told her. Picking up a report on his desk, he said, "Thirty minutes ago, a call came in from the Tetons headquarters. We have a missing two-year-old girl named Susie, who wandered away from the Colter Bay tent camping area."

Shelby scowled. "That's not good. That whole area is heavy with grizzlies."

"No need to tell me." He looked up and said, "Why don't you switch back into your civilian clothes? I need a tracker and Dakota isn't here. Are you willing to do it?"

"Sure. Just take me off the duty roster." She grinned. "I'd much rather track than cruise around looking to hand out a speeding ticket."

Cade smiled. "I thought so. Okay, here's the contact info. You're going to have to talk with the parents first. I got a deputy already on scene, Ken Hutchinson. You can talk to him, too. I'm also arranging a larger volunteer group, but that's going to take a couple of hours. Getting you there right now is going to help us find that lost baby."

"Right you are." She started toward the door. "Oh, when Dakota comes back in, tell him where I am? He's probably going to be exhausted and go to bed like he usually does, but he should know where I am. He's a worrywart."

Cade nodded. "I will." He glanced at his watch. "He should show up any time now. You might even meet him on the way out."

Shelby lifted her hand. "I'm off. I'll be in contact once I'm out at the campsite and have interviewed the parents."

SHELBY GLANCED AT THE position of the sun. It was 8:00 a.m., the morning very cool as it always was at this time of year. The sky was cloudless, a light blue. The parents were distraught and that was understandable. The other deputy, Ken Hutchinson, remained with them as she followed the child's tiny tracks from the campfire area to the asphalt parking lot nearby. He'd picked up small prints on the other side of the road. There was a sign that said Day Trail, and that's where the child's print was, he thought. The water from Jackson Lake could be seen from the camping area.

Shelby quickly went to the black sand and searched for Susie's footprint. To her relief, she found none. If she had, it could be an indication the child had walked into the water and drowned. Then her body would be found by dredging. It wasn't something Shelby wanted to do.

Pulling the rifle over her shoulder, Shelby went to the day track trail sign, knelt down and saw the print. The area was thickly wooded with trees and brush, the trail damp and narrow. The child had wandered off in the direction of the boat ramp, about a thousand feet on the other side of this thicket of woods. Colter Bay was a major area for boaters, both with engines or kayaks and canoes. There was a huge launch area and Shelby wondered if the girl had made it to the other side. If she had, she could be in real danger of falling off the unsteady movable wharfs.

Slowly rising, Shelby keyed her hearing, all senses online. Susie had disappeared at 7:00 a.m. when the mother was making breakfast over the campfire. She had been busy and distracted. The father was down at the Jackson Lake boat area, getting their fishing boat ready to take out for the day. It was easy to have a young child wander off in such a situation, Shelby knew. But the child had only an hour's lead and she felt confident she could find Susie shortly.

The other worry for Shelby was the high grizzly bear population around Jackson Lake. Right now there was a mother grizzly with three cubs known to frequent this area near the boat launch ramp. It was the bear's turf. That wasn't good for anyone who was lost. Particularly a small child. If the child started to cry or call out for her parents, the bear, if close enough, would hear it and come running. A young human's voice sounded like the mewing of a baby elk calf calling for its mother.

A shiver ran through Shelby as her thoughts went in that direction.

The woods closed in, the muddy track a thin brown ribbon. Mouth tightening, Shelby followed the toddler's fresh, muddy tracks. Soon, the forest grew quiet and silence thickened around her. She was starting to sweat and halted. Once she pulled off her thick jacket, she stuffed it in her knapsack. She rolled up the sleeves on her pink blouse, took a drink of water and then continued toward the wall of brush ahead of her.

Shelby stopped about two feet from the stand. What was she looking at? Kneeling down on one knee, she studied the disrupted soil. She saw the toddler's track, but there was another, much larger boot track on either side of the child's prints. *What the hell?* She pressed her hand into the soil and leaned closer. Her mind moved over possibilities. Mostly not good. Measuring the length of the track, as well as the width, she figured it to be male, not female. The boot was simply too large for a woman's foot.

Looking up, Shelby studied the gloomy forest surrounding her. Heart squeezing with fear, she wondered if a man had come upon Susie and taken her. To what end? A sexual predator who just happened upon the child? She swallowed hard. She didn't want to think those thoughts, but she was a law enforcement officer and she couldn't afford to ignore the possibility.

She'd seen Susie's mother's and father's boot prints at camp. And this print did not match their boots. Taking the radio from the side of her pack, she stood and called in to Cade Garner. When he answered, she told him what she'd found. His voice went dark with worry.

"Welton?" he demanded.

"I don't know," Shelby said, continually looking around now, feeling a sense of danger. "We can't leave him out of this scenario."

"Damn. Okay, Dakota is on his way out there right now. Give me your GPS coordinates and I'll send them to him."

Some relief filtered through Shelby as she looked at her GPS guide and gave him the info. "How soon will he be here?"

"Thirty minutes. He just got back and is exhausted. He had a run-in with a grizzly where he was."

Her brows flew up. "Oh no. Is he all right?"

"Yeah, and so is the bear. It was a female and he fired a couple of warning shots up in the air and she decided to leave instead of attacking him."

Sighing, Shelby said, "Close call."

"I know. Look, you want to wait there for him?"

"No, I'll push on. I'm going to track south on the path now because that's where the boot prints are leading. I'm sure he'll be able to track me from here. Out."

Worried for the child, Shelby put the radio back into her pack, turned and continued to follow the prints. Whoever it was was in a hurry, the stride lengthening. When she went back to the original track and compared it to what she was seeing later, it was clear the man had picked up the toddler. The depth of the tread was deeper, indicating he was carrying more weight, perhaps the child in his arms?

Shelby tried to figure out other scenarios as she slowly moved parallel to where the boot prints were leading her. Could a fisherman have happened by? Maybe he was carrying the toddler back to the main forest ranger headquarters of the Tetons? That was equally possible. Still, her nerves were stretched as she followed the track toward the lake area.

A second, curving wall of brush and willows rose in front of her. Shelby saw the tracks turn and follow around them. Suddenly, she heard a cry, a child's whimper.

She stopped near the end of the thicket, surrounded by forest and no other humans in sight. Her heart rate tripled. She hurried around the end of the stand and headed toward the sound. The child continued to cry.

Shelby let out a sigh of relief as she saw Susie

sitting just inside a wall of brush. To the child's right was another large thicket.

"Hey," she crooned, kneeling down in front of the dirty, scratched child, "it's okay, Susie." She gently touched the toddler's black hair and smiled at her. "I'm Shelby. I'm going to get you out of here and home to your mommy and daddy...."

Just as she leaned forward, her hands extended to slide around the toddler's waist, something stirred behind her.

Shelby twisted a look to her right, her eyes widening. Too late! There was Welton's leering face, his smile crooked as he jabbed a hypodermic needle into her upper arm. The bite of the syringe exploded through her.

"Too late, bitch," he breathed, yanking the syringe out of her arm. "You're mine...."

Shelby spun around, her arm smarting with pain. As she started to go for her pistol, Welton's boot flashed out. The boot toe caught her in the shoulder, knocking her off her feet. Landing with a thud, Shelby felt her mind starting to short out. She rolled to the left as Welton came at her, his fists clenched, a snarl on his lips. Her hand fell over the pistol.

"No, you don't!" Welton jerked her hand away and yanked the pistol out of her holster. Standing above her, he grinned, breathing hard. "Just be a good girl and let the drug do its work." He chuckled as he saw the woman's eyes begin to close, her body sinking back onto the forest floor. "The last thing you're going to remember is my face, you bitch. You put me away, you killed Hartley. Now I'm going to make you pay for all of it...."

DAKOTA SCOWLED, LOOKING at the extra boot tracks along with the toddler's. He was breathing hard, having trotted to the GPS coordinates Shelby had given him. Exhaustion pulled at him and he rubbed his reddened eyes. For the past week he'd spent twelve hours, dusk to dawn, searching every cabin up on the slopes of the Tetons, hoping to find that Welton had moved to new digs. He'd found nothing. *Now this.* He pulled the radio from his pack and called Shelby.

No answer.

Fear arced through him. Shelby would answer. She couldn't be that far away. Toddlers don't walk miles. They usually walk in a circle of sorts. He called in to Cade Garner.

"Has Shelby called in?" Dakota demanded, his gaze ranging over the wild territory. Grizzlies were everywhere. They could easily hide in the thickets that ringed Lake Jackson.

"No. Not yet. Are you there?"

"Yeah, just arrived." His mouth turned down. "This isn't good. She should be answering her radio."

"Maybe it's low on batteries?"

"Maybe…" The hair on the back of Dakota's neck stood up. Shelby was in trouble. He could feel it. "Look, I'll follow her track and call later. Out."

Stuffing the radio on his belt, Dakota loped down the slight incline. He followed her tracks, which were fresh and easy to read. It was now 9:00 a.m., the heat of the day beginning. Somewhere beyond him was Jackson Lake. He could smell the scent of water in the air. Where was Shelby? Why wasn't she answering her radio? *Damn!*

Dakota followed the tracks down to a huge wall of willows that grew for about a tenth of a mile. Beyond that was a major tourist hiking trail that went around the lake. He saw her track stop for a minute, noticed a dirt impression where she'd knelt down on one knee as if looking at something more closely. As he lifted his head, Dakota's eyes narrowed. Shelby had stood up. But now her boot track changed. She was running, the toe of her boot deeper than the rest of the print. What was she running toward? He hurried around the edge of the thickets. His SIG Sauer rode low on his right thigh so his hand could just naturally reach out and touch the butt of the German pistol. The restraining strap was off and he had easy access to it, if needed.

Dakota turned and stopped. There in front of him was the toddler! She was crawling around in the dirt, playing with it, her tiny hands and arms dusty. Dakota felt a terrible chill move through him as he walked toward the child. The prints became muddled and choppy in the nearby dirt. Frowning, he studied them intently. And then his heart slammed into his ribs. God, there was Welton's boot track! He recognized it because he'd seen it at the original cast at the forensics lab.

Leaning down, he sucked in a breath, a cry strangling in his throat. There were Shelby's tracks. He quickly followed them. There was a depression in the dirt farther down near the thickets. It was a partial imprint of the side of her body. Turning on his heel, Dakota swallowed hard. He rose and went over to the toddler to make sure she was all right. Susie looked up at him with smiling green eyes, a handful of dirt in her tiny fist. Dakota gave the toddler a cursory inspection, and couldn't find any injury.

Jerking the radio off his belt, he called Cade Garner. His voice was dark and hard-sounding. "I've got Susie. But the bad news is, Welton has got Shelby. Their tracks converge here, Cade. I think Welton stole the kid to sucker Shelby into tracking so he could capture her." His nostrils flared as he looked at the surrounding area. "He's got her. I'll get this kid back to her parents and then I'm going after that son of a bitch because he's going to kill Shelby...."

As he trotted back toward the camp with the

toddler in his arms, Dakota's mind churned at a
high rate. He had Shelby's sheriff's jacket on the
seat of his truck. Storm was with him. As soon as
he'd given Susie back to her relieved parents, he
would get to his truck. The wolf was good at tracking, too, but her nose could hold a scent and follow
it for a long time. He'd be stuck following tracks,
but Storm could speed things up.

His chest hurt until Dakota felt as if he was
going into cardiac arrest. As he loped through the
woods, his long legs taking him closer and closer
to the camp, he wanted to cry out in rage and frustration. Shelby had walked right into a trap set by
that bastard! Terrible photos of Ellie taken after
she was found rose in front of him. *Oh, God, don't
let that happen to Shelby. I'll do anything for you.
Just don't let Welton torture her. Oh, God, please...*

He ran on powerful legs, his boots digging in
hard, dry surface. As a SEAL, he could run thir-
teen miles with ease, even with a sixty-five-pound
pack on his back. His mind went forward. He carried his M-4 rifle in the truck, his major hiking
pack filled with medical first-aid items, water and
food. Approximating the time as he ran, the thickets swatting at his lower body, Dakota moved into
complete military mind-set.

It would take every bit of his ten years as a
SEAL to find Shelby before it was too late. He'd
keep his cell phone on so Cade Garner could con-

tinuously track his whereabouts. A helicopter was out of the question because it couldn't see through the thick forest. Nor could it land if the pilots could locate Shelby and Welton. He wasn't sure if Shelby was conscious or not. He'd find out soon enough, going back to track them just as soon as Susie arrived safely in her parents' awaiting arms.

His whole world anchored on Shelby. She'd gone through so damn much already. And he felt helpless, unable to find Welton before the bastard lured her in and captured her. Angry with himself, angry with the convict, he sprinted the last quarter mile, the camp now in sight.

The only thing between Shelby and Welton was him. The steel resolve coming up through him was a familiar one. He always got that sense of hunting when he and his team were about to infiltrate and connect with the enemy. This time was no different. The only thing on Dakota's side of this terrible situation was that he was a damned good tracker, fast and best of all, he had a wolf that could follow Shelby's scent. He had to bring all his deadly skills together in order to find and rescue her. And kill that son of a bitch in the process. By the time this day was done, Welton was a dead man. The convict just didn't know it yet.

CHAPTER TWENTY-THREE

HEART POUNDING, DAKOTA headed out from the campsite once the toddler was given to the happy parents. He wasted no time in telling Deputy Hutchinson, who was with them, what had happened. Moving back into the forest, retracing his steps, his eyes on the ground, Dakota kept his M-4 rifle in his hand. He'd given Storm a smell of Shelby's coat. The wolf bounded ahead of him, following the exact trail he'd just retraced.

As he ran, the breath tearing out of his mouth, stomach-churning photos he'd seen during the trial of Hartley and Welton ran through his mind. He'd tried to put those photos of Ellie so damn deep down inside him they'd never see the light of day again. But now they hung like specters of the past coming back to taunt him all over again.

The first thing the sexual predators had done to Ellie was use a sharp knife and they'd made six cuts on the bottom of each of her feet. That way, it would be impossible for her to escape them. He cried for what his sister must have felt as they cut her soles to red, bleeding ribbons.

Dakota halted at the site of thickets where the struggle had taken place. All his SEAL training went online. The hatred for Welton and the fear he had for Shelby's life mixed like a toxic shake in his gut. As he was paralleling her footprints, he could tell Welton had done something to Shelby because he was carrying her. The footprints were much deeper and somewhat off balance. Shelby was a tall woman and she had weight to go with her height.

Dakota was intimately familiar with this area, a major tourist trail. That was to his advantage. His mind whirled with questions as to where Welton was going. He knew there was a parking lot nearby. Could he get to it in time? Was that where Welton was headed? Uncertain, he saw Storm stop and lift her nose to the air. Skidding to a halt, Dakota looked around. Where were Welton's tracks? Storm bounded down the incline between the thick stands of trees, heading toward the water. Turning on his heel, he followed the wolf, desperately trying to find tracks.

There! Dakota picked up Welton's boot prints again. He was trying to hide his tracks by remaining in islands of grass here and there. As he trotted behind his wolf, the prints fresh and obvious, Dakota fought photos from the past. He remembered sitting in the courtroom with his parents. When the prosecutors put up slides of Ellie's mouth, he had felt nauseated. The second thing Welton and Hartley did was take a pair of pliers and pull out four of her lower molars in her mouth. The prosecutors theorized that Ellie had fought them, screaming, and they wanted to silence her while they raped her. Wiping his mouth, his eyes watering for a moment, Dakota felt nausea crawling up his throat. Would Welton do the same thing to Shelby? *Oh, God, no. No, please let me find them. Let me find them….*

They rushed to the edge of Jackson Lake. This part of the lake had much less tourist traffic than farther north. Dakota looked across the rippling lake. No one was in sight. Usually, there were canoes and fishing boats. The lake was lapping at the small pebbled beach where he stood. Breathing hard, his M-4 in his right hand, he watched Storm pace back and forth along the beach, trying to pick up a scent.

The terror swelled inside him as he postulated that Welton had some kind of boat or canoe waiting here. Perspiration dotted his face and he wiped his brow with the back of his sleeve. His mind cartwheeled with possibilities. Where did Welton go? Where could he go from here?

"Storm," he called to the wolf. "Come!" He dug the toes of his boots into the sand and pebbles, leaping up the bank and running parallel to the edge of the lake. Dakota knew there was a small boat ramp on the end of the lake. And a parking lot. It was possible Welton had a vehicle stashed there. It was a huge risk to take, but the only logical choice for Welton. He ran hard and fast, the branches and leaves of brush swatting at his lower body. There were no tourists around, no hikers. It seemed as if the world were holding its breath as he tried to locate Shelby.

The past fueled his determination, his fear for Shelby. Those photos. The slides of Ellie, her hands and ankles tied to the posters of the bed, naked, unconscious, slammed into him. His mother had cried out when the photos had been flashed to the jury. Dakota had pressed his palms against his eyes, crying softly for his dead sister.

The forensics people testified that Ellie had been repeatedly, brutally raped. They couldn't say how many times, but there was no doubt that Hartley and Welton had both raped her. Dakota's heart had torn into small pieces as the forensics expert droned on in robot fashion about the rapes, the many rips and tears and blood found in her vagina. He sat there in shock. His father and mother sobbed, holding each other. He sat there alone, feeling horror and a murderous rage toward the two convicts.

Dakota called on the radio as he approached the wharf and parking area. Cade was mounting a search team as swiftly as possible, but Dakota knew he had the lead and he was Shelby's only hope under the circumstances.

Seeing a fisherman standing on the wood wharf, Dakota signed off, put the radio on his belt and approached the older man with a fishing hat on his silver hair.

"Excuse me," he called, breathing raggedly. "Have you seen anyone with a woman around here in the past half hour?"

The man frowned, fishing rod in hand. "Yes, yes, I did. Strangest thing."

Dakota wanted to scream as the older man halted to think.

"There," he said, pointing up toward the parking lot. "A guy with a woman who was unconscious went up to a green Chevy pickup. He put her in the passenger side and then burned rubber getting out of here."

"A green Chevy pickup?" Dakota's hopes rose.

The elder nodded, a worried look on his face. "I asked him if the woman was all right. She was passed out cold. He was dragging her out of the boat over there and having a tough time doing it. I went over to ask if she was okay. He told me she'd drunk too much liquor and had passed out. He was taking her home."

Stomach turning, Dakota tried to steady himself. "How long ago?"

"Maybe five minutes at the most," he said, studying the watch on his wrist.

"Did you get anything else on the truck? A license plate number?" He hoped against hope that the elder did, knowing in all probability, he hadn't.

"Well," he said, smiling a little as he pulled out a piece of paper from his pocket, "I did. I called the Forest Service headquarters and told them about it. Something didn't feel quite right about it. The truck turned south on the road out there, heading back, I think, toward the entrance to the Tetons Park. Are you law enforcement, by any chance?"

"The woman you saw, what color was her hair?"

"Blond. Real pretty, but she was very pale. I got worried. Are you with the forest service?" He looked at the military rifle in Dakota's hand.

"Yes," he lied, taking the paper. Relief poured through him as he saw the wobbly handwriting and the license plate number the fisherman had jotted down. Quickly, he called Cade on his radio, giving him the intel.

"Is the woman in trouble?"

Nodding, Dakota rasped, "She's been kidnapped." He pulled a photo from his pocket. "Was this the guy who had her?" It was a photo of Welton.

"Why…goodness. Yes, it was." He frowned. "She's not drunk, then?"

"No," Dakota said, his voice low with worry. "She's a kidnapping victim and he probably drugged her."

The fisherman took off his hat and scratched his head. "Listen, you need to get after her, then.

He left here only five minutes ago." He fumbled round in a pocket of his fishing vest, pulling out a set of keys. "My name is Harold Porter. That red Jeep over there is mine. Here's the keys. I'm too old to drive high speed, but my Jeep might get you to her in time."

Grateful, Dakota said, "Thanks. You staying at the Jackson Lake Lodge?"

"I am. When you can, return my Jeep to me?"

"I will," Dakota promised. "Thanks."

"I hope you get to her in time," he called.

As Dakota raced up the hill toward the Jeep, Storm was on his heels. *Hurry! Hurry!*

They both leaped into the open-air Jeep. Dakota jammed his foot down on the accelerator and roared out of the parking lot. He got on the radio again with Cade Garner and filled him in. Dakota's mind leaped with possibilities. Would Welton try driving out of the park? If he did, there was a blockade of deputies and cars waiting for him at the entrance. But there were so many dirt roads he could take instead and head up into the high country and disappear. If he did that, Dakota knew he could lose him.

The Jeep screamed at a hundred miles an hour, the wind tearing at Dakota as he drove intently on the only road in the park. He'd risked passing several slower-moving vehicles. The speed limit was forty miles an hour. It couldn't be helped. There was a long curve up ahead and two roads that turned right and moved up into the slopes of the Tetons.

Just as he made the curve, he saw an SUV parked on the berm near one of the roads. It wasn't the green Chevy pickup. He called Cade and demanded to know if the deputies had spotted Welton at the entrance. They had not. Braking hard, he pulled up behind the SUV. Leaping out, Dakota ran up to the man who was standing at the front of the vehicle, looking under the hood.

"Hey, have you seen a green Chevy pickup pass this way in the past few minutes?"

The man, in his forties, looked up. "Yeah, I did. What's wrong?"

"Which way did it go?" Dakota demanded.

Shrugging, the man said, "He turned up one of those roads."

"Which one?"

"I don't know. I was looking at my carburetor when he came roaring around in front of me. I thought he was going to hit me. He scared the hell out of me."

Frustrated, Dakota nodded. "Okay, thanks." He turned and trotted back to the Jeep, giving Garner the new intel.

Dakota headed for the first dirt road. The roads were a tenth of a mile apart on the same side of the highway. Which one had Welton taken? He braked and got out. Storm remained in the Jeep as he rap-

idly studied the dirt road. It was almost impossible
to tell if Welton had turned into this road. There
were so many sets of tire tracks and he didn't know
which set might belong to the Chevy truck. Loping
down the berm to the second road, Dakota halted
and studied the entrance area. The dirt looked more
disturbed, as if a vehicle had turned at higher speed
than normal and skidded sideways.

Hesitating, his gut still churning, Dakota considered both roads. This second road, a forest service one, looked like the best possibility. He called
Garner as he ran back to the Jeep and gave him
the GPS coordinates. Dakota slammed down on
the accelerator, the vehicle fishtailing as he moved
off the berm around the stalled SUV and made for
the second road.

Dakota headed up into the woods, speeding and
kicking up a rooster tail of thick yellow dust in the
wake of the vehicle. Both hands on the wheel, the
Jeep bounced and skidded on the soft dirt. If he
hadn't had his SEAL training with desert patrol
vehicles, he'd have crashed this civilian Jeep. The
road twisted and turned. They were leaving six
thousand feet and moving up to nearly nine thousand feet. He relentlessly pushed the vehicle, his
mind moving over all the cabins up in this area.

Welton had a plan. Dakota knew there were six
cabins in the area. Which one was he going to?
Each cabin was more than half a mile to a mile off

this forest service road. Each would take time to stop and check out. Shelby didn't have that kind of time. Mouth tightening, his knuckles white on the steering wheel, he tried to figure out a way to tell which driveway Welton would take.

SHELBY SLOWLY BECAME CONSCIOUS. She was aware of being bounced and tossed around in the back-seat, the car roaring and skidding around. Opening her eyes, her senses muddied, she tried to under-stand where she was. Her arm hurt and she lifted her hand. Blood met her fingertips. What had hap-pened? She was slammed against the door, hitting her head. *Oh God!* Her eyes flew open as she tried to fight the powerful effects of the drug. *Welton!*

Jerking a glance to her right, she saw the con-vict's profile. He was driving like a madman, hands gripping the wheel, the truck shrieking as it flew over the rutted dirt road.

Her mind didn't want to work. She was in trou-ble. Adrenaline kicked in and erased some of the drugged sensations she fought. Welton had set her up. He'd captured the child to lure her in. Mouth dry, Shelby lifted her badly shaking hand. *Escape!* She had to escape!

Welton had not bound her, so she was able to raise her head just enough to look between the seats. She saw no pistol. Her own holster was empty. He had removed the weapon. Shelby's only priority was to escape. The truck was lurching and jumping around on the bumpy road. Shelby tried to estimate how fast they were going. Did she even have a chance to escape?

Ellie Carson hadn't had a chance. Shelby remembered the woman's trauma at Welton's hands. Her mouth tightened. The choice between staying and leaving was clear. She might break her neck or kill herself opening the door and rolling out. But it was a risk worth taking. Shelby slowly stretched her hand upward, so as not to distract Welton, who was driving erratically. The door clicked open when she pressed a button.

As she slowly turned on her side, her trembling hand moving to the door handle, Shelby thought of Dakota, how much she loved him. He was a wounded vet, but he had a magnificent heart and soul. Saying a quick prayer, Shelby took a deep breath and shoved the door open.

Welton saw something out of the corner of his eye. *What the hell!* The rear right door flew open.

Too late!

The woman launched out the door, headfirst. *The crazy bitch!*

Shocked, Welton instantly slammed on the brakes. The truck fishtailed at high speed. It lurched slowly sideways, out of control. Welton snarled a curse as he felt the truck become airborne. Dammit, anyway! He clung to the wheel, the truck sailing off the road, across a gully and nose-diving toward a stand of trees.

Shelby hit the road hard. She tucked and rolled, trying to absorb the slamming pressure of hitting the earth. A cry tore from her as pain reared up her right shoulder. The truck engine suddenly raced, the sound like a roar. Rolling to a stop, she watched the green truck sail through the air, headed for a stand of fir trees.

Without waiting to see what would happen, Shelby dove off the road into the area where head-high thickets stood. The burning sensation in her right shoulder made her think she'd torn something. Breathing hard, wobbling on shaky knees because the drug was still in her system, she pushed off with the toes of her boots and lunged into the forest. The faster she could get away, the less Welton was likely to find her.

She'd gone a few feet when she heard a crunching, crashing noise. The truck had hit a tree! Had it killed Welton? Shelby wasn't going back to find out. He had weapons and she knew he'd come hunting her. Turning, she moved in weaving motions, stumbling, tripping and catching herself. The terror of what Welton could do to her spurred her on at full speed, regardless of her shaky equilibrium.

Steam erupted from the destroyed radiator, a noise she quickly left behind. The deeper Shelby ran down the slight incline, the less she heard.

Good. Because she had to put distance between them or Welton would kill her. Mind churning, Shelby looked around, trying to get her bearings, but it was impossible. Douglas fir surrounded her, thick and silent. The soft pine needles hid her boots somewhat as she thunked along. Breathing raggedly, her breath tearing out of her mouth, Shelby pushed onward. The hill sloped downward. Somewhere below, she had to hit flatland or a trail. There were hundreds of hiking trails throughout the slopes of these mountains. If only she could find a trail, Shelby knew it would eventually lead to help. *Oh, God, let me survive this!*

CHAPTER TWENTY-FOUR

WELTON SNARLED A CURSE as he leaped out of the overturned Chevy. He grabbed the deputy's pistol and hightailed it into the forest. She couldn't have gone far! As he made a diagonal run, Welton's anger soared. How could he have been so damned stupid not to tie the bitch up? He'd been so sure he gave her enough of the drug to keep her unconscious until he reached the cabin. He ran hard and fast, weapon in his hand.

Shelby wove drunkenly through the Douglas fir. She kept seeing black dots dancing threateningly in front of her eyes. No! She couldn't lose consciousness! She just couldn't! Pumping her legs, wobbling and off balance, she stumbled on a hidden root and went flying down the incline. She landed on her belly, let out a groan and rolled. Miraculously, as she pushed up to her hands and feet, she realized she was on a major horse trail. Shelby spotted hoof prints. The trail curved just above where she'd fallen. Hope flared in her.

Her knees were weak. She tried to get fully upright, but her knees buckled beneath her. Fear shot through her as she tried again. The drug was powerful and no matter what Shelby did, she couldn't force her exhausted body to overcome its paralyzing effects.

Suddenly, a horse and rider came trotting around the curve. Shelby's eyes widened. It was Curt Downing! Her mind kept blipping out, but she remembered he was an endurance rider and rode nearly every day to keep his Arabian black stallion in shape for the coming endurance race in September.

Curt yanked back hard on the reins, his stallion grunting and dropping his hindquarters, skidding to a stop, almost running over the woman in the middle of the trail. He gawked, unsure of what he was seeing.

"Shelby?" he called, sitting up in the saddle, disbelief in his voice. She was kneeling on the trail, her hands scratched and bloodied. Her blond hair was disheveled around her taut face. "What's going on?" he called, trying to get his horse to stand still.

"H-help me, Curt," she called, stretching her hand out toward him.

Welton came bounding down the incline. "Don't touch her!" he yelled at Downing.

Curt jerked around toward the sound and scowled as he saw the convict scramble down the slope to the trail, pistol in hand. "What the hell is going on here?" he yelled.

With a gasp, Shelby tried to get up, but she fell to her side on the trail just as Welton reached out for her. His fingers tangled in her hair and he jerked her upright. Pain radiated through her scalp and she cried out.

"Stop!" Downing roared, going for the pistol he always wore at his side. No way was he going to stand back and let Welton harm her. He knew the convict's past, and no woman, not even a woman deputy, deserved to be tortured by the bastard.

Welton snarled. "Like hell I will…" He lifted the pistol and shot twice.

With a cry, Shelby saw both bullets strike the rider. Downing was thrown backward by the power of the bullets slamming into him. He tumbled off the back of his frightened horse. The stallion's eyes rolled. It leaped to the side of the trail, frightened by the booming sounds.

Welton cursed as the careening animal struck him in the shoulder. His hand was jerked off the woman's hair, flying through the air, the pistol knocked out of his hand.

Shelby collapsed on the trail. Her vision blurred. She scrambled to her hands and knees as she saw her pistol flying out of Welton's hand. The horse had run into him, frightened by his rider falling off. Downing lay on the trail, groaning, his arms flopping weakly, blood pumping out of his chest.

With her last ounce of strength, she lurched to

her feet. Shelby had to get to the pistol that had landed no more than ten feet away from her.

Welton snarled and cursed, rolling down the trail. He flew to a stop, his head striking a fir. For a moment he grunted as if stunned. Then he caught sight of the deputy weaving unsteadily on her feet, heading for the pistol. He jumped up.

"Leave it alone, bitch!" he screamed. Welton hurled himself toward her.

DAKOTA HEARD THE TWO shots. He skidded to a halt, M-4 in hand. Storm surged ahead, speeding toward the noise. His heart plummeted as he breathed raggedly, orienting and trying to locate the direction of the sound. Had Welton found Shelby? He hurled himself down the hill, on the heels of his gray wolf, who ran with her ears pinned against her skull.

The slippery, loose pine needles made him skid as he moved down the steep incline. Between the trees, Dakota spotted a wide horse trail. The noise had come from that direction. As he flipped the safety off on his M-4, he kept running with his focus on finding Shelby. Who had fired that pistol?

Dakota wove around a large thicket near the trail, his heart rate tripling. There, on the trail, was Welton and he had Shelby on the ground. Dakota's gaze jerked to the left. Another man lay lifeless on the trail a hundred feet away. He turned back to Shelby. She was kneeling on the trail, her hands tied in front of her, her neck stretched back against Welton's thigh as he held the pistol to her temple.

"Welton!" he roared, skidding to a halt, the M-4 jammed to his shoulder, the stock tight against his cheek. He had the convict's snarling face in his scope, the crosshairs painted against his sweaty, angry face.

Welton jerked his head upward toward the bellowing sound. His mouth dropped open for only a second. Shelby was drugged and it was easy to get some rope he'd carried with him tied around her hands. She struggled feebly, but his tight grasp on her hair forced her to remain where she was. "Back off!" he screamed at the man with the rifle two hundred feet above them. Who was this bastard? Whoever he was, Welton knew he was military by the way he stood frozen with that rifle. He pressed the pistol into Shelby's temple.

"Drop your weapon or I blow her head off!"

Dakota's entire focus was through the Nightforce scope. "Drop your pistol or I'm putting a round through your head, Welton." His heart pounded wildly in his chest. He tried to compensate for his ragged breathing as he kept the crosshairs steadied on Welton.

"Like hell I will," Welton snarled. His finger curved against the trigger.

Suddenly, out of nowhere, a gray wolf flashed toward Welton.

Dakota saw Storm crash out of the brush to the left of the convict. She charged Welton, mouth open, lips curled, revealing long white canines, aimed directly at him.

It was just the diversion Shelby needed. As Storm burst out of the bushes, she jerked up her left elbow and struck Welton in the crotch.

Welton cried out as her elbow connected with his genitals. The pistol jerked away from her temple. He doubled over, his hand releasing her hair as he aimed the pistol at the charging wolf. Shelby cried out, collapsing on the trail, the last of her energy dissolving.

Dakota took the shot. One to the head. The M-4 bucked savagely against his shoulder. The booming sound echoed loudly. The shot hit Welton and flung him backward a good three feet. By the time Storm leaped upon him, Welton was dead, half his skull blown away.

Dakota sprinted down the hill. Shelby was rolling over, trying to get up, still fighting to survive. He skidded down the hill and onto the trail.

"Shelby, lie still!" he ordered harshly. He just wanted to make sure the bastard was dead, and he was. Storm panted nearby. Dakota ran to check on the other man on the trail. He turned him over and was stunned. What was Curt Downing doing in this mess? He pressed two fingers to the man's exposed throat and found no pulse.

Dakota jerked the radio from his belt and reported it all to Cade. He went toward where Shelby was sitting up, giving the GPS coordinates. They were in deep forest and there was no way a helicopter would get into the area. Signing off, he jammed the radio into his belt and knelt down in front of her. He laid the M-4 aside. Dakota quickly untied the ropes binding her wrists and threw them aside.

His hands came to rest on her shoulders. She was trembling. "Shel, it's all right. You're safe now. Are you hurt?" Of course she was and Dakota examined her from head to toe. He saw no gunshot wounds, no massive bleeding anywhere else on her body. Relief coursed through him. Her eyes were wild, her pupils abnormally dilated. She'd definitely been drugged.

"Come here," he rasped, dragging her into the safety of his arms. "You're going to be okay, Shel. God, I love you." He held her tightly against him. Her breath came out in choking sobs. Her face was dirty, scratches across her cheek and her hands were bloodied. As she quivered uncontrollably, he had new worries. He kissed her tangled hair. "He drugged you, didn't he?"

Shelby felt herself falling off the edge of an invisible cliff, her consciousness beginning to disintegrate. "Y-yes," she forced out, the rest of the words hung up in her mind, not accessible to her mouth. She felt the strength and power of Dakota's arms around her. The shock of it all made her shake uncontrollably. Welton had been about to kill her. She heard Dakota's heart racing against her ear as he shifted. He slid one arm beneath her legs and the other around her shoulders.

"Hang on," he growled, standing and pulling her into his arms. "I'll get you help. Just hold on, Shel…."

They were the last words she heard as he crushed her against himself and turned on the trail. *Help.* She was going to get help. The rough weave of the damp shirt beneath her cheek gave her solace. She was safe….

"SHE'S COMING AROUND," Jordana told Dakota quietly, who anxiously waited nearby. She adjusted the IV drip into Shelby's arm. "Just be with her. She's going to need some orientation."

Dakota nodded. He'd not left her side since getting Shelby down to a major trailhead where the sheriff's deputy cruiser was waiting for them. A U.S. Forest Service helicopter was nearby, rotors already turning, to take Shelby and him to the Jackson Hole Hospital.

The door softly shut and the light blue private room became silent once more. Moving forward, Dakota slid his hand over Shelby's shoulder. In the past hour since they'd arrived, Jordana McPherson had overseen her care. Shelby had been given a cocktail of drugs to combat the drug Welton had given her. All Dakota could do was wait while the doctor and nurses cared for her.

Cade Garner had already stopped by. The two bodies had been recovered at the trail and were now in the city morgue, waiting to be examined by the medical examiner.

Dakota watched as Shelby's long blond lashes began to flutter, a sign of consciousness. He hadn't had time to clean up. He was filthy, dusty and sweaty, but he didn't care. He wasn't ever going to leave Shelby's side until she was awake and he was convinced she was going to be all right. She had gone into convulsions on the helicopter flight to the hospital. The paramedic on board had stabilized her, but it showed the power of the drug Welton had given her. Jordana told him later that she would have died from an overdose and Dakota had found her just in time.

Dakota noticed her lips parted and he saw her swallow. Leaning down, he pressed a kiss to her wrinkling brow.

"It's okay, Shel. You're here in the Jackson Hole Hospital. You're going to be all right."

Dakota gently squeezed her shoulder as he watched her. Jordana had warned him that coming off the drug would cause her to be cold, weak and shaky. Antidrugs given to her earlier would annul the virulent effects of the drug Welton had given her. She would survive, but the withdrawal would be brutal, too.

Shelby could hear Dakota's low, deep voice near her ear. She'd felt the warmth of his lips on her sweaty forehead, his moist breath soothing her. Fighting for consciousness, Shelby oriented her focus to his large hand on her shoulder. It was warm. Some of her fear began to dissolve. It took every bit of strength for her to lift her lashes. As she did, everything was blurry.

"Don't fight so hard," Dakota rasped, touching her cheek. "You're coming out of a drug overdose, Shel. You're okay. You're safe." This seemed to appease her and she ceased her struggles. Even now she was trying to fight. Fight to survive. He cupped her jaw and brushed her dry, cracked lips with his mouth. He wanted to breathe his life into her, erase the death that still held her in its grip. He kissed her tenderly. His heart mushroomed with such love for Shelby that he had to force himself to ease away from her mouth. As he did so, her cloudy blue eyes opened for the first time. He smiled. Her pupils were no longer so dilated.

"Shel?" he called softly, his face inches from hers. Their breaths mingled. "You're doing fine. You're coming out of it…" He threaded his fingers gently through her hair.

A lump stuck in Shelby's throat as she drowned in the glittering gold-brown of Dakota's eyes. They burned with love for her, the raw emotions in them, the care so apparent in his expression. The hardened SEAL mask disappeared. In its place, a man deeply shaken by many conflicting emotions. Closing her eyes, she forced her lips to work. "I love you...."

Her whispered words shattered him. Dakota pulled back a little more, his large hand cupping her pale cheek. "I know you do. And I love you, too, Shel. I'm here and I'm not leaving your side."

It took another hour before Shelby was truly conscious. Her vision cleared, the blurriness dissolving and everything in sharp, clear detail. Dakota was sitting in a chair at the side of her bed, facing her, his hand wrapped firmly around her cool, chilly one. Blips of her experience began to tease her spotty memory. Horror and terror riffled through Shelby like pulverizing ocean waves. She clung to Dakota's warm, strong hand because it fed her strength and helped ground her back in the present. Here. With him. She took a deep breath, her voice raspy.

"Welton?"

Dakota eased out of the chair. He saw clarity in her shadowed blue eyes. "Dead. I shot him."

The finality, the tightly held rage he held in check, pummeled her. Now the SEAL mask was back in place, the implacable warrior who had saved her life. She swallowed hard. "Thank you…" She frowned. "The other man…Curt…?"

"Welton must have shot him. He was dead when I arrived."

Nodding, her mouth dry, she whispered, "Yes, Curt rides his horse on the trails. He was in the wrong palce at the wrong time. He tried to stop Welton." She then uttered, "He shot Curt." Dakota nodded and said nothing. Shelby felt a bit more strength flow into her limbs. "Can you help me sit up? I need some water. I'm dying of thirst."

In moments, Dakota had the bed levered upward so that she was sitting up at a comfortable angle, pillows behind her back. He poured water from the blue plastic pitcher into a glass. He slid his arm behind her shoulders, holding her as he gently pressed the rim of the cup to her lower lip. She drank all of it.

"More?"

"No…thanks…" Shelby sighed as he eased her back against the pillows. She closed her eyes for a moment, her emotions crashing through her like the huge up-and-down drafts of a thunderstorm. Tears leaked from beneath her lashes.

It was heartbreaking for Dakota to see the silvery paths of tears down her taut, pale face. He moved closer to her bedside and gently smoothed them away. He still didn't know what had happened between her and Welton. He was afraid to ask. Jordana had inspected her closely and found nothing but bruises and scratches. He pushed away strands of blond hair from her face, just as she opened her eyes once more. They were dark and filled with emotions he couldn't decipher.

"God, I feel awful. What the hell did he shoot me up with?"

"A drug to knock you out." Dakota wouldn't tell her she'd been given a lethal dose. She didn't need to hear that right now. Maybe much later.

"It did that." Shelby felt more aware, more in her body. She held Dakota's worried stare. "I'm remembering things now...." She reached out, sliding her hand into his. As his fingers wrapped around hers, she sighed. "After he jumped me at the bushes, where the child was, I blacked out."

"The little toddler is safe and sound," he reassured her, seeing the question in her eyes. "Back with her parents."

"Thank God. Welton stole the baby to lure me into his trap."

"Yeah, I finally put that part together, too," Dakota muttered.

"Took me a while to figure it," she said with distaste.

"Hey," he called softly, touching her chin, "don't be hard on yourself, Shel. No one could have seen this coming."

"Maybe not." She shrugged, which caused sharp

pain in her shoulder. She reached up, sliding her fingers across it and remembering more. "I woke up in a truck. I was lying on the backseat. I was coming out of the drug haze and seeing Welton driving like a demon."

"A fisherman at the wharf where he tied up the boat saw him drag you out of it and into a green Chevy pickup truck. Do you remember any of that?"

Shaking her head, she licked her dry lips. "No… nothing."

"That fisherman not only had the license plate of Welton's truck, but he gave me the keys to his Jeep so I could pursue him."

"That was so kind of him," she murmured, touched. "As evil as Welton was, we have people like that fisherman who tipped the scales in the opposite direction."

Dakota breathed a sigh of relief. Shelby seemed almost completely present, her voice stronger, her mind working. He continued to hold her hand. "Welton had chosen one of two dirt roads that were close together. I stopped and talked to a driver of an SUV who had engine problems, and he saw the truck race by, but didn't see which road Welton took. I parked and ran over to both of them to try to figure it out. There were a lot of fresh skid marks on one, and that's the one I took. It was the right road."

"I knew I had to get out of the truck. I knew once he stopped, I was dead. I unlatched the rear door and somehow dived out it." Shelby shook her head. "I felt like a rag doll. My legs wouldn't work right. I was weaving around. I couldn't run a straight line if I tried."

"I don't know how soon after I got to where he crashed the truck." Dakota felt some satisfaction as he added, "Storm already had your scent and when I turned her loose, she headed back down the road where you had apparently fallen out of the truck. She led me directly to you."

Rubbing her brow, a headache coming on, Shelby whispered, "Bless Storm. She made the difference. Curt Downing surprised me. He was riding his horse around the corner at a trot. He damned near ran over me. I couldn't even move to get out of his way. I was helpless. By that time, Welton had caught up to where I was." She shook her head. "Curt Downing tried to help me, but Welton shot him off his horse." She looked up at Dakota's grim expression. "That horse went ballistic and crashed into Welton, knocking him away from me."

"And that's when I arrived on the scene."

"I saw you put the rifle to your shoulder. He had a hold of my hair and I couldn't do anything. The drug was taking me under. I had no fight left in me."

"You had enough left in you to jam your elbow

into the bastard's crotch. You gave me a clear shot, Shel." Dakota reached over and looked deeply into her marred eyes. "You fought with everything you had. You never backed off even with the drug in your system." His voice lowered, unsteady. "You're the bravest woman I've ever seen. You were magnificent. I don't think anyone else would ever have done what you did. You saved yourself from Welton."

CHAPTER TWENTY-FIVE

"I WANT TO GO HOME." Shelby looked up at Jordana and then Dakota, who stood nearby. The doctor frowned as she checked her vitals and the IV.

"Shelby, you nearly died from a drug overdose." She took out a penlight and held Shelby's jaw lightly. "Look into my eyes," Jordana said, moving the light slowly from one eye to the other.

Dakota said nothing, just watched Shelby's eyes dilate properly and then move back to their normal size. It had been four hours since she'd regained consciousness.

"Okay," Jordana said, concern in her tone. She looked across the bed at Dakota. "I know you were a trained combat medic."

"That's right."

Jordana turned back to Shelby. "You're not out of the woods yet. But what I can do is let Dakota take you home and stay with you. He knows the signs of drug overdose, of convulsions. I'll give him some medicine in case you need it."

Shelby swallowed hard. She was so grateful. "Thanks. I owe you one...."

"I'm so glad to be home," Shelby whispered as she was led to her bedroom with Dakota's hand beneath her elbow. Her knees were still unsteady and he was afraid she'd fall.

"You have a beautiful house," he said, looking around. Entering the bedroom, he noticed a pink, flowery spread across the queen-size bed. The drapes were open, allowing in light.

"I feel safe here," Shelby said. She'd called her parents earlier and let them know she was all right. They were going to travel back to Jackson Hole tomorrow to see her and take up residence once more in their home.

Dakota helped her sit down on the edge of her bed. "God, I feel weak. How long is this drug going to make me feel like this?" she asked. His expression was readable, his eyes filled with vigilance. He hadn't cleaned up yet. His beard darkened his face, making him look more the warrior she knew he was and always would be.

"Probably in another twelve hours you should be past most of these symptoms. Would you like a bath? A shower?"

Shelby shook her head. "I'm just tired." She moved her palm across the well-worn spread. It was soft and comforting to her. "I need two things," she told him huskily, meeting and holding his dark gaze. "I need sleep and I need you holding me tonight." The sky was bright with afternoon sunlight.

She lifted her chin and waited for his answer. She saw a glint come to his eyes.

"Anything you want, Shel," he said in a low voice. Reaching out, Dakota grazed her hair. "Do you want help undressing? Do you want to wear your nightgown?"

She caught Dakota's hand and pressed a kiss to the back of it. She drew his hand to her cheek. "I'll get myself to bed. You come when you want."

"I'll get a shower and shave first. I stink," he said.

A slight smile pulled at the corner of her mouth. Shelby released his hand and he felt softened tingles moving heatedly across his skin. How badly he wanted to love Shelby. He wanted to make things right. Make the fear he saw banked in her eyes go away forever. He knew he could do it. "I'll be back in a little while," he promised.

NEARLY TWO HOURS LATER, Dakota slid into bed beside Shelby. She was sleeping soundly on her side, one hand tucked beneath her cheek. There was now a faint blush across her cheeks. It hurt him to see the deep scratch across her temple where she'd run through brush to escape Welton. As he pulled the drapes closed, the sun hanging lower on the western horizon, the room grew shadowed.

Dakota moved slowly to Shelby's side so as not to awaken her. She was as naked as he was. He smiled and gently eased one arm behind her neck and the pillow. He curved his body against hers and placed his other arm across her waist, holding her close. Holding Shelby safe.

Dakota didn't know how long he lay awake. It didn't matter. Beneath his arm, he could feel the slow rise and fall of her breasts as she slept. After he started to hold her, Shelby seemed to breathe more evenly and sink into a deeper slumber. It told him she felt safe in his arms. *Protected*.

He thought about Ellie. The court trial. The horrifying pictures flashed for the jury to realize what had been done to his sister. As Shelby slept soundly in his arms, cocooned by his body, he felt profound relief and the soul-eating guilt over Ellie's death was released. He'd only been seventeen years old at the time, unable to help Ellie at all. Now it was as if he'd been given a second chance to avenge her death. Only this time, he was a SEAL, trained to use controlled violence when demanded. As he inhaled the sweet scent of nutmeg through the silky strands of Shelby's hair that tickled his jaw, he reveled in the fact that he had been able to save Shelby. It didn't minimize Ellie's death. But it helped Dakota to put it all into perspective.

SEAL training gave him the tools, the dangerous edge he needed to find Shelby when no one else could have. Storm had done her part, too. She'd sped up the process of finding her. The wolf had made all the difference.

Dakota closed his eyes. The woman now in his arms, resting safe against him, was the one he wanted in his life until he took his last breath. He knew Shelby loved him as fiercely as he loved her. And he silently promised her that he would show her every day just how much she meant to him and his badly injured heart. Shelby was healing him, whether she knew it or not.

Rising on his elbow, Dakota could see her profile in the gray light. Tears still fell down her cheeks. She was deep in sleep, probably reliving the nightmare of yesterday. Leaning down, Dakota placed his lips over the swollen cut on her temple. Whispering her name, he told her she was safe. He rested his chin against her hair. Almost instantly, the tears stopped and once more, the tension left her body. Humbled that he had a healing effect on Shelby, he slowly resumed his sleep position once more.

Dakota had never thought it possible that a human could heal another. Yet that was what he'd just experienced. Love was deeply healing. He loved Shelby.

And then his old fears came back to haunt him at a moment when he was completely vulnerable. He was far too damaged to be with Shelby. Was it fair to her to burden her with someone like him? Dakota was always afraid of his PTSD. He'd broken a nurse's arm when she'd touched him while he'd been asleep. He lived in silent terror of doing something like that to Shelby. Shutting his eyes tightly, Dakota tried to get a handle on those damn demons of his. He'd never had anyone challenge them until Shelby walked boldly into his life. His love and his darkness were at war. He wasn't sure which side would win.

Dakota wished with all his heart he could remove the pain and trauma Shelby suffered. The body, the emotions, remembered those times, as he knew too well himself. And he was sure that in the coming days, weeks and months, Shelby would experience all of them in their jagged, cutting intensity.

He had suffered similar effects from war. Trauma was trauma. At least he'd be at her side to guide her through. He'd never had support, but she would. The love Dakota felt for her swelled his chest, filled him until he thought he might die of joy. He'd never experienced this before.

Somewhere in the coming night, Dakota heard an owl calling near the window. Exhaustion washed over him as he, too, relaxed and gave in to the tiredness of his body and his wounded soul. Dakota slept with the woman he loved, grateful she was safe, in his arms.

SHELBY AWOKE WITH A start. Her entire body spasmodically jerked. And just as swiftly, she felt Dakota's reaction, his arms automatically holding her a little more tightly, a little more surely, as if to tell her she was safe. *Safe.* Weak morning light filtered in around the drapes. The room was muted with gloom, but she relaxed, an anguished breath escaping her. Her heart was pounding. She felt his long, callused fingers splayed out across her torso, holding her against his warm, strong body.

"All right?" Dakota asked, his voice thick with sleep.

Automatically, Shelby slid her hand over his forearm. "Just images..." she managed, her voice hoarse, emotions still riffling through her. The terror was still with her. But she had Dakota and he needed her, too. It was a frightening thought and she was too vulnerable, too much in shock to absorb it. Was she the woman he needed? Would he always come if she needed him? He'd been there for her without fail. Dark, questioning emotions warred with her heart. The trauma forced her to question everything.

Dakota instantly came awake; it was a natural SEAL reaction. From exhausted sleep to total alertness, as if an enemy were nearby. He pushed up on his elbow and he eased Shelby onto her back so he could look directly into her eyes.

Inwardly, Dakota winced as he saw tear tracks down her drawn cheeks. It hurt him to see her like this. He could stand anything but a woman or child crying. His chest felt as if it were being twisted in two by a vise. Reaching out, Dakota coaxed strands of blond hair away from her cheek. "Bad dream?"

Holding his alert golden gaze, her pulse still pounding, she nodded. "I—I'm a little emotional right now...."

"You're coming off that drug, that's why. It makes you feel crazy and you question everything," he quietly reassured her, holding her shattered blue gaze. Her pupils were okay, but Dakota not only felt but saw the savage emotions working through her. Shelby was struggling to contain them, to combat and suppress them. *Not this time.* "Come here," he rasped, pulling her tightly against him as he rolled over onto his back. "You need to get it out of your system, Shel. I'll hold you. Go ahead..."

The gruff tenderness in his voice comforted her. She turned and curved her body against his, head nestled in the crook of his shoulder. "I—I have this terror in me. I feel like it's eating me alive, making me question everything." Shelby slid her hand across his massive, darkly haired chest. She shut her eyes, fighting back the lump in her throat.

"Shel, I've been where you are. It's a kind of demon that wants to control you. It isn't about drugs, it's about trauma. The key is—" he pressed a kiss to her brow "—to fight it."

As much as Shelby struggled to suppress the sob, it tore out of her throat. The sound that came out sounded like that of a wounded animal. Her entire body convulsed against his. Dakota pulled her as tight as he could, as if to shelter her from the storm within her.

Dakota closed his eyes, jaw resting against her hair. Shelby's arms tightened around him as she sobbed her pain. He did not let her go. Her fingers dug frantically into his flesh, opening and closing almost spasmodically. Dakota understood the depth of her uncontrolled fear. Shelby was familiar with Ellie's trial. She'd been a witness for the prosecution, seen the horrific pictures. She understood what Hartley and Welton would have been capable of doing to her. Dakota buried his face in the strands of her soft hair, her sweet scent mingled with the animal-like sounds tearing out of her. He simply held her, absorbing as much of her pain as he could.

Shelby lost track of time, of place. She felt out of her body, as if her soul were fragmenting, tearing slowly apart into jigsaw pieces. Only Dakota's arms, his quiet strength held her together. Her tears tangled and soaked into the dark hair across his chest. Shelby couldn't stop weeping, controlled by her emotions, the drugs in her system, the overwhelming desire to live.

She felt like a leaf torn off a tree during the most savage storm she'd ever experienced. It was Dakota's low, vibrating voice near her ear, his moist breath flowing across her cheek, that allowed her to hold on, to ride out this violence swirling within her. She fought her own demons now. But he was here, supporting her, feeding her with his strength. His hand ranged slowly up and down her spine, soothing her, taming the violence she felt moving out of her. Each touch of his scarred fingers trailing across her spine, brought her a little more peace and a little less agony with each stroke.

Finally, Shelby lay utterly exhausted in his arms, but he didn't stop stroking her shoulders and spine. He knew she needed this contact with reality, this grounding, to finally loosen the grip of the horror of the past two weeks. And then she slept. Really slept in his arms, his body a barrier against the terror in her life, a protection and promise of better times ahead.

The next time Shelby awakened, she was fully aware of resting on Dakota's shoulder. His chest hair tickled her chin and nose. Unconsciously, Shelby moved her hand languidly across his powerful expanse, fingers tangling in the soft, silky hair of his chest. She felt his flesh tense and a ragged sound escape his lips. His hand moved across hers.

"Shel?" His voice was drowsy, filled with concern.

"It's okay," she whispered, pressing a small kiss to his chest wall. Again, she felt him tense, as if controlling himself. "I want you. All of you," she whispered, pulling her head back just enough to meet his narrowing eyes.

"Are you sure?" he asked, his arm moving across her shoulder. Dakota had no idea of time, only that the room was bathed in eastern sunlight. His mind was groggy, desperately needing more sleep. But right now he was hotly aware of Shelby's body against his, the amazing and stunning clarity in her blue eyes. He could see real life in them for the first time since the incident. His Shel was home. There was no doubt that she was fully present. Dakota felt himself harden, wanting her so damn bad. Yet he knew when people were traumatized, they did things they were sorry for later. Trauma was a chameleon and he had no wish to make love with her if she really wasn't fully aware of what she was asking for. Sex could wait. He was far more concerned about healing her fragile emotional and mental state.

"Do I not look sure?" Shelby arched her brows and gave him a reckless smile. She lifted her hand, her fingertips tingling as she cupped his cheek. "I need you, Dakota. All of you. I know what I'm doing. I know what I need—*you*." She saw his hesitation, maybe his concerns stirring? *To hell with it.*

Leaning up, she pushed him back on the bed, moving her body over his, their hips meeting and branding each other. She planted her elbows on either side of his head, looked deeply into his eyes.

Her fingers moved gently across his scalp, his hair soft as she tangled and engaged the short, clean strands. Their noses almost touched.

"I love you. You saved my life. You held me when I was hurting. Now," Shelby whispered before she placed her lips lightly upon the hard line of his mouth, "I want to celebrate life. I want to love you, Dakota. I'm bruised, not broken. And yes, I'm a little stiff in the shoulder but nothing that won't go away in a few days." Shelby sighed against his mouth. She felt him tremble, as if giving himself permission to return her slow, teasing wet kiss.

His hands roved from her shoulders, down the length of her long, strong spine to her flared hips. Curving his hands down to where her thighs melted into her hips, Dakota heard her moan. His callused fingers enflamed her flesh and slowly, deliberately caressed her. Her mouth deepened against his as he moved his fingers closer to her center of moistness and warmth. His body hardened beneath her cajoling hips, scalding his erection as their mouths clung hotly to each other.

Lost in the strength and tenderness of his mouth, Shelby eased onto her back with Dakota on top of her. The sheets were cool against her heated flesh. His body hard and tense, his flesh hot against her own, sent her arching hips to meet his.

As powerful as Dakota was, Shelby could feel him monitoring the amount of weight he placed against her body, monitoring the amount of pressure against her hungry lips. She ached to feel more of him. Frustrated, she dug her fingers into his flesh, letting him know she wasn't any china doll that would break. She thrust her hips solidly against his erection and instantly felt him tense, a low animal growl vibrating through his chest. She loved the sound rumbling through him, resonating within her body. She placed her lips against his mouth.

"My turn," she whispered against him, and she eased herself across his hips, moving on top of Dakota. She settled her thighs against him. The smoldering look in his eyes scorched her body and her entire lower body spasmed. There were so many small and longer scars across his torso, chest and shoulders. Dakota had suffered so much and she purposely ran her fingers across each one, memorizing each one, licking his flesh, kissing it and wanting to remove the memory forever. He quivered each time her lips lightly grazed each one, heightening her hunger of him. Even though he was a man with demons, he'd risen above his own tortured existence and had held her while she hurt and cried out her pain. Now Shelby was going to help dissolve the memory of each of those battle scars he'd gotten over the years.

Dakota's lips lifted away from his gritted teeth as she moved her wet core slowly up and down him. Automatically, he captured her sweet hips, staring up into her glinting blue eyes that reminded him of a hunter stalking her prey. He was no prey, and lifted her just enough to sheathe deeply into her. In that instant, Shelby froze, her back arching, a moan of pleasure tearing out from between her parted lips. Her eyes closed, head tipped back, a vulnerable smile across her lips as she welcomed him into her silky, wet confines. Dakota lifted his hands and slid them around the soft globes of her breasts. He leaned up as she sank downward. His lips met the first hardened nipple, suckling strongly on it, and then the other. She trembled violently beneath his touch. Hunter had turned into prey with soft, malleable flesh between his large hands. He thrust deeply into her, and her eyes closed. She absorbed his male strength into her yielding body, a flush spreading rapidly across her cheeks.

Shelby was strong, pliant and hungry. He brought her into a frantic, plunging rhythm with himself. Breasts teasing him against his chest, Dakota hotly took her mouth, thrusting his tongue deeply into her. He felt her stiffen, felt more than heard a cry of raw satisfaction originate from very deep within her body. Her spine grew taut as the heat exploded between them, deluging them with feverish outward ripples of intense primal pleasure.

He was grateful for the fire that rolled through him. Shelby clung to him, her fingers still digging frantically into his thick shoulders. He prolonged her orgasm, moving his hands to her hips, thrusting deep and keeping the pressure against her core. She cried out suddenly and he removed that steel control over himself. She languished in continuing orgasms beneath his onslaught. Drawing in air between his clenched teeth, Dakota gripped her tightly against him, his face pressed against her slender neck, lost in the fusion of scalding oneness. His release went deep into her writhing body. Her breath sharpened against his as she sought and found his mouth. Her lips curved across his, taking him to places he had never known existed before this moment.

CHAPTER TWENTY-SIX

"WELCOME BACK, SHELBY."

"Thanks, Cade. Good to be back." Shelby gave her boss a smile as she picked up her weapon. For the past two weeks she'd been on medical leave. It felt great to be working again.

"How's Dakota doing?"

She slid the gun into the holster on her right hip. "Moving down here to my home." Wrinkling her nose, she added, "Not that he has that much to move. The guy was living off the land. Some clothes, but that's all."

Cade leaned back in his chair and studied her. "You're happy?"

Shelby's smile grew. "You're the first to know, Cade." She held up her left hand to show him a small diamond engagement ring.

"I already noticed that when you walked in," he said drily, his grin widening. "Couldn't happen to two better people. Congratulations. Have you set a date?"

"Thanks. We're looking at an October wedding.

We want everyone to attend. My mother is helping me with the invitations as we speak."

"We'll look forward to being there to see you two married off."

She sighed and said in a quieter tone, "He's an incredible person, Cade. I guess it took this incident with Hartley and Welton for me to really see him.

"He's a SEAL whether he's still in the navy or not. And everything he'd ever been taught was put into play to save my life."

"He was worried about his PTSD and living with you," Cade said.

Nodding, Shelby sobered and sat down in the chair in front of the desk. The morning sun was strong in the east office. "Dr. Jordana McPherson has him on an adaptogen to lower his cortisol levels. That's part of what causes PTSD. She's had success with other people who have had PTSD symptoms. I'm crossing my fingers it will help him."

Cade became grave. "Then Dakota can come and live among the rest of us and feel part of us, not alone any longer."

Shelby gave her boss a soft smile. "No one can live alone like he did. The first time I met him in at E.R., my heart just tore in two for him. Seeing the look in his eyes…"

"You pulled him out of that darkness, Shelby.

Maybe neither of you realized it for some time, but I saw it."

She nodded. "He'd talk to me about his demons from war. And I tried to understand and I couldn't, no matter how hard I tried." She took in a deep breath and admitted, "Until I got my own demons from Welton. Then I understood."

Cade's face grew sympathetic.

"Trauma is highly underrated, but we know that, as law enforcement. Firefighters see it, too, and so do paramedics. With the right woman in his life, Dakota will make the transition from being a loner to part of a group that respects and admires him. And I know he'll help you, too, Shelby. Sometimes two wounded people can be healers for each other."

Shelby folded her hands in her lap. Her voice trembled when she said, "Love heals us, Cade. But you know that from your own experience." He'd lost his wife and child in an accident years earlier. And later, he met a woman and they fell deeply in love. Cade hadn't believed he could love twice in his life, but he was proven wrong. Shelby saw his eyes warm.

"Love can heal the deepest of wounds," he agreed. "Changing topics, what's Dakota going to do with his female wolf? I know Fish and Game isn't going to like a gray wolf prowling around in the city limits of Jackson Hole."

"It got resolved by nature," she told him wryly,

smiling. "Three days ago when we were up at Dakota's cabin, a beautiful black wolf, a male, was standing just inside the tree line. Dakota and I watched Storm trot over, tail wagging, to meet him. They took off and disappeared. Yesterday, when I was helping him pack his clothes, we saw Storm and her new boyfriend again. It's as if she came back to tell us she was in love, too. Then they took off. Dakota thinks this young black wolf will start his own pack. Storm will be his alpha female."

"Two packs in the valley," Cade murmured. "Well, why not? It's a big valley. And we've wanted the wolf population to grow around here."

"Dakota talked to the guys over at Fish and Game yesterday and told them what had happened. They're deliriously happy about it. The head guy, Frank, thinks they'll mate. Storm is fully matured and Dakota's hoping at some point to see her pups. Another happy ending."

Sitting up in his chair, he chuckled. "Good, because I was having nightmare visions of people calling the sheriff's department, reporting a gray wolf trotting through their yard."

"It's taken care of," Shelby promised wryly, understanding his position.

"I like happy endings."

"So do I. Did you know that one of Dakota's SEAL buddies is going to visit today? This is an officer he worked with in his platoon. I haven't seen Dakota this excited about anything."

"Except you," Cade intoned with a grin.

She felt heat sweep up her throat and into her face. "Well…" she said, avoiding his humored look, "yes, except me." Dakota made her feel as if she were the only woman in the world. He loved her deeply and opened up like a book to her, sharing everything. Her heart swelled with a fierce love for the military veteran. Dakota had seen too much and survived when others did not. She became serious and held Cade's gaze. "He's had so much taken away from him. His sister…his family dying four years later. He had no one, Cade. His grandparents are gone, too. I think, in some ways, the SEALs are a brotherhood, another type of tight-knit family group that gave him the support and love he needed to survive all those other losses."

Grimly, Cade nodded. "I wouldn't disagree. So, his friend? Who is he?"

"Captain Jake Ramsey. He was AOIC, assistant officer in charge of Dakota's squad. After I agreed to marry Dakota, he called Jake and told him. So Jake is coming here to check me out." She grinned.

"Oh?"

"Yeah, I guess from what Dakota told me, in the SEAL community if a guy thinks he's fallen in love and wants to get married, someone from the platoon has to come and make sure."

"Make sure of what?"

Shelby chuckled. "Well, you have to hear the rest of this story. In the community they have a saying. If you haven't dirt-dived the woman, then you shouldn't be marrying her."

His brows rose. "Dirt-dived? What the hell does that mean?"

"That's what I asked Dakota because the slang brought up all kinds of weird pictures for me," Shelby said, her smile increasing. "In SEAL training, you get sandy, wet and dirty. It means you've dived down, done the training, absorbed the learning and experience to know it inside out. Dirt-diving means knowing everything about your subject, or," she said as she laughed, "in that case, Dakota learned the width, breadth and depth about me. He knows me as well as he knows himself, so that by getting married, there are no surprises, no hidden agendas. He said the SEAL community is very protective of their wives and children. Jake is coming to make sure Dakota has done his homework." She continued, "And really, I think Jake is coming because he and Dakota are like brothers. They've never been out of contact since Dakota left the SEALs. And from what Dakota has said, Jake lost his wife and baby to a drunk driver a number of years earlier. I guess Jake wants to see Dakota happy because he once had a family himself."

"That's a sad story," Cade said, no doubt feeling a kinship since his wife and child had been torn from him. "Where's he staying and how long is Jake visiting?"

"We have a guest bedroom at my—our house. Jake has three days before he has to fly to Washington, D.C., to the Pentagon for a top secret assignment."

"I'm sure he and Dakota are going to have a good time sharing and catching up."

Shelby rose and grinned. "Yes, I'm sure they will. Me? I'll just make Jake home-cooked meals while he's here and he'll be fat, dumb and happy about it."

Chuckling, Cade raised his hand. "Be safe out there, Shelby. You're back on the roster and back on duty."

She opened the door. "It feels good, Cade. Maybe my life will settle down now."

Grinning, Cade said wryly, "I don't know. Now you're going to be dirt-dived by this SEAL friend of his."

"Oh," she said and laughed, "all Jake is going to do is meet me and find out how much I love Dakota. I think they'll spend some quality time together at the house while I'm out in my cruiser giving speeding tickets and handling calls of bears or moose in backyards."

Shaking his head, Cade matched her laugh. "I'm

keeping you on day rotation for a month. I think you and Dakota can use that time wisely."

Would they ever! But Shelby said nothing and waved goodbye to her boss. Shutting the door to his office, she felt so happy she didn't even feel her boots touching the floor. She glided out the rear of the building to get her cruiser. Pushing open the rear door, Shelby looked up. The summer sky was a light blue with long, graceful strands of high cirrus clouds moving across it. She knew how excited Dakota was to see his teammate. By the time she got off duty and drove home, she'd get to meet this man whom Dakota felt so close to.

She chose a black Tahoe cruiser with *Sheriff* written in gold on both doors, opened it up and began to arrange the gear before she climbed in. Dakota would have all day alone with Jake Ramsey. She was sure they'd have plenty to talk about. She'd already put in a huge beef roast into a Crock-Pot, replete with carrots, potatoes and celery. When she got home at five tonight, she'd have dinner ready, except for making the gravy. Dakota assured her Jake would die and go to heaven with that kind of delicious, home-cooked meal.

Shelby smiled as she turned on the various radios situated below the dashboard. The familiarity of her job made her even happier. The worst was over. Her questioning whether she was the right woman for Dakota had been laid to rest. They'd had a long and deep emotional talk about their individual demons. And Dakota had finally realized that he could live with her, despite his PTSD. He was aggressively pursuing help from Dr. McPherson, which gave her relief. Plus, Shelby knew in her heart of hearts, their love for each other would build an unbreakable bridge between them. Love trumped all. She knew that. She was living it every day with Dakota.

As she pulled out into traffic to begin her shift, Shelby sighed, happy. Being Dakota's wife was an unexpected dream come true. She loved him with a fierceness that defied description. He loved her with an equal fierceness, her body still glowing after their lovemaking this morning. Yes, life was good. It didn't get any better than this.

WHEN SHE ARRIVED HOME, Shelby heard the laughter of two men out back on the patio of the house. Dakota's laughter was easy to recognize and she automatically smiled, dropping her keys in a bowl on the desk in the foyer. She knew Dakota would hear her come in to greet her. He was so damned alert and missed nothing.

She was right. He met her in the kitchen, his gaze growing warm as she walked into his arms. His mouth touched hers lightly and he kept his hand around her waist.

"How was your first day back at work?" he

asked, grazing her blond hair that she'd released from its ponytail.

"Great. It felt so good." She grinned. "Jake arrived?"

"Yeah, come on. I want to introduce you to my AOIC when I was a SEAL."

Shelby was more than a little curious about meeting this man who had been Dakota's officer in charge. As she moved out the opened door, she saw a deeply tanned man with military-short black hair and piercing gray eyes that reminded her of an eagle watching his prey. He wore a collegiate type of short-sleeved light blue shirt and pressed tan chinos. Jake Ramsey had the same kind of explosive, tightly held energy she'd encountered around Dakota. He was ruggedly handsome with a square face and as he stood, he appeared to be at least six feet tall. He wasn't muscle-bound, but clearly in top shape, not an ounce of fat anywhere on his body. Shelby saw a number of white scars on his leanly muscled arms.

"Jake, meet Shelby," Dakota said, releasing her waist so she could walk over and shake his hand.

"Ma'am," Ramsey said, nodding deferentially as he offered his hand to her. "It's nice to meet my best friend's lady."

Shelby looked down at his hand, feeling the thick calluses across his palm, many nicks and small white and more recent pink scars across his long, well-shaped fingers. Sliding her hand into his, she said, "Just call me Shelby. Welcome, Captain Ramsey. I'm glad you could visit Dakota. He really misses his SEAL family."

The man seemed to monitor the amount of strength in his grip and then released her hand. There was an aura of command around Ramsey, his shoulders thrown back, chin held level, his gaze moving across her face, as if memorizing it. If Shelby didn't know Dakota, didn't know that SEAL operators' lives depended upon their alert intelligence, she'd have been unsettled by his swift, intense inspection.

"Yes, ma'am, and we miss him equally as much." Ramsey smiled a little, his gaze moving to Dakota, who stood behind her. "He'll never tell you this, but he was our best operator in our platoon. As LPO, lead petty officer, he took care of the other seven shooters, as well as me and our OIC."

Part of his military lingo was lost on her. Shelby smiled and decided she'd ask Dakota for a translation later, when they were alone. She didn't wish to embarrass Ramsey for his military-speak. "I believe it." She turned and gazed warmly up at Dakota, who stood near her left shoulder. "I hope he told you he saved my sorry ass a couple of weeks ago?"

A reluctant, thin smile crossed the officer's serious features. "Yes, ma'am, he did. I'm not surprised. He saved all of us at one time or another Down Range."

Dakota snorted. "Hey, let's get off the topic of me, okay?" He placed his hands across Shelby's shoulders. She was still in uniform. "Want to get into civilian clothes and join us for some beer and chips before dinner?"

"Sounds like a great way to end my day. I'll see you two in a few," she said.

Dakota watched her leave, the sway of her hips making him want Shelby all over again. They had made love every night for the past two weeks, unable to get enough of each other. He turned and saw his AOIC staring at her with a frown.

"Problem?" Dakota asked, sitting down at the table and spreading his legs out in front of him.

Ramsey sat down. "I just find it hard to believe she's an effective law enforcement officer."

"Oh, here we go again," Dakota griped good-naturedly. He pulled the bag of opened potato chips over and poured more into a nearly empty bowl. "This is your women-are-weak bullshit rearing its ugly head again, Ramsey."

"You had to save her life. Isn't that the point?"

Dakota drilled a hard look into the SEAL officer's eyes. "Don't go there," he growled. "You don't know the full story. Shelby took out Hartley, who attacked her from behind, all by herself. You don't give women enough credit, Jake. Don't throw your bad experience with your sick mother on her. She's a damn good sheriff's deputy and she can have my back any day."

Jake chewed thoughtfully on the potato chip, hearing his LPO's passionate warning. "Thank God women aren't allowed in the SEALs. I'd have a real problem, then," he muttered.

Dakota knew when he said Shelby could have his back, that it was a SEAL operator's highest compliment he could pay to his—or her—comrade in arms. And he could see the emotional reaction in Ramsey's carefully arranged face. Normally, Jake was damned hard to read. He gave little away, if ever. As an operator, he was cool, calm and collected. The men were loyal to him and they trusted him out on an op. The only chink in his armor was women, one way or another. Ramsey had had a lousy childhood, a caretaker for a chronically ill mother. His father, a SEAL of great reputation in the ranks, was never home to care for her. Jake got saddled with caregiver duties for eighteen years of his life. He grew up fast and he matured quickly. Maybe, Dakota thought as he sat there in silence with his friend, that was the wound through which he saw all women.

"She's pretty."

"Yeah, I made the mistake of calling her a Barbie doll when I first met her. She shut me up real fast on that one." Dakota grinned fondly in remembrance of their first meeting. Then he allowed emotion into his voice. "She's got a good heart, is scary smart and has SEAL alertness," he told Ramsey in a quiet tone.

SHELBY SNUGGLED AGAINST Dakota's warm, strong body. It was nearly midnight, the house quiet once more. Moonlight filtered around the drapes, giving her just enough light to see his rugged profile. He lay on his back, his arm wrapped around her shoulders, bringing her solidly against his frame. "You're worried?"

Cutting a glance down at her, he pursed his lips. "I'm worried for Jake. He's like a brother to me, Shel. Something's eating away at him. It has been for years. It's taking him down in a way I can't reach, touch or change."

"You said he lost his wife and baby in an accident years ago?"

He nodded. "Yeah." His nostrils flared and he pushed his fingers through his short hair in frustration. "He's never gotten into a relationship since his wife died. He avoids women like the plague." And then Dakota scowled. "I should amend that. He had a woman in his past, Captain Morgan Boland. They had a red-hot love affair the last two years they were at Annapolis together. She accidentally got pregnant, miscarried his child and he ran from her."

"Ouch. Not the right thing to do," Shelby murmured, moving her hand across his chest, slowly sifting the thick, silky hairs through her fingers.

"Yeah, it was bad. And that's not like Jake. He's as steady and solid an officer any SEAL could ask for. He never runs from a fight."

"Because he took care of his mother for eighteen years? He saw this as a similar trap, maybe?"

Turning on his side, he studied Shelby's shadowed green eyes. "They met again in Afghanistan two years ago. I was there. I saw it. They've always had this fatal attraction for each other since they were twenty. They're twenty-nine now. And out of bed they fight like cats and dogs. It was Christmas and they spent it together. I was happy for Jake. I know Morgan has always held his heart, but I don't think he'll ever admit it or realize it." Scowling, he said, "They had one hell of a fight the third morning when we were saddling up to leave. You could hear them screaming at each other clear across the village. Morgan can't be tamed. She's a strong, intelligent and resourceful woman like you. I just don't think Jake can handle it or her. Not that you 'handle' a woman."

"Morgan sounds like my kind of gal. They're out there, Dakota. I'm one of them. Is he blind?"

"He's got to be. Whatever is stuck in his craw about women being weak is his Achilles' heel.

Maybe that's why he's had no one in his life since that Christmas two years ago."

"What woman worth her salt would want to stay with a guy like that? There's got to be respect between the two or it's not going to work."

"You're smart as a whip. You know that?" Dakota threaded his fingers through her hair, watching the pleasure dance across her face.

"Don't give me too much credit. In law enforcement, you learn a lot of psychology on the job regarding people's actions, reactions and motives. You have to take them into consideration in order to work positively with them."

"You're still a very intelligent woman, Shel." He caressed her lower lip with his thumb. "I'm a lucky man."

"Tell me something," she said, catching his hand and kissing it. "Why was Jake looking at me like I was some kind of alien from another planet? I tried to be nice to him. Not screw up and embarrass you. Did I say or do something wrong to earn that kind of look from him?"

Chuckling, Dakota pulled her against him, her head coming to rest on his chest, her hair a gold coverlet across it. "Don't let him bother you, Shel. He's got problems with any woman in combat."

"What?"

"Yeah, he thinks no woman can handle combat of any kind. Doesn't matter whether it's a woman in the military or outside in a civilian agency, like being a law enforcement officer or firefighter, for example."

Shelby absorbed the slow thud of Dakota's heart beneath her ear. He loved her and she had never felt so happy. "That's such a crock of bull."

"You and I know it. He doesn't."

"So I'm like some kind of bug under his prejudicial microscope of life?" Jake had agreed to be his best man at their wedding in early September.

"That pretty much sums it up."

"You know what I wish for him?" Shelby eased up on her elbow to meet his glittering eyes that burned with desire for her. "I wish with all my heart he someday meets his match. Only it's a woman who sits his ass in place this time around."

As he caressed her reddening cheek, Dakota felt her anger. "Calm down, Shel. I'm a believer. Women handle combat of all types, all the time. It might not be a war overseas, but there are plenty of wars on the streets of towns and cities. Women in the military are in ground combat in the Middle East right now." He lightly touched her nose and added, "You're in combat as a law enforcement officer every day."

Some of her frustration dissolved as he traced her brow with his thumb and his fingers trailed tantalizingly across her jaw and neck. His touch was electric. Provocative. And it made her hungry for him. "Okay, white flag. I'm in bed with you, not him, thank God."

Grinning, Dakota chuckled and hauled her over on top of him, their legs tangling among one another. "You should feel sorry for him, not angry." He slid his hands across her mussed hair and slowly moved his fingers down across her shoulders, tracing the outline of her long torso to her flared hips.

"Do you think he'll be home in time from this op to be your best man at our wedding?"

"I don't know, Shel. He's been pulled in on a top secret assignment. And once he knows what it is, he can't tell me. We'll just have to wait and see if we hear from him. I'm sure he's going Down Range. Back into combat. Jake has my email address. He knows where I live and I know he'll stay in touch with me."

Lying against his hard body, feeling the muscles shift and tense as she suggestively moved her hips against his, Shelby shook her head in frustration. "I hope for your sake he can, Dakota. I know he's like a brother to you."

Dakota needed all the cosmic family he could get. No one went through life alone. Soon, though, this fall, he would be absorbed into her loving family. Her father respected Dakota, and they got along like father and son. Her mother doted on him. She'd been baking him his favorite chocolate chip cookies once a week. No, Dakota would easily become part of her family. He deserved that kind of good dharma. He deserved her.

Leaning down, she grazed the hard line of his mouth, feeling him begin to relax, to focus on them…on her. Shelby saw the unspoken worry in his eyes for Jake. They had two more days together and she knew that time with his friend meant the world to Dakota. She silently promised not to make an issue of Jake any longer. Time was too short and she wanted the man beneath her to enjoy it with Jake. He deserved to be happy.

"I love you, Shel," he growled, capturing her face, tilting her chin to just the right angle to kiss.

A soften whisper slipped from her lips as she allowed Dakota to guide her mouth down upon his. "You are my life, my love, forever…."

* * * * *

A timeless seduction
A unique temptation
And a whole world of dark desires...

From *New York Times* bestselling author

GENA SHOWALTER

And from debut author

KAIT BALLENGER

It all happens in AFTER DARK

Available wherever books are sold!

Be sure to connect with us at:

Harlequin.com/Newsletters
Facebook.com/HarlequinBooks
Twitter.com/HarlequinBooks

www.Harlequin.com

REQUEST YOUR FREE BOOKS!

2 FREE NOVELS
FROM THE ROMANCE COLLECTION
PLUS 2 FREE GIFTS!

YES! Please send me 2 FREE novels from the Romance Collection and my 2 FREE gifts (gifts are worth about $10). After receiving them, if I don't wish to receive any more books, I can return the shipping statement marked "cancel." If I don't cancel, I will receive 4 brand-new novels every month and be billed just $6.24 per book in the U.S. or $6.74 per book in Canada. That's a savings of at least 22% off the cover price. It's quite a bargain! Shipping and handling is just 50¢ per book in the U.S. and 75¢ per book in Canada.* I understand that accepting the 2 free books and gifts places me under no obligation to buy anything. I can always return a shipment and cancel at any time. Even if I never buy another book, the two free books and gifts are mine to keep forever.

194/394 MDN F4XY

Name _____ (PLEASE PRINT) _____

Address _____ Apt. # _____

City _____ State/Prov. _____ Zip/Postal Code _____

Signature (if under 18, a parent or guardian must sign)

Mail to the **Harlequin® Reader Service:**
IN U.S.A.: P.O. Box 1867, Buffalo, NY 14240-1867
IN CANADA: P.O. Box 609, Fort Erie, Ontario L2A 5X3

Want to try two free books from another line?
Call 1-800-873-8635 or visit www.ReaderService.com.

* Terms and prices subject to change without notice. Prices do not include applicable taxes. Sales tax applicable in N.Y. Canadian residents will be charged applicable taxes. Offer not valid in Quebec. This offer is limited to one order per household. Not valid for current subscribers to the Romance Collection or the Romance/Suspense Collection. All orders subject to credit approval. Credit or debit balances in a customer's account(s) may be offset by any other outstanding balance owed by or to the customer. Please allow 4 to 6 weeks for delivery. Offer available while quantities last.

Your Privacy—The Harlequin® Reader Service is committed to protecting your privacy. Our Privacy Policy is available online at www.ReaderService.com or upon request from the Harlequin Reader Service.

We make a portion of our mailing list available to reputable third parties that offer products we believe may interest you. If you prefer that we not exchange your name with third parties, or if you wish to clarify or modify your communication preferences, please visit us at www.ReaderService.com/consumerchoice or write to us at Harlequin Reader Service Preference Service, P.O. Box 9062, Buffalo, NY 14269. Include your complete name and address.

ROM13R

LINDSAY McKENNA

77710 THE DEFENDER	___ $7.99 U.S.	___ $9.99 CAN.
77616 THE LAST COWBOY	___ $7.99 U.S.	___ $9.99 CAN.

(limited quantities available)

TOTAL AMOUNT	$ _____
POSTAGE & HANDLING	$ _____
($1.00 FOR 1 BOOK, 50¢ for each additional)	
APPLICABLE TAXES*	$ _____
TOTAL PAYABLE	$ _____

(check or money order—please do not send cash)

To order, complete this form and send it, along with a check or money order for the total above, payable to Harlequin HQN, to: **In the U.S.:** 3010 Walden Avenue, P.O. Box 9077, Buffalo, NY 14269-9077; **In Canada:** P.O. Box 636, Fort Erie, Ontario, L2A 5X3.

Name: _____

Address: _____ City: _____

State/Prov.: _____ Zip/Postal Code: _____

Account Number (if applicable): _____

075 CSAS

*New York residents remit applicable sales taxes.
*Canadian residents remit applicable GST and provincial taxes.

⊕ HARLEQUIN® HQN™
www.Harlequin.com

PHLM0713BL

DAILY WISDOM FOR
MOTHERS

A 365-Day Devotional

Michelle Medlock Adams

BARBOUR
PUBLISHING

ISBN 1-59310-175-9

Cover image © Getty Images

Published by Barbour Publishing, Inc., P.O. Box 719, Uhrichsville, Ohio 44683
www.barbourbooks.com

Our mission is to publish and distribute inspirational products offering exceptional value and biblical encouragement to the masses.

Member of the
Evangelical Christian
Publishers Association

Printed in the United States of America.
5 4 3 2 1

DAILY WISDOM FOR
MOTHERS

DEDICATION

For my mother, Marion, who is full of wisdom.
Thanks for always believing in me.
And for my mother-in-law, Martha.
Thanks for raising such a wonderful son.
I love you both!
Michelle (a.k.a. Missy)

INTRODUCTION

Let's face it. Life is busy—especially for moms. As a mother of two young girls, I find it challenging some days just to make time for a shower, let alone time to spend with God. I'm sure you face the same thing—you desire a deeper relationship with the Lord, but you don't have hours to spend in His Word every day.

That's why this book is perfect for moms like us. I wrote it with you in mind. Within these pages you'll find a quick, easy-to-read devotional for each day of the year. A Scripture and a short prayer complete each day's reading. Every month we'll tackle a different aspect of being a mom—so by the end of the year, we'll have become stronger and wiser in every area of our lives!

January's theme is "Casting Your Cares"—dealing with the worries, expectations, and obligations of being a mother. In February, the topic is "Loving Unconditionally," learning to show love to your children no matter what. March is all about "Taking the Time" and treasuring every moment of raising our children—even the 2 A.M. feedings. April's theme is "Becoming Mother of the Year"—giving up the quest for perfection and learning to see yourself as God sees you. In May, we'll spend time considering "Having a Thankful Heart" and learning to appreciate the everyday blessings, big and small. June's topic is "Dreaming Big Dreams" and allowing yourself to have dreams of your own—even in the midst of soccer practices and bake sales. In July, it's "Surviving the Good, the Bad, and the Ugly," learning to lean on God when being a mom seems too hard. August's theme, "Taming the Tongue," is about allowing God to use your words to edify and speak wisdom into your children's lives. For September, we'll discuss "Daring to Discipline" and following God's leading on the path to raising godly kids. October's topic is "Living to Give"—embracing the motherhood role and giving it all you've got! In November, we'll encourage "Praying More" and learning the importance of time on your knees as it relates to your children. Finally, in December, the topic is "Giving Your Kids to God." We'll explore trusting God totally with our children and teaching our kids about having a real relationship with Him.

I hope that you'll look forward to your devotional time each day. Grab a Diet Coke or a cup of java and spend some time with God today. Maybe you can squeeze it in while the kiddos are napping. Or maybe your best time with God is right after you put the children to bed at night. It doesn't really matter—whenever you sit down with this book, it'll be the right time. I pray that God will open your eyes and your heart as we take this daily journey together.

MICHELLE MEDLOCK ADAMS

"Come to me,
all you who are weary and burdened,
and I will give you rest."
MATTHEW 11:28

Ahhh. . .rest. Who wouldn't love a day of rest? But let's face it. Mothers don't really get a day of rest. If we rested, who would fix breakfast? Who would get the children ready for church? Who would do the laundry so your son can wear his lucky socks for the big game on Monday?

No, there's not a lot of rest in a mother's schedule. But, that's not really the kind of rest this verse is talking about. The rest mentioned in this verse is the kind of rest that only Jesus can provide. Resting in Jesus means feeling secure in Him and allowing His peace to fill your soul. That kind of rest is available to all—even mothers.

So, in the midst of the hustle and bustle of your life (even if you're elbow deep in dishwater), you can rest in Him. Start by meditating on the Lord's promises and His everlasting love for you. Make a mental list of the things in your life that you are thankful for, and praise God for each one. Allow His love to overwhelm you. . .and rest.

MOM TO MASTER
Lord, help me to rest in You—even when I'm overwhelmed with the "to-dos" of each day. I want more of You in my life. I love You. Amen.

CASTING YOUR CARES

JANUARY 2

*Cast all your anxiety on him
because he cares for you.*

1 PETER 5:7

Ever have one of those days? The alarm clock didn't go
off. The kids were late for school. The dog threw up
on the carpet. You spilled coffee down the front of
your new white blouse. Ahhh! It's one of those "Cal-
gon, take me away!" days, right?

But it doesn't have to be. No matter how many
challenges you face today, you can smile in the face of
aggravation. How? By casting your cares upon the
Lord. That's what the Lord tells us to do in His Word,
yet many of us feel compelled to take all of the cares
upon ourselves. After all, we're mothers. We're fixers.
We're the doers of the bunch. We wear five or six fe-
doras at a time—we can handle anything that comes
our way, right?

Wrong! But God can. When the day starts to go
south, cast your cares on Him. He wants you to! As
mothers, we can handle a lot, but it's true what they
say—Father really does know best. So, give it to
God. C'mon, you know you want to. . . .

MOM TO MASTER
*Lord, help me to turn to You when my troubles
seem too big to face alone and even when they don't.
Help me to trust You with all of my cares.
I love You, Lord. Amen.*

CASTING YOUR CARES

God is our refuge and strength,
an ever-present help in trouble.
PSALM 46:1

"MOM!" Allyson shrieked.

It was one of those "mom cries" that sends mothers into an instant panic. I heard my then five-year-old screaming for me, but I couldn't find her.

"Mom, hurry!"

Finally, I found her. She was way up in our live oak tree that stood in our front yard. . .and she was stuck. Trying to remember how to climb a tree, I inched my way up. Finally, when I could reach her, she clung to me like she'd never clung before. Once we were safely on the ground, I reminded Allyson that she wouldn't have been stuck in our tree if she'd been obedient. After all, she wasn't supposed to leave the backyard, and she certainly wasn't supposed to climb our tall tree—not without help.

Allyson's tree trauma is similar to how many of us walk with God. We do our own thing—and when we get stuck, we holler, "Help, God, and hurry!" After He rescues us, we cling to Him until we're safe. Then, we go about our own lives until we need Him again.

Wouldn't it be better if we just stayed close to God all the time—not just in troubled times? Then we wouldn't have to holler. He'd already be there.

MOM TO MASTER
Father, help me to stay near You all the time. Amen.

CASTING YOUR CARES

JANUARY 4

*"Who of you by worrying can add
a single hour to his life?"*
MATTHEW 6:27

If you're an '80s lady, you probably remember that catchy song "Don't Worry, Be Happy." (I bet you're singing it right now, aren't you?) You know, there's a lot of truth in that silly little song.

So many times, as mothers, we think it's our job to worry. After all, if we don't worry about the children, who will? Someone has to worry about their grades, their health, and their futures—right?

Well. . .not exactly. God tells us in His Word that worry is a profitless activity. Worrying about our children may feel like a natural thing to do as a mother, but in reality it's sin. Here's why. If we are constantly worrying about our kids, that means we're not trusting God to take care of them. It's like saying to God, "I know that You created the universe, but I'm not sure You know what's best for my children. So, I'll handle these kids, God."

When you put it that way, it sounds ridiculous, doesn't it? We would never say that to God, yet each time we give in to worry, that's the message we're communicating. So, do like the song says, "Don't Worry, Be Happy." God's got you covered!

MOM TO MASTER
*Father, I give all of my worries to You.
I trust You with my children. I love You. Amen.*

All you need to remember is that
God will never let you down;
he'll never let you be pushed past your limit;
he'll always be there to help you come through it.

1 CORINTHIANS 10:13 MSG

Overwhelmed. Yes, sometimes I feel like that's my middle name—"Michelle Overwhelmed Adams." I bet you share that feeling sometimes, too, don't you?

Being a mom is the toughest job any of us will ever have. Sometimes the demands are so great, I'm not sure I can do it all. From laundry to parent/teacher conferences to homework help—it's a lot to pack into one day. And, as grateful as we are to be mothers, we still get stressed.

Whether you work outside the home or at home—you're busy. When you feel that overwhelming sense of "I don't think I can do one more thing today" taking over—stop! Breathe deeply and remember that God promised He'd never give you more than you can handle. Isn't that good news?

So, when you're on your way to Wal-Mart at 10 P.M. to retrieve art supplies for your child's project that is due tomorrow—don't sweat it! Don't let the stresses of the day overwhelm you. Just smile and know that God has equipped you to handle anything.

CASTING YOUR CARES

MOM TO MASTER

Please be the Lord over the little and big things in my life. Thank You, God, that I don't have to feel over-whelmed today. Amen.

> *I call on you, O God, for you will answer me;*
> *give ear to me and hear my prayer.*
>
> PSALM 17:6

When Allyson was only three, she encountered an eight-legged friend who wasn't so friendly. That spider left his mark—a large, black circle on my little girl's right calf. I hadn't noticed the bite that morning because Allyson had dressed herself. But shortly after I arrived at work, the phone rang.

"Michelle, you need to get Allyson to a doctor right away," urged my daycare provider. "I think she's been bitten by a Brown Recluse."

Quickly, I drove to the daycare, scooped up Allyson, and headed for the doctor's office. Panicked, I called my husband and unloaded. Then, I called my mother and cried some more while Allyson sat calmly in her car seat—no tears, no fears.

Then I heard her sweet little voice say, "Don't cry, Mama. I prayed and Jesus is taking care of me."

In all of the confusion, I had neglected to call on the Great Physician. Thankfully, Allyson hadn't forgotten. She knew who to go to, even if her spastic mother didn't.

Allyson taught me a lot that day. She showed me that prayer should be instinctive. God should be the first One we "call" in every situation. Make sure He is first on your speed dial.

CASTING YOUR CARES

MOM TO MASTER
Lord, help me to pray without ceasing—
especially where my children are concerned. Amen.

"For I know the plans I have for you,"
*declares the L*ORD*, "plans to prosper you and not to*
harm you, plans to give you hope and a future."
JEREMIAH 29:11

Do you ever feel like you're not doing enough for your children? Sure, you enrolled them in ballet, karate, and gymnastics, but you forgot to sign them up for soccer—and now it's too late! The recording in your head begins playing, "You're a bad mother."

I hear that same recording. Sometimes, it plays nonstop.

I worry that I'm not providing my children with the opportunities that will bring success. What if they don't make the middle school soccer team because I didn't sign them up for summer soccer camp? What if they miss out on those academic scholarships because I didn't spend enough time reading with them when they were little?

What if? What if? What if?

You know, God doesn't want us dwelling in the land of "What If." He wants us to trust Him with our children. He wants us to quit "what if-ing!" God has a plan for their lives—better than you could ever imagine. So, relax. You're not a bad mother because you missed soccer camp sign-ups. If you've given your children to God, you've given them the best chance to succeed that you could ever give them!

CASTING YOUR CARES

MOM TO MASTER
Lord, I give my children to You. Thank You, God, for
Your plans. Amen.

JANUARY 8

*"But seek first his kingdom and his righteousness,
and all these things will be given to you as well."*

MATTHEW 6:33

Are you a planner? Are you a list maker? I think most mothers have to-do lists longer than their legs. You know, my list making became so addictive that I found myself making lists during our pastor's sermon on Sunday mornings. Of course, it looked like I was taking notes, but I wasn't—I was planning out my week.

The pastor was preaching about spending more quality time with God, and I was scheduling a fifteen-minute devotional time for Him somewhere on Thursday. Pretty sad, huh?

Well, I'm happy to say that there is life after lists. I am a recovering to-do list maker. It was a gradual process, but now I can actually sit through a sermon and truly focus on what the pastor is saying.

I've found such freedom in trusting God with my daily activities. Sure, I still have reminder sticky notes scattered around my house, but now I'm not ruled by a list. I've learned there is sweet rest and freedom in trusting God with my day.

So, before your feet hit the floor each morning, simply pray, "God I give this day to You." Let Him make your list. Trust me, His list is easier to accomplish and much more fulfilling.

MOM TO MASTER
*Lord, I commit this week to You. Help me to plan
wisely and follow Your leading. Amen.*

CASTING YOUR CARES

*I can do everything through him
who gives me strength.*
PHILIPPIANS 4:13

Remember that powerful song "I Am Woman" performed by Helen Reddy? I was just a youngster when it hit the charts, but I remember my mother belting out the lyrics: "I am strong. I am invincible. I am WOMAN!"

She sang that song with such passion. I didn't understand that emotion then, but I certainly understand it now. Aren't those empowering words?

There are some days when I can't muster the courage to sing, "I am woman, hear me roar. . . ." In fact, I feel more like singing, "I'm a worm on the floor." How about you? Do you ever feel less than powerful?

Well, I've got good news, and it's even better than Helen Reddy's song. God's Word says that we can do *all* things through Christ who gives us strength. All means all, right? So no matter how you feel today, you can accomplish whatever is on your plate. See, you don't have to *feel* powerful to *be* powerful. The God in you is all-powerful, and He will cause you to triumph. After all, you are more than a woman—you are a child of the Most High God. Now that's something to sing about!

MOM TO MASTER
Thank You, Lord, that even when I feel powerless, You are powerful. Help me to be courageous for You. Amen.

CASTING YOUR CARES

JANUARY 10

"Be still, and know that I am God."

PSALM 46:10

It was late, and the storm raged on.

Where is she?

Abby, my then nine-year-old, had gone to a theme park with her best friend. I had felt okay about letting her go—but that was before the tornado warnings had been issued. Now, I just wanted her home—crouched in the hall closet with the rest of us. I wanted to know she was safe. I wanted to hug her. I wanted to protect her.

My husband, Jeff, and I prayed that God would watch over her. Still, worry filled my heart. I needed to know she was all right.

Why don't they call?

Just then, the front door opened. Abby was home.

In those prior moments of worry, I had heard that still, small voice saying, "Be still, and know that I am God." But, I couldn't be still. My mind was filled with horrible thoughts and doubts. I wanted to trust God, but this was my baby!

Isn't that ironic? As moms, we're sometimes afraid to trust God with our children. But, what we fail to realize is this—He loves them even more than we do. He loved them before we ever held them in our arms. We can trust Him with our kids.

MOM TO MASTER
Thank You, Lord, for watching over my children—
even when I can't be there for them. Amen.

I will say of the LORD,
"He is my refuge and my fortress,
my God, in whom I trust."
PSALM 91:2

Somewhere deep within all moms lurks "Warrior Mom—Protector of Her Young." And, when Warrior Mom surfaces—look out!

My Warrior Mom alter ego surfaced not long ago when a little girl began bullying my oldest daughter. I was just about to call this child's mother and give her a piece of my mind when I heard: *Giving her a piece of your mind won't bring peace.*

Still, I longed to verbally annihilate this woman for raising such a mean-spirited daughter. But, God prompted me to pray for them. Of course, that was the last thing I wanted to do. Warrior Mom isn't a prayer, she's a fighter! But, I listened to that still, small voice and prayed. Do you know what happened? Abby and that little girl became friends, and later I was given the opportunity to pray with her mother during a family crisis.

If I had acted on my Warrior Mom instincts, I would never have had the opportunity to pray with this family. God didn't need Warrior Mom to handle the situation. He just needed me to follow His leading. So, the next time Warrior Mom is awakened in you, remember that God's got a better way.

MOM TO MASTER
Thank You, Lord, for taking care of my children better than I can. Amen.

JANUARY 12

There is a time for everything,
and a season for every activity under heaven.

ECCLESIASTES 3:1

If they gave an award for "World's Coolest Mom," my friend would win. She's nice and fun, and she throws the most elaborate birthday parties for her little girl. From games to treats to goodie bags—her parties rock!

Just before her daughter's seventh birthday, my friend was at it again. But in the midst of party-planning, her daughter kept asking, "Mama, will you play with me?"

After saying no several times, my frustrated friend answered, "I can't play right now. I'm busy planning *your* birthday party. Now, isn't that more important?"

Her little girl looked up at her and thoughtfully said, "No. I'd rather cancel the party and just have you play with me. That's the best present."

Even as my friend shared the story with me, tears came to her eyes. Her daughter didn't care about an elaborate birthday bash. She simply wanted her mom's attention.

Many times in our quest to be the perfect mom, we lose sight of the big picture—our children need our love and attention more than anything. So, stop trying to *plan* the perfect party games and actually *play* some games with your kids today. It's time.

CASTING YOUR CARES

MOM TO MASTER
Lord, help me to make time for
the most important people in my life,
and help me to keep things in perspective. Amen.

*"The LORD does not look at
the things man looks at.
Man looks at the outward appearance,
but the LORD looks at the heart."*
1 SAMUEL 16:7

I'm sure you know her. She's the mom who has a flat belly, long legs, and perfect hair. Admit it, you occasionally wish she'd fall into a cotton candy machine and gain thirty pounds. Her very presence makes you feel less than attractive, doesn't it?

Guess how I know these things? Because I know a Miss America mom, too, and I feel like one of Cinderella's ugly stepsisters whenever she's around.

Comparing yourself with others is never a good thing, and it's not a God thing, either. God isn't concerned with whether or not your belly is as trim as it was before childbirth. His Word says that He looks on the heart, not on your outward appearance. He's more concerned with the condition of your heart, not the cellulite on your legs. Of course, that doesn't mean we shouldn't strive to be the best we can be—both inside and out—but it certainly relieves some of that pressure to be perfect.

Give your jealousies and feelings of inadequacy to God and find your identity in Him. He loves you just the way you are—even if you're not Miss America.

MOM TO MASTER
*Father, help me not to compare myself with others.
Help me to see myself through Your eyes. Amen.*

CASTING YOUR CARES

*You shall rejoice in all the good things
the LORD your God has given
to you and your household.*

DEUTERONOMY 26:11

"Rejoice in the Lord always. Again I will say, rejoice!" (Philippians 4:4 NKJV). That's what the Word says, but that's not always the easiest task. . .am I right? What about when your child's teacher says something ugly about Junior during your parent/teacher conference? Or, how about when another driver pulls right in front of you and steals your parking spot at the grocery store? Or when your toddler knocks over your red fingernail polish, spilling it all over your bathroom rug? Not wanting to rejoice too much at that point, are you?

Daily aggravations will be a part of life until we get to heaven. That's a fact. So, we just have to learn how to deal with those aggravations.

Here's the plan: Today if something goes wrong— stop, pause, and praise. I don't mean you have to praise God for the aggravation. That would be kind of silly. I'm saying just praise God *in spite* of the aggravation. Before long, the "stop, pause, and praise" practice will become a habit. And that's the kind of habit worth forming! So go on, start rejoicing!

MOM TO MASTER

*Father, I repent for the times when I am less than
thankful. I rejoice in You today. Amen.*

As far as the east is from the west,
so far has he removed our transgressions from us.
PSALM 103:12

"So I'll put you down for two dozen chocolate chip cookies, okay?" asked the perky voice on the other end of the receiver.

"Sure," I mumbled. "I can bring those on Friday."

If only she'd called after I'd had my morning Diet Coke, I could've come up with an excuse. But it was too late now. I'd have to produce the cookies.

Friday arrived and I still hadn't baked them. So, I did what any resourceful mom would do—I drove to the Wal-Mart bakery. After purchasing a box of cookies, I cleverly transferred them to one of my own storage containers.

Those cookies were a hit. Everyone commented on my wonderful baking ability! I just smiled. I couldn't bring myself to confess my secret. Allyson knew I hadn't baked them, but she kept quiet.

I had gotten away with it, but I'd been a poor witness for my daughter. Later that night, I apologized to Allyson, admitting my wrongdoing.

"It's okay, Mom," she said. "We all make mistakes."

Boy, that's the truth, and I surely make my share of them. I'm thankful that God wipes the slate clean each time we repent. That's good news no matter how the cookie crumbles.

MOM TO MASTER
Thank You, God, for wiping the slate clean. Help me to do better. Amen.

> *For as high as the heavens are*
> *above the earth, so great is his love*
> *for those who fear him.*
>
> PSALM 103:11

Honor Day. That should be a wonderful, happy day, right? Well. . .this particular Honor Day was not so fun. It was the first Honor Day that my daughter, Abby, who was normally a straight-A student, had ever gotten a B on her report card.

Of course, we assured Abby that a B was good. Still, it was traumatic for my nine-year-old daughter. She ran off the stage in tears, and I chased after her. I hugged her and said those magic words: "Do you want to go get a chocolate doughnut and a Cherry Coke?"

She nodded, and we were off.

Abby and I both lived through the first B on her report card—sad as it was. She felt badly even though we were quite proud of her eighty-eight percent in math.

So many times as a mother, I feel like I've just received the dreaded B on my Mom's Report Card. Ever been there? You've tried really hard to do everything right, but in the end, your best didn't feel good enough? On those days, I'm thankful that my heavenly Father is there with a spiritual chocolate doughnut and Cherry Coke to cheer me up. It's nice to know that He loves us no matter what—just like we love our kids.

CASTING YOUR CARES

MOM TO MASTER
Thank You, God, for loving me unconditionally. Amen.

Trust in the LORD with all your heart
and lean not on your own understanding;
in all your ways acknowledge him,
and he will make your paths straight.
PROVERBS 3:5–6

When I was eight years old in Vacation Bible School, I memorized the above Scripture. At the time, my motivation for learning this important passage was a blue ribbon. Ahhh. . .the lure of a shiny blue ribbon! Now, more than twenty years later, I've lost that ribbon, but those words are still imprinted on my heart. They pop into my mind at the times when I need them the most.

Today, as the mother of two little girls, I try to motivate my children to memorize Scripture, too. We recite them on the way to school every morning, which has become a fun way to start the day. Sometimes we try to see how fast we can say the verses. Other times, we make up songs with them. With every recitation, we're putting more of God's Word in our hearts.

As a mom, that's so comforting to me because I know that those memory verses will pop into their minds whenever they need them most. God's Word will be there for them even when I can't be—and that's even better than a shiny blue ribbon!

MOM TO MASTER
Thank You, God, for Your Word. Please help my children to love Your Word even more than I do. Amen.

> *"Martha, Martha," the Lord answered,*
> *"you are worried and upset about many things,*
> *but only one thing is needed. Mary has chosen what*
> *is better, and it will not be taken away from her."*
> LUKE 10:41–42

Do you remember when you were pregnant? In the midst of weird food cravings, swollen ankles, and raging hormones, you spent time dreaming of your baby. You wondered things like: "What will he or she look like?" "What will be his or her first words?" "Will he or she be healthy?" and "How will I ever care for a tiny little baby?"

I think every mother worries. It seems like the natural thing to do. Most first-time moms worry that they won't be equipped with the appropriate parenting skills needed to be a good mom. Then, the baby comes—and with it, a whole new set of worries. As the child grows, the worries grow, too. Sometimes, the worries can become almost suffocating.

When I feel overwhelmed with the worries that accompany motherhood, I realize I've forgotten to figure God into the equation. With God, all things are possible—even raising good kids in a mixed-up world. God doesn't expect mothers to have all the answers, but He does expect us to go to Him for those answers. So, if worries are consuming your thoughts—go to God. He not only has the answers, He *is* the answer!

CASTING YOUR CARES

MOM TO MASTER
God, I trust You with my children,
and I give You my worries. Amen.

*Jesus answered,
"I am the way and
the truth and the life."*
JOHN 14:6

Do you ever get lost? I am what you might call "directionally challenged." My children think it's pretty funny, seeing their old mom talking to herself in the front seat, repeating directions in chantlike manner, and praying quite a lot. Still, it seems that no matter how I try, I get lost on a regular basis. Of course, in my defense, Texas *is* a big place, and you can never return the same way you arrived. It's never a matter of simply reversing the directions.

Getting lost used to really frustrate and frighten me. Now, I consider it more of a fun adventure. I find that something good usually comes from it. For example, recently when I lost my way, I discovered this great garden shop with the most beautiful iron bench. Now that bench adorns our yard—it was meant to be! Other times, these extended trips in the SUV give us more family time—precious moments to laugh and share.

You see, it's all in the perspective. I no longer worry when I'm lost. I just enjoy the journey. Life is the same way. There's no sense worrying your way through each day—just enjoy the trip. After all, if we know Jesus as our Lord and Savior, we're on the right road because He is the Way!

MOM TO MASTER
Thank You, God, for guiding my every step. Amen.

CASTING YOUR CARES

Let us fix our eyes on Jesus,
the author and perfecter of our faith.

HEBREWS 12:2

When we were trying to break Abby from her pacifier, this verse took on new meaning for me. I'd never fully understood the meaning of the word *fixed* until I witnessed Abby's fixation on her pacifier. We thought we had thrown away every one of them. I'd pitched at least fifteen of them, but still, Abby found the last one. There it sat atop her dresser, slightly hidden by a basket of hair bows. When I walked into her room, she was standing on her rocking chair, reaching toward her "pacy," and staring intently upon her prized possession.

I picked her up, grabbed the pacifier, and quickly tossed it into the kitchen sink. I didn't think Abby had seen me, but she had. For the next hour, she stood beneath the sink, reaching upward, crying for her pacifier. Her eyes were fixed. In fact, they were fixed until she finally fell asleep right there on the kitchen floor.

Her determination really spoke to me. I thought, *If only I could be as determined to keep my eyes fixed on Jesus as Abby is to keep her eyes fixed on that pacifier, my faith would not falter*. Even today, that image of Abby's pursuit of her pacifier stays with me, reminding me to stay fixed on the Father.

CASTING YOUR CARES

MOM TO MASTER
Lord, help me to keep my eyes fixed on You. Amen.

Dear children,
do not let anyone lead you astray.
1 JOHN 3:7

Do you ever worry about the friends that your children are making? I do. I often wonder, *Will they be good influences on my children? Will they hurt my children? Do they know Jesus as their Lord and Savior? Will they be lifelong, trustworthy friends?*

While I don't know the answers to all of these questions, I do know one thing—Jesus will be their lifelong friend. They will always be able to count on Him. He will come through for them time and time again. He will stand by them no matter what. How do I know these things? Because He's been there for me when nobody else was.

I discovered early in life that friends sometimes let you down—even your best friends—because they're human. If you put your hope in friends, disappointment and hurt are inevitable. But, God is a sure thing.

I realize that I can't pick my children's friends, and I know that I can't protect them from the hurt that comes from broken friendships and disloyalty. But, there are two things I can do—I can teach them about Jesus, and I can pray that the Lord sends them godly friends. You can do the same for your kids. You can start today.

MOM TO MASTER
Lord, please send my children good friends. I'm thankful that You're their best friend and mine. Amen.

JANUARY 22

"Love each other as I have loved you."
JOHN 15:12

"Stop it!" Allyson wailed.

"You stop it, stupid head!" Abby screamed.

And on and on it goes. . .

There are days when I wonder if my girls will ever be friends. Sure, they love each other because they have to—they're sisters. But, will they ever *like* each other?

I think all moms wonder that same thing—especially after witnessing an hour or two of nonstop fighting between their children.

Then, just about the time I've given up and think my kids are doomed to be enemies, the Lord gives me a glimpse of their true feelings. Another child comes against one of them, and the other sister steps up in her defense—just like that! Or, I find them asleep, side by side on the living room floor. That's a scene that always makes me smile.

The Lord knew what He was doing when He put our families together. He knew that our kids would fight, and He knew they'd need each other. And here's another comforting thought—God loves your children even more than you do, and He desires for them to be buddies, too. So, the next time your children are bickering, don't get discouraged. Just thank the Lord for His love in your home.

MOM TO MASTER
Lord, thank You for my children. Please help them to appreciate each other more. Amen.

Many are the plans in a man's heart,
but it is the LORD's purpose that prevails.
PROVERBS 19:21

Stage mothers. They aren't bad people. They're just overzealous. A few years ago, I was in charge of the annual elementary talent show at my daughters' school, and I encountered moms who verbally assaulted me over their children's placement in the program. (Did I mention it was a volunteer position?) At the time, I couldn't understand their irrational behavior. I thought, *These moms must be nuts!* Little did I know that I also had a nutty stage mother inside of me.

Later, while watching my daughters' gymnastics team practice, I made casual conversation with another mom until she huffed and puffed that my daughters were taking too many turns, causing her daughter to miss practice time. Immediately, the stage mother in me arose. I should've let it go, but I didn't. She may have huffed and puffed, but I blew her house down.

At once, I understood why those moms had attacked me over the talent show details. Their abominable behavior had been motivated by an intense love for their children—same as mine. The only way to control the stage mom in all of us is to realize that God is the best director. He doesn't need our input. He has a starring role for our children—if we'll only take our places backstage.

MOM TO MASTER
Lord, please direct my children in all things. Amen.

CASTING YOUR CARES

> *"Be careful, or your hearts will be
> weighed down with dissipation,
> drunkenness and the anxieties of life,
> and that day will close on you
> unexpectedly like a trap."*
> LUKE 21:34

Do you know that worry never changed a single thing? Worry never turned a single thing around. (Well, it's turned a lot of hair prematurely gray, but that's about it.)

You know, worriers are called "worrywarts." Think about that—a wart isn't exactly a beautiful sight. No, it's an eyesore. What do we do with warts? We put medicated drops on them and make them disappear. That's exactly what we should do with our worrywart personalities—make them disappear.

While there's no magic "worrywart potion" on the market, you have easy access to one that you might not have considered—God's Word! It will obliterate worry if you'll only believe it. If you truly believe that "No weapon formed against you (or your children) will prosper" (Isaiah 54:17), then you shouldn't waste time worrying about unforeseen tragedies. God's got you covered! Isn't that comforting? Doesn't that make the worrywart inside of you shrink and wither away? It should!

God must have known we'd worry. I think that's why He put so many Scriptures about worry in His Word. Find those today and meditate on them. Worry never changed anything, but God's Word always does.

MOM TO MASTER
Father, I give my worries to You. Amen.

CASTING YOUR CARES

I know, O LORD,
that a man's life is not his own;
it is not for man to direct his steps.
JEREMIAH 10:23

We had just moved cross-country, and now we had to find a school for Abby, who was starting kindergarten in the fall. Several of my coworkers suggested a Christian school nearby. My husband and I met the principal and completed all of the necessary paperwork for Abby's enrollment—still, I wasn't sure. At my urging, we also investigated the public elementary school, just minutes from our home.

Abby didn't care where she attended school as long as she could take her Little Mermaid lunchbox. But, Jeff and I worried. We didn't want to make a wrong decision. We prayed about which school would be best for our girls, but neither of us felt like we'd received a definite answer from God. I was hoping the clouds would part and Jesus would utter the right choice. That never happened, so we went with our gut instinct and chose the public school. It was a wonderful decision, although at the time, we weren't sure.

I often worry when we have to make big decisions concerning our children. I'm so afraid I'll stray from the path that God has for us, but you know what I've discovered? Even if we stray, God finds us.

MOM TO MASTER
Father, I trust You with all my decisions. Amen.

CASTING YOUR CARES

JANUARY 26

"I, the Lord,
have called you in righteousness;
I will take hold of your hand."

Isaiah 42:6

Even now, I instinctively grab Abby's and Allyson's hands when we cross the street. At ages ten and eight, my girls do not think this is cool, but I can't help myself. By taking their hands, I feel I am protecting them from traffic, strangers, and all other dangers. I bet you do the same for your children. As I often tell my daughters—it's a mom thing.

I'll probably be reaching for their hands until they leave the nest. But, you know what? That's not such a bad habit. In fact, if I could get in the habit of reaching out to God and taking hold of His hand more often in my day-to-day activities, I'd be farther down the road in my faith walk.

I'm not sure why I neglect to reach for His hand when I'm crossing the busy streets of life. I guess, like my daughters, I think I'm mature enough to handle it on my own. Or, as my mother would say, I get "too big for my britches." I'm so thankful that we have a loving heavenly Father who reaches down to take our hands when we need Him the most. If you haven't taken hold of God's hand in awhile, why don't you grab it today?

Mom to Master
Father, I take hold of Your hand today. Amen.

Look in the scroll of the LORD and read.
ISAIAH 34:16

Just saying the words, "It's devotion time," used to make my girls roll their eyes. In a world of PlayStation, DVDs, CDs, and computers—keeping our kids' attention on what's important is a tough task. So, we try to make our devotion time into a question/answer game. This ensures our children will pay attention because no one wants to lose the Bible Quiz game!

This game tactic works for our family devotion time, but getting our children to have their personal devotional time is even tougher. That worries me. You know what else worries me? I once heard a preacher say, "Your children may not be reading their Bible regularly, but you can bet they are reading you." Ugh! I sure hope they weren't reading me the other day when that lady took my parking spot at Wal-Mart.

As you know, we're not supposed to worry. So, I have given my worries to God over this situation. Daily, I ask Him to help me live out my faith. If my life is an open book before my girls, I want to make sure it's full of God's Word. How about you? Encourage your kids to read God's Word and then live your life according to His Word. That's a one-two punch against the devil!

CASTING YOUR CARES

MOM TO MASTER
Father, help me to live out Your Word before my children. Amen.

Trust in the LORD forever,
for the LORD,
the LORD, is the Rock eternal.
ISAIAH 26:4

Did you ever have a pet rock? I think we all did. I remember painting them, gluing funny eyes on top, and naming each one. Crazy, isn't it? And, can you believe that pet rocks are actually making a comeback? My girls are loving them! Of course, I know it's just a phase they'll soon outgrow. When the next fad rolls around, they'll throw their pet rocks into their desk drawers, never to be seen again.

That's how fads are—totally hot one minute and completely forgotten the next. In a world of fad diets, fad fashions, and fad everything else, I want to make sure that my children don't think of God as a passing fad. I know you wish the same for your kids. So, how can we ensure that our children will view God as a steadfast part of their lives? If only there were a magic pill we could give them that would guarantee they'd love God until the end of time. . . .

Well, there's no pill to give them, but we do have God's Word to feed them. We can also let our children see us loving God and His Word. Most importantly, we can pray that our kids will always love God—the real Rock.

CASTING YOUR CARES

MOM TO MASTER
Father, help my children to love You
more than anything or anyone else. Amen.

"Therefore I tell you,
do not worry about your life."
MATTHEW 6:25

It amazes me sometimes just how much I worry. The Bible clearly says to cast all of your cares on Him, yet I choose to keep those cares to myself. By nature, I'm a fixer; I'm a doer. And sometimes that works against me. While my self-sufficient nature enables me to get a lot accomplished, it also causes me to worry over things that I should hand over to God.

Are you a worrier, too? To some extent, I think all moms are worriers. Worrying just seems to be part of our job description, right underneath the "take care of your children until you die" part. While worrying may come naturally to you, it's not God's will for your life. He wants you to live in perfect peace, and worrying is a peace destroyer. It's the opposite of peace. So, why not give your worries to God today?

It won't be easy at first, but you can do it. Here's the plan: The very minute that your thoughts turn into worries, say aloud, "I cast (fill in the blank) on God right now." Pretty soon, casting your cares will become a habit and worrying will be a thing of the past.

CASTING YOUR CARES

MOM TO MASTER
Father, transform my thinking. Help me to quit worry-
ing and simply trust You with every part of my life.
Amen.

> *"Therefore do not worry about tomorrow,*
> *for tomorrow will worry about itself."*
>
> MATTHEW 6:34

"No worries."

I've been told that is a common Aussie expression. Well, if that's true, I'd say those folks down under are right on top of things. What a great attitude! If only I could look in the face of trouble and say, "No worries." Instead, I usually list all of my worries and wallow around in them for awhile.

You know, as Christians, we really should be able to look in the face of trouble and say, "No worries." After all, if we're really trusting our heavenly Father, we won't have any worries. Now, I didn't say we wouldn't have any problems. As long as we're on this earth, there will be trouble. God tells us that in His Word, but He also tells us not to fret over them. That means it's actually possible to encounter stress and problems and still have no worries. That should be our goal.

If we could live like that, we'd be better wives, better mothers, better daughters, better friends, better Christians—better everything! Life would simply be better if we stopped worrying. Worrying is a time stealer, so put worry in its place! The next time you encounter trouble, say, "No worries!" and mean it!

MOM TO MASTER
Father, help me to have a
"no worries" attitude from now on! Amen.

CASTING YOUR CARES

Plans fail for lack of counsel,
but with many advisers they succeed.
PROVERBS 15:22

Vacation is supposed to be a fun time, right? But, if you're a planner or a list maker like me, even vacations can stress you out and cause worry.

Recently, we took our girls to Disney World in Orlando. I ordered the free vacation planning video. I purchased the Disney World Vacation Planning Guide. I visited numerous Disney World Web sites, collecting research. I even called six different families who had recently been to Disney World and interrogated them.

While research and planning have merit, I went overboard. I became so involved that I began overanalyzing every decision about the trip. It stole my joy. Instead of eagerly anticipating our family vacation, I became burdened with the responsibility of planning the "Best Disney Vacation Ever!" I drove everyone in our house totally nuts! Finally, my husband (seeing that I was on overload) hired a travel agent to plan the vacation for us. Whew! It was off my shoulders, and I could rest in the fact that an expert was on the job.

Well, we have a life expert *always* on the job— God. So, the next time you get overloaded with the cares of the world, call on Him. He will take care of everything, and He doesn't even charge a commission!

MOM TO MASTER
Father, I give all of my "to-dos" to You. Amen.

FEBRUARY 1

*Satisfy us in the morning
with your unfailing love.*
PSALM 90:14

Let's face it. There are days when it's tough to show love to your children. Of course, you always love them—they're your kids! But, if you're like me, there are days when you don't particularly love everything about them.

We had one of those days recently. My in-laws were in town, and I had asked the girls to be on their best behavior. That SO did not happen. They fought nonstop. At one point, Ally actually had Abby in a headlock. I threatened, spanked, grounded, and hollered until I was totally defeated. By day's end, I was sure I had to be the worst mother in the world.

As I kissed my girls good night, I wanted so badly to hit the rewind button and start the day over again. Unfortunately, that was impossible. As I moped down the hallway to my bedroom, I took heart in one thing—God does have a rewind button! He lets us start over every time we fail. So, the next time your children are acting less than lovely and your love walk has become more of a crawl, ask God to hit the rewind button.

MOM TO MASTER
*Lord, help me to love my children even when they act
unlovely. Help me to love them like You love me. Amen.*

LOVING UNCONDITIONALLY

"My grace is sufficient for you,
for my power is made perfect in weakness."
2 CORINTHIANS 12:9

It's the mother's curse. I'm sure your mom has used it on you before: "I hope you have a child just like you when you grow up!" And, chances are—you did! In my case, I had two. You know what's interesting about raising children that are exactly like you? You tend to see all of your faults in them. It's as if there is a gigantic magnifying glass, constantly revealing their weaknesses, which happen to be the same weaknesses that you struggle with on a daily basis.

This, of course, is the breeding ground for fighting, resentment, and hurt. So, as mothers, we have to break that "mother's curse" and celebrate our children. We need to smash that magnifying glass that focuses in on their flaws and love our kids—weaknesses and all. Ask the Lord to help you see your children as God sees them. And, ask Him to help you see yourself through His eyes, too.

In other words, give your kids and yourself a break. Don't expect them to be perfect, and don't expect perfection from yourself, either. God loves you and your kids—flaws and all. Remember, His power is made perfect through our weakness.

MOM TO MASTER
Lord, help me to nurture my children's strengths and pray over their weaknesses. I give them to You. Amen.

LOVING UNCONDITIONALLY

God is love.
Whoever lives in love lives in God,
and God in him. In this way,
love is made complete among us.
1 JOHN 4:16–17

Remember that popular '70s song "Love Will Keep Us Together"? I was in grade school when it hit the radio airwaves, and I can remember singing it at recess with my gal pals. We knew every word by heart. Well, there's a lot of truth in that title, especially where our families are concerned.

Life gets complicated, and families fall apart. It happens. It even happens to Christian families. It may have happened in your own family. But, I'm here to tell you that love is the answer. When nothing else will, love will keep your family together. No, I'm not talking about that fair-weather kind of love. I'm talking about the God kind of love—an everlasting, unconditional love from heaven.

So, even if your teenager has left home or turned his back on God, love will draw him back. Not the sermons you've preached nor the rules you've enforced—only love will turn your situation around. Let God's love live big in you. Let God's love be the superglue in your family, binding you with one another for a lifetime. Live the love and reap the results.

MOM TO MASTER
Father, I ask that Your love flow
through me to my children. Amen.

"Love each other as I have loved you."
JOHN 15:12

"You love Allyson more because she's a blond like you!" Abby, then nine, screamed at me as she slammed the door.

Following Abby's logic, that statement would've been inaccurate because I'm only blond thanks to Clairol. (I don't even remember my natural color, but I think it's closer to Abby's brown locks.) At any rate, I had a problem that ran much deeper than the color of my roots.

I was baffled, befuddled, bewildered, and all those other *b* words, too.

I had always tried to treat my children equally. I certainly didn't love one daughter more than the other. I thought I had the "no favoritism" thing down. Apparently, that was not true, as Abby had so eloquently let me know.

As I pondered Abby's feelings of mistreatment, I checked into "Hurt Hotel." Indignant, I huffed, *How could she say such a thing?* Then, I took a "guilt getaway" and said a few "Woe is me, I'm a bad mom" mantras. Finally, I hit my knees in desperation. That's where I found answers and insight that gave me hope for a better tomorrow. I may not always get it right where my kids are concerned, but if my heart is right, God will cover me. He'll help me to show them just how much I love them. He'll do the same for you.

LOVING UNCONDITIONALLY

MOM TO MASTER
Father, help me to love my children like You love me. Amen.

Knowledge puffs up,
but love builds up.
1 CORINTHIANS 8:1

There should be a retreat reserved for all mothers of "tween" girls. As it turns out, once a girl hits age ten, mothers are stupid. I know this firsthand because I am now a member of "The Stupid Mom Club." It's not a membership I like very much, and I'm constantly trying to prove that I don't belong in this club. I find myself saying things like: "Do you know that I was on the honor roll all through school? I never even got a B until high school!" Or, "I am three times your age, and I know more than you'll ever know!"

Ever used that one?

Of course, all of this self-elevating talk accomplishes absolutely nothing. I could talk until my lips fall off, but my words won't change how Abby views me. But, God's Word will! Proverbs 31:28 says, "Her children arise and call her blessed." Oh, yeah! I am living for that day, how about you? During your prayer time, say, "Lord, I thank You that my children arise and call me blessed," and watch your kids' attitudes change. Soon, we'll all be out of "The Stupid Mom Club." That's a promise!

LOVING UNCONDITIONALLY

MOM TO MASTER

Father, give me patience to love my children—
even when they don't treat me nicely.
Help me not to take it personally. Amen.

*"I have loved you with
an everlasting love."*
JEREMIAH 31:3

Looking down into the face of my first newborn baby, I couldn't imagine loving anyone more than I loved her at that moment. She was everything I had dreamed of during those nine months of pregnancy. Jeff and I did all of the annoying baby talk and silly noises that all new parents do. We were absolutely captivated by her every sound, move, and facial expression. We adored her!

So, when I discovered I was pregnant with Baby Number Two on the eve before Abby's first birthday, I wondered, *Will I ever love another child as much as I love Abby?* I was worried. I just couldn't fathom loving another child as much as I loved "Baby Abbers," as we affectionately nicknamed her.

Then, Allyson Michelle Adams came into this world on August 15, 1994—bald and beautiful. I looked into her sweet face and fell in love all over again. Jeff and I discovered that we could love another baby just as much as our first. We always tell our girls, "You are *both* our favorites!" Do you know that is exactly how God sees us? He doesn't love you or me more than anyone else—we're all His favorites! Meditate on that today and embrace the Father's love.

MOM TO MASTER
*Father, help me to accept and
celebrate Your love for me. Amen.*

LOVING UNCONDITIONALLY

FEBRUARY 7

Love is patient.

1 CORINTHIANS 13:4

Have you ever really meditated on the Love Chapter—1 Corinthians 13? I had to memorize the entire passage when I was a member of our church's high school Bible quizzing team. Even now, fifteen years later, I can still quote the entire chapter. I wish I lived those verses as well as I can recite them.

You know which one really gets me? Love is patient. Uh-oh! Patience is one of those virtues that you admire in others but you're sure is not an option for you, right? This is especially true when it comes to our kids. It seems they know exactly which buttons to push. If you're in a hurry, Junior will lose your keys. If you're expecting company, your daughter is sure to spill nail polish on the carpet. If you're on the telephone, every child suddenly needs your undivided attention.

Let's face it—moms get a patience test every day. I've often failed that test. That's why I'm so thankful that God offers "make-up exams." Through His Word and His unconditional love, we don't have to fail those patience tests anymore. The Lord can help us walk in love—even patience—if we'll only ask for His intervention. So, ask Him today.

MOM TO MASTER

Father, fill me with more of Your love, and help me to have more patience—especially with my family. Amen.

Do not let any unwholesome talk
come out of your mouths,
but only what is helpful for building others up.
EPHESIANS 4:29

Have you ever been around a parrot? I've never owned an actual parrot, but I do have two little "parrots" running around my house. Abby and Allyson repeat much of what I say—good and bad. I bet you have some parrots in your house, too.

Recently, my youngest daughter overheard one of my "girlfriend gab sessions" and later repeated something I'd said. In her cute little eight-year-old voice, she said, "Bite my hiney," to her sister! Goodness, it had sounded so harmless when I'd said it, or had it? Either way, my parrot had repeated something that was what the Bible might call "unwholesome or unlovely talk." I was busted!

This parrot episode has made me watch my speech a lot more carefully, looking for unlovely talk and asking the Holy Spirit to keep a watch over my words. It's not only about setting a good example for my children, it's also about truly living love in every area of my life. Catty remarks, unwholesome talk, and sarcasm really have no place in our conversations—not if we're really living the God kind of love. So, walk and talk love, and give your parrots something worth repeating.

MOM TO MASTER
Father, put a watch over my mouth.
Help me to walk and talk love. Amen.

FEBRUARY 9

*[Love] always protects, always trusts,
always hopes, always perseveres.*

1 CORINTHIANS 13:7

Recently, our pastor preached a sermon I'll not soon forget. His topic? Love. I've heard hundreds of sermons about love, but I'd never heard it preached quite like this. He said, "Love always believes the best in others."

Yikes! Just when I thought my love walk was shaping up, he zapped me! I wrote it down this way in my journal: "Love always believes the best—especially in my children."

It's a tough world out there and getting tougher all the time. Our children are faced with many challenges. Sometimes, we're the only ones believing the best in them. We're the only ones cheering them on to victory. We're the only ones making them feel special. Sometimes, we're the only ones on their side.

Believing the best in our children doesn't mean turning our heads when they act inappropriately. Rather, it means giving them the benefit of the doubt. If they say they turned in their homework and yet you receive a note that says they didn't, you believe them, assuming the teacher has misplaced it. Then, pray with your child that the teacher will find the missing homework. You know, if we believe the best in our children, we'll get the best from our children.

MOM TO MASTER

*Father, thank You for my precious children.
Help me to always believe the best in them. Amen.*

*Be imitators of God. . .
and live a life of love.*
EPHESIANS 5:1–2

Valentine's Day is just around the corner. Department stores are splashed in red and pink. Radio stations are playing sappy love songs. And heart-shaped boxes of chocolates are calling your name! Love is in the air, so why not celebrate it?

If you're married, schedule a sitter and steal some time away with your mate. Drink flavored coffee at your favorite café or pop some popcorn and rent *An Affair to Remember*. Just enjoy each other. If you're a single mom, don't let Valentine's Day be a sad holiday for you. Instead, celebrate the love you share with your children! Take the kids out for a night of bowling or catch a kids' flick together. Tight on cash? Simply stay home and read funny poetry books or play fun board games as a family. Just spend quality time with each other.

This is also a great time to send a special note to your grown children, letting them know how much they mean to you. Go ahead. You have an excuse to be mushy! It's Valentine's Day, so spread the love, share the love, and celebrate the love! And, by all means, eat a few pieces of chocolate, too!

MOM TO MASTER

*Lord, thank You for placing such wonderful people
in my life. May they always know this week—
and always—how much I love them. Amen.*

LOVING UNCONDITIONALLY

Love is patient, love is kind.
1 Corinthians 13:4

It never fails. When I get on the telephone, suddenly my children need me. It's almost instantaneous. As soon as the receiver goes to my ear, my daughters appear. It's one of those "mom phenomena."

One afternoon while I was on a long distance phone call with my best friend, the clamoring for my attention began. One after another, my girls interrupted. All at once, I lost it. I put my hand over the phone (so that my best friend couldn't hear me holler), and I shot out some verbal bullets. It was ugly.

Both daughters retreated to their bedrooms to sulk and recover from my outburst. As I hung up the phone, I realized how unlovely I had acted. The Bible says that love is patient and kind, and I hadn't been either of those things.

Funny, I had practiced patience and kindness all day long with friends, coworkers, and strangers, but I couldn't show my children the same love aspects. I repented to God and then I asked for my daughters' forgiveness. It's easy to act ugly, but it takes work to walk in love—especially with our children. Love is a choice. Choose to show your family love today.

Loving Unconditionally

Mom to Master

*Father, help me to walk in love—
especially where my children are concerned.
Help me to be more like You. Amen.*

I trust in God's unfailing love for ever and ever.
PSALM 52:8

We use the word *love* an awful lot. "I *love* your new purse," or "I *love* that dress on you," or "I *love* Hershey kisses." I bet if you kept track, you'd find yourself using the word *love* more than a dozen times each day. Because we use it so much, *love* has lost some of its punch, some of its luster, some of its meaning.

But, real love—the God kind of love—is so much more than the "love" that has become so clichéd in our culture. The God kind of love is an everlasting love. His love stretches as far as the east is from the west. His love is deeper than the deepest ocean. His love is higher than the highest mountain. His love covers a multitude of sins. His love is unconditional. His love is truly awesome!

Now, that's the kind of love I want to walk in. How about you? I want to receive the Father's love, and I want to extend His love to others—especially to my children. As moms, we should have the aroma of love. So, if your love aroma is a little funky (like that green cheese in the back of the fridge), ask God to refresh your love today!

MOM TO MASTER
Lord, I pray that Your love—
the real thing—
shines in me and through me. Amen.

LOVING UNCONDITIONALLY

*In the beginning God created
the heavens and the earth.*

GENESIS 1:1

"Love makes the world go 'round." I've heard that expression all of my life, but I've never really pondered its meaning. . .until this week. I flippantly said it, and my ten-year-old gave me a blank stare and uttered, "Huh? What does that mean?"

Here's what I concluded after a few serious moments of reflection. The world's kind of love doesn't make the world go 'round. In fact, the kind of shallow, temporary love the world has to offer makes the world go crazy, not 'round. But, the God kind of love—*that* is the kind that makes the world go 'round. It keeps it spinning when nothing else will.

If your world is no longer going 'round. If your household is less than heaven on earth. If you've forgotten what it feels like to really experience unconditional love. . .run into the Father's arms right now. Your heavenly Father longs for the opportunity to "love on you," in the same way that you adore loving on your children. So, spend some time with the Father today. His love not only makes the world go 'round, His love *created* the world! Awesome!

MOM TO MASTER

*Father, I want more of Your love. Wrap me in Your
arms today that I might experience the kind of love
that truly makes the world go 'round. Amen.*

LOVING UNCONDITIONALLY

"Love your neighbor as yourself."
LEVITICUS 19:18

Love is an active verb, but sometimes we forget that in today's society. Since February is the month we celebrate love, I thought it might be nice if we activated love in our various communities. Here's the plan for "Activation Love." Do at least one "love in action" activity each day for the rest of this month. It doesn't have to be a big thing. Small gestures such as calling a relative just to say "I love you" count.

Here are some other ideas to get you started: Enlist your kiddos' help and volunteer at a nearby soup kitchen one Saturday. Go grocery shopping for the church shut-ins and deliver the bags of food as a family. Buy some dog and cat food, and drop it off at your local humane society/animal shelter. Begin a letter-writing campaign this week, and write letters of appreciation to President George W. Bush, the servicemen and women of this nation, the pastoral staff at your church, the teachers at your children's school, etc.

You'll be surprised how much your kids will enjoy "Activation Love." You'll be doing good works on behalf of the Father, and you'll be teaching your children that love truly is an active verb. So, go for it! Let's put our love to work!

LOVING UNCONDITIONALLY

MOM TO MASTER
Lord, help me to love others
the way that You love me. Amen.

Oh, how I love your law!
I meditate on it all day long.
PSALM 119:97

Don't you just love *The Grinch Who Stole Christmas* by Dr. Seuss? Do you remember the scene where the Grinch's heart grows ten times bigger? Then the Grinch who once wore a scowl wears a big Grinchy smile! Doesn't that make you feel warm and fuzzy inside?

Well, that scene is played out in my life every time I spend time in God's Word. Many mornings I wake up like the Grinch, scowling as I try to find a Diet Coke to revive me. I stumble through the morning, saying as little as possible, until I finally get time alone with God. During those moments, my heart grows ten times bigger in order to make room for all of my Father's love. After I get my "love fill-up," I'm ready to face my family again and give out the love I've just received.

As moms, we can't run on empty love tanks. We are expected to give love all day long, so if we don't have a full supply, we'll start to resemble old Mr. Grinch. If your love tank is low today, pull up to the Word of God and spend some time with the Lord. His love is waiting for you, and it's premium stuff! Ready? Begin fueling.

LOVING UNCONDITIONALLY

MOM TO MASTER
Lord, fill up my love tank until
it is overflowing. Amen.

A gentle answer turns away wrath.
PROVERBS 15:1

I recently saw a T-shirt with the printing "Love is my final answer" on it. I thought that was pretty good. Think about it. When you answer with love, you give strife no place to go.

The other day, Abby wanted to go boating with her friend. Normally, we would say yes to this request, but this was a holiday weekend. And, according to the news reports, there would be many alcohol-filled boaters on the lake. We just didn't have peace about it, so we told Abby, "No, not this time."

Abby *really* wanted to go, so she began retaliating in a big way. It was ugly. As she huffed and puffed, I decided to try out the "love answer." So, I said, "Abby, honey, we love you too much to let something bad happen to you. There will be lots of drunken boaters out there today, and we just aren't willing to take that chance. You are too precious to us." To my surprise, she was okay with that answer. While she was disappointed that she couldn't go to the lake, she understood our reasons and resumed normal behavior. Wow! I didn't even have to raise my voice or threaten to ground her!

Let love be your final answer today. It really works!

MOM TO MASTER
Lord, help me to make love my final answer in every situation. Amen.

LOVING UNCONDITIONALLY

FEBRUARY 17

Show the wonder of your great love.
PSALM 17:7

Do you have unstoppable love? Do you have the kind of love that overflows to everyone around you? I wish I could answer yes to those questions, but I'd have to say, "Not really." But, that is my desire.

A firefighter at our church recently shared with us that firefighters use a piece of equipment called a deluge nozzle for really big fires. This nozzle puts out fifteen hundred gallons of water per minute. Now that's a lot of water!

Wouldn't it be neat if they could invent a deluge love nozzle, guaranteed to put out fifteen hundred gallons of love per minute? Then, each time I feel impatience, irritability, or frustration rising up inside of me, I could just reach for the deluge love nozzle and spew some love around. I can hear it now—I'd start to holler, and my kids would say, "Hurry! Get Mom her deluge love nozzle!"

Well, there may not be a deluge love nozzle in existence, but we have something even better—Jesus Christ. He's our secret weapon of love. And He can cause you to spew more love than even a deluge nozzle. So, call on Him today. He's got enough love to totally soak your family.

MOM TO MASTER
Lord, thank You for being my secret love weapon.
Help me to share Your love today. Amen.

LOVING UNCONDITIONALLY

[Love] bears all things.
1 CORINTHIANS 13:7 NKJV

"Mommy, guess what Abby did?" Allyson asked in a singsongy voice.

My then blond-haired, blue-eyed, six-year-old couldn't wait to tattle on her big sister. She was almost bursting with the news, hoping to get Abby grounded for her misdeed.

"I don't know what Abby did, but before you tattle on your sister, you'd better be sure it's worth it," I interjected. "Because I ground the one who is exposed, *and* I ground the tattler."

Allyson's eyes didn't look quite as bright as she pondered the temptation to tattle. Slowly, she retreated to her bedroom. Her desire to expose her sister had passed, and I was glad. Tattling is a bad habit that extends way beyond childhood—as adults we call it gossiping. Both are despicable in God's eyes.

Tattling and gossiping are roadblocks in many of our love walks. Exposing each other's shortcomings and failures is the exact opposite of love, because love bears all things. The word *bears* in that sentence means "covers." So, the next time your little tattlers run up to you with some juicy information about another sibling, turn 1 Corinthians 13:7 loose on them. Your words may not be effective, but God's Word packs quite a punch! Tattling and gossiping have no place in our homes. Let love root them out!

LOVING UNCONDITIONALLY

MOM TO MASTER
Lord, help me to raise my children to walk in love. Amen.

FEBRUARY 19

I trust in God's unfailing love
for ever and ever.
PSALM 52:8

Sometimes it's harder to walk in love than others. Can I get an "Amen!" on that? There are days when my love walk has quite a limp. On those days, I often wonder how God can still love me. Ever wondered that yourself? I'll think back over something I've said or done that was less than lovely, and my insides cringe.

This is especially true when it comes to my children. Of all the people in my life, I want to make sure I show my kids that unconditional, always-there-for-you kind of love. So, when I fail to accomplish that goal, my heart hurts. But, it's in those times that I sense the Father's presence in a big way. I can literally feel His love wrapping around me like a cozy sweater.

No matter how many times I fail, God still loves me. And, on those days when I know I'm definitely not in the running for "Mother of the Year," that's good to know. God loves us even more than we love our children. In fact, the Word says that we're the apple of His eye. I like that. So, the next time your love walk becomes more of a crawl, remember—God adores you.

MOM TO MASTER
Heavenly Father, thank You for loving me
even when I am less than loving. Amen.

LOVING UNCONDITIONALLY

"I have loved you with an everlasting love."
JEREMIAH 31:3

"I love you more than a million red M&Ms."

That's one of our favorite lines from a contemporary movie. It's what the daughter says to her mom in the beginning of *What a Girl Wants*.

My daughters and I have come up with a few of our own "Love you more thans. . . ." Here are our top five:

1. I love you more than a bag of Hershey's kisses.
2. I love you more than a fluffy, fuzzy puppy.
3. I love you more than McDonald's French fries.
4. I love you more than shopping at Limited Too.
5. I love you more than a Sno-cone with extra flavoring.

This is such a fun game to play on road trips. (It's especially effective to stop petty fights in the backseat, as well as discontinue comments such as "Mom, she's touching me!") Also, it's a great way to say "I love you" in a non-mushy, kid-friendly way. As my girls inch toward those preteen years, they tend to become embarrassed by just about everything—especially affection-showing parents.

So, find lots of new ways to say you love your children today. Then, have each child come up with a new way to express love to our heavenly Father. There's nothing quite like a day of love.

LOVING UNCONDITIONALLY

MOM TO MASTER
Lord, I love You more than _____. Amen.

[Love] is not self-seeking.

1 CORINTHIANS 13:5

Love means putting others' needs and desires before your own. Of course, as moms, we are well aware of that fact. When my girls were toddlers, they had many needs and desires. In fact, it seemed that one of them needed something from me all the time. If I had taken a shower by 3 P.M., I was doing well.

Especially when our children are little, we get to learn firsthand that aspect of love. And, some days, it's not easy. There were times when I prayed, "Please, God, just let them nap at the same time today so I can take a long, hot bath." (Hey, I would've paid a thousand dollars for a bubble bath back then!) Those were precious times, but boy, they were busy times, too!

Maybe you're living those busy days right now. Maybe you're reading this and thinking, "Precious days? I want to escape!" Well, don't despair. God cares about your crazy, busy days. He knows that this "mom gig" isn't an easy job. He wants to give you rest and peace, and He is well pleased with your well doing. So, the next time you hear "Mommy!" and you want to run the other direction—take heart! You are growing in love.

MOM TO MASTER

Lord, help me to appreciate even the busiest of days and help me to show Your love today. Amen.

LOVING UNCONDITIONALLY

" 'Love your neighbor as yourself.' "
LEVITICUS 19:18

Remember memorizing "Love your neighbor as yourself" back in Sunday school? That was an easy one to learn but not so easy to apply. In fact, there are days I still have trouble with that love commandment.

I recently had one of those days when I volunteered to oversee the annual talent show at my daughters' school. It was scary! Every stage mother came out of her closet and decided to make herself known. Either their children were in the wrong part of the show or they didn't like the way I ran dress rehearsal. Talk about a love challenge! I did not want to "love my neighbor" at that juncture. Actually, I wanted to throttle my neighbor and repent later. Ever been there?

I discovered that sometimes love means biting your tongue really hard. But, it's in those times that we find out how much love we truly have inside of us. It's sort of like a tube of toothpaste. If there is toothpaste inside the tube, toothpaste comes out when you squeeze it. Well, when we are squeezed under pressure, if love is on the inside of us, love comes out. But, if we have other junk in there, that comes out, too. So, build yourself up in love. Trust me, you'll need it later!

MOM TO MASTER
Lord, help me to love all of Your people. Amen.

"Man looks at the outward appearance,
but the LORD looks at the heart."

1 SAMUEL 16:7

"Can't Buy Me Love" is a catchy little song with a power-packed message. Of course, kids don't always agree with its message. When my husband told our daughters he wouldn't buy them a Go-Kart, they cried and said, "You just don't love us!"

Maybe you've heard that same retaliation in your home. It's a common kid manipulation, but totally ineffective and way off base. In fact, the reason we wouldn't buy our daughters the Go-Kart is because it was dangerous for them to have one in our neighborhood. It wasn't that we didn't want to get them one, it's that we wanted to protect them from dangers they didn't understand.

God is like that, too. As our heavenly Father, He has to say no to some of our requests. He sees those hidden dangers that we don't. But, when He says no, occasionally I'll come out with that old manipulation that never works—"You didn't answer my prayer, so You must not love me." Of course, that is not true. I know that in my heart, but sometimes I pray out of hurt. I'm so thankful that God looks on the heart, not the hurt. Show your kids that same mercy the next time they say, "You just don't love me."

MOM TO MASTER
Lord, help me to show Your mercy
to my children. Amen.

LOVING UNCONDITIONALLY

" 'Love your neighbor as yourself.' "
LEVITICUS 19:18

Did you know this commandment is listed nine times in the Bible? I've used it several times in this devotional. It's just so good. I've probably read this Scripture a hundred times, but I usually focus on the "Love your neighbor" part; however, the verse doesn't stop there. It says, "Love your neighbor *as yourself.*" That means that we have to love ourselves before we can really love others.

I don't know about you, but since I've had children, things have shifted. There are definitely parts of my body I don't love anymore. And, there are things I'd like to change about my personality, too. I wish I were more patient and more organized. Bottom line—there are a lot of days that I don't love myself. How about you? It's hard to love ourselves. We tend to focus on all of our imperfections. We hone in on all of our faults.

If you have trouble receiving a compliment or if you are constantly belittling yourself—you need to get in the "self-love mode." Ask God to fill you up with His love and help you to see yourself through His eyes. When I look at myself through His eyes, I look great! It's like the best airbrush job ever! So, love yourself today. It's not a biblical suggestion. It's a commandment!

MOM TO MASTER
Lord, help me to love myself today. Amen.

LOVING UNCONDITIONALLY

FEBRUARY 25

*But from everlasting to everlasting
the LORD's love is
with those who fear him.*

PSALM 103:17

There are some days when I can't see past the end of my nose. Life is just so busy! Deadlines, overflowing laundry baskets, soccer practice, grocery shopping. . . Tomorrow seems an eternity away, and I can't even wrap my mind around the concept of eternity. So, when I read a verse that says God's love is with us from everlasting to everlasting, I don't always get it.

Lately when having my Bible study time, I've been asking God to turn off the to-do list part of my brain so that I can really hear God's voice through His Word. And, you know what? It works! Suddenly, His Word leaps off the page, and all at once, I get it! This has now become one of my very favorite verses! To think that someone—especially the Creator of the universe—could love me forever and ever is so great! What a wonderful promise!

As moms, we don't have a lot of time to meditate on God's Word, so we have to make the most of those moments with the Master. Ask God to help you really focus as you read the Bible. Ask Him to show you what He has especially for you on that day. It's exciting!

LOVING UNCONDITIONALLY

MOM TO MASTER
Lord, help me to meditate more on Your Word. Amen.

"For I, the LORD your God,
am a jealous God."
EXODUS 20:5

Remember your first love? I married my high school sweetheart. I remember the first time we held hands. I remember the first time we kissed. I remember the exact outfit I was wearing when he first said he loved me. I remember it all! Even after twelve years of marriage, I still smile and get all sappy when I hear "our song" on the radio.

God wants us to love Him even more than we love our spouse and children. He tells us that He is a jealous God. He wants us to remember those special times with Him—the moment you gave your heart to Him, the miracles He has performed in your life, the times He came through when no one else could. . . He wants us to sing praise songs to Him as a love offering. He says if we won't praise Him, the rocks will cry out. I don't want any rock doing my praising for me. How about you?

Start today and keep an "I Remember" journal. Record what God does for you each day—even the smallest things. It'll be sort of a daily "love letter" to the Father. If you've grown cold to God, you're sure to fall in love with Him again.

LOVING UNCONDITIONALLY

MOM TO MASTER
Lord, help me to keep You as my first love. Amen.

> *"I tell you the truth,*
> *if you have faith as small as a mustard seed,*
> *you can say to this mountain,*
> *'Move from here to there' and it will move."*
>
> MATTHEW 17:20

LOVING UNCONDITIONALLY

The girls are at it again. I find it rather ironic that I'm writing about love while my daughters wrestle on the ground. Obviously, God has a sense of humor. Deep down, beneath their "I'm too cool for words" attitudes—they do love one another. I occasionally see glimpses of that love. It's sort of like the morning mist—there for a few moments and then gone almost instantly. Still, their love for each other remains— buried within them somewhere.

On the days when I can't see even a shadow of that love, I continue to thank the Lord that it's there. Abby will call Allyson a "stupid head" and Allyson will give Abby a crack on the head. After I discipline them, I raise my hands and I say, "Thank You, Lord, that my girls love each other. I thank You, God, that they will be lifelong friends." Sometimes, I say it purely out of faith because there is no evidence of that love, but faith of a mustard seed is all I need—that I've got! Put your faith to work today, and watch the love grow in your home.

MOM TO MASTER
Thank You, Father, that my children
love You and each other. Amen.

Love one another deeply, from the heart.
1 PETER 1:22

"Mommy, will you always love me?" Abby asked, looking up at me with her big green eyes.

"Of course, I'll always love you," I said, kissing her on the head. "That's what mommies do."

Abby smiled, satisfied with my answer.

At that moment, I thought, *I hope she will always be able to feel my love—no matter what.* Or, if she can't feel my love, I want her to feel God's love. His love is much more far-reaching than mine.

Today's world is very unsure. In fact, it's crazy many days. In the hustle and bustle of day-to-day life, our children need our affirmation. They need to know that we'll always love them. And more importantly, they need to know that their heavenly Father will always love them. So, take this opportunity to tell them that you love them and that God loves them even more than you do—and that's a lot!

Love is the answer. Even if your children wander from "the straight and narrow path," love will bring them back. If you're discouraged today because your children don't seem to be accepting your love or embracing God's love—hold on! God's love has a way of penetrating even the hardest of hearts.

LOVING UNCONDITIONALLY

MOM TO MASTER
Thank You, Father, for Your love.
Help me to show Your love to my children. Amen.

*"Look at the birds of the air;
they do not sow or reap or store away in barns,
and yet your heavenly Father feeds them.
Are you not much more valuable than they?"*

MATTHEW 6:26

"Mommy, hurry!" Abby called from the middle of the driveway. "It's a baby bird!"

Sure enough, right in the middle of our driveway was a sweet, fluffy, baby dove. He was probably five weeks old. He had all of his feathers, but the dainty dove still couldn't fly. After calling the Texas Wildlife Headquarters, I was instructed to move the bird into a makeshift nest in a hanging basket near the tree where he had fallen. As I planned my emergency bird rescue, I rushed to the front door to watch our little feathered friend. That's when I saw one of the most beautiful sights I'd ever seen—the mother dove nuzzling her baby bird—right in the middle of our driveway. She was protecting her baby at all costs.

We would do the same for our children. We'd give our life for our kids, wouldn't we? Do you know that's how God feels about us? He adores us! He cares about each one of us. When we fall out of our respective nests, He is right there, hovering over us, protecting us, loving us.

MOM TO MASTER
*Thank You, Father, for always being there for me—
protecting me and loving me. Amen.*

You too,
be patient and stand firm.
JAMES 5:8

One of my best friends just had her second baby—
Baby Aimee. She is so precious and innocent and tiny.
Every time I hold a newborn, I'm still amazed. For
nine months we wait and dream and anticipate, and
then finally the baby comes. At that moment, when
you see your sweet baby for the first time, all of those
months of waiting are so worth it.

Waiting is not easy, especially when you're waiting
for something as monumental as the birth of a child.
But, even if you're waiting on God to perform a miracle in some other area of your life, it's tough. We're not
a patient people. When days turn to weeks and weeks
turn to months and months turn to years, you can't
help but wonder if God is still working on your behalf.
But rest assured, He is! Just as your children were born
when they were ready, your dreams and miracles will
hatch at their appointed times. So, hang in there and
wait with joy. Whenever you are able to finally embrace whatever it is you're believing God for, it will be
more than worth the wait!

MOM TO MASTER
Lord, thank You for giving me the patience
to wait with joy. I love You. Amen.

TAKING THE TIME

MARCH 2

"As long as the earth endures, seedtime and harvest,
cold and heat, summer and winter,
day and night will never cease."

GENESIS 8:22

Somehow that verse is comforting to me. Just knowing that God can keep all of the earth's functions—seasons, temperatures, etc.—in order, makes me feel good. Often, I find myself stressing about time-related issues, such as: *Am I spending enough quality time with my children? Will I meet my book deadline? Will I have enough time to lose ten pounds before my next high school reunion?*

I recently heard a preacher on the radio talking about time management, and he asked, "Are you spinning your wheels or are you on a roll?"

Well, I thought, *it depends on which day you ask me!*

Some days I have it all together—everything is running on schedule and I feel in complete control. (Okay, realistically I have only three days a year like that.) Most of my days are filled with unexpected visitors, last-minute hair appointments, school activities, and putting out fires. Can I hear a collective "Amen!"?

But, we can rejoice in knowing that if God can keep the world spinning, He can certainly handle the tasks before us each day. So, the next time you're running in circles, call on Him.

MOM TO MASTER

Lord, I recognize Your ability to keep everything in
order. I give every part of my life to You. Amen.

*Jesus said, "Let the little children come to me,
and do not hinder them."*
MATTHEW 19:14

I once read an article that said children spell love T-I-M-E. As I pondered that statement, I had to agree. Sometimes, as parents, we think that our kids spell love M-O-N-E-Y because our society has become so materialistic, but in reality, kids just want to be with us. Abby and Ally would rather spend an afternoon watching old Doris Day movies on my big bed than practically anything I could give them. They actually enjoy being with me, and that's something I am so thankful for. I realize that as they get older, that may not always be true, so I want to take advantage of each and every opportunity to snuggle together, eat buttery popcorn, and watch Doris Day work her onscreen magic with Rock Hudson.

Find some activities that you and your children enjoy doing together like going hiking, going fishing, doing crafts, reading stories, baking cookies, playing board games. . . Just find some common ground and make time for your children. Even if you have to "pencil in" a day of baking cookies with kids in your daily planner—do it! Don't just say you love your children—show them! Spend some time together.

MOM TO MASTER
*Father, I want to thank You for every moment
I get to spend with my children.
Help me to treasure this time. Amen.*

MARCH 4

Be joyful always.
1 THESSALONIANS 5:16

Slowly you open one eye, trying hard to focus on the clock—2 A.M.

How could she be hungry again? you wonder.

As the baby wails on, you stumble down the hallway in your fuzzy slippers and tattered bathrobe. Such is the life of a mommy.

We are a rare breed. A royal sisterhood. A mommy sorority. We operate on only a few hours of sleep, never finishing a meal, and usually juggling ten balls at once. Let's face it—this mom thing is no easy gig, which is why moms can be occasionally crabby—especially moms of newborns. C'mon, admit it! You've bitten a few heads off in your lifetime, too! I can remember thinking, "I can't do this one more day! God must not have known what He was doing when He made me a mom." But, you know what? He did know.

I found out that He had equipped me with everything I needed to be a good mom. And, He was more than happy to help me make it through when I felt my weakest. He will do the same for you. No matter how dark your dark circles are. No matter how ugly you've acted today. No matter what—God loves you and believes in you.

MOM TO MASTER
*Father, help me not to be crabby as
I learn how to be a mom. Amen.*

TAKING THE TIME

"For I know the plans I have for you,"
declares the LORD, "plans to prosper you and not to
harm you, plans to give you hope and a future."
JEREMIAH 29:11

We recently went to MGM Studios in Walt Disney World in Orlando—such fun! We rode the Tower of Terror. We went upside down several times on Aerosmith's Rockin' Rollercoaster. We had a total blast!

As evening fell, we only had time for one more ride. That's when I read the description of the Disney Animation Tour. I knew that as a budding artist, my ten-year-old Abby would love it! I would have rather gone on the Tower of Terror again, but I knew Abby would be greatly inspired by the animation tour. So, that's what we did. We watched clips from classic Disney movies. We listened to actual artists talk about the process of making animated films. We saw drawings from an upcoming movie. It was interesting, and for Abby, it was magical. It confirmed something inside of her.

The whole way back to the hotel, we discussed the beauty of Disney art. Abby talked passionately of how God would someday use her art. I was so thankful that we hadn't missed the opportunity to fan Abby's dream. Why not look for ways to encourage your children's dreams today?

MOM TO MASTER
Father, help me to fan the dreams
You've placed within my children. Amen.

He who heeds discipline
shows the way to life.
PROVERBS 10:17

"That's it. You're in the time-out chair!" I hollered to my then four-year-old Allyson. She had rolled her eyes at me one too many times that afternoon. Slowly, she cowered over to the time-out chair, positioned in the corner of her room. She detested time out. Just hearing the words *time* and *out* in the same sentence made her cringe. But as much as she hated it, she spent a lot of time in that little wooden chair. Her rebellious streak simply took over from time to time.

I find myself in God's time-out chair almost as often as Allyson frequented hers as a preschooler. It seems I also have a rebellious streak. But, God's time-out chair isn't a place where He puts you to punish you; rather, you put yourself there when you disobey Him. It's a place where the blessings of God no longer flow. I don't like it there anymore than Allyson liked her little wooden chair. But the best thing about God's time-out chair is you can get up at any time. All you have to do is repent and move on. So, if you're in the time-out chair today, don't worry. Your chair time is almost up.

MOM TO MASTER
Father, help me to follow You all the time. Amen.

TAKING THE TIME

"Is not wisdom found among the aged?
Does not long life bring understanding?"
JOB 12:12

As we strolled through our local Wal-Mart, my then three-year-old Abby found a stuffed animal that she just couldn't live without. I told her no, and that was it. Abby threw herself on the floor and proceeded to have the mother of all tantrums. Ally, who was one at the time, let out some sympathy cries, adding to the scene. Once Abby's breathing returned to normal, we headed to the checkout lane.

It was at that exact moment when I saw this sweet elderly man from our church. He looked into the faces of my little girls and whispered to me, "They are so precious. These are the best years of your life. Treasure each moment!"

I smiled politely, but on the inside I was thinking, *Are you kidding me? Did you just see the tantrum I had to deal with back there? Give me a break!* That was more than seven years ago, but his words have stayed with me.

Those were precious years. I can see that now. Sometimes, when I was elbow deep in dirty diapers, I couldn't see it. So, if you're in the middle of your children's preschool years take some advice from the wise old man at my church—treasure each moment.

TAKING THE TIME

MOM TO MASTER
Father, help me to treasure each moment
with my children. Amen.

> *Let the wise listen*
> *and add to their learning.*
> PROVERBS 1:5

Listening. It's almost a lost art form in today's world. Yet, according to the International Listening Association, "Being listened to spells the difference between feeling accepted and feeling isolated." Wow, that's pretty strong, isn't it?

In professional circles, I am a good listener. I understand the importance of listening to my colleagues; yet, I sometimes fail to listen to my children. I find myself interrupting them, trying to get them to "get to the end of the story" while I am still young. But, that's not what I should be doing as a caring, accepting mom. The Lord convicted me about this very thing not long ago, and I've been working on my listening skills ever since.

Are you a good listener? Do you really give your kids your full attention when they are talking to you? Do you nod your head and smile, letting them know that you're truly into what they are saying? If not, you may need to ask God to help you improve your listening skills, too. If we fail to listen to them now, we'll be sorry later when they no longer choose to tell us things. So, go ahead. Open up your ears and your heart and listen to your children!

TAKING THE TIME

MOM TO MASTER
Lord, please help me to listen to my children
the same way that You listen to me. Amen.

*He gives strength to the weary
and increases the power of the weak.*
ISAIAH 40:29 NIV

Are you too busy? Is your calendar so marked up that you have to pencil in potty breaks? Moms are busy people. That's just a fact of life, but if we allow ourselves to become too busy, we'll miss out on quality time with our families. We'll be running around so much that we won't know if we're coming or going. Even good things can be bad if they take us away from our families.

For instance, if volunteering to head up the crafts committee for this year's Vacation Bible School consumes so much of your time that you can't play with your kids an entire month of the summer—it's not a good thing. Or, if teaching the ladies' Bible study on Tuesday nights conflicts with going to your son's baseball games all spring—you might need to step down from that leadership role.

Like the catchy anti-drug campaign slogan, I've had to learn to "Just say no!" to some things. It's not my nature to say no. I am usually the first one to jump in and volunteer—many times at the expense of my husband and children. But, I'm doing better these days. So, if you're like me, learn to "Just say no!" Your family will thank you.

MOM TO MASTER
*Lord, help me to make wise decisions
where my time is concerned. Amen.*

TAKING THE TIME

Oh, how I love your law!
I meditate on it all day long.
PSALM 119:97

Don't you just love to soak in a big bathtub full of bubbles? The beautiful bubbles tickle your toes and the fresh, flowery fragrance fills the room. It's one of my most favorite things to do. If I could, I would soak in the tub so long that my entire body would become "pruney." There's just nothing like a bubble bath—it's pure heaven! It's time well spent, as far as I'm concerned. Soaking in bubbles totally de-stresses me and brings a quiet rest to my soul. And what mom doesn't need more of that in her life?

Do you know what else brings peace and rest? Soaking in God's Word. When you spend time in the Word of God, it transforms you from the inside out. It replaces stress with peace; sickness with healing; anger with compassion; hate with love; worry with faith; and weariness with energy. Soaking in God's Word every day will keep you balanced and ready to tackle whatever comes your way. It's time well spent. You'll become a better person—a better wife and a better mom. And you won't even get "pruney" in the process.

MOM TO MASTER

Lord, thank You for Your Word. Help me to
soak it in more and more each day. Amen.

TAKING THE TIME

*"But seek first his kingdom
and his righteousness."*
MATTHEW 6:33

The joke around our house is, "I bought a book about time management. I just haven't had time to read it." As a fellow mom, I'm sure you can relate. We have about a hundred things to do before noon! Listen, I'm all for time management. I have interviewed experts about time management and written very informative articles using their comments and advice; however, I am not very efficient when it comes to actually practicing time management principles.

I truly want to do better, but I feel overwhelmed before I even get started. Instead, I rush around in a thousand directions—wrapping presents a minute before we're supposed to leave for the birthday party, making my bed while I brush my teeth, etc. You get the idea. Then one day it dawned on me—God is a great time manager. He can get a lot done in a short amount of time. I mean, hey, He made the entire world in a week!

At that moment of revelation, I asked God to help manage my time. I asked Him to reveal the activities, volunteer positions, assignments, and friendships that needed to go. Then I asked Him to replace that "free time" with things He would have me do. And, you know what? He really knows what He's doing.

MOM TO MASTER
Lord, help me to be a better time manager. Amen.

TAKING THE TIME

MARCH 12

*This is the day the LORD has made;
let us rejoice and be glad in it.*

PSALM 118:24

"Kodak moments." Aren't they great? I love to look through photographs from past vacations, honor days, field trips, sporting events, family gatherings, holidays, and more! And, when I have time, I enjoy scrapbooking—to really showcase our precious pictures. As I was putting together a recent scrapbook for my father, I noticed that almost every picture I'd taken featured smiling, happy folks. Some were posed "cheesy" pictures, but even the candid shots showed intense happiness. Whether it was Abby finishing her round-off back handspring series at the last gymnastics meet or Ally enjoying some fresh watermelon—happiness just oozed from each photograph.

Like the commercial says, those are the moments you cherish. Sometimes, you have to hold onto those happy memories to make it through until the next Kodak moment. Life is difficult, and traumatic events can uproot your entire life in an instant. So, we need to live each day mindful that these are precious times—special moments with our loved ones—treasured times that are gone like the mist in the morning. Enjoy each moment with your children—even the not-so-pleasant ones—and thank God for the Kodak moments.

MOM TO MASTER
*Lord, I thank You for filling my life with
Kodak moments. Amen.*

*"By this all men will know
that you are my disciples,
if you love one another."*
JOHN 13:35

When was the last time you slowed down long enough to make mud pies with your kids? When was the last time you read funny poetry by a candlelight pizza dinner? If it's been awhile, then plan a special day to do nothing but fun stuff with your children. Of course, this works much better if your kids are willing to spend an entire day with you. Once they reach puberty, Mom is sort of on the "nerd list." But, if you still have little ones or tweens running around, why not host an all-out fun-filled day?

Begin with pizza for breakfast. Watch funny, family films in your jammies until noon. Then, if the weather is nice, take a bike ride together or go on a scavenger hunt in a nearby park. Play board games until nightfall. Finish the day with devotions and prayer time. Just bask in each other's presence, soaking it all in.

At the end of the day, you will have made some magnificent memories. When your kids are old, they'll look back on that day and smile. They may not remember exactly what you did, but they'll remember the love.

TAKING THE TIME

MOM TO MASTER

*Lord, help me to spend more quality time
with my family. Amen.*

MARCH 14

*And pray in the Spirit on all occasions
with all kinds of prayers and requests.*

EPHESIANS 6:18

I once saw a bumper sticker that said, "Seven days without prayer makes one weak." At first I thought it was a typo, but then I realized it was a clever play on words. The more I thought about it, the more I liked it—and the more convicted I became.

I'm really diligent about reading my daily devotions. I regularly go to church. But then I started evaluating my prayer life. Wow—it seemed almost nonexistent.

I started thinking about the times I had spent more than a few minutes in prayer, and it was always at a time when I was going through bad stuff. In other words, I only spent quality time talking to God when I needed Him. I spent all of my prayer time asking Him for stuff. I would throw in "Thank You, Lord, for such and such" every now and then, but most of my time was spent requesting His intervention. I rarely took time to listen to Him, in case He had something He wanted to say to me in that still, small voice.

Is your prayer life rushed and one-sided? If it is, don't despair. Just begin spending quality prayer time with the Father today. He's been waiting for you.

MOM TO MASTER
Lord, I want to hear from You. I love You.

Taking the Time

The living, the living—they praise you,
as I am doing today;
fathers tell their children about your faithfulness.
ISAIAH 38:19

"There's no time like the present."

That's what my mother always used to say when she wanted me to clean my room. Now, I find myself using that very same line on my girls. Of course, they look at me the same way I used to look at my mom when she used that expression on me. (Yes, I rolled my eyes at my mom, too!) Still, the fact remains that it's a true statement. There really is no time like the present.

So, if there is something you've been longing to do, or someplace you've been dreaming of going, or someone you've been wanting to visit—go for it. Do it today. Seize the moment! What are you waiting for?

We're not promised tomorrow, which is why we need to live each day as if it were our last. Love a little more. Laugh a little more. Hug your kids more. Serve God with all of your heart. Don't let the sun go down without telling your family how much you love them. Make sure your kids know how much Jesus loves them. Think of today as a gift from God—because it is.

MOM TO MASTER
Thank You, God, for every minute of every day. Amen.

Jesus said,
"Let the little children come to me,
and do not hinder them."

MATTHEW 19:14

"No."

That was always the answer I received from one of my former bosses. No matter what idea I'd offer—even if it had been the best suggestion in the world—his answer was always, "No." I nicknamed him "Negative Ned." Though I tried to joke about it, his negativity almost crippled me on the inside.

After being shot down so many times, I quit offering suggestions. I quit sharing my thoughts. I went into my "survival mode" with all of my defenses up. God eventually freed me from that supervisor, but I learned a lot during those months of drifting in the Sea of Negativism. Those lessons have stayed with me, and I often think of Old Ned when I'm parenting.

As moms, it seems our duty to say no. And sometimes, no is the correct response. But, don't be so quick to always say no, or your children will quit asking you stuff. They'll go into their survival mode and put up their defenses—just like I did with my boss. As moms, we should take time to really listen to our kids' requests before saying no. If we don't, we just might become "Negative Nellie."

MOM TO MASTER
Lord, help me to be open-minded and approachable—
especially with my children. Amen.

*"Do not judge,
or you too will be judged."*
MATTHEW 7:1

"You're not like other moms," commented one of my daughter's friends. "You rock!"

That may be the highest compliment I've ever received in these thirty-plus years. Abby's friend thought it was cool because I knew all of the words to Aaron Carter's latest release, "That's How I Beat Shaq."

Okay, so that's not exactly a spiritual hymn, but the point is, I had taken the time to be interested in my nine-year-old daughter's musical preferences. While scanning her CDs for offensive language (which results in an immediate eject), I discovered that some of her music was kind of fun. I borrowed a few of her CDs and began listening to them when I power-walked. Hey, you've never lived unless you've power-walked to a Jump 5 song!

Besides discovering some fun new tunes, I also discovered something else—taking time to know your kids and their likes and dislikes is very cool. It brings you closer to them. It puts you right in the middle of their world and helps you better understand their turf, their dreams, their struggles, and more. I highly recommend it. It's exciting and fun. And, you might just find out that you really like that Sponge Bob guy after all. (It's okay; I'll never tell.)

MOM TO MASTER
Lord, help me to better understand my kids and their preferences. Amen.

TAKING THE TIME

> *"I have swept away*
> *your offenses like a cloud,*
> *your sins like the morning mist."*
> ISAIAH 44:22

Do you remember that great song by Cher called, "If I Could Turn Back Time"?

Okay, that's about the only line from the entire song that I actually remember, but that line is really good, isn't it? I mean, have you ever really pondered the concept of turning back time? What would you do differently? (Besides that terrible mullet hairstyle you had in the early '80s, what else would you change?) What would you keep exactly the same?

I wrote an entry in my journal about this very topic, and I discovered some key things. I wouldn't change any of the big decisions I'd made—choosing to follow God, choosing to marry Jeff, choosing to go into journalism, having children early in our marriage. . . But my journal entry was filled with little regrets and misguided priorities. I wrote, "If I could turn back time, I would spend more time playing in the sandbox with my girls. I would spend more time enjoying my children instead of just caring for them."

Well, we can't turn back time, and there's no sense living in regret. God doesn't want us to do that. But, we can begin correcting those things today— spend more lazy afternoons with your kids. The housework will wait—time won't.

MOM TO MASTER
Lord, help me prioritize my life. Amen.

*Don't let anyone look down on you
because you are young.*
1 TIMOTHY 4:12

They say that once you learn to ride a bike, you never forget. I beg to differ. Okay, so I haven't really ridden a bike (unless you count the stationary ones at the YMCA) in about fifteen years. But, last month when we bought our daughters two new, shiny bikes, I wanted one, too! Suddenly, I had to have one. So, my husband bought me a beautiful silver bike—with gearshifts and everything!

I could hardly wait to get home and try it. The girls thought it was really funny seeing their old mom on a new bike, but they were supportive in between giggles. Abby showed me how to use the gearshifts while Ally reviewed the whole kickstand thing with me. The bike felt quite foreign as I shakily began down our driveway. My heart pounded with fear. It was as if I'd never ridden a bike in my whole life. Thankfully, my children were there to teach me all of the skills I had forgotten.

You know, we're never too old to learn, and sometimes we neglect to recognize the teachers living in our own homes. Our kids may be younger, but in some ways they are much wiser. Why not let your kids teach you something today?

MOM TO MASTER
*Father, help me to never get too old
to enjoy my kids. Amen.*

TAKING THE TIME

> *. . .that is, that you and I may be*
> *mutually encouraged by each other's faith.*
>
> ROMANS 1:12

It was the last day of horse camp, and all of the parents were on hand to see the campers' presentation of the skills they'd learned that week. Smiling proudly, Abby rounded the corner on her horse. Then, all at once, the old, stubborn horse stopped. He simply wouldn't budge. Abby ever so gently kicked the horse in the ribs. Still, the horse wouldn't go. Then Abby whispered, "Walk on, Prissy. Walk on." Finally, the horse started moving forward. Every time the stubborn animal stopped, Abby would simply say, "Walk on," and the horse would begin moving again.

As I watched Abby maneuver that large animal around the ring, I learned something—encouragement is vitally important. Each time our kids start to get off that straight and narrow path, we should softly whisper, "Walk on." By encouraging our children, we can give them the confidence to move toward their dreams, to conquer their fears, and to fulfill the destiny that God has for each of them. Sometimes, all they need is a little nudge and a soft, encouraging word to move forward.

Sure, offering encouragement takes time, but it'll be time well spent. So, why not look for opportunities to whisper "Walk on" today? Like Abby's horse, your children will respond positively.

MOM TO MASTER
Father, help me to ever so gently
encourage my children. Amen.

Be very careful, then, how you live—
not as unwise but as wise,
making the most of every opportunity.
EPHESIANS 5:15–16

Did you know that there are 1,440 minutes in every day? Our youth group at church recently changed its name to "14:40" to signify that our kids are learning to follow God every minute of every day.

"Make the most of the minutes!" our youth pastor shared.

Wow. That's good, isn't it? If we really lived every minute for God, wouldn't this be a different world? As our youth pastor spoke passionately about "14:40," my heart started beating so hard that I thought it would pound right out of my chest. I got excited, challenged, and convicted, all at the same time. Now it's a daily goal around our house to make the most of those 1,440 minutes. The girls have really embraced the idea. It causes them to think about their decisions and actions throughout the day. It does the same for me.

Sure, we miss it. There are minutes in our day that we wish we could do over, but God knows our hearts. He knows that we are focused on making the most of the minutes for the Master. Why not start a 14:40 campaign in your house?

MOM TO MASTER
Father, help me to make the most of every minute today.
Help me to live each minute for You. Amen.

TAKING THE TIME

MARCH 22

Make the most of every opportunity.
COLOSSIANS 4:5

It was my thirteenth birthday, and I was very much into drama. I loved being in plays. I loved going to the theater. And I loved *Annie*. It was my all-time favorite musical, and it was coming to Bloomington, Indiana, on my birthday! I knew tickets would be scarce, but my heart was set on going. My mom knew it, and she must have called every ticket vendor in the entire state of Indiana to track down tickets. After weeks of sleuth work, she was finally able to nab three fifth-row tickets to the show. I will never forget that night. I'm not sure if it was so special because the show was wonderful or if it was because I knew how hard my mom had worked to make that night possible.

Each time my daughters' birthdays roll around, I think about that "Annie" birthday. Even if we can't purchase expensive tickets to a Broadway musical every year, we always try to make each birthday celebration very special. I bet you do the same. Or, if you haven't made a big deal of your children's birthdays in the past, it's not too late. You'll have an opportunity every year! Start planning now. Let your children know that you are so thankful to be their mother.

TAKING THE TIME

MOM TO MASTER
Lord, help me to make my children
feel loved every day—
especially on their birthdays. Amen.

And my God will meet all your needs
according to his glorious riches
in Christ Jesus.
PHILIPPIANS 4:19

Abby and Allyson were drawing pictures of our family a few years ago, and Abby proudly displayed her artwork on the fridge. When I passed by later in the day, I saw the picture of me that she had drawn. It broke my heart. There was a picture of Daddy fishing with them and there was a picture of me typing at my computer.

"Oh, no!" I cringed. "Is that how they see me? As just a writer at my computer—never having any time for them?" I panicked. I cried. And then I prayed. I asked God to work a financial miracle in my life so that I wouldn't have to work so many hours and miss out on the fun family stuff. God was faithful to answer my prayer. I have been able to turn down some of the lesser-paying, more time-consuming jobs, still make the car payment, and have more time with my children.

God will do the same for you. The Bible says that He is no respecter of persons. So, if it's your desire to work fewer hours to be with your children more, just ask God. He has the answer.

MOM TO MASTER
Lord, please work a financial miracle
in my life that would allow me to spend
more time with my family. Amen.

TAKING THE TIME

MARCH 24

*Jesus Christ is the same yesterday
and today and forever.*

HEBREWS 13:8

As I waited for Abby's highlights to process, I read a hair magazine. I was so relieved to discover that "Big Hair Is in Again!" Finally, my '80s "do" is back in fashion!

In fact, the '80s are coming back with a vengeance! Allyson recently told me about a new kind of pants she likes. She described them like this: "They have zippers and pockets all over them, and they make this weird swishy noise when you walk."

I said, "You mean parachute pants?" *Ding. Ding. Ding.* That was the right answer! I cannot believe that parachute pants are back in style. (I thought they were a fashion fiasco the first time around!) It's really true what they say—if you hang onto something long enough, it will eventually come back in style.

Isn't it good to know that no matter if you're sporting a mullet, "The Rachel," or a classic bob, Jesus loves you? His love never changes. In fact, He is always in season. His Word is as current and applicable today as it was a century ago. So, even if our clothing, hairdos, and musical preferences are considered "totally uncool" by our offspring, we can offer them the One who will never go out of style—Jesus.

TAKING THE TIME

MOM TO MASTER
*Thank You, Lord,
for being my Savior all the time. Amen.*

Man is like a breath;
his days are like a fleeting shadow.
PSALM 144:4

Attention shoppers! Christmas is only nine months away. Hurry! Hurry! You don't want to be caught in that last-minute yuletide frenzy.

Okay, so in reality, few people begin shopping for Christmas in March. Oh sure, there are some of those eager beavers who start shopping for the next Christmas on December 26, but most of us wait until Thanksgiving dinner is settled in our tummies before we hit the malls, right?

As far off as December 25 may seem, it's just around the corner. Time has a way of slipping by us. It's like the introduction to *Days of Our Lives* says—"like sands through the hourglass. . ."

It seems like only yesterday that we were celebrating birthdays at Chuck E. Cheese. Now, we're having boy/girl skating parties. What happened to those years? They sneaked past me when I wasn't looking. Wouldn't it be great if we could keep our children little forever? But we can't, so don't miss one moment of their growing-up years. We can't get those years back. Enjoy them as much as you can right now. (Oh, and go ahead and start buying a few Christmas presents each month to avoid the retail rush!)

MOM TO MASTER
God, help me to make good use of my time,
cherishing every moment with my kids. Amen.

TAKING THE TIME

"To God belong wisdom and power;
counsel and understanding are his."

JOB 12:13

"You are ruining my life!"

That's what the daughter screamed at her mother in the recent remake of Disney's *Freaky Friday*. We took the girls to see that movie earlier this month, and all of us enjoyed it—especially me. I could totally relate to the mother in the film. I, too, am a member of the "You've ruined my life!" club. Abby has told me that more than once.

You know, on days when your beloved child looks you in the face and says, "You're ruining my life," you don't want to be nice. Actually, you want to be defensive. You want to say, "Listen, kiddo, do you have any idea what I do for you every single day? You couldn't make it without me!" (And yes, I have said those things.)

But, what the mother discovers in *Freaky Friday* is that she lacks understanding where her daughter is concerned and vice versa. Once the mom and daughter see things through the other's eyes, understanding comes. If you're also a member of the "You've ruined my life" club, ask God to give you understanding so that you can see things through your kids' eyes. If you do, I have a feeling your membership in that club will soon expire.

MOM TO MASTER
God, help me to understand my children
the way that You understand me. Amen.

TAKING THE TIME

*"But my salvation will last forever,
my righteousness will never fail."*
ISAIAH 51:6

Okay, admit it. You watched every episode of the very first *American Idol* season, didn't you? Well, if you didn't, I'll bet your kids did. It was an amazing journey. Of course, we Texans were quite thrilled when our home girl Kelly Clarkson won the coveted title. My daughters and I jumped and cheered as if we'd won!

Soon after, Kelly released her single "A Moment Like This," and it became an instant hit. Like millions of other Americans, we scrambled to Wal-Mart to buy our copy, and we played it over and over again. I love these words: "A moment like this. Some people wait a lifetime. For a moment like this. Some people search forever. . . ."

There are very few "Moments Like This" in life. We treasure those monumental moments, such as our first prom, graduation day, our wedding day, the birth of our children. Those are tender times. But, do you know what the most special "Moment Like This" moment is? The day you made Jesus the Lord of your life.

Make sure that you celebrate all of the "Moments Like This" with your children. But most importantly, make sure that your children experience that most important moment so that they won't be searching forever.

MOM TO MASTER
*God, help me to never miss a special moment
with my children. Amen.*

TAKING THE TIME

> *Finally, brothers, whatever is true,*
> *whatever is noble, whatever is right,*
> *whatever is pure, whatever is lovely,*
> *whatever is admirable. . .*
> *think about such things.*
>
> PHILIPPIANS 4:8

"What time is it, kiddies?"

"It's time for *Cowboy Bob's Corral!*"

Even today, twenty-five years later, I can still remember the theme song to the *Cowboy Bob's Corral* kiddy show that aired on Channel 4 in southern Indiana in the 1970s. It was my very favorite show. I loved Cowboy Bob's horse. I loved the cartoon segments. And I loved how Cowboy Bob closed every show with, "Remember, if you can't say anything nice, don't say anything at all." Then he'd ride off into the sunset, and I'd wave good-bye to Cowboy Bob until the following afternoon.

Those were great afternoons spent with Cowboy Bob. Every show, that crafty old cowboy would sneak in moral advice, and we'd soak it all up because if Cowboy Bob said it, it just had to be true.

I'm sure Cowboy Bob has long since retired, and now my kids head home from school just in time to watch *Lizzie McGuire*—with me. Are you monitoring your kids' TV shows? If not, you should be. I don't mean you should become the TV gestapo, but you should find out what they're watching and what they'll be remembering twenty-five years from now. . . .

MOM TO MASTER
God, help me to help my children
make good viewing choices. Amen.

But when you pray,
go into your room,
close the door and pray to your Father,
who is unseen.

MATTHEW 6:6

Do you have a sort of bedtime ritual with your children? Some parents read a storybook to their children every night. Other parents share a Bible story or two. Some even make up their own stories to share. Whatever your bedtime routine might be, I hope that prayer is part of it.

Saying a bedtime prayer with your children is one of the most important things you can do for them. It accomplishes several things, such as teaching your kids to pray by hearing you pray aloud, giving prayer a place of importance in their lives, making prayer a habit for them, drawing the family unit closer, and enriching their spiritual side. To put it in the words of my daughter Allyson, "PRAYER ROCKS!"

We spend so much time just doing "stuff" with our kids—running them to soccer practice, helping with homework, playing board games—and all of that is good. But if we don't figure prayer time into the daily equation, we're just spinning our wheels. Prayer time is a precious time. Don't miss out on it even one night. It's a habit worth forming!

MOM TO MASTER
Father, help me to teach my children
the importance of prayer time. Amen.

Remember the days of old;
consider the generations long past.

DEUTERONOMY 32:7

Do you ever take a stroll down memory lane and take your kids with you? If not, you might want to put on your mental walking shoes and head down that path. Trust me, they'll like it!

My girls love to hear about "the olden days." They love to hear stories of when Jeff and I were high school sweethearts. They almost hurt themselves laughing when I share my most embarrassing moments. And they especially love the story about the time I met Shaquille O'Neal.

Funny, isn't it? Our children enjoy hearing about our youth. Sometimes I think our children believe we were born old. So when we share stuff from our past, they feel more connected to us. When my children found out that I was a cheerleader in high school and college, they were blown away! All of a sudden, Abby said, "Cool! Can you teach me?"

Sure, that does wonders for the old ego, but more than anything else, it establishes a line of communication that wasn't there before. It gives you a common ground with your kids. So, go ahead. Share some funny stories from your youth. Your kids will love it.

TAKING THE TIME

MOM TO MASTER

Thank You, Lord, for giving me such wonderful
memories that I can share with my children. Amen.

*"If it is the Lord's will,
we will live and do this or that."*
JAMES 4:15

I zipped past my father carrying an armload of dirty laundry. A few seconds later, I zipped past with a basket of clean laundry. Ten minutes later, I was wrapping Allyson's birthday presents while talking on the phone. As soon as I put down the receiver, my father sighed.

"You are too busy, honey," he said, sitting in the La-Z-Boy chair, watching "The Price Is Right."

I realized that I had totally ignored my precious visitor while trying to accomplish the tasks on my to-do list that morning. My seventy-nine-year-old dad had just wanted me to sit down and spend some quality time with him and Bob Barker. So, I did. I let the answering machine get the rest of my calls, and I watched TV alongside my dad, making conversation on commercial breaks. Dad has suffered several strokes over the past three years, so every moment we have with him is a precious one.

There are times when those to-do lists serve us well, and there are other times when we need to crumple them up and toss them into the trash. That morning taught me something—don't be too busy with life to enjoy life. It's all about prioritizing, really.

MOM TO MASTER
*Lord, help me to prioritize my day in a way
that is pleasing to You. Amen.*

For where envy and self-seeking exist,
confusion and every evil thing are there.

JAMES 3:16 NKJV

Two years ago I was asked to cohost the Christmas party for my daughter Allyson's first-grade class. I felt overwhelmed—especially since I was cohosting with "The Perfect Mom." She was June Cleaver, Carol Brady, and Donna Reed all rolled into one. As she talked of creative crafts, groovy games, and adorable homemade treats, I realized my ideas were not nearly "Martha Stewart-y" enough. I quickly retreated and took direction from her.

I helped her create the Winter Wonderland party, but inside I was having a pity party. As I cleaned up the leftover goodies, Allyson threw her arms around my waist and squeezed her biggest squeeze.

"Thanks for coming today, Mommy," she said.

I hugged her back. In her eyes, I was a success. She didn't care that I couldn't get my snowman cakes to stand up. She didn't care that none of the games were my ideas. She loved me—flaws and all.

That's how God is. Many times we compare ourselves to others and feel we don't measure up, but God loves us—flaws and all. I may never be "The Perfect Mom," but as long as I'm the best mom I can be—that's enough.

MOM TO MASTER

Lord, help me to keep my eyes on You
and not on my shortcomings.
I repent for feeling jealous sometimes. Amen.

BECOMING MOTHER OF THE YEAR

"Come to me,
all you who are weary and burdened,
and I will give you rest."

MATTHEW 11:28

There are days when I'm sure the side of my SUV must say "TAXI." We run to gymnastics. We race to cheerleading practice. We rush to art class. We hurry to Girl Scouts. We eat fast food on the way to computer class.

I want to stand up and say, "Stop the world from spinning! I want to get off!"

There is such pressure these days to make sure our children are in every extracurricular activity that sometimes I wonder if it's all too much. Have you been wondering the same thing?

We're moms. It's only natural that we desire to give our children the best. So, it's no wonder we sign them up for all of these wonderful extracurricular opportunities. But be careful. Make sure you're not pushing and nudging your children right into burnout. We don't want our kids to be so overwhelmed with activities that they have no time to be kids. They only get one childhood. Ask God to help you enhance their growing-up years without overwhelming them with "stuff." Even good stuff, if there's too much of it, can be bad.

MOM TO MASTER

Lord, help me not to pressure my children
with too much "stuff." But, help me to encourage
the gifts that You have put inside them. Amen.

APRIL 3

As I climbed into bed, I felt lower than a snake's belly. I knew I had blown it.

My mind replayed all of the times I'd lost my temper with the girls throughout that day. Granted, Abby and Allyson had acted absolutely awful, but I had acted even worse. I wanted to bury my head under the covers and hibernate for at least six months.

Nobody likes to fail, but until we get to heaven, we're going to fail. We're going to have bad days. We're human! I think, as moms, we sometimes forget that fact. We set such high standards for ourselves— so high that they are unattainable by humans. So, if you've been feeling lower than a snake's belly lately, take heart! God isn't mad at you. He loves you— temper tantrums and all. Just repent for your wrongdoings and ask Him to help you do better today. You can start fresh right now.

Determine to love more than you yell and laugh more than you nag. If you can do those two things today, you can go to bed tonight feeling really good! You may not be able to do those things in your own strength, but God can help you. Just ask Him.

MOM TO MASTER
*Father, I ask for Your forgiveness. Help me to be
quick to love, not quick to yell. Amen.*

Aim for perfection, listen to my appeal,
be of one mind, live in peace.
And the God of love and peace will be with you.
2 CORINTHIANS 13:11

Dictionary.com defines perfection like this:

> perfection (pr-fkshn) *n.* The quality or condition of being perfect. The act or process of perfecting. A person or thing considered to be perfect. An instance of excellence.

Wow. If I am supposed to be "excellent" all the time, I'm in a heap of trouble. There are some days when I might earn that "Blue Ribbon of Excellence," but there are a lot of days when I wouldn't even qualify for an honorable mention. How about you?

That's why I like the Christian definition of perfection a lot better. One inspirational author defines "Christian perfection" like this: "loving God with all our heart, mind, soul, and strength."

Now that seems more doable to me. In other words, I don't always have to "get it right," but if my heart is right and if I'm truly seeking God, I can walk in Christian perfection. And, guess what? You can, too! We may never win another blue ribbon the rest of our lives, but we can still be winners. Who says nobody's perfect? If we're in love with God, we are!

MOM TO MASTER
Father, help me to attain Christian perfection
every day of my life. Amen.

You need to persevere so that when
you have done the will of God,
you will receive what he has promised.

HEBREWS 10:36

Taebo. Pilates. Curves. Yep, I've tried them all (and I'm still trying most of them) to achieve that perfect body. You know—the bodies we had before pregnancy? I look at pictures of myself from my early twenties, and I'm amazed. You could actually see my abdominal muscles! Those were the days. . . .

But, being a determined woman in my mid-thirties, I decided to regain my youthful figure. So, I started exercising more than usual. I traded in my nightly power walk for an intense hour-long Winsor pilates workout. Once I was able to walk again, I added a thirty-minute resistance workout to my weekly routine. This has been going on for the past three months. Let me just share that I hurt myself in places I didn't even know existed! But, I am making progress. And, I've learned some things along the way.

Striving for perfection is a painful process no matter if you're trying to achieve the perfect body or the perfect walk with God. Perfection is a myth, really. We are made perfect through Christ Jesus—not through working it as hard as we can. If we keep our eyes on Jesus, He will cause us to succeed.

MOM TO MASTER
Father, help me not to get overwhelmed with the
desire to be perfect. I want You to perfect me. Amen.

BECOMING MOTHER OF THE YEAR

"I have loved you
with an everlasting love."
JEREMIAH 31:3

I absolutely love the quirky things about my kids. I love the way Abby laughs uncontrollably at movies. I love the way Allyson likes wearing clothes that match mine. I love the way they only like purple grape juice because white grape juice just doesn't make sense. I love the way they fall asleep in the car—even if it's only a ten-minute drive to Wal-Mart! I love these little things about my girls because they are my precious children.

Do you know that God feels the same way about you and your little quirky habits? He loves you—everything about you—period! Isn't that good to know?

So many people feel they have to become perfect before God will ever accept them, but that's simply not true. It's a lie that the devil likes to whisper in our ears to keep us from having a relationship with God. The truth is this: God loves us just the way we are! We don't have to be perfect. When we make Jesus the Lord over our lives, He gives us a clean slate. When the Father looks down at us, all He sees is the Jesus inside of us, and Jesus is pure perfection.

MOM TO MASTER

Father, help me to appreciate and celebrate the quirkiness of my kids the same way that You love and celebrate me. Amen.

*In the same way,
the Spirit helps us in our weakness.*

ROMANS 8:26

There's a great line from a movie that says, "You have to pass a test to get a driver's license, but they'll let anyone be a parent."

Of course, that line was said in jest, but it's actually true. Sometimes I feel like I received way more training to get behind the wheel than I did to raise two precious little girls. I had driver's education in high school. My father let me practice parallel parking in his car. I had lots of help, and I needed lots of help.

But when it came time to have my children, there was no mandatory parenting class. If it hadn't been for my mother and sister, I would've really been in trouble. I didn't know the first thing about sterilizing bottles. I had no clue how to work the Diaper Genie. I was hoping a genie would come out and do the forty-two loads of laundry awaiting me. I felt pretty inadequate to fill the "mommy shoes."

I discovered that I had to quit focusing on my inabilities as a mother and begin focusing on my abilities. God had chosen me to be a mom, and if He had chosen me, I knew that He had equipped me. He has equipped you, too!

MOM TO MASTER
*Father, thank You for equipping me
to be a good mother. Amen.*

Each one should test his own actions.
Then he can take pride in himself,
without comparing himself to somebody else.
GALATIANS 6:4

If there were an award for "World's Most Creative Mom," my buddy Angie would win hands-down. She doesn't just call the bakery at Wal-Mart to reserve a birthday cake. Are you kidding? She creates her own masterpiece! One year, she made a barnyard scene cake, using snack cakes for the silo. Another year, she made these adorable bug cupcakes, playing on the *A Bug's Life* theme.

Angie is very creative and very fun. If I were a kid, I'd want her to be my mom. As you can imagine, Angie's creativity is hard to match. I used to feel like a big nerd compared to her. I'd worry that my children would end up on *Oprah,* telling the world that their mother never loved them enough to bake a barnyard cake.

One day while I was wishing I were more creative in the kitchen, the Lord convicted me. The gist of His message was simply, "Get over it!" God wanted me to know that He had given me special abilities that He hadn't given anyone else. Once I grasped that concept, I no longer felt nerdy. I still order Wal-Mart cakes for my children, but I do so with great joy!

MOM TO MASTER
Father, help me to be the best mom that I can be. Amen.

BECOMING MOTHER OF THE YEAR

For we are God's workmanship,
created in Christ Jesus to do good works,
which God prepared in advance for us to do.
EPHESIANS 2:10

I've always loved this Scripture. Did you know that the word *workmanship* indicates an ongoing process? So, if we are God's workmanship, we are God's ongoing project. In other words, He isn't finished with us yet! Isn't that good news? I am so glad! I'd hate to think that I was as good as I was going to get.

So, if you are feeling less than adequate today, thinking that you are a terrible mother and wife and Christian—cheer up! God is not through with you yet! In fact, He is working on you right now—even as you're reading this devotional. He knew that we'd all make big mistakes, but this Scripture says that He created us in Christ Jesus to do good works. He's prepared the road for us. He's been planning our steps long before we arrived here, so don't worry!

We may not be where we want to be today, but as long as we're further along than we were yesterday, we're making progress. We're on the right road. After all, we're God's workmanship, and He only turns out good stuff!

MOM TO MASTER
Thank You, God, for working on me,
perfecting me from glory to glory. Amen.

*"Before I formed you in the womb I knew you,
before you were born I set you apart."*
JEREMIAH 1:5

While I was pregnant, I read a book titled *What to Expect When You're Expecting* and learned the exact week that my baby would be able to hear sounds outside the womb. That's when I began reading stories to my belly. I even put headphones around my large middle section and let the baby listen to inspirational music. Jeff and I talked to my tummy saying silly things like, "Hey, little girl! Can't wait to see you!"

Looking back, we were completely captivated by the entire experience. We felt as though we knew our daughters before they were ever born. After all, we'd been "interacting" with my belly for months—talking to it, reading to it, singing to it. I bet you did the same thing. Isn't it amazing how much you loved the baby you were carrying even though you'd never actually met that little person?

Having gone through that experience has given me a new appreciation for Jeremiah 1:5. To think that God knew me before I was ever born—wow! One translation says that God knew me and approved me. So, if you are struggling with a poor self-image today, snap out of it! You've been approved by Almighty God!

BECOMING MOTHER OF THE YEAR

MOM TO MASTER
*Lord, thank You for approving me
before I was even born. Amen.*

> *So also, the tongue is a small thing,*
> *but what enormous damage it can do.*
>
> JAMES 3:5 NLT

"I'm fat!" Abby said, stepping off the bathroom scales.

"Wonder where she's heard that before?" Jeff asked, raising his eyebrows at me.

Yes, I've been known to be a slave to the scales. And, yes, Abby has heard me say that before. Well, I'm not fat, and neither is she. But, it seemed that my negative body image had been passed down to my ten-year-old daughter. With bulimia and anorexia affecting so many girls and women today, I realized the seriousness of Abby's statement.

I took Abby's face in my hands, and I said, "You are not fat. You are the perfect size, and even if you weren't, that wouldn't change how special you are to me, your daddy, and your heavenly Father."

She smiled and took off to play with her sister.

Our words are powerful. They have an effect—either good or bad. That encounter with Abby made me reevaluate my words. I repented, and I asked God to uproot those negative seeds that I'd unintentionally planted into Abby's heart and mind. Then, I thanked God for His love and for His protection of my children.

If your mouth has been spewing words that aren't uplifting or godly, ask God to uproot those bad seeds. He knows our hearts, and He is a merciful God.

MOM TO MASTER
Thank You, God, for protecting
my children from wrong thinking. Amen.

A heart at peace gives life to the body.
PROVERBS 14:30

Are you at peace with the person God made you to be?

If you don't have peace within yourself, you'll never have peace with other people. God could send you another mom to be the friend you've been praying for, but if you're not at peace with yourself, that relationship won't work. You've got to be happy with who God made you to be first before you can experience healthy relationships.

If you're focused on your imperfections and are constantly wishing you were someone else, you're allowing the devil to steal your peace and replace it with wrong thinking. Don't get caught in that trap. That's a miserable way to live. Learn to celebrate the person that God made you to be.

The devil will try to convince you that you're a weak worm of the dust. He'll try to get you thinking wrong about yourself. But you need to declare out loud, "I am a child of the Most High King, and He thinks I'm great."

You may not be happy with every aspect of yourself, but you need to be happy about the basic person that God created you to be. When you start practicing that mindset, your peace will return. And that's a great way to live!

BECOMING MOTHER OF THE YEAR

MOM TO MASTER
Lord, I pray that Your peace overtakes me today. Change my wrong thinking. Amen.

Be strong and take heart,
all you who hope in the LORD.
PSALM 31:24

Do you ever just wake up and think, "Forget it! I'm not even going to try anymore!" I sometimes do—especially if the scale says I've gained a pound or two and I've truly been trying to eat better. Or if my house is a total wreck and I have spent several hours the day before cleaning and "de-cluttering" it. Or, if my workload is massive and every editor is breathing down my neck at the same time. That's when I hit overload and basically shut down. That's when you'll find me in the fetal position, under the bed, with chocolate in hand.

A better way to handle those days when stress and feelings of inadequacy try to overtake us is to run to Jesus. Some people forget that Jesus is Lord over every part of our lives—even the stressful parts. Tell yourself, "My hope is in the Lord. I don't have to have everything figured out. He has already gone before me, ensuring my victory." Now, rejoice! Be strong! Take heart! And, sure, have a piece of chocolate if it makes you feel better!

MOM TO MASTER

Father, I am feeling stressed out and inadequate today. Help me to handle every part of my life with Your loving touch and Your infinite wisdom. I love You. Amen.

Therefore, if anyone is in Christ,
he is a new creation; the old has gone,
the new has come!

2 CORINTHIANS 5:17

My sister, Martie, is a genius at her craft. She is a professional interior designer, and her eye for detail is unbelievable! She can take most any room and make it lovely. It's pretty amazing, really. Using the same furniture, the same pillows, and the same accessories, she can arrange them in such a way that the entire room is transformed into something beautiful.

With just a tweak here and a new seating area over there, voila! My living room looks great! Who would have dreamed it could look so wonderful? And, I didn't even have to get new furniture to get a "new look."

Well, let me introduce you to another Master of Design—the Almighty Himself! God is so masterful that He can take our old lives and with a tweak here and a tweak there, He can transform us into beautiful creatures. Our once old and ugly hearts are revived, rejuvenated, and transformed by the Master's touch. So, if you're in need of a heart transformation today, go to the Master Designer. He's got a new look just waiting for you!

MOM TO MASTER
Father, I am in need of a makeover.
Please mold me and make me into the beautiful
creature that You've called me to be. Amen.

BECOMING MOTHER OF THE YEAR

Finally, brothers, whatever is true,
whatever is noble, whatever is right,
whatever is pure, whatever is lovely,
whatever is admirable—if anything is excellent
or praiseworthy—think about such things.

PHILIPPIANS 4:8

"Don't go there, girlfriend!"

I have a friend who always says that to me when I am heading toward the self-pity pit. Funny as that expression sounds, it packs a lot of wisdom. If we can stop ourselves before we start wallowing in that self-pity pit, we'll be a lot better off in the long run. See, once you get down in that pit, it's hard to claw your way back out.

For me, all it takes is dwelling on something negative for a few minutes. I'll start to think about the fight I had with my daughters that morning, and the next thing I know, I am looking up from the center of that yucky pit.

I believe that's why the Bible tells us to think on good and lovely things. God knew that if we thought on the other stuff for very long that we'd wind up in that old, yucky pit. So, if you're in that pit today, reach up! God is reaching out to you, ready to help you out. Think on Him—not your past failures.

MOM TO MASTER

Lord, help me to spend time thinking on good
and lovely things—not my past failures. Amen.

I will praise you as long as I live.
PSALM 63:4

Have you ever watched a college cheerleading squad? Their motions are perfectly timed, in sync, on beat, and very sharp. If one member is behind a half a count, you'll be able to tell. Even minor flaws and mistakes are greatly magnified when the rest of the team is so good.

Do you ever feel like that cheerleader who is a half step behind the entire routine? Me, too. Sometimes it seems that all of the moms I know have it all together, and I'm kicking with the wrong leg. The devil loves to point out our shortcomings and whisper things like, "Hey, you are the worst mother ever. If you were a better mom, your children would be doing better in school."

See, the devil knows what buttons to push in order to make you feel the very worst, but don't let him have access to your buttons. When you start to compare yourself with another mother, stop yourself. Right then, begin thanking God for giving you the wisdom and strength to be the best mom you can be. When you respond to the devil's button-pushing with praise for the Father, you will send the devil packing.

MOM TO MASTER
Father, help me to be the best mom that I can be.
Help me to stop comparing myself with others.
I praise You. Amen.

God does not show favoritism.
ACTS 10:34

Did you ever see the movie *The Princess Diaries* starring Julie Andrews and Anne Hathaway? If not, you'll want to rent it sometime. It's a wonderful story of an "ugly duckling" who is turned into a "lovely swan." We loved the movie so much that we also purchased the soundtrack, which features a song called, "What Makes You Different." I love this song by the Backstreet Boys. The chorus says, "What makes you different makes you beautiful to me."

Isn't that cool? As moms, wouldn't it be great if we could communicate that message to our kids on a daily basis? I want Allyson to know that her cute little beauty-mark-of-a-mole above her lip not only makes her different, but also makes her beautiful. And more importantly, I want my girls to know that God adores their differences and that He thinks they are beautiful.

I wish I'd learned that truth early on. As an adult, it's harder to accept God's unconditional love and approval. Some days, I look at all of my shortcomings, and I wonder how anyone could love me. On those days, it's hard to feel beautiful. Yet, in my quiet time, I can hear God singing softly in my ear, "What makes you different makes you beautiful to me. . . ." Let God sing to you today.

MOM TO MASTER
*Thank You, Father, for Your
unconditional love and acceptance. Amen.*

But the man who looks intently into
the perfect law that gives freedom. . .
he will be blessed in what he does.
JAMES 1:25

My niece Mandy and I always tease each other saying, "You SO want to be me." Of course, that comment must be followed with a smirk and a head toss for the full effect. While we're just having fun, there are some days when I'd rather be anyone but me. Ever been there? How about when you're fifteen minutes late for your child's parent/teacher conference? Or, how about when you forget to send out your daughter's birthday invitations? Yes, I've done both of those dastardly deeds. Guilty!

Isn't it good to know that God doesn't expect us to be perfect? He understands that we are going to drop the ball once in awhile. We're human! He knows that because He created us. You're allowed to make mistakes. Whew! Good thing, eh?

As I get older, I have learned to relax a bit more. Or, as they say here in Texas, "I've learned to let stuff roll off of me like water off a duck's back. . . ." (Okay, so I'm not exactly sure what that expression means, but it's a good visual, isn't it?)

So, relax. If you make a parenting mistake, God's got you covered. Look to His Word for wisdom and guidance. We should all "SO want to be like Him."

MOM TO MASTER
Lord, thank You for loving me even though
I am not, nor ever will be, perfect. Amen.

APRIL 19

*When they measure themselves by themselves
and compare themselves with themselves,
they are not wise.*

2 CORINTHIANS 10:12

Our assignment was to make a poster encouraging parents to join the PTA. Sounds easy enough, right? Well, this easy task turned into an all-day fiasco. Once I was informed that each class would have its own poster, I got nervous. That meant that our poster needed to be extraordinarily good because it would be compared to all of the other PTA posters. This poster for Abby's fifth-grade class became more than a task—it became a mission!

Using our newly purchased art supplies, Abby and I began creating a very peppy poster. The theme was "Join the Team!" so we cut out pictures of sports figures and glued them all over the blank poster board. Then we wrote the words "Join the Team!" and decorated each letter with glitter. I was quite proud of our creation—until I saw all of the other posters.

They were masterpieces! Our best hadn't been good enough. Suddenly, I was sad for Abby because her mommy was such a poor artist. But she wasn't one bit disappointed! In fact, she thought our poster was the best. You see, it's all in the perspective. Ask God to give you back your childlike perspective today.

MOM TO MASTER
*Lord, help me to be satisfied with my best.
Please give me a childlike perspective. Amen.*

Let us fix our eyes on Jesus,
the author and perfecter of our faith.
HEBREWS 12:2

We were planning a bridal shower at my house for a dear friend of mine. Her maid of honor asked that we all wear pink—Camille's main wedding color. I thought that was a lovely idea; however, I look like Ronald McDonald in pink! My hair has a lot of gold in it—and yes a bit of red—and pink is one color that makes my hair look brassy. When I wear pink (which is hardly ever), my husband and kids call me "the Heatmiser." (Remember the Heatmiser cartoon villain from *Scooby Doo*?)

As I whined about wearing pink, my ten-year-old daughter, Abby, spoke something I'll never forget.

"Don't worry about what you'll look like," she said. "All eyes will be on Camille anyway. It's her party."

Wow, what insight from a ten-year-old!

She was right. I was so focused on looking presentable that I'd lost sight of the whole reason we were having the shower—to honor Camille.

Many times, I become so self-absorbed that I lose sight of the real mission. Do you do that, too? The Word tells us to fix our eyes on Jesus. If you have your eyes on Him, you'll remain focused on the mission—not yourself. Where are your eyes today?

BECOMING MOTHER OF THE YEAR

MOM TO MASTER
Lord, help me to keep my eyes on You. Amen.

*I can do everything through him
who gives me strength.*

PHILIPPIANS 4:13

I've got big dreams—so big that I'd be embarrassed to share them with anyone. Sometimes, I'll write about my dreams in my journal, and later when I read over them, I even embarrass myself. I get that whole attitude of, "Who do you think you are? You could never accomplish those things."

That "Negative Nellie" voice rears her ugly head from time to time, and I have to silence her with the Word of God because it says I can do *all* things through Christ who gives me strength. It's not me—it's Him! The God in me can accomplish things even bigger than I could ever dream.

The God in you can do "big, huge" things, too—as my daughter Allyson likes to say. So, get your big, huge faith on, and go after those dreams! Maybe you've always wanted to write a children's book or teach a women's Bible study. Chances are, God placed those dreams in your heart, so He will help you accomplish them.

Isn't that great news? God has caused you to dream big dreams, so you can expect Him to help you BIG TIME! You've got big dreams and a big God—that's a powerful combination!

MOM TO MASTER

*Father, I know that You are the author of my dreams,
so I am asking You to assist me as I pursue them. Amen.*

But thanks be to God!
He gives us the victory through
our Lord Jesus Christ.

1 CORINTHIANS 15:57

It's been one of those days. You know the kind I mean—when no matter what you do, you end up frustrated. It's on those days when perfection seems an eternity away. It's on those days when I'm sure I'll never measure up. It's on those days when I have to stop and crawl into my heavenly Father's lap and let Him reassure me.

He reminds me that I am an overcomer through Him. He tells me that I am the apple of His eye. He whispers, "You can do all things through Me." Suddenly, I am restored, revived, revved up, and ready to go.

You know, we need to do the same thing for our kids. There are many days when my children come dragging in from school—lower than a snake's belly. I can tell that they've encountered some "yucky stuff" that day. That's when we as moms can speak life into them—just like our heavenly Father does for us. We can restore, revive, rev up, and send them back out ready to go.

So, get yourself reenergized so that you'll be ready to give to your children. Remember, you are victorious through Jesus. Shout your victory today!

MOM TO MASTER

Thank You, Father, for loving me when I
fall way short of perfection. I love You. Amen.

> *Do you not know that*
> *in a race all the runners run,*
> *but only one gets the prize?*
> *Run in such a way as to get the prize.*
> 1 CORINTHIANS 9:24

I used to run track. Okay, it's been *many* years since I ran competitively, but I remember what it was like to race toward that finish line, giving it everything I had. I didn't always win, but I sure gave it my all. Our track coach never expected any more than our best performance. He was happy with us if we ran our hardest, even if we didn't win first place.

You know what? God feels the same way. He doesn't expect you to be the best in every situation. He just expects you to do your best every time. If you go for the gold and only bring home a silver, that's okay.

Like the Bible says, press toward the mark. Run a good race. Step out in faith. Then, even if you don't get the prize, you'll be able to hear God whisper, "Well done, My good and faithful servant," because you gave it your all.

So, lace up those spiritual track shoes and get back in the race. The finish line awaits!

MOM TO MASTER
Thank You, Father, for giving me
Your approval even when I don't win the race.
Help me to always give it my all. I love You. Amen.

To all perfection I see a limit;
but your commands are boundless.
PSALM 119:96

You know the problem with trying to be perfect? You always end up disappointed in yourself and others. During the seasons of my life when I've been on the "Polly Perfectionist" kick, I've noticed that's when I become more critical of myself and others. When I get in that perfectionist mode, I not only find fault with everything I do, but also with everything that others do. As you might imagine, I don't have a lot of friends who want to hang out with me when I've got on my "Polly Perfectionist" hat.

Bottom line—no one is perfect. No matter how hard we try, we'll never achieve perfection until we get to heaven. That doesn't mean we shouldn't strive to be and do our best, but it does mean we should give ourselves and others a break. Take your eyes off of your shortcomings, stop finding fault with others, and look to God.

Rest in the Lord and meditate on His perfection. After all, He is the only Perfect One. He doesn't expect perfection from you, so you shouldn't expect it from others. If you're in that "Polly Perfectionist" mode, ask God to help you accept yourself as human and move on.

MOM TO MASTER
Father, help me to strive for perfection
but accept when I fall short. Amen.

BECOMING MOTHER OF THE YEAR

APRIL 25

We all stumble in many ways.
If anyone is never at fault in what he says,
he is a perfect man.

JAMES 3:2

I'm so thankful that God chooses to use imperfect people to accomplish His will on this earth. Take Moses, for example. He killed an Egyptian for mistreating an Israelite and later got so angry that God's people were worshipping a golden calf, that he smashed the Ten Commandments—yikes! Or what about Peter? He cut off a guy's ear and denied that he ever knew Jesus—not once. . .but three times! Wow! Isn't it good to know that even Moses and Peter messed up once in awhile? Somehow, I find that comforting.

Okay, so I haven't cut off anybody's ear lately, but I have bitten off a few heads. And while I haven't smashed any commandments recently, I've broken a few of them. My husband and children would be the first to tell you that I'm not perfect. But, I am a work in progress. Just like Moses and Peter, we are all attaining from glory to glory. And thank the Lord that He uses imperfect people just like us. He knows our limitations, and He still loves us. So, if you're having a "Commandment-smashing, ear-cutting-off" kind of day, don't worry. God can still use you!

MOM TO MASTER
Thank You, Lord, for using me—
even though I am less than perfect. Amen.

But he said to me,
"My grace is sufficient for you,
for my power is made perfect in weakness."
Therefore I will boast all the more gladly
about my weaknesses,
so that Christ's power may rest on me.

2 CORINTHIANS 12:9

Nobody likes to admit weaknesses, but hey, we've all got them. The good news is this—God can work with weakness. In fact, His Word tells us that His power is made perfect in our weakness. Pretty cool, eh? So, why is it so difficult to admit we have weaknesses?

I'll be honest, I hate to admit that I have weaknesses—especially with my children. I like to appear perfect and "superhero-like." I want Abby and Allyson to think they've got the coolest mom in the world—a mom who loves God, loves them, and can still skateboard with the best of them. But, over the past few years, I am pretty sure my daughters have figured out that Mom has got some weaknesses—definitely! The cat is out of the bag, so to speak.

And I'm okay with that. If we let our children see our shortcomings, they'll feel better about their own weaknesses. So quit trying to disguise your weaknesses or make excuses for them. Just admit you've got them and let God's power be made perfect in them.

MOM TO MASTER
Father, thank You for working through
my weaknesses. Amen.

BECOMING MOTHER OF THE YEAR

*Every good and perfect gift is from above,
coming down from the Father of the heavenly lights,
who does not change like shifting shadows.*

JAMES 1:17

When Abby and Allyson were born, I wrote in their baby books "My Gifts from Up Above." That's exactly how I felt about each one of my daughters. As I looked down into their faces, I couldn't believe how blessed we were. I bet you felt the same when you had your children. Whether you gave birth to them or adopted them, they were the best gifts you'd ever received, weren't they?

I remember thinking, "They are so perfect, and I didn't do anything to deserve these precious children. God just gave them to me. He loves me that much!"

God is like that. He just loves to give gifts to us—that's what daddies do.

So, even on the days when your little darlings are less than perfect and you're thinking, "I thought that Scripture said the Father only sends good and perfect gifts. . ."— rejoice! You are blessed. Send up praise to the Father for your children, your spouse, your home, your extended family, your friends. God loves sending blessings our way—especially when we appreciate the ones He's already sent.

MOM TO MASTER

*Father, thank You for every gift that You've
sent my way. I am especially thankful for
my children. I appreciate You. Amen.*

There is no fear in love.
But perfect love drives out fear.
1 JOHN 4:18

Okay, so I've accepted the fact that I'll never be perfect. But, it's good to know that God's perfect love is available to me and that His love drives out fear. You know, as moms, we encounter a lot of fears concerning our children. We fear they won't develop properly when they are growing inside of us. We fear we'll do something wrong as parents. We fear they aren't learning like other children. We fear we aren't spending enough time with them. . .and on and on and on.

But Romans 8:15 tells us that we did not receive a spirit that makes us slaves to fear; rather we received the Spirit of sonship. That entitles us to the right to cry out to God as our Abba, Father. He wants us to run to Him when we're fearful. He wants to cast that fear right out of our hearts.

So, if you're struggling with fears of inadequacy, or if you're worried about your children to the point that your stomach is in knots—run to God! Let Him replace your fear with His perfect love. Now that's a deal you can't refuse!

MOM TO MASTER
Father, thank You for Your perfect love.
I will not fear because You are my God. Amen.

APRIL 29

Clothe yourselves with. . .patience.

COLOSSIANS 3:12

BECOMING MOTHER OF THE YEAR

Have you ever noticed that everybody seems to have an opinion concerning how you should raise your children? Oh yeah—even the woman at the dry cleaners said I should take away my daughters' pacifiers before long because if I didn't, their teeth would rot. That was an interesting tidbit of information I hadn't counted on when dropping off my "Dry Clean Only" laundry.

Many times you'll receive parenting advice from your own mother or your mother-in-law—whether you ask for it or not. They feel it's their duty to impart their nuggets of knowledge. If you're like me, you sometimes tire of endless advice. You've read the parenting books. You are prayerfully parenting your kids. Admit it, there are times when you want to yell, "Back off! They're my kids, and I'm doing the best I can do!"

But before you verbally attack your mom the next time she criticizes the type of detergent you're using on your baby's garments, pray. Ask God to help you receive everyone's input with graciousness and gratitude. You certainly don't have to follow their advice, but grin sweetly as they relay their theory of potty training. Someday, you'll be the one dishing out advice. It's true, you know. We do become our mothers!

MOM TO MASTER
Father, help me to receive advice with grace and gratitude. Amen.

"As for God, his way is perfect;
the word of the LORD is flawless.
He is a shield for all who take refuge in him."

2 SAMUEL 22:31

"It's my way or the highway!" I heard my voice shout to Abby as she stormed out of the room.

We were having a rather spirited discussion about her disobedience. I let her know that she would follow the rules of the house, or she would spend a lot of time grounded to her room—period! At age ten, Abby wasn't too keen on the whole "grounded for life" scene. So, my declaration of "It's my way or the highway!" seemed quite effective.

While it's a catchy phrase, it's not very correct in God's eyes. It's not my goal to parent my children my way, because my way is rarely the right one. My instincts are often wrong, and I'm way too emotional to make good, solid decisions every time. God's way is WAY more effective. Funny, though, how I sometimes forget that until I've already tried it my way and fallen flat on my face. Ever been there?

So, if you're trying to handle everything on your own today—don't! Give it to God. Ask for His divine intervention. His way is best. After all, He is the Way!

MOM TO MASTER
Lord, I want to do things Your way—
all the time. I love You. Amen.

MAY 1

*You should praise the LORD
for his love and for the wonderful
things he does for all of us.*
PSALM 107:21 CEV

Don't you just love to give gifts to your children? Isn't it exciting to surprise them with something they've really been longing for—like a new bike or a trip to Disney World? It is so much fun to see their eyes light up and their enthusiastic smiles and giggles commence. I love to bless my children. When Abby and Allyson give me big hugs and squeal "Thank you!" my heart melts. I can hardly wait until the next time I can do something nice for them.

You know, God is the same way. He loves to bless His children. He loves to surprise us with the desires of our hearts. He delights in sending us unexpected gifts and blessings. But He also expects us to acknowledge His blessings. He expects us to have grateful hearts. So, make sure the next time the Father sends down a blessing, you immediately stop and thank Him for His wonderful gift. Go ahead. Tell Him right now just how thankful you are today. He does so much for all of us. He is worthy to be praised!

HAVING A THANKFUL HEART

MOM TO MASTER

*Thank You, Lord, for all that You do for me.
I appreciate You, and I am so thankful for
the many blessings in my life. Amen.*

Give thanks to the LORD,
for he is good;
his love endures forever.
PSALM 107:1

Have you ever heard the expression, "You better thank your lucky stars!" People say it all the time. In fact, you may have even said it a time or two. Or how about, "Well, thank goodness!" Funny how sayings slip into our speech without us really giving them much thought. But we really should be more careful with our speech—especially when we're dishing out thanks.

When something good happens to you, don't thank your lucky stars or goodness—they didn't have anything to do with it! Thank your loving heavenly Father who lavishly blesses us every day. Get into the habit of immediately recognizing the Lord for His goodness right when it happens. If I get a parking spot up front at Wal-Mart, I say, "Thank You, Lord, for holding that spot just for me." Make thanking God a habit, and you'll find that you have many reasons to praise Him. It puts you in an attitude of gratitude, and that's a great place to be!

MOM TO MASTER
Thank You, Lord, for everything that You do
for me each day. Help me to be better at recognizing
every blessing that You send my way. Amen.

HAVING A THANKFUL HEART

Great peace have they who love your law,
and nothing can make them stumble.

PSALM 119:165

Did you know that God's Word contains approximately seven thousand promises in its pages? It has promises to cover any circumstance or problem that you'll ever encounter. If you're ill and need God's healing touch, the Word says, "by his wounds you have been healed" (1 Peter 2:24). If you're struggling financially, the Bible says, "my God will meet all your needs according to his glorious riches in Christ Jesus" (Philippians 4:19). If your teenagers are rebelling against you and God, the Word says, "But from everlasting to everlasting the LORD's love is with those who fear him, and his righteousness with their children's children" (Psalm 103:17).

No matter what is going on in your life today, God has got you covered. If you can find a promise in His Word, you have something solid to stand on and build your faith upon. Aren't you thankful for that today? God's Word has all of the answers, and we have access to those answers twenty-four hours a day. We live in a country that enjoys religious freedom, so we can even read His promises in public. Praise God for His promises today.

HAVING A THANKFUL HEART

MOM TO MASTER
Thank You, Lord, for Your Word. I praise You for
the many promises contained in its pages. Amen.

And do not forget to do good
and to share with others,
for with such sacrifices God is pleased.
HEBREWS 13:16

Remember that '80s song "What Have You Done for Me Lately?" by Janet Jackson? While I like that song (You're humming it right now, aren't you?), I do not like that attitude—especially when I get it from my children. The other day I carted home several new outfits from Limited Too, my daughters' favorite store. They were ecstatic—for about twenty minutes.

Later that evening when I wouldn't drop everything and run them into town for a McDonald's fix, I heard one of my angels say, "You never do anything for us." I wanted to flush their new outfits down the toilet! But I didn't. Instead, I shut my bedroom door and brooded. During that time, the Holy Spirit revealed to me that I sometimes act that same way with God. He will give me a huge blessing, and I'll rejoice for awhile, but two days later, I am whining around about how God has forgotten me simply because something didn't work out exactly as I'd desired.

Do you do the same thing? If so, repent and ask God to rid you of your "What Have You Done for Me Lately?" 'tude.

MOM TO MASTER
Thank You, Lord, for all that You do for me.
Help me to never forget Your goodness. Amen.

HAVING A THANKFUL HEART

*I urge, then, first of all,
that requests, prayers, intercession and
thanksgiving be made for everyone—
for kings and all those in authority,
that we may live peaceful and quiet lives
in all godliness and holiness.*
1 TIMOTHY 2:1–2

Ever since the U.S.A. experienced the tragedy of September 11, 2001, I've looked at life a little differently. I think we all have. September 11 made us realize that we're not promised tomorrow, so we'd better be thankful for today.

It's made me more thankful for every minute of every day. It's made me hug my children more often. It's made me call my husband just to say I love him. It's made me share my faith a little more aggressively. It's made me reprioritize my life. And, it's made me appreciate the freedom and privileges that come from being an American.

Are you thankful today for your rights as an American? Then join with me and commit to praying regularly for our leaders and our military personnel who defend and protect this country. Let's thank God for His covering over this nation and praise Him that we can worship Him without fear. And, let's encourage our kids to do the same. With prayer and praise, we give the devil a one-two patriotic punch!

HAVING A THANKFUL HEART

MOM TO MASTER

*Lord, I pray for my nation today, and I thank You
for allowing me to live in a country
that was founded on Christian beliefs. Amen.*

*"But seek first his kingdom
and his righteousness,
and all these things will be
given to you as well."*
MATTHEW 6:33

Do your kids ever get the "gimme syndrome"? You know, the "gimme this and gimme that" phase. We've lived through a few of those in our house. Of course, there are the "terrible twos" when everything is "mine!" And, then the tweens seem to bring out the "gimmes" in a more expensive way. Instead of "Gimme that sucker," it's "Gimme that Go-Kart." (I wonder if the teen years will give birth to the "Gimme that Corvette!")

No matter the season, the "gimme syndrome" is bad. You see, "gimmes" always lead to more "gimmes." The Bible might say it like this: "gimmes beget gimmes." Once you fulfill the first "gimme requests," there are always more to follow. It's continual!

But, if we seek God first, all of our wants and "gimmes" will be fulfilled. We need to keep our "gimmes" under control and focus our energies on seeking God. If we breed little "gimme" kids, they'll carry that mentality over into their relationship with God. Their prayers will be filled with, "Hi, God. Gimme this and gimme that. Amen." Ask God to get the "gimmes" out of your household today. That's one request He'll be happy to fulfill!

MOM TO MASTER
*Lord, I pray that You remove the "gimme" attitude
from my household. I love You. Amen.*

*A man of many companions
may come to ruin,
but there is a friend who
sticks closer than a brother.*
PROVERBS 18:24

HAVING A THANKFUL HEART

Sometimes being a mom is a lonely gig. Before my children were born, I was quite the social butterfly, fluttering my way to social event after social event. After Abby and Ally came along, I was lucky to get a shower by noon. So I lost contact with a lot of those social friends—the ones you only see at events. And, even some of my dearest buddies from college sort of ditched me once I was a mom. After all, they were still single and living a totally different life. That left me with a few mommy friends I'd met through my MOPS (Mothers of Preschoolers) group and our church. I wasn't very close with any of them, and there wasn't much time for building close relationships with two toddlers in the house. So, I cried out to God for a friend. That's when I heard that still, small voice say, "I'm your Friend."

Wow. I'd totally forgotten that I had a friend in Jesus—even though I'd sung that hymn a thousand times in my life. So, if you're feeling isolated and friendless today—look up. You've got a friend in Him. I'm thankful for His friendship today.

MOM TO MASTER
Lord, thank You for being my best Friend. Amen.

That my heart may sing
to you and not be silent.
O LORD my God,
I will give you thanks forever.
PSALM 30:12

We teach our kids to say "please and thank you," and that's a good thing. Manners are very important; however, I often wonder if we're just teaching our kids to "go through the motions" without the proper motivation. In other words, do they just say "thank you" because they know they're supposed to, or are they really thankful?

If I do nothing else right, I want to raise my girls to be thankful, appreciative children. Of course, I'd like them to truly mean their "thank you" responses in day-to-day life. But more than anything, I want them to be thankful to our Lord Jesus Christ for His many blessings.

I think the best way to teach our kids to have thankful hearts toward our heavenly Father is by example. If they see us—their moms—praising God and acknowledging His goodness in everyday life, they'll follow our lead. So, take time to not only teach the manner part of "thank you," but also teach the heart part of "thank you." Let's enter His gates with thanksgiving in our hearts every day! He is worthy of our praise, and our children need to know that. So go on, get your praise on!

HAVING A THANKFUL HEART

MOM TO MASTER
Lord, thank You for being my heavenly Father.
I praise You today! Amen.

*They were also to stand
every morning to thank
and praise the LORD.*

1 CHRONICLES 23:30

I've never been much of a morning person. This was especially true when I was a child. I'd wait until the absolute last possible moment to get out of bed. But, my morning "wake-up call" began at 6 A.M. every weekday, courtesy of my mother, Marion, who *is* a morning person.

She didn't just knock on the door and say "Time to get up." Oh, no—she was far too joyful for that. My mother had an entire musical extravaganza worked out. She'd begin with her rendition of "This is the day that the Lord has made. We will rejoice and be glad in it." All of this singing was accompanied by very loud handclapping, and if that didn't do the trick, she would flip the lights on and off in time to her singing.

As you might have guessed, I proudly carry on this tradition. I even sing the same song, accompanied by loud handclaps and my own light show. And my kids moan and groan, much the same way I did. Nevertheless, we begin each day praising God and thanking Him for another day—some of us a little more than others! We're starting the day on the right note—why not join in the fun?

MOM TO MASTER
Lord, thank You for another day to praise You. Amen.

HAVING A THANKFUL HEART

Give thanks to the LORD,
call on his name;
make known among the nations
what he has done.

1 CHRONICLES 16:8

Did you know there are several places in the Bible where we are instructed to tell what God has done for us? In other words, when God blesses us, we need to shout it from the rooftops. My kids are really good about this.

Last year, Abby could hardly wait to tell everyone how God had blessed her with tickets and backstage passes to the Newsboys concert in Dallas. She had prayed that God would enable her to go because she'd never been to a concert, and miraculously, God came through BIG TIME! It was pretty amazing. The Lord "just happened" to have one of the band members come to one of my book signings. And my daughters "just happened" to be with me, and he "just happened" to give us tickets and backstage passes. Isn't it spectacular the lengths that God will go to in order to bless His children?

So, go ahead and testify about God's goodness in your life. Encourage your children to share their praise reports, too. In fact, you might even schedule a special time each week for "Family Praise Reports." It could be fun, and God will love it!

MOM TO MASTER
Lord, You are so good to us, and I want to
shout Your goodness from the rooftops! Amen.

HAVING A THANKFUL HEART

> *Praise the LORD.*
> *Give thanks to the LORD,*
> *for he is good;*
> *his love endures forever.*
> PSALM 106:1

When my girls were really little, I used to listen to them pray at night. They thanked God for everything under the sun—grasshoppers, popcorn, mud pies, Oreo cookies, puppies, swimming pools, kittens, chocolate bars, ballet classes. . .everything! In fact, one of Allyson's prayers actually inspired my board book, *Why I Love You, God.* She totally cracked me up, thanking God for the littlest of things—even lollipops!

But, you know, besides being cute, our children's prayers should be a model for our grown-up prayers. When they count their blessings, they *really* count their blessings. Many times, as adults, we rush through our evening prayers without really thanking God for anything specific. We just send up a generic prayer and hope for the best. If we come to the Lord like little children, as the Word says, we are sure to get it right. So, follow your children's lead. Thank the Lord and *really* count your blessings!

MOM TO MASTER

Lord, I want to thank You for all of the blessings
in my life—Your unconditional love, my children,
my mate, my extended family, sunny days,
springtime flowers, my pets, my church, my friends,
Doris Day movies. . .everything! Amen.

HAVING A THANKFUL HEART

You are my God,
and I will give you thanks;
you are my God,
and I will exalt you.

PSALM 118:28

When I think about my earthly father, I always smile. My dad is the kind of dad who dotes on his children. My sister teases that she's his favorite, and I tease back that I am, but in all honesty, he makes both of us feel like the favorite child. And if you asked my brother, he'd say *he* was Dad's favorite! That's just how my dad is, and that's exactly how God is, too. He is a doting Dad. He loves us so much. In fact, He adores us!

But I don't love my dad because He is good to me or even because he makes me feel like I'm his favorite. I love my dad simply because he is Dad. You know, we should love our heavenly Father for that very same reason—not for what He can give us or do for us—but simply because He is our Father. That's what Psalm 118:28 says to me: "You are my God, and I will give you thanks." Tell Him today how much you love Him—just for being Him.

MOM TO MASTER
Father, I want to praise You today just for being You. I am so thankful that You are my heavenly Father. Amen.

MAY 13

*Let us come before him with thanksgiving
and extol him with music and song.*
PSALM 95:2

When I think of attacking someone in battle, I think of a "sneak attack." I envision a great army in camouflage, quietly approaching the enemy at night when all are asleep. If I were going to plan an attack, that's probably how I'd do it. But, you know what? God didn't plan attacks like that. Over and over again in the Old Testament, God sent "the praise and worship team" ahead of the troops, singing and playing music unto the Lord. You can bet they weren't sneaking up on anyone, not with all the singing and shouting going on up front.

Obviously, God was trying to communicate something to us—praise and worship are very important! There are days when I don't feel much like praising God. You know the days I'm talking about, right? Like when your child's teacher calls to tell you that he is failing math. Or, when your boss tells you the company is downsizing and you're being let go. Those are not joyous times; however, we are supposed to praise God in spite of the circumstances. Why? Because when we praise Him—especially in the bad times—we ensure our victory. If you're in need of a victory today, praise the Lord!

MOM TO MASTER
*Father, I praise You today in spite of
the bad stuff in my life. Amen.*

Let the word of Christ dwell in you
richly as you teach and admonish
one another with all wisdom,
and as you sing psalms, hymns
and spiritual songs with gratitude
in your hearts to God.

COLOSSIANS 3:16

The phrase "with gratitude in your heart" appears over and over again in the Scriptures. You know what that says to me? It says, "Hey, Michelle. Just thanking God isn't enough. Your heart has to be filled with gratitude." You may fool your family and friends with your false gratitude or pitiful praise, but God looks on the heart. He sees what's really in there.

I find myself doing this with my kids, too. Abby or Allyson will draw me a picture and hand it to me (usually when I'm right in the middle of something hugely important), and I'll say, "Thanks, honey. That's really nice." Hardly giving it a glance, I slap it up on the fridge. Ever been there? See, we should not only have a heart filled with gratitude when we praise God, but also when we thank our family. Kids are perceptive. They may not be able to see your heart, but they sense when you're just going through the motions.

So, do a heart check today. Is your heart full of gratitude? If not, get a refill. God's got gratitude with your name on it. Just ask Him.

MOM TO MASTER
Father, I praise You with my whole heart today.
I love You and appreciate You. Amen.

HAVING A THANKFUL HEART

Always [give] thanks to God
the Father for everything.
EPHESIANS 5:20

She was one of Abby's friends, but this little girl bugged me. I love kids. I even write children's books! But she was a challenge. One afternoon, I took Abby and her little friend shopping. While in the Bible bookstore, I purchased a cute cross bracelet for each of them. Abby hugged and thanked me. But the little friend didn't even say thanks! She just slipped on the bracelet and went on her merry way.

I kept thinking, "If she were my daughter, I would be disciplining her right now." But you know what? It wasn't my place to discipline her. My job was simply to show her the love of Jesus. See, God expects us to show grace and mercy to others the same way that He shows grace and mercy to us. And, I know there have been times when God has sent down a blessing, and I've "slipped it on" and went on my merry way. How about you? If you've been less than grateful lately, repent and spend some time thanking God for His goodness today.

MOM TO MASTER
Father, help me to always have a grateful spirit.
Help me to be an example for You. Amen.

HAVING A THANKFUL HEART

*"But be sure to fear the L*ORD
and serve him faithfully with all your heart;
consider what great things he has done for you."
1 SAMUEL 12:24

Ever heard that catchy little praise and worship chorus that says, "Look what the Lord has done!" It's one of my all-time favorites. I love the tune, of course, but I especially like the words, "Look what the Lord has done!" That's why I like to keep a journal, so I can look back and see what God has done.

I have a little notebook (pretty ratty looking at this point) that I call my "Prayer and Praise Journal," and I record various requests and prayer concerns inside. Then, when God answers my prayers, I go back and check them off, recording the details of God's miraculous intervention. It's exciting to look back and see what the Lord has done.

I encourage you to begin keeping a prayer and praise journal if you don't already. Maybe you can create a family prayer and praise journal so the kids can participate, too. Incorporate the journal into your family devotion time. You'll be surprised how often God comes through in a big way. We just tend to forget unless we've recorded it somewhere. So, celebrate God and look what He has done!

HAVING A THANKFUL HEART

MOM TO MASTER
Father, thank You for Your faithfulness.
I am amazed at all that You've done in my life. Amen.

*Why, you do not even know
what will happen tomorrow.
What is your life?
You are a mist that appears
for a little while and then vanishes.*

JAMES 4:14

Not long ago, our pastor posed this question to us: "If you were told you only had a week left to live, what would you do?"

Wow. I hadn't ever thought about that before. Of course, I'd want to spend every second with my family, giving them love and hugs. I wouldn't let the daily stresses of life get to me. I'd focus on the positives. And I think I'd spend a lot of time thanking the people in my life for the love they've always shown me. I'd want them to know how much their love had meant in my life before I headed to heaven.

As I was contemplating these things, our pastor said, "So, why wait? Go ahead and do those things now. You don't need a negative diagnosis to act on those things, do you?"

Well, I guess not. My pastor was right. We can show our love, give hugs, and display our gratitude today. We don't have to wait for a terrible health crisis to shake us up. So, go ahead. Live today like it's your last, because someday it will be.

HAVING A THANKFUL HEART

MOM TO MASTER
*Father, I want to thank You for another day of life.
I love You. Amen.*

Consider it pure joy, my brothers,
whenever you face trials of many kinds.
JAMES 1:2

I recently visited a Web site that made me feel a bit guilty for all the times that I've complained about everyday stuff. Its headline said, "Things to be thankful for:

* The taxes I pay—because it means that I'm employed.
* The clothes that fit snugly—because it means I have enough to eat.
* The mounds of laundry—because it means I have clothes to wear."

Okay, be honest. Have you ever been thankful for taxes, extra weight, or loads of laundry? Me neither. But, it is an interesting concept. It does make you think, doesn't it? We should be looking for reasons to be thankful—even in the stuff that would not ordinarily fill our hearts with gratitude.

And, we should impart that same attitude into our kids. They'll be much happier children if they'll take that stance in life. So, when your daughter doesn't get invited to "the big party," she can be thankful that she has a mom who will take her to the movies instead. Or, when your son doesn't make the football team, he can be thankful that he has more free time to practice his guitar. It's really about looking for that silver lining in every gray cloud. Find that silver lining today.

HAVING A THANKFUL HEART

MOM TO MASTER
Lord, I praise You for the good
and not-so-good things in my life. Amen.

We were not looking for praise from men,
not from you or anyone else.

In fiction writing, your characters always have to have a motivation for their actions. If your reader doesn't understand that motivation, the characters' actions seem contrived and unnatural. Motivation is key.

In life, motivation is key, too. I found this out the hard way. You see, I have always been a people pleaser. I'm the one who will volunteer to bake seventeen pies for the annual bake sale, simply because I want the PTA members to like me and think I'm a really devoted mother. Maybe you're a people pleaser, too.

Being a people pleaser is not only exhausting but also very pointless. First of all, you'll never be able to please everyone. And secondly, if you're doing things for people just to gain their adoration and approval, your motivation is wrong.

Think of it like this—would you still be serving in that way if you weren't going to be recognized or appreciated for your actions? If your answer is yes, then your motivation is right. But if you are doing things simply to gain praise, your motivation might be off. Even if no one ever recognizes your good deeds, take heart—God knows. He's keeping track. And He thinks you're great!

HAVING A THANKFUL HEART

MOM TO MASTER
Lord, help me to keep my motivation
pure when serving You and others. Amen.

*Be kind and compassionate
to one another.*
EPHESIANS 4:32

Do you know that some people never hear a "thank-you?"

You'll be able to spot these folks. They are usually the grouchy ones. I encountered one the other day at a shoe store. She was checking me out (with a scowl on her face, I might add) when I noticed that she had charged me full price for my shoes. So, I said, "Miss, according to that sign over there, these shoes are on sale for thirty percent off."

She looked at the sign, then the shoes, then the sign again, and said, "These aren't the same shoes."

"I think they are," I said, "because I checked the SKU number against the advertisement."

She huffed and puffed and slammed the shoes down on the counter. Then, she stomped over to the sale area and did her own investigation. After a few minutes, she came back, still scowling, and said, "You're right. They are on sale. I'll have to redo the whole transaction."

It was obvious she was having a hard day. So, I made it my mission to encourage her. I thanked her for redoing my receipt. I praised her for her efficiency. We ended up having a nice conversation. She even smiled. Make it your mission to appreciate someone today. Start with your kids!

HAVING A THANKFUL HEART

MOM TO MASTER
Lord, help me to seize every opportunity to bless others.

A friend loves at all times.

PROVERBS 17:17

Did you ever watch the sitcom *The Golden Girls*? I still catch the reruns sometimes. I love that show, and I especially like the theme song "Thank You for Being a Friend" by Andrew Gold. The lyrics still make me smile: "Thank you for being a friend. Travel down a road and back again. Your heart is true, you're a pal and a confidante."

Who wouldn't want a friend who fits that description? Good friends are hard to find and even harder to keep. That's why we should be very thankful for our friends. As moms, we're so busy being moms that we rarely take time for our friends. But we need friends. If you haven't taken time lately to tell your friends how much you appreciate them, why not tell them today? Drop a card or place a call. Send a bouquet of flowers. Bake her some cookies. Schedule a lunch date with her.

While you're at it, tell your children how much you value their friendship, too. As my girls get older, I realize how blessed I am to have their friendship. They are my best shopping buddies! Go ahead, reach out to a friend today.

HAVING A THANKFUL HEART

MOM TO MASTER

Lord, thank You for my friends. Help me to be a better friend to those special people You've put in my life. I love You. Amen.

I will proclaim the name of the LORD.
Oh, praise the greatness of our God!
DEUTERONOMY 32:3

Have you ever heard the expression, "Praise and be raised, or complain and remain?" Now that's a phrase that really packs a punch! It means if you complain about your current circumstances, you'll remain there a lot longer than if you'd just praise the Lord in spite of it all.

Sure that's easy to say, but it's not so easy to do. I don't know about you, but praising God during difficult times is the last thing I want to do. I'd rather retreat to my bedroom with a box of Junior Mints and sulk awhile. But sulking won't change things any more than complaining will.

By praising God during the dark times, we're telling God that we trust Him—even though we can't see the daylight. Anyone can trust God and praise Him on the mountaintop, but only those who really know God's faithfulness can praise Him in the valley. And it's during those valley times that we truly feel God's tender mercy and experience extreme spiritual growth. So, praise God today—even if you don't feel like it. Through your praise, you open the door for God to work in your life.

HAVING A THANKFUL HEART

MOM TO MASTER
Lord, I praise You in spite of the difficulties in my life.
Help me to resist complaining and praise You instead.
Amen.

> *"How long will this wicked community grumble against me? I have heard the complaints of these grumbling Israelites."*
>
> NUMBERS 14:27

Have you ever read about the children of Israel's forty-year journey to the Promised Land? In actuality, that journey should've only taken them about forty days. As it turned out, they were their own worst enemy. God had just rescued them from slavery, caused the Egyptians to give them clothes and riches, parted the Red Sea so that they could walk across, provided manna from heaven for food, and yet they still complained! In fact, they whined about the manna that God had been faithfully sending down every morning. They wanted something different. They were basically saying, "Hey, could you send down some waffles? We're really bored with the whole manna thing."

Unfortunately, we occasionally have that whole Israelite attitude at our house. I'll make meatloaf with potatoes and carrots, and Abby will whine, "Why'd you make meatloaf? You know I don't like meatloaf."

Or, I'll buy wheat bread and Allyson will say, "I only like white bread. I'm not eating that!" Can you relate?

Complaining is not only aggravating to us, it's aggravating to God. So, don't let Connie and Connor Complainer exist in your house. Let's keep teaching gratitude. Our kids will finally get it, or they'll have to stay in their rooms for forty years!

MOM TO MASTER
Lord, help me to teach my kids to be praisers, not complainers. Amen.

"Now, our God, we give you thanks,
and praise your glorious name."
1 CHRONICLES 29:13

Just the other day I was rounding up the dust bunnies from underneath our bed, when I found something special. It was a letter I'd written to my cousin Judy but never mailed. The letter was five years old! Apparently, it had fallen out of my old address book. As I read my words, I had to smile. I told of all the wonderful things that God had done in our lives over the past six months. He had healed Jeff from a terrible infection. He had opened up the door for me to write for a Christian magazine. He had caused our house to sell for full asking price—so many praises!

As I finished reading the letter, I knew why I had never mailed it. God wanted me to find it five years later. The words of that letter caused me to reflect on that time in our lives—a time when we didn't have very much. I wasn't working full time, and we were living from paycheck to paycheck. Still, God always provided.

I spent the rest of that afternoon reflecting on the faithfulness of God. Why not take some time today and remember the times God has come through for you? It's a trip down memory lane worth taking!

HAVING A THANKFUL HEART

MOM TO MASTER
Lord, thank You for always coming through
for me. I love You. Amen.

> *You should praise the LORD for his love*
> *and for the wonderful things*
> *he does for all of us.*
> PSALM 107:21 CEV

"Thank You, Lord, for saving my soul. Thank You, Lord, for making me whole. Oh, thank You, Lord, for giving to me—Thy great salvation so rich and free." Those are the words to a little chorus that I always sang in children's church growing up. Do you know what I remember most about that little song? It's how Ivan Hunter, a wonderful man who led our worship time, looked when he sang it. His face almost glowed. Even as a kid, I knew that Ivan was singing about something he truly believed in and cherished.

Ivan took every opportunity to thank the Lord. He'd testify to anyone who would listen—whether it was the garbage man or the mayor. Well, Ivan went to heaven a few years ago, but his memory lives on. And we're doing all that we can to carry on the testifying tradition. On more than one occasion, I've heard Abby tell her friends about something that God has done for her. And Ally often reminds me of the blessings in my life—especially if I'm in "one of those moods." Jeff does the same. You see, it's good to be bold for Jesus. Make testifying a habit in your household.

MOM TO MASTER
Lord, help me to be bold for You. I praise You. Amen.

Then Jesus looked up and said,
"Father, I thank you that you have heard me."
JOHN 11:41

I totally understand why Jesus wants us to come to Him like little children. When kids pray, they have no doubt that God hears their requests and will answer them. That's how we all ought to pray.

I used to send up a "Wheel of Fortune" prayer. I'd petition the Lord, and then I'd "spin the wheel of prayer," hoping I'd land on the right one that would really touch God's ears and cause Him to act on my behalf. Silly, isn't it? Maybe you've done the same thing.

But since I discovered this verse in John, I haven't been sending up "Wheel of Fortune" prayers anymore. Instead, I petition the Lord and thank God for hearing my prayers. I figure if Jesus thought it was a good idea to thank God for hearing His prayers, it's probably a good idea for me, too. Plus, I really am thankful that He hears my prayers. Sometimes, God is the only One who will listen to me. (If Cartoon Network is on, forget about it—my kids totally tune me out!) So, go ahead. . .talk to God. Tell Him your dreams, setbacks, and heartaches. Pray in faith, and thank Him for hearing you. It will make all the difference.

MOM TO MASTER
Lord, I want to thank You for hearing my prayers.
You are an awesome God. Amen.

HAVING A THANKFUL HEART

Because of the surpassing grace
God has given you.
Thanks be to God for his indescribable gift!

2 CORINTHIANS 9:14–15

Grace. We say grace. We name baby girls Grace. But do we really understand how wonderful God's grace is in our lives? I wouldn't want to live one second without it operating in my life. Grace is defined as God's unmerited favor. In other words, we didn't earn it. We certainly didn't deserve it, but God gave us His grace anyway. How great is that?

And where you find grace, you almost always find mercy alongside it. Whew! That's good news, isn't it? People who lived under the Law didn't have the luxury of grace. When they broke even the teensy-weensiest rule, they were in a lot of trouble. I'm so thankful for God's grace, because I mess up on a regular basis. But when I do mess up, I can run to Him. I don't have to hide, because when I repent, He gives me grace. He says, "That's okay, Michelle, you'll do better next time."

In the same manner that God shows us grace, we should show our children grace. They aren't perfect. They are going to mess up once in awhile. But, if we show them grace, they'll run to us when they get into trouble. They won't hide from us.

HAVING A THANKFUL HEART

MOM TO MASTER
Father, I praise You for the gift of grace. Amen.

May the God of hope fill you with
all joy and peace as you trust in him,
so that you may overflow with hope
by the power of the Holy Spirit.

ROMANS 15:13

One of my favorite praise and worship CDs is "Thank You, Lord, for the Holy Ghost" by Keith Moore. When I first bought this CD, I began singing the words, "Thank You, Lord, for the Holy Ghost," but in actuality, I hadn't ever really thanked God for His gift of the Holy Spirit.

The Holy Spirit truly is a gift. The Word of God calls the Holy Spirit our comforter. As a mom, there are days when I definitely need comfort. Do you ever have those "feel sorry for yourself" kind of days? On those days, I feel unworthy. I feel like a failure as a mother. I feel unlovely. At times, I don't even know what to pray. But that's when I turn to the Holy Spirit. He comforts me. He helps me know what to pray. He leads me to Scriptures in the Word that pertain to my exact circumstances. He gives me a pick-me-up greater than any B-12 shot could ever offer! The Holy Spirit will do the same for you. So, if you haven't ever thanked God for the Holy Spirit, why not do so today?

MOM TO MASTER

Father, thank You for the gift of the Holy Spirit. Amen.

HAVING A THANKFUL HEART

> *"Now, our God, we give you thanks,*
> *and praise your glorious name."*
>
> 1 CHRONICLES 29:13

Muchas gracias! Okay, that's about the only phrase I remember from my college Spanish classes. No matter what the language, "thank you" is pleasing to the Father. Praising His holy name should be second nature for us. Do you know the Bible says that the angels continually praise the Lord? I always picture them face down before His throne, praising Him 24-7. That's a pretty good gig, don't you think?

Since I've become a more avid praiser, I now understand why God seeks our praise. It's not that He is on some ego trip. He certainly doesn't need our praise. He knows that praising Him and having a thankful heart changes us on the inside. If you're praising, you can't be complaining. If you're praising, you're opening up what I like to call "the blessing highway." While a negative spirit and complaining attitude puts up roadblocks on that superhighway, a thankful heart clears the road!

So, praise Him today—in every language you can think of! He is worthy of our praise! Get your kids involved. Think of lots of reasons to give thanks. Maybe have each child learn to praise God in a different language. Make it fun, and make a joyful noise!

HAVING A THANKFUL HEART

MOM TO MASTER
Father, I give You all of the praise and honor today.
You are worthy! Amen.

He blesses the home of the righteous.

PROVERBS 3:33

I love to give my children things that they adore. I think that's why I love Christmas shopping so much. I Christmas shop all year long. If I see something that I know Abby or Allyson will adore, I'll buy it and store it away for the holidays. However, I'm always tempted to give those Christmas presents to the girls right away. In fact, a lot of times, that's exactly what I do. I can't stand it. I just have to give them their gifts early! I bet you do the same thing. We're moms. It's our nature to give to our kids. We can't help ourselves!

As much as we love to give our kids the desires of their hearts, it pales in comparison to how much our heavenly Father enjoys blessing us. Where do you think that desire to give unto our children comes from? God.

He is the best present-giver. He can hardly wait to give you that new set of wing chairs that you've been longing for. He wants you to have that Walt Disney World vacation. He loves to see us enjoying the blessings He sends our way. So, enjoy your blessings today. By doing that, you're blessing the Father.

MOM TO MASTER
Father, I appreciate all of the special gifts
that You give to me.
Thanks for loving me so much. Amen.

HAVING A THANKFUL HEART

He who is kind to the poor lends to the LORD,
and he will reward him for what he has done.

Have you ever seen those commercials on TV that show the boys and girls overseas who don't have anything to eat? I can hardly watch them. It's heartbreaking to see the poverty and hopelessness that they encounter daily. Upon the prompting of my children, we currently support a little girl overseas named Carmen. The girls love to write letters to Carmen and send her snapshots of our family and pets. They also love to send her presents. While we're not allowed to ship anything too bulky, we can send small tokens now and then.

We like picking out paper dolls for her, and we've been told she loves them. Most children in the United States wouldn't think paper dolls were too exciting, but if you've never had anything, a paper doll would seem really cool. You'd probably be truly grateful for a paper doll.

That's the kind of attitude I want to have—a "paper doll thankfulness." I want to be grateful for even the smallest gesture or gift. I want my heavenly Father to know that I'm thankful whether He sends down a paper doll or a Cadillac Escalade. I want the same grateful attitude for my children. Let's teach our kids that kind of thankfulness.

HAVING A THANKFUL HEART

MOM TO MASTER

Father, I praise You today for the big
and little blessings in my life. Amen.

Then the LORD answered me and said:
"Write the vision and make it plain on tablets,
that he may run who reads it."
HABAKKUK 2:2 NKJV

Have you ever heard the expression, "Run with the vision"? Like many expressions, this one is based on a Scripture. It's sort of the sound bite version of Habakkuk 2:2. This is one of my favorites. In fact, for the longest time I had it taped to my computer so that I would see it every day and be reminded of "the vision."

While my vision or dream may be different from yours, in order to see our visions come full circle, we have to do the same thing—keep the vision before us! That means meditating on Scriptures that pertain to our vision, praying over our vision, talking about our vision with those of like-minded faith, and believing God to bring our visions to pass.

If you've lost your dream, ask God to restore it in you. He has placed dreams and visions on the inside of every one of us. Your dream may be dormant, but it's there. Ask God to reawaken it today. Then, write your vision in your journal so you'll never forget it again.

MOM TO MASTER
Thank You, Lord, for placing that special vision
in my heart. Help me to keep it before my eyes. I trust
You to make it come to pass as I follow You. Amen.

DREAMING BIG DREAMS

*I can do everything through him
who gives me strength.*

PHILIPPIANS 4:13

For a long time, I didn't think it was okay to have other dreams besides being a mom. I thought it was selfish to want more. But those thoughts were not right thinking. I discovered that God had placed those dreams and desires inside of me. He is the One who caused me to dream in the first place, so why should I feel guilty?

Maybe you've always desired to write children's books, but you thought it was just a crazy whim. If you're passionate about it—if writing books for children burns in your heart—it's more than a whim. It's probably part of God's plan for your life. Ask Him to show you His plan today. He may not show you all of it (because it would totally overwhelm you to see the entire plan), but He will show you enough to take the initial steps toward the fulfillment of your dream. Isn't that exciting?

Being a mom is the greatest gig we'll ever have, but God doesn't want us to limit ourselves. He can use us—even in the midst of motherhood. Nothing is too big for Him, and nothing is impossible with Him. So, dream on and get with it!

DREAMING BIG DREAMS

MOM TO MASTER
*Lord, help me to follow You down the road
that leads to my dream. Amen.*

*"If you believe,
you will receive whatever
you ask for in prayer."*
MATTHEW 21:22

Have you watched TV lately? I was already familiar with the Crocodile Hunter, but I had no idea we also had Snake Wranglers. I couldn't help but watch as these two people used a big stick and a bag to capture a brown poisonous snake in Australia—scary!

Can you imagine waking up and saying, "You know, I'd like to chase and capture poisonous snakes for a living someday"? Obviously, these folks who deal with dangerous and deadly animals enjoy what they do. If you watch Steve Irwin, the Crocodile Hunter, you know he loves it. He is truly walking in his dream—as odd as that dream is to most of us.

That's what I love about our heavenly Father. He gives each of us unique dreams, and then He equips us to accomplish those dreams if we'll only believe. There is no dream too silly, scary, adventurous, or extreme for our God. It gives Him great joy to see us pursuing the ambitions He has placed within us. He can't wait to see you walking in your dream—even if that dream is chasing crocs in the Outback!

MOM TO MASTER
*Lord, thank You for placing unique dreams
in my heart. Help me to follow after them
without any fear or hesitation. Amen.*

DREAMING BIG DREAMS

Where there is no vision,
the people perish.

PROVERBS 29:18 KJV

I've seen it happen with people who retire early in life. They lose their drive. They lose their vision. They lose their reason for getting up in the morning. But you don't have to be of retirement age to lose your vision. I've also seen young mothers lose their hope and drive. The devil loves to discourage us and steal our hope.

No matter where we are in life—a mother of a newborn or a mom whose last child just graduated high school—we need to have a goal, a dream, a vision. If we don't, the Word says we'll perish. I don't think it means we'll perish physically, but we'll die spiritually. That's why it's so important to find out God's plan. Do you know God's plan for your life?

If not, ask God to show you His vision for your life. Seek His plan, and once you discover it, write it down, and keep it before you. Thank Him for that vision every day. Keep the vision close to your heart, and only share that vision with people you can trust. Your vision is something to be treasured and celebrated.

MOM TO MASTER

Lord, help me to never lose my vision or my drive.
I want to move forward with You. Amen.

DREAMING BIG DREAMS

Teach me to do your will,
for you are my God.
PSALM 143:10

"A dream is a wish your heart makes. . . ." Remember those lyrics from the theme song in the Disney movie *Cinderella*? I've always loved that movie. I was so excited when my daughters were over Barney and old enough to appreciate Cinderella. And I've always loved those lyrics. There's a lot of truth in those words.

A dream isn't just a thought your mind comes up with on its own. Instead, it's a vision your heart comes up with before it ever reaches your brain. You see, the real dreams in our lives are birthed in our spirit—deep down inside of us. Dreams are more than passing fancies. They are more than whimsical mind wanderings. They are much more. They are of God.

If you haven't let your heart make any dreams lately, ask God to show you the dreams that He has for you. He hasn't forgotten about them and neither should you. Get excited about your dreams. Be thankful that God finishes the things that He authors. He authored your dreams, so you know He's going to bring them to pass. Go ahead and dream. Dream big!

DREAMING BIG DREAMS

MOM TO MASTER
Lord, reawaken the dreams on the inside of me—
the ones that You placed there. I love You. Amen.

*A heart at peace gives life to the body,
but envy rots the bones.*

PROVERBS 14:30

Have your dreams ever ripped at the seams? Mine have.

There have been times when I've wondered if God even cared about my dreams, wishes, goals, or desires. I'd look around and see good things happening for everyone else, and I'd wonder if God had forgotten about me. I'd get the whole "What about me?" mentality. Ever been there? It's an unpleasant place to be. That "What about me?" mentality eventually leads to jealousy, envy, bitterness, and hopelessness. So, if you're on that road, hurry to the nearest exit!

If you can't be happy for your friend when she finally gets to move into her dream home, God will never be able to bless you with your dream house. If you can't do the dance of joy with your sister when she wins an all-expense-paid cruise, God will never be able to bless your family with a dream vacation. In the midst of everybody else's dreams coming true, we have to keep our hearts right. If we don't, we'll never get to walk in ours. Keep your eyes on the Master, and He will make your dreams come true, too. Don't worry when you see others getting blessed. God has more than enough blessings to go around.

MOM TO MASTER

*Lord, help me to be happy when others realize their
dreams because I know my dreams will come true, too.
Amen.*

DREAMING BIG DREAMS

But those who hope in the LORD
will renew their strength.

ISAIAH 40:31

"Any contractions today?"

"Not yet," I mumbled. "Maybe I'll try running up and down the stairs a few times."

I ran the stairs. I walked around the block. I took castor oil. I did everything I could think of to start my labor, but that baby wasn't budging. She didn't care that I was seven days overdue. She didn't care that I was really anxious to have her. She wasn't coming out until she was good and ready. When she finally decided to make her descent, we welcomed Abby Leigh Adams into the world. She was perfect and right on time in God's eyes.

Waiting. That's one of the toughest things we have to do as our dreams percolate inside of us. Have you ever noticed that God's timing never seems to be our timing? And it doesn't matter how much we cry out to Him, He won't bring about our dreams until it's the right time. It doesn't matter if you spiritually run the stairs or walk around the block, your dream won't be birthed until God says it's time. So, if you're pregnant with a dream, and you're tired of waiting—hold on. Your promise is on its way!

MOM TO MASTER
Lord, thank You for my dream. Help me to wait
patiently and faithfully until it is birthed. Amen.

DREAMING BIG DREAMS

> *Now faith is being sure of what we hope for*
> *and certain of what we do not see.*
>
> HEBREWS 11:1

Abby, my ten-year-old, is an aspiring writer who is always coming up with stories. So, like her mom, she likes to carry a notebook with her. That way, if she comes up with a great idea, she can jot it down before she forgets it. The other day in a store I found a royal blue notebook with the words "Dare to Dream" written in silver across the cover. I had to buy it! It spoke to me. What a great message for Abby— and what a great message for all of us!

Dare to dream.

You know, dreaming is a bit daring. It requires mentally sticking your neck out. Dreaming big dreams requires taking big steps of faith. It's not always a comfortable place to be, but it's definitely an exciting one. It's what I like to call living on the edge.

God likes those who dare to dream. Remember Peter? He was the only one who dared to dream and stepped out of the boat. He was doing great, too— until he took his eyes off of Jesus. But, here's the good news. When Peter started to sink, Jesus rescued him. He'll do the same for us. So get out of the boat and dare to dream!

DREAMING BIG DREAMS

MOM TO MASTER

Lord, help me to be daring when it comes to
the dreams that You put inside me. Amen.

"Do not give dogs what is sacred;
do not throw your pearls to pigs.
If you do, they may trample them under their feet,
and then turn and tear you to pieces."

MATTHEW 7:6

Have you ever heard the expression "Don't cast your pearls before pigs"? My mama used to give me that advice when I'd share my dreams with a friend at school, only to be teased. Today, I find myself sharing that same wisdom with my girls.

You see, not everyone is going to embrace our dreams and celebrate our victories with us. It's true! Even your Christian friends may not want to hear what God has placed in your heart—especially if it's bigger than the things they have in their hearts. Unfortunately, the green-eyed monster lives in some Christians, too.

So, be careful whom you choose to let in your inner circle. Don't share your dreams with just anyone. Your dreams are too precious to waste on the dogs and pigs. Only share your dreams with your family and close Christian friends—the ones who will be happy for you and celebrate with you. If you don't have anyone like that in your life, pray that God will send you someone you can trust. And remember, you can always trust Him.

DREAMING BIG DREAMS

MOM TO MASTER
Thank You, Lord, for giving me such precious dreams.
Help me to be careful when sharing them with others
that I don't confide in the wrong people. Amen.

God gives a man wealth,
possessions and honor,
so that he lacks nothing his heart desires.

ECCLESIASTES 6:2

Did you know there is actually an association designated for the study of dreams? There are many people who have devoted their lives to interpreting and
discovering the meanings of various dreams and images. Wild, huh?

If you're like me, you're probably thinking,
"Don't you actually have to go to sleep for an extended period of time to have dreams?" If you're in
that "mother of newborns or toddlers" stage, you're
probably not racking up a lot of REM time. Hang in
there; those dark circles do have silver linings!

Too much pizza or something we've watched on
TV can trigger the dreams we have at night, but the
dreams that beat deep within our hearts come from
a different source—God! We don't need any association or expert to interpret their meaning for us. God
is the originator of those dreams, so just ask Him. He
has all the answers, and He is willing to share His
wisdom with you. So, meditate on the dreams that live
within you, and always remember who placed them in
your heart. He wouldn't have placed them there if He
weren't going to make sure those dreams came true.

DREAMING BIG DREAMS

MOM TO MASTER

Thank You, Lord, for the dreams you've placed inside of
me. Please reveal them to me so that I can understand
them more fully. Amen.

*I can do everything through him
who give me strength.*

PHILIPPIANS 4:13

"What do you want to be when you grow up?" I asked my daughter, Ally, when she was only four.

She thought for a moment and then she answered matter-of-factly, "A movie star."

"Great," I responded. "Then you can pay for Mommy's and Daddy's retirement condo in Florida."

Children know how to dream big. Do you know why? Because no one has told them yet that they can't dream big. I love that about kids. They don't have that inner voice going that says, "You can't be a movie star. You're not good enough. You're not pretty enough. You'll never be able to accomplish your dream." No, they believe they can do anything. And you know what? They're right! God's Word says that we can do all things through Christ who gives us strength. All means all, right?

That's why Jesus said we should have childlike faith. We should be able to believe BIG when it comes to the dreams and ambitions that God has placed within us. God wouldn't have placed them there if He weren't going to help us achieve them. So, learn from your kids. Get back that childlike faith, and start believing.

MOM TO MASTER
Lord, help me to believe You like my children believe You. Help me to dream big like they do. I love You. Amen.

> *"If you have a message of encouragement*
> *for the people, please speak."*
>
> ACTS 13:15

Dream squashers. They seem to be everywhere. Recently, I taught at a Christian Writers' Conference where I sat on a magazine panel with editors of prestigious publications and other professional writers. As the questions came in from the audience, the panel members unleashed their dream squasher personalities. One by one, they told these people who longed to be writers that they wouldn't be able to make a living as writers. "The competition is stiff." "Magazines don't pay very much per story." "Don't quit your day jobs!"

I wanted to stand up on the middle of the table and say, "It's not true! You can make it! If I can make a living as a professional writer, so can you! God is no respecter of persons. What He did for me, He will do for you!"

I did say a bit to ward off the dream squashers, and you wouldn't believe how many people came up and thanked me. Wow! That experience really opened my eyes. People are hungry for encouragement. They are tired of the dream squashers.

If you are surrounded by dream squashers, let me encourage you today. God believes in you. Ignore the dream squashers. In truth, they are afraid to believe, and they resent you for stepping out in faith. Pray for them, but avoid them at all costs.

DREAMING BIG DREAMS

MOM TO MASTER
Lord, help me to never be a dream squasher. Amen.

*My guilt has overwhelmed me
like a burden too heavy to bear.*
PSALM 38:4

Have you taken any guilt trips lately? Oh yeah, I've
been on a few. Just last week I had to miss my daughters' Honor Choir performance because of a business
commitment. It hurt my heart not to be there. Sure it's
captured on video, but I can't get that live performance
back—it's gone forever! Even now as I tell you about
it, I feel guilty.

Sometimes living out our dreams comes with a
price. As a writer, I occasionally have to travel to promote my books. I'm not gone very often, but when I
miss something as important as an Honor Choir concert, I begin questioning my commitment as a mom.
Then, I start wondering if I am even a good mom. If
I let my mind stay there very long, I begin wondering
if I should give up writing altogether.

Then, God reminds me that He is in control of
my life. He has already ordered my steps. He knew
that I'd have to miss that Honor Choir performance,
and He enabled my husband to go and videotape it for
me. So, if you've been on a guilt trip lately, unpack
now! Guilt doesn't come from God, so don't go there!
Thank God for the good things in your life.

DREAMING BIG DREAMS

MOM TO MASTER
*Lord, help me to avoid those intense feelings of guilt.
I give them to You right now. Amen.*

> *"Again, I tell you that if two of you*
> *on earth agree about anything you ask for,*
> *it will be done for you by my Father in heaven."*
> MATTHEW 18:19

I have a niece who collects these cute little chubby angelic figurines called "Dreamsicles." Maybe you collect them, too. I have a couple in my daughters' rooms. You know what I like about these little figurines? I like their name—Dreamsicles. So much of today's merchandise that represents dreamers takes on a New Age feel. That's not the case with these little guys. My niece likes them because they are little reminders that say, "Hey, believe in your dream! Dare to dream! Don't give up!"

Who doesn't need to be reminded to do those things? Even if you don't have Dreamsicles throughout your home, you need to remind yourself to dream. Let your mind dwell on your dreams. See yourself walking in your dreams. Share your dreams with your children and allow them to share their dreams with you. Remind each other of your dreams and encourage one another. Then, as a family, you can pray over those dreams every night. Finally, when those dreams begin to manifest, you can celebrate together as a family. When a family gets its faith on, look out! Those dreams are just around the corner.

MOM TO MASTER
Thank You, Lord, for my dreams. Help me to
follow after them and to encourage my kids
in their dreams, too. Amen.

Now to Him who is able to do
far more abundantly beyond all
that we ask or think, according to the power
that works within us.

EPHESIANS 3:20 NASB

When I was a little girl growing up in Indiana, I was the classic daydreamer. I'd sit in class, look out the window, and dream of being anywhere but in Mrs. Webster's room. I couldn't wait to grow up and have a life that didn't include homework. Now that I'm all grown up, I still daydream. I've traded homework for housework, but basically I feel like that same little girl on the inside.

I still have hopes and dreams that I think about on a daily basis. I still believe that God is going to do big things for me. And now, twenty-five years since I was in Mrs. Webster's fourth-grade class, I know that God is capable of doing the impossible in my life. He has proven Himself to me time and time again.

Has God proven Himself to you? Do you have confidence that He is able to do above all that we could ever ask or think? Now, I don't know about you, but I can ask and think of a lot of stuff, so that verse totally excites me. It should totally excite you, too. If you've never seen the power of God in your life, ask Him to show Himself strong to you today. He will. He's just been waiting for you to ask.

MOM TO MASTER
Father, I believe that You will do above all I could ever ask or think, and I thank You for working in my life. Amen.

DREAMING BIG DREAMS

> *"You may ask me for anything in my name, and I will do it."*
>
> JOHN 14:14

Have you ever seen a shooting star whiz past in the night sky and whispered to your children, "Hurry, make a wish!" We love to look into the night sky and see who can spot the first shooting star. It's lots of fun—especially if you're out in the country where the sky is so awesome, away from the city lights.

But you know, the last time we saw a shooting star and I said that to my girls, I heard that still, small voice whisper something to me. He said, "You don't need a shooting star to make a wish. You can ask Me for anything." Wow! That was quite a revelation. I guess I'd always known that I could ask my heavenly Father for anything—big or small—but I'd never thought of it in quite that way.

We need to quit wishing on shooting stars and make our requests known unto God. Tell your dreams to the Father. Let Him know your innermost desires. Wishing never got anyone anywhere, but prayer changes things for the better. Faith-filled prayers will change your situation. So, go ahead. Pray about your dreams today—you don't even have to wait on a shooting star.

DREAMING BIG DREAMS

MOM TO MASTER

Father, I am asking You to accomplish _____ in my life. I believe You can bring it from a wish to a reality. Amen.

This is the confidence
we have in approaching God:
that if we ask anything according to his will,
he hears us.
1 JOHN 5:14

When my girls were really young, they used to ask me the funniest stuff. They thought Mommy could do anything! Once, Abby asked if I could touch the stars. I guess to her three-year-old pint-sized body, my five-foot-three-inch frame seemed pretty tall. In her eyes, I *could* touch the stars. She believed in me.

That's how our heavenly Father wants us to feel about Him. He wants us to look up to Him in total amazement and trust and ask, "Father, can You touch the stars?" But, unlike me, He can answer yes because He can do anything—He *made* the stars!

Sometimes when I think about the future and how I fit into His plan for my life, I think, "I can't do that! I don't have what it takes." And I'm right—I don't, but He does. We just have to know Him. Do you know Him?

If you don't know Him, ask Jesus to be your Lord and Savior today. All you have to do is tell Him you're sorry for your sins and ask Him to take over every part of your life. The One who can touch the stars wants to live in your heart. . .so go ahead, ask Him.

MOM TO MASTER
Lord, please take over every part of my life.
I love You. Amen.

DREAMING BIG DREAMS

*Joseph had a dream,
and when he told it to his brothers,
they hated him all the more.*

Some dreams are just not meant to be shared. Take Joseph's dreams, for example. Remember when he told his brothers about his dreams? They were less than thrilled to learn that little bro had dreamed they would someday bow down to him. I can only imagine what my older brother and big sister would have said if I'd told them that God had given me a dream of them bowing down to me. I would probably not be alive to write this devotional!

You see, there are some dreams you're just supposed to keep to yourself. Not everyone is going to want to celebrate with you. That's why keeping a journal is such a good idea. When you want to share your dreams with others, but you're pretty sure God wants you to keep them just between the two of you—write them in your journal! It's a way of recording the very things that God has placed in your heart. Then, when they come to pass, you can go back and reread what God revealed to you months earlier and celebrate with your close friends and family.

MOM TO MASTER

*Lord, thank You for the dreams You've given me.
Help me to know when it's the right time to share
and when it's not appropriate. I love You. Amen.*

DREAMING BIG DREAMS

"Have faith in God," Jesus answered.
MARK 11:22

Lately, my pastor has been preaching about getting a new faith attitude. Here are the questions he's been using to challenge us:

*Are you maintaining, or are you in hot pursuit?

*Are you holding the fort, or are you taking new ground?

*Are you dry-docked, or are you launching out into the deep?

*Are you settled into the status quo, or are you reaching up to the next level?

*Are you throwing in the towel, or are you going in for the next round?

*Are you retreating, or are you advancing?

*Are you circling the wagons, or are you leading the charge?

*Are you chasing after your dreams, or are you running them down?

Wow! I want to be so full of faith that I am running down my dreams—not just chasing after them. But, that kind of faith only comes from the Lord. Visualizing and meditating on our destinies isn't enough. We have to meditate on God's Word and spend time in prayer before we'll have the kind of courage it takes to launch out. If you'll spend time with God, He'll enable you to answer those questions with aggressive faith.

MOM TO MASTER
Lord, help me to run down my dreams. Help me to be aggressive and determined when it comes to my faith. I love You. Amen.

DREAMING BIG DREAMS

Finally, brothers, whatever is true,
whatever is noble, whatever is right,
whatever is pure, whatever is lovely,
whatever is admirable—if anything is excellent
or praiseworthy—think about such things.

PHILIPPIANS 4:8

Have you ever talked yourself out of a blessing? It's called thinking too much about the wrong things. I am guilty of it. God will place something in my heart, and by the time it reaches my head, I've already thought of ten reasons why it won't work.

When my girls were just toddlers, my sister taught a Bible study at our church in Bedford, Indiana. It was so great. My sister would dig things out of the Word that really ministered to the ladies. But, God called my sister and her husband to another city to serve as pastors, leaving the Bible study without a leader. My cousin Aimee said she believed God was calling me to step up to the plate, but I was much more comfortable watching from the sidelines. Secretly, I'd also felt the Lord's leading to fill my sister's shoes, but I was scared. I hadn't been to Bible school. I was just a mom, and sometimes I wasn't even very good at that!

Finally, I agreed to do it, and God met me. He enabled me to teach things I didn't even know. See, He didn't call me because I knew a lot. He called me because I knew Him. What is God calling you to do today? Be obedient. He isn't looking for pros; He is looking for willing hearts.

MOM TO MASTER
Lord, help me to be obedient the first time You call. Amen.

DREAMING BIG DREAMS

The tongue also is a fire, a world of evil among the parts of the body. It corrupts the whole person, sets the whole course of his life on fire, and is itself set on fire by hell.
JAMES 3:6

Over the course of Abby's and Ally's elementary years, I have served on every PTA committee known to man. From talent shows to school carnivals, the girls are quick to volunteer dear old Mom. Running an elementary talent show was certainly not a childhood dream of mine, but I accepted that task because there was a need.

That talent show experience was quite difficult, but I certainly learned some things about working with people. Looking back, it was great preparation for serving on the faculty for writers' conferences because whenever you get around a bunch of writers, you're going to encounter some egos.

Having battled with stage mothers during the talent show, I was much more prepared when I received cutting comments from other writers at these conferences. So, when a fellow faculty member said to me, "I'm sorry, you're not allowed to dine in here. This is for faculty only," I was able to smile sweetly and say, "Well, that's good because I'm a faculty member." Had God not helped me train my tongue during the talent show ordeal, I might've throttled this "guardian of the faculty dinner door" and repented later.

So, don't despise small beginnings. Do whatever you're called to do now to the best of your ability. Just consider it preparation work for your dream—it'll be worth it!

MOM TO MASTER
Lord, help me to be the very best I can be today. Amen.

DREAMING BIG DREAMS

"For I know the plans I have for you,"
declares the LORD, "plans to prosper you
and not to harm you,
plans to give you hope and a future."
JEREMIAH 29:11

I recently told Allyson that when she was only eight weeks old, growing inside of my belly, the doctors thought I would miscarry. In fact, they sent me home to wait for "the inevitable." I had been bleeding quite heavily, and the prognosis was not good. But, God is the Great Physician, amen. He stepped in where medicine stopped, and I was able to carry Allyson almost full term. She came just three weeks early—perfect in every way.

After hearing this story, Ally looked up at me with her big blue eyes and said, "I'm pretty special, aren't I, Mom?"

I smiled and said, "Yep, you sure are. God must have a very special plan for you, my dear."

No one will ever be able to convince Allyson that God doesn't have big plans for her because she knows it in her knower. We all need to grasp that revelation today. We need to know that God thinks we're special and that He has awesome plans for our lives. Even if your life has been difficult up to now, that doesn't change the facts—God has a special plan for you. Grab hold of that today. Meditate on it. Begin to thank God for His plan, and then watch as He unfolds it.

MOM TO MASTER
Lord, thank You for the plans You have for me.
Help me to walk in them. Amen.

I gave you milk, not solid food,
for you were not yet ready for it.
Indeed, you are still not ready.

1 CORINTHIANS 3:2

Do you know that God doesn't dangle carrots just to tease us? No, if God dangles a carrot in front of us, He plans on giving it to us. He would be an unjust God if He placed a dream in our hearts with no intention of helping us achieve that dream. We serve a just and loving heavenly Father. He doesn't like to withhold stuff from us, but sometimes He has to—because we're not ready.

When our kids were babies, they couldn't wait to grow up. They wanted to do all the stuff the big kids were doing, right? But, as parents, we had to protect them from the "big kid stuff" because they weren't yet big kids. I remember Abby wanting to climb the monkey bars at the park so badly. She would stand at the bottom, reach her arms toward the top of the bars, and cry. Her little lip would quiver and my heart would break. But I couldn't let her climb those bars—she wasn't big enough. She didn't know enough.

It's the same way with God. If you haven't yet realized your dream, it's not that God has forgotten you—you just may not be ready yet. If we'll just hang in there, we'll be on the big kid monkey bars before we know it!

DREAMING BIG DREAMS

MOM TO MASTER
Lord, help me to be patient as
I wait for my dream to come true. Amen.

> *Let us draw near to God*
> *with a sincere heart*
> *in full assurance of faith.*
> HEBREWS 10:22

If you're the mom of boys, you may have sat through hours of Little League games. How many times have you heard the coach yell, "Keep your eye on the ball!"? Probably hundreds.

You know, that's pretty good advice for us, too. If we'll just keep our eyes on the ball—our dreams—we'll stay focused and determined. But if we're looking in the stands at everybody else's fulfilled dreams, we'll never achieve the level of success that God has for us.

I've always loved the scene from the movie *Runaway Bride*, where Maggie (Julia Roberts) is trying to stay focused on walking down the aisle instead of bolting like she usually does, and her "sports nut" of a fiancé says, "Come on, honey, be the ball." That, too, is good advice. If we can train our minds and hearts to stay so focused on God's plan for us, we'll finally become that plan. We'll enjoy the things that God has had planned for us since the beginning of time.

So, keep your eye on the ball. Be the ball! Go forward with God, and before you know it, you'll be doing the chicken dance in the end zone. (Go ahead and spike the nearest football—you know you want to!)

MOM TO MASTER
Lord, help me to keep my focus on
You and Your plans. Amen.

DREAMING BIG DREAMS

For you did not receive a spirit that
makes you a slave again to fear,
but you received the Spirit of sonship.
ROMANS 8:15

Are you afraid that you won't ever accomplish your dreams? Do you worry that you're not good enough or smart enough or talented enough to do the things that God has placed in your heart? I think we all face those issues of self-doubt and fear. But we can't allow fear to dwell in our lives. Fear is lethal to our joy level. It's lethal to our self-esteem. And, it's lethal to our walk with God.

Think of it this way—where fear begins, failure starts. So, if you're allowing fear to rule your mind, you're not allowing yourself the opportunity to succeed. Fear is the opposite of faith, so you can't be in fear and in faith at the same time. You have to choose. So, choose faith!

Stop the fear tape that's playing in your head. Ask God to fill you with so much faith that there won't be room for any fear. Don't let the devil stop God from using you. Don't let the devil stop you from walking in your dreams. This is your time, and his time is up.

MOM TO MASTER
Lord, fill me with faith. I give You my fears. Amen.

> *"If you believe,*
> *you will receive whatever*
> *you ask for in prayer."*
> MATTHEW 21:22

I love to read children's stories that end in ". . .and they all lived happily ever after." Yeah, right! If only it were that easy, eh? In reality, our homes aren't always so happy. A good marriage takes work. A happy home takes work. But, both are possible.

We must base our marriages and our families on the Word of God. That's the only way we'll ever have "heaven on earth" in our homes. That's the only way we'll ever experience the "happily ever after." Find Scriptures in the Word that apply to your family situations and stand on those.

Begin praying for your husband and your children today. I don't mean just a quick, "Bless my husband and my kids," line in your morning prayer. I mean really commit some time to praying for them. You don't have to know exactly what to pray. The Holy Spirit will help you. The point is this—happily ever after *is* possible. Through prayer and Word time, you can live the dream of heaven on earth in your home. Now, that's a dream worth having and standing for!

MOM TO MASTER
Lord, thank You for my spouse and my children. Help
me to be the wife and mother that You've made me to
be. Please increase the happiness in my home. Amen.

And he said: "I tell you the truth,
unless you change and become like little children,
you will never enter the kingdom of heaven."
MATTHEW 18:3

Children have the best imaginations. Last week, my husband and I worked at our daughters' school carnival. We ran the "first aid" booth where we treated fake wounds with gauze, adding fake blood and fake hospital bands. It was a big hit! But the most fun part was listening to the stories each child came up with concerning the fake wounds. One little boy told his friend, "See this? It's a shark bite." Another said he was injured outrunning a wild pack of donkeys. I think that one was my favorite!

Listening to the kids share wild and outrageous stories all day made me realize why it's so easy for them to dream big dreams. They have the most amazing imaginations. It's nothing for them to dream big dreams. God doesn't have to work through all of that doubt unbelief like He does with us. As we get older, we lose much of that ability to imagine and dream. We become cynical, loaded down with baggage.

We can learn from our kids. If we will dream without limitations like our children, God will be able to do big things with us. So, go ahead. Let your mind become like a child, and dream.

MOM TO MASTER
Lord, thank You that my children have such vivid imaginations. Help me to learn from them. Amen.

DREAMING BIG DREAMS

Great is the LORD,
and most worthy of praise.

PSALM 48:1

Are you grateful when God opens the doors to your dreams? Do you immediately recognize that He is the door opener, or do you credit your success to good luck, chance, or your own skill? Sometimes when God answers our prayers and promotes us to the places we'd only dreamed about, we forget to thank Him.

Whenever my children forget to thank me for something major that I've done for them, I'm disappointed and occasionally hurt, but I still love them. God feels the same way. He doesn't stop loving us because we neglect to thank Him, but He certainly deserves our praise and adoration. So, be sure that you take every opportunity to praise Him when He answers a prayer, opens a door, or gives you divine insight.

God longs to hear us praise His name. So, look for opportunities to praise Him. When you get an unexpected promotion at work, immediately praise the Lord. If you inherit some money from a relative you didn't even know existed, thank the Lord. If you get a scholarship to return to school to finish your degree, thank the Lord. He is the opener of the doors to your dreams, and He deserves our praise.

MOM TO MASTER

Lord, I praise You for being the deliverer of my dreams.
You are awesome, and I love You. Amen.

DREAMING BIG DREAMS

The fear of the LORD leads to life:
Then one rests content, untouched by trouble.
PROVERBS 19:23

Have you ever heard the expression, "Be happy where you are on the way to where you're going"? If you're always looking to the future with longing, you'll miss the good stuff going on right now. You have to find the right balance.

My daughters do this from time to time. When they were younger, they'd get so many presents for Christmas that they couldn't enjoy the ones they'd already opened because they were so focused on opening the next gift. They would hardly look at the roller skates they'd just received before they were on to the next package. It wasn't until all of the presents were unwrapped that they could actually enjoy the blessing load they'd been given.

Have you been guilty of that, too? Are you looking for the next present to unwrap instead of enjoying the blessing load all around you? It's easy to do—especially if you're in the diaper, teething, can't-get-back-into-your-prepregnancy-clothes stage. Some days it's hard to find the "gift" in all of it, but look closely. There are gifts all around. Enjoy this wonderful motherhood journey. Don't miss a minute of it. Every moment should be treasured. You have to enjoy today before you'll ever really appreciate tomorrow.

MOM TO MASTER
Lord, help me to enjoy every minute
of this journey. Amen.

DREAMING BIG DREAMS

> *The Master said, "Martha, dear Martha,*
> *you're fussing far too much and getting*
> *yourself worked up over nothing.*
> *One thing only is essential,*
> *and Mary has chosen it."*
>
> LUKE 10:41–42 MSG

In the midst of carpools, cheer practice, gymnastics practice, Honor Choir, church youth group, and homework, my girls have little time to "chill" these days. They are so busy, I doubt they even have time to daydream. We'd have to schedule a daydream on Tuesdays between 4:00 and 4:15 P.M. for that to take place.

It's easy to see that today's kids are too busy for their own good, but what about us? Who do you think they learned it from? In addition to driving them to and from practices, we have our own activities and commitments. There's not much time to dream or meditate on the things God has placed in our hearts, either.

But we need to *make* time. It is vitally important to our spiritual health. Take time to read over your journal notes, meditate on a Scripture or two, talk to God about your dreams, or thank Him for His goodness. I can't go a day without that time, and neither should you. Our kids also need that time, so let's encourage one another to take time for God. He's worth it.

DREAMING BIG DREAMS

MOM TO MASTER

Father, help me to meditate on Your goodness
every day. And help me to teach my children
that You are worth their time. Amen.

Trust in GOD. Lean on your God!
ISAIAH 50:10 MSG

Do you remember that song "Lean on Me" by Al Green? I think Club Nouveau remade it back in the '80s. I love the words to that song. I've always thought of it as rather inspirational in nature. Do you remember the words? "Lean on me. When you're not strong. I'll be your friend. I'll help you carry on." (You're singing along right now, aren't you?)

If there's anything moms need, it's someone to lean on from time to time. Can I get an amen, sister? When the dishwasher is broken, the car is in the shop, the kids are sick, and your bank account is empty and payday is a week away. . .we all need somebody to lean on.

I'm so thankful that we have God to lean on during difficult times. Even if our husbands or our children or our friends don't understand our feelings and even if there's no one else around to lean on, we've always got God. He promises in His Word to never leave us nor forsake us. We can lean on Him, and He's happy to let us. So, if you're having a lousy day, a lousy week, or even a lousy year, God understands and He loves you. Go ahead—lean on Him. He will be your Friend.

MOM TO MASTER
Thank You, Lord, that I can lean on You.
Thanks for always being there for me. Amen.

SURVIVING THE GOOD, THE BAD, AND THE UGLY

Cast all your anxiety on him
because he cares for you.

1 PETER 5:7

When my friend had a stillborn baby several years ago, we were all devastated. I remember when I got the call. I was stunned. None of us knew what to say or do. There were no explanations. And there were no words to comfort her. The only comfort for her pain came from *the* Word—God's Word. The Lord was there for my friend and her family during this horribly painful time, and that's what pulled them through.

Maybe you've lost a child, or maybe your child has run away from home. I can't pretend to know exactly what you're going through, but God knows. Whatever pain you're experiencing, God is there for you. He loves you, and He cares about your loss. He hurts when you hurt. He longs to comfort you. All you have to do is ask.

While I'll never understand why my wonderful friend lost her baby, I've come to understand one essential thing—God is there for us when we're hurting. He will never leave us. So, cast your cares on Him. He really does care for you—more than you'll ever know.

MOM TO MASTER
Lord, I give my hurt and sense of loss to You today.
Thank You for being there for me—
no matter what. I love You. Amen.

SURVIVING THE GOOD, THE BAD, AND THE UGLY

O LORD, hear my prayer,
listen to my cry for mercy;
in your faithfulness and righteousness
come to my relief.
PSALM 143:1

"I hate you!" Abby screamed, followed by an intense door slam.

"Well I'm not too crazy about you right now, either!" I yelled back, stomping down the hallway toward my bedroom.

That kind of lethal word exchange will instantly turn any day into a bad one. And yes, it's happened at our house before. In fact, it happened not long ago when I wouldn't let Abby go over to a friend's house until her closet was in order. Abby lost her temper, and I lost mine. Ever been there?

There are days when I wonder if I'm cut out for this motherhood role, especially the days when my children yell, "I hate you!" That will bring on the self-doubt in a big way. On those days, I want to eat a big bag of M&Ms and drink a two-liter of Diet Coke. But that only leads to guilt and extra treadmill time. So, I've learned a better route—give it to God. He has all the solutions. He cares about you. He wants to comfort you. And, you'll feel better. Plus, prayer is calorie-free. Partake today!

MOM TO MASTER
Lord, help me not to take offense when my children say
ugly things to me. I give my hurt to You. Amen.

JULY 4

Backyard barbecues. Family picnics. Patriotic pa-
rades. Red, white, and blue Sno-cones. Fireworks at
the park. Ahhhh. . .I love the Fourth of July. But, I
love this day for many more reasons than the ones I
just listed. I love it because, as Americans, we celebrate our freedoms on this day.

Every time I hear that song by Lee Greenwood
that says, "I'm proud to be an American," I'm moved
to tears. Every time I sing the National Anthem at a
ball game, I get chills. I am so thankful to live in the
United States. I'm so thankful to be able to raise my
children here—in the land of the free, home of the
brave. We enjoy so many liberties here.

Let's take this moment to thank God for America, and let's pray for our leaders and the men and
women who defend this country. Encourage your children to pray along with you. Make it a habit to pray for
America and those who lead this mighty land—not
just today, but every day. Happy Fourth of July!

MOM TO MASTER
*Thank You, Lord, for America. I pray for
the leaders and the military personnel today.
Lead them and protect them. Amen.*

"For your Maker is your husband—
the LORD Almighty is his name—
the Holy One of Israel is your Redeemer;
he is called the God of all the earth."
ISAIAH 54:5

I have a very good friend who is a single mother. She is an amazing woman. She works long hours to pay the bills, and she still finds time to read stories to her little girl. She attends most every school event, and she does it all with a smile on her face. I am in awe of my friend.

When I compliment her, she always says the same thing: "You just do what you have to do." And to be honest, there are days when she doesn't know if she can do it all. She worries about paying the bills on time. She wonders if she'll be able to buy her daughter those designer tennis shoes. She gets lonely. But she knows the most important thing—that God said He would be her husband. She has learned to trust Him for everything in her life. That's how I want to be. I'm thankful for my friend, and I'm thankful for all that she is teaching me about trusting the Lord.

MOM TO MASTER

Lord, please take care of all of the single moms in the world. Thank You for being there for all of us. Amen.

*"Man looks at the outward appearance,
but the LORD looks at the heart."*

1 SAMUEL 16:7

Every morning when I look in the mirror, I seem to have changed a bit. The more I study my face, the more little lines I see forming around my eyes. How did those get there? It's not as easy to look good in my thirties as it was in my twenties. Can I get an amen? I am now slathering every magic potion on my face and neck. Firming. Toning. Anti-wrinkle. Anti-blemish. Anti-aging. Antioxidants. You name them, I'm using them. Maybe you are, too.

Well, here's the good news: Even if we can't turn back the hands of time, even if our faces have a few more lines than they did ten years ago, even though we're growing older—God still adores us. He loves us on our very worst day. He thinks we're special, not because of our outward appearance, but because of our heart condition. The Word says that man looks on the outward appearance while God looks on the heart. So, go ahead and slather on those beauty creams, but make sure you spend time basking in God's presence through His Word and through prayer. That's the only true and lasting beauty treatment, so go for it!

MOM TO MASTER
*Lord, thank You for loving me
just the way I am. Amen.*

"No weapon formed against you shall prosper."
ISAIAH 54:17 NKJV

Do you remember the song "I Will Survive" by Gloria Gaynor? I bet you're singing it right now, aren't you? There are days when "I Will Survive" becomes my theme song. Do you know the days I'm talking about? I'm talking about the days when everything goes wrong—your son finds out he is failing four of his six classes; your daughter needs $850 for cheerleading dues and uniform fees; your husband gets the pink slip; the dog throws up on your new carpet; and your home hair-coloring job turned your coif a lovely shade of orange.

On those days, the fighter in me screams—I will survive! It's sort of like saying, "Go ahead, devil. Bring it on. I will survive!" Of course, I wouldn't have the courage or strength or will to go on if it weren't for my heavenly Father. He is the One whispering in my ear, "It's okay. Don't worry about that. I've got you covered. You're coming out on top! Hang in there! Press forward!"

If you don't have God as your cheerleader on those really challenging days, you'll probably be singing the blues instead of "I Will Survive." So, go ahead. Ask God to help you today.

MOM TO MASTER
Lord, I need Your help today. Thank You for being my biggest cheerleader—especially when I need an extra boost of encouragement. Amen.

SURVIVING THE GOOD, THE BAD, AND THE UGLY

JULY 8

And the people, that is,
the men of Israel,
encouraged themselves.
JUDGES 20:22 NKJV

Do you ever encourage yourself in the Lord? As moms, we encourage everybody else—our husbands, our children, our friends, our extended family, and our neighbors. But we rarely take time to encourage ourselves. Instead, we're overly critical of ourselves. We allow the devil to beat us up, telling us how awful we are. If we'll listen long enough, the devil will convince us that we're unworthy to be servants of God. He'll tell us that we're horrible parents and wives. He'll tell us that we're failures in life. The devil will serve us condemnation with a side of guilt as often as we'll let him. So, tell him, "NO MORE!"

We have to stop allowing the devil to deceive us. Don't dwell on his lies; meditate on God's Word. The Bible says that you are fully able to fulfill your destiny. It says that no weapon formed against you is going to prosper. It says that you can do everything through God's strength. Stop focusing on what you can't do and start focusing on what you can do. Quit looking at how far you've got to go, and start looking at how far you've already come. Encourage yourself in the Lord today! It's your turn.

SURVIVING THE GOOD, THE BAD, AND THE UGLY

MOM TO MASTER
Thank You, Lord, for giving me the ability to
fulfill my destiny. Help me to stay encouraged. Amen.

"If all you do is love the lovable,
do you expect a bonus?
Anybody can do that."
MATTHEW 5:46 MSG

Do you realize that we have golden opportunities to show love to others every single day? It's true! When that telemarketer interrupts your dinner and you're tempted to hang up right in that person's ear, don't do it. Show mercy and kindness. Or, when you encounter rudeness when checking out at the grocery store, don't return rudeness with more rudeness. No, counter that evil with goodness.

Why? The Bible says we're supposed to do unto others as we would have them do unto us. If we'll discipline ourselves and show kindness when we want to react rudely, God will reward us. This is especially true when it comes to our children. Try it! The next time one of your kids gives you the "whatever" sign and blows you off for no reason, smile sweetly and say, "You are so precious to me. I love you." It won't be easy. Your flesh will want to scream, "Listen, kiddo, you'll not 'whatever me' and get away with it! I am your mother. So don't even go there with me!"

Make kindness a habit. You'll find that if you sow seeds of kindness, you'll reap a mighty harvest of kindness. Now that's the kind of crop I want in my life, how about you?

MOM TO MASTER
Lord, help me to show love and kindness
to those who are unlovely and unkind. Amen.

SURVIVING THE GOOD, THE BAD, AND THE UGLY

> *Gideon said to him, "Me, my master?*
> *How and with what could I ever save Israel?*
> *Look at me. My clan's the weakest in Manasseh*
> *and I'm the runt of the litter."*
>
> JUDGES 6:15 MSG

Do you ever feel incapable of being a good mother? Are there days when you think, "God, are You sure I can do this?" If you ever feel inadequate, you're not alone. Women all over the world struggle with those same feelings of insecurity, self-doubt, and hopelessness. Even though you feel less than able to do all of the things on your plate, God sees you as more than able to do everything He has called you to do.

Even great leaders in the Bible felt inadequate at times. Remember what Moses said when God called him to tell Pharaoh to let the Israelites go? Moses said that he couldn't possibly do it. He told God that He had the wrong guy before finally agreeing to do it. And what about Gideon? When God called him to lead His people against Midian, he said, "I'm the weakest in Manasseh—the runt of the litter." Still, God addressed him as "You mighty man of valor." See, God didn't see Gideon as a weak worm of the dust. He saw Gideon as a mighty man of valor. God sees you as mighty and strong and capable, too! Ask God to help you see yourself as He sees you.

MOM TO MASTER
Lord, help me to see myself as You see me.
I love You. Amen.

*"And I tell you that you are Peter,
and on this rock I will build my church,
and the gates of Hades will not overcome it."*
MATTHEW 16:18

Did you know that God loves to use ordinary people to do extraordinary things? Look at Peter. He was just a fisherman, but God called him "the Rock upon which I'll build my church."

What about Mary? She was a teenager who wasn't yet married, but God chose her to give birth to Jesus. How about David? He was the little guy in the family. When his brothers went to war, he had to stay at home and watch over the sheep. Still, God called him to defeat the giant. Amazing, isn't it?

So, if you're feeling like you're not cut out for this motherhood job, cheer up! God is using you to do extraordinary things for the Kingdom of God. He wouldn't have entrusted you with your precious children if He didn't believe you could handle it. Of course, it's difficult some days. But, hey, God is a big God—bigger than all of our doubts, transgressions, and faults. You don't have to be perfect. You just have to be available. Open your heart and let God restore your hope today. He has more extraordinary things in store for you!

MOM TO MASTER
*Lord, do the extraordinary in me
and through me today. Amen.*

SURVIVING THE GOOD, THE BAD, AND THE UGLY

*For great is the LORD
and most worthy of praise.*

1 CHRONICLES 16:25

The other day I was in Wal-Mart (my home away from home), and I noticed a mom struggling with her toddler son. He was doing the whole "I want that toy!" sobbing routine. I smiled to myself, remembering the many times I'd gone through the exact same situation with Abby and Allyson. I felt for her. I wanted to tell her, "It will be all right. Someday, you'll look back on this episode and smile." But I was afraid if I shared those sentimental words of wisdom with her at that moment, she might bop me over the head with the bat her little boy had a death grip on!

We all encounter difficult parenting moments, but if we can keep things in perspective, we'll lead much more joyful lives. When Abby and Allyson used to throw those fits in public, I'd feel humiliated. I'd let the devil steal my joy for several days over one of those crying fits. Looking back, that was wasted time. I should've spent that time enjoying my kids, not beating myself up for their behavior. Don't let Satan steal your joy—no matter how ugly it gets. Just smile and praise the Lord for every parenting moment—good and bad.

MOM TO MASTER

*Lord, thank You for every parenting moment—
even the difficult ones. Help me to keep my joy. Amen.*

And let us not grow weary while doing good,
for in due season we shall reap
if we do not lose heart.
GALATIANS 6:9 NKJV

Do you ever wonder if you're getting through to your children? There are times when I impart words of wisdom to Abby and Allyson, and I can actually see it bouncing off their little heads into the great beyond. This is especially true if I'm imparting while Cartoon Network or *Lizzie McGuire* is on TV.

Well, take heart! It turns out they actually do listen to us and internalize some of what we say. I saw evidence of this just the other day. As we prepared to head over to the much anticipated elementary school carnival, Ally began crying. She had a horrible red rash all over her face and arms. She'd obviously had an allergic reaction to something. As I fumbled around for Dr. Yee's telephone number, Ally began praying over herself. Within five minutes, the red rash faded to a light pink. Within ten minutes, it was completely gone! Jeff, Abby, and I were amazed. I don't know if I was more amazed that God had healed her or that Ally had thought to ask Him to heal her. Both were miracles worth celebrating.

So, don't grow weary in teaching your kids. Some of that wisdom is getting in there—I promise!

MOM TO MASTER
Lord, help me to take advantage of every teaching
opportunity where my children are concerned. Amen.

SURVIVING THE GOOD, THE BAD, AND THE UGLY

*"Get wisdom! Get understanding!
Do not forget, nor turn away from
the words of my mouth."*
PROVERBS 4:5 NKJV

When you're the mother of little ones, it seems that everyone feels entitled to pass on advice. As if this motherhood thing isn't hard enough, people from all walks of life feel the need to share their nuggets of wisdom with you.

When Abby was two, she still loved her pacifier. I couldn't get it away from her. She just had to have her "pacy." It apparently bothered others because everywhere we went, people shared ways I could help Abby leave her pacifier behind. After about the eighth tidbit of wisdom concerning her pacifier addiction, I stopped listening. Sure, I'd smile sweetly, nod my head occasionally, and say thank you, but I was singing Barry Manilow tunes in my head.

None of the advice that had been passed on to me worked, by the way. You know what worked? Prayer. That's right, Jeff and I simply prayed for wisdom concerning the pacifier dilemma, and God gave us a "Purge the Pacy Plan." Guess what? It worked. So, when everyone is trying to tell you what to do, smile sweetly, nod, and sing "I Write the Songs" in your head, but go to God for answers. Advice can be cheap, but wisdom from God is priceless!

MOM TO MASTER
*Lord, help me to be gracious to those who offer advice,
but I am asking for Your wisdom in every situation.
Amen.*

SURVIVING THE GOOD, THE BAD, AND THE UGLY

"Do not sorrow,
for the joy of the LORD
is your strength."
NEHEMIAH 8:10 NKJV

Do you know a person who is a "gloom and doomer"? You know the type—the person who *never* has a good day. The person you never ask, "How are you?" because you'll be there listening to her misfortunes, bad luck, and illnesses for hours. Maybe you're a gloom and doom kind of gal. If you are, there's hope.

You don't have to live with a dark cloud over your head anymore. God is your way out of gloom and doom. He will help you make joyful living a way of life.

Determine today to become a positive person—not only for your sake but also for the sake of your kids. They pick up on our defeatist attitudes. They will become mini gloom and doomers if we allow that spirit of hopelessness and depression to invade our homes. So, let's get all of the gloom and doom out of our lives once and for all. Get in the habit of saying these confessions every day: "I am well able to fulfill my destiny. God has made me an overcomer. No weapon formed against me is going to prosper. The joy of the Lord is my strength." Before long, that dark cloud that's been blocking the Son is sure to move out!

SURVIVING THE GOOD, THE BAD, AND THE UGLY

MOM TO MASTER
Lord, help me to be a positive person. Amen.

*Whatever I have, wherever I am,
I can make it through anything in
the One who makes me who I am.*

PHILIPPIANS 4:13 MSG

Have you seen that reality show *Survivor*? If not, here's the skinny on it: Basically, they take a group of men and women and put them in a remote, difficult place where they have to "survive" the game. The last one who is not voted off wins the million dollars. I've often thought they should hold the next *Survivor* series in my house. See how many of them can do three loads of laundry a day, get the kids up and ready for school, pack lunches, write six deadline stories, work out, get ready, pick up the kids at school, taxi the kids to and from their after-school appointments, go grocery shopping, fix dinner, help with homework, spend time with God, return phone calls, and on and on and on! I'm exhausted just typing all of the things that we moms do every day. *Survivor*? Give me a break! After being a working mom, I'm ready for any of them.

I'll bet you are, too! Keeping all of the balls in the air is tough. In fact, some days it seems practically impossible. But on those days, I look to God. He says I can do all things through Him, so I'm holding Him to that. You should do the same!

MOM TO MASTER

*Thank You, Lord, for giving me the strength
and ability to tackle all challenges. Amen.*

"Ask and it will be given to you."
MATTHEW 7:7

"Nobody knows the troubles I've seen. Nobody knows the sorrows. . . ." Remember that little chorus? You have to sing it in a real "bluesy" voice to get the full effect. It's funny to tease about singing the blues, but it's not so funny if you're actually in a blues state of mind.

After I had Abby, I went through a bit of that postpartum depression that you hear so much about these days. Maybe you experienced that terrible condition, too. I remember breastfeeding Abby and sobbing at the same time, wondering why I was even crying. I remember trying to fasten my Levi's and crying as they lacked two inches from meeting. I remember feeling helpless, hopeless, and clueless. I hadn't the first idea how to be a mom. But, thank the Lord, God did know. He had all the answers, and after I got around to asking for His help, I came out of that "blue funk."

If you're feeling down today, look up. God is there for you. He has all of the answers you need. And He is ready and willing to impart that wisdom to you. All you have to do is ask.

MOM TO MASTER
Heavenly Father, please deliver me from
this depression. I want to walk in joy. Thank You
for all of the blessings in my life. Amen.

SURVIVING THE GOOD, THE BAD, AND THE UGLY

*For God is working in you,
giving you the desire to obey him
and the power to do what pleases him.*

PHILIPPIANS 2:13 NLT

Do you ever feel rebellious? My mother calls that a "mean streak." It seems my mean streak is a mile wide at times. Bottom line? I sometimes have a hard time being obedient. Maybe you have that same challenge. But here's the good news: Whether or not you realize it, God is at work on the inside of you. He is constantly fixing you so that you'll want to obey Him. He loves us so much that He is willing to work on us until our mean streaks are entirely gone. He will never give up on us! He doesn't dwell on our disobedience. He sees us through eyes of love. The more we understand that love, the more we'll want to walk in obedience. The more we embrace our Father's love, the more we'll want to please Him.

Here's more good news: God is doing that same work on the inside of our children. So, when they want to disobey, He is willing to go that extra mile to help them *want* to obey. See, He loves our children even more than we do. As we become more obedient to God and His ways, we'll become better examples for our children. It's a win/win situation.

MOM TO MASTER

*Heavenly Father, thank You for helping me
become more obedient. Amen.*

SURVIVING THE GOOD, THE BAD, AND THE UGLY

Never forget your promises to me your servant,
for they are my only hope.
PSALM 119:49 TLB

When something devastating happens to one of our children, it's hard to go on. We're mothers. We're programmed to hurt when they hurt. We'd do anything to take their pain for them. We want so badly to make everything all right for them, but sometimes that's not in our power. When your child has been arrested for drinking and driving. . .when your baby is diagnosed with cancer. . .when your mentally challenged child is being tormented at school. . .that's when it's time to run to the Word of God. When you need God the most, He is there for you. And you'll find Him in His Word.

When we were preparing to move from Indiana to Texas, I was concerned that Abby and Allyson would have trouble making friends in their new home. I worried they'd miss their grandparents and friends too much. I feared we were making a mistake. After crying for awhile, I opened God's Word and began reading in Joshua.

Now, I'm not a big Old Testament gal, but on this day the Holy Spirit directed me to Joshua 1:9. That's when I read these words, "Do not be terrified; do not be discouraged, for the LORD your God will be with you wherever you go."

God knew I needed reassurance that He would be with me during the move, and He would be with my daughters, too. His Word comforted me. It will comfort you, too. So, go there today.

MOM TO MASTER
Heavenly Father, thank You for Your Word. Amen.

SURVIVING THE GOOD, THE BAD, AND THE UGLY

*When I pray, you answer me,
and encourage me by giving me
the strength I need.*

PSALM 138:3 TLB

My daughters love to sing that song "Supergirl" that goes, "I'm Supergirl, and I'm here to save the world." As they were serenading me with those lyrics the other night, I thought to myself, "That should be my theme song!" Sometimes I try to be Supergirl, thinking it's my job to save the world, and that's when I really get myself in a mess.

Moms are fixers. While that determination and can-do attitude works in our favor much of the time, it can also work against us if we become too self-sufficient. If we rely on ourselves too much, we take God out of the equation. Of course, that leads to total chaos, confusion, and ultimate failure.

So, c'mon, Supergirl, rip that *S* off of your shirt and put God back into the equation. He's got the strength you need. He's got the answers you need. He's got it all! Second Corinthians 12:9 tells us that He is made perfect in our weakness, so it's okay if you're feeling stressed out and incapable of fulfilling the demands that are on you right now. Hey, you're in the perfect situation for God to do His best work.

MOM TO MASTER
*Lord, I realize that I try to do too much on
my own, so I'm giving it all to You today.
Please take control of every area of my life. Amen.*

"Oh, that we might know the LORD!
Let us press on to know him!
Then he will respond to us as surely as
the arrival of dawn."

HOSEA 6:3 NLT

I'm not much of a morning person. I'm more of a night owl. But it seems that when I travel, most of my flights are very early morning. So, about three or four times a year I actually get to see the sun rise. Wow, Texas has the most gorgeous sunrises! Because the land is so flat here in Fort Worth, you get a really spectacular view. God's handiwork is definitely apparent—makes me want to get up early more often!

Even though I rarely see the sun rise, I know that it always does. That's one thing you can depend on—no matter where you happen to be in the world—the sun always rises. That's why I like Hosea 6:3 so much. It says to me, "Hey, as long as the sun rises, the Lord is going to be there for you." Isn't that good news? That means no matter what you're going through right now, God is there for you, ready to respond to your needs.

So every time you see the sun up in the sky, let it be a reminder of God's promise to you. He is there—ready, willing, and able to intervene on your behalf.

MOM TO MASTER
Lord, thank You for always being there for me. Amen.

SURVIVING THE GOOD, THE BAD, AND THE UGLY

*"But as for me and my family,
we will serve the LORD."*

JOSHUA 24:15 NLT

Are your children serving the Lord? Have they made Jesus the Lord of their lives? If you have a wayward child, I know the heartache you must be experiencing. But remember this: It ain't over until the fat lady sings, and she hasn't even stood up! It may look like your child is rebelling against you and God, but keep praying. Keep believing. Find Scriptures to stand on. Have faith that God is working behind the scenes to bring your child into the Kingdom.

It may look hopeless right now, but God is our hope and glory. He loves your child more than you do. He is able to turn situations around without even getting up from His throne. So, don't worry. Only believe. During this time of praying for your child's salvation, surround yourself with the Word of God. Listen to praise and worship music. Watch Christian TV. Read the Word. Read Christian books. Immerse yourself in God and let Him build your faith.

Remember the story of the prodigal son in Luke 15? I'm sure that father thought he'd lost his son for good. But he hadn't. The son returned. Your child will return, too. Don't give up. Stand your ground and wait for your miracle.

MOM TO MASTER

*Lord, thank You for protecting my wayward child.
I praise You that my child is coming into
the Kingdom. In Jesus' Name. Amen.*

For I am the LORD,
I change not.
MALACHI 3:6 KJV

I couldn't believe it. Today, Abby asked if she could borrow Jeff's ties. She said, "It's cool to wear men's ties. All the kids are doing it." I had to laugh! We wore men's ties in the '80s! If you're an '80s chick, you probably wore a tie or two in your time. (Not to mention parachute pants, leg warmers, and neon plastic bracelets.) Wow, the '80s were a fashion fiasco, eh?

Abby, my ten-year-old, thinks her generation is the first to wear men's ties and plastic bracelets. I guess it's really true what they say: If you hold onto something long enough, it will eventually come back in style. . . . Wonder where I put those parachute pants?

Well, styles come and go. Fashion and hairstyles change from season to season and year to year. One moment your mullet is in style, the next minute it's out. In this ever-changing world, I'm so glad that Jesus never changes. The Word says He is the same yesterday, today, and forever. Hallelujah! A relationship with Jesus—that's the one thing we can give our kids that will never go out of style.

MOM TO MASTER

Lord, thank You for being the same yesterday,
today, and forever. I love You. Amen.

SURVIVING THE GOOD, THE BAD, AND THE UGLY

The disciples woke him up, shouting,
"Master, Master, we're going to drown!"
So Jesus rebuked the wind and the raging waves.
The storm stopped and all was calm!

LUKE 8:24 NLT

It never failed. With the first boom of thunder, Abby and Allyson were crawling into bed with us. As little girls, they were very afraid of storms. Even now, when one of those Texas-sized thunderstorms makes its way across the Lone Star State, the girls retreat to our bedroom. I can totally relate because I was also afraid of storms when I was a little girl. I can remember pulling the covers over my head and praying, "God, please make the storm go away!"

Today, I find myself praying that same prayer when the storms of life get too scary. When my father had a severe stroke and they called in the family to say our good-byes, I prayed for God to stop the storm. And just when I thought I couldn't handle one more black cloud, God intervened. My dad pulled out of it and continues to amaze us all.

God will quiet the storms in your life, too. He doesn't always calm the storms in the way that we want or anticipate, but He will do it. All we have to do is have faith. So, come on out from under the covers and call on the One who can calm the storms.

MOM TO MASTER
Lord, thank You for settling the storms
in my life. Amen.

How can I know all the sins
lurking in my heart?
Cleanse me from these hidden faults.
PSALM 19:12 NLT

Allyson's walk-in closet is always a mess. Sometimes I can't even get inside of it. About once a month, we have to aggressively motivate her to clean out her cluttered closet. Of course, I have a hard time punishing her for her messy closet when mine doesn't look much better. How are your closets?

What about your "life closet"? Got any skeletons in there? We all have a few skeletons in our closets—things we're ashamed of and hope nobody ever discovers. But isn't it great to know that Jesus loves us—skeletons and all? When Jesus comes into our lives, He totally cleans out our closets. In fact, He not only cleans them out, He totally remodels them. He replaces hopelessness with hope. He replaces fear with love. He gets rid of sickness and puts in healing.

We no longer have to be ashamed of the skeletons in our closet because Jesus has already taken care of those. He has cleansed us from them. We are new creatures in Christ Jesus. So, don't worry about those skeletons anymore. Jesus adores you, and He makes no bones about it!

MOM TO MASTER
Lord, thank You for making me a new creature. Thank You for getting rid of the skeletons in my closet. Amen.

SURVIVING THE GOOD, THE BAD, AND THE UGLY

So let us come boldly to the throne of our gracious God. There we will receive his mercy, and we will find grace to help us when we need it.

HEBREWS 4:16 NLT

We have a system at our house. We keep a "Good Behavior Chart" on the fridge, and that chart keeps track of Abby's and Ally's good deeds and completion of assigned chores. Earning A's on report cards is worth several check marks. But mouthy, disrespectful attitudes earn several X's, which cancel out the check marks. This system really works! When the girls wanted to get their ears pierced, we challenged them to earn twenty-five marks. It wasn't long before both of them had met their quota, and we were off to the mall for an ear-piercing celebration.

Aren't you glad that God doesn't have a check mark system? We can never earn our way to heaven. We can't be good enough—no matter how hard we try. It's only by God's grace and mercy that we get in on all of His promises.

As a child, I thought I had to be good all the time in order for God to love me. That's a warped perception of God, isn't it? Let's make sure that our kids know that God loves them—even when they don't behave perfectly. Let's make sure they know that God isn't out to get them—He's out to love them.

MOM TO MASTER
Thank You, Father, for loving me even when I behave badly. Amen.

SURVIVING THE GOOD, THE BAD, AND THE UGLY

Remember that in a race everyone runs,
but only one person gets the prize.
You also must run in such a way that you will win.
All athletes practice strict self-control.
They do it to win a prize that will fade away,
but we do it for an eternal prize.

1 CORINTHIANS 9:24–25 NLT

I have a neighbor who is preparing to run a marathon. We started out walking/jogging together. My attitude was, "Let's get this over with so I can get on with my day." But her attitude was different. She began to love jogging. It wasn't long before I could no longer keep up with her. I would jog my two and a half miles, and then she would continue for another eight or ten miles.

She is serious about this new endeavor. She now subscribes to magazines about running. She has purchased several outfits specifically designed for long distance runners. And, she is only eating foods that go along with her training program. She doesn't want to just finish the race—she wants to win this race!

As moms, we need to approach life in much the same way. We are running the most important race there is—raising our children. And, yes, sometimes it seems like we're never going to cross that finish line. Sure, there are days when you'd rather trade in your running shoes for bunny slippers, but hang in there! Keep feeding on the Word of God—that's your training food. The finish line awaits!

SURVIVING THE GOOD, THE BAD, AND THE UGLY

MOM TO MASTER
Lord, help me to finish this most important race. Amen.

> *"There is no other god who
> can rescue like this!"*
>
> DANIEL 3:29 NLT

Keith Moore sings a song that goes, "There is no God as big as mine. Too big of a problem you cannot find." I love that song. I sing it all the time just to remind myself that we serve a very big God—a God who is able to handle any problem.

Children have no problem with this concept. When Abby is upset over something, and I say, "Don't worry about that. God is in control. He is way bigger than your problem," she's totally okay. She knows that God is a big God. But, as we get older, we pick up doubt, unbelief, and other baggage. Sometimes, those things can hinder our faith. They can block our faith eyes from seeing that God is bigger than anything we could ever encounter.

I want to challenge you today to get a vision of the vastness of our God. If you keep a journal, I want you to write down all of the problems you're facing today. Maybe you're facing bankruptcy. Maybe your husband has asked for a divorce. Maybe your children are failing school. Whatever it is, write it down. Now, write these words over the top of your problems: "My God is bigger than all of these things!"

We serve a big God!

MOM TO MASTER
*Lord, I praise You for being bigger than
all of my problems. Amen.*

SURVIVING THE GOOD, THE BAD, AND THE UGLY

And I sought for a man among them,
that should make up the hedge,
and stand in the gap before me for the land,
that I should not destroy it: but I found none.
EZEKIEL 22:30 KJV

We all know that we need God, but have you ever thought that God might need us, too? Sure, He is Almighty God. Still, God needs His people. In fact, He needs people like you and me, working for Him and accomplishing His goals here on earth. More than anything, He is looking for willing hearts to take the message of His Son around the world.

As moms, we can do that in our own neck of the woods. Our world might be our children's ball games, the grocery store, Wal-Mart, the dry cleaners, our workplace, our neighborhood, our children's school. . . We don't have to travel to Africa to evangelize. We can touch the people in our little corner of the world with His love.

Look for opportunities to share God with others. If you're at the grocery store and you notice that your checker is having a hard day, say, "How are you doing today?"

If she says, "Well, I'm not feeling very well," simply ask, "Do you mind if I pray for you? I'd be happy to do that while you're ringing up my items." I've never had anyone say "no" yet. They are grateful, and God is pleased.

MOM TO MASTER
Lord, help me to touch my world with Your love. Amen.

SURVIVING THE GOOD, THE BAD, AND THE UGLY

> *Let them turn to the LORD*
> *that he may have mercy on them.*
> *Yes, turn to our God,*
> *for he will abundantly pardon.*
> ISAIAH 55:7 NLT

One thing about my children, they are pretty quick to repent. When Allyson was only four, she loved to play with my china. She wanted to have tea parties with her stuffed animals. Of course, her tea set wasn't fancy enough. She wanted to use my good stuff. (You know, the kind that stays in the china cabinet until Thanksgiving dinner!) I had already told her not to touch my fine china, but she just couldn't help herself. Unfortunately, her little hands weren't so careful. When I heard a crashing sound coming from the living room, I knew what she had done. She had dropped one of my saucers on the hard, tile floor and it was lying there in several pieces.

Before I could even round the corner, her tiny little voice was chanting, "I'm sorry. I'm sorry. I'm sorry. I'm sorry," just as fast as she could say it. I couldn't help but laugh. She knew the best way out of her disobedience was repentance, and she was right.

You know, we could all learn from our children when it comes to quick repentance. When we're disobedient to God, it's best to go right to Him and confess our sin and move on. He wants us to run to Him, not away from Him.

MOM TO MASTER
Lord, thanks for being quick to forgive. Amen.

SURVIVING THE GOOD, THE BAD, AND THE UGLY

*Don't you know that the LORD
is the everlasting God, the Creator of all the earth?
He never grows faint or weary.
No one can measure the depths of his understanding.
He gives power to those who are tired and worn out;
he offers strength to the weak.*

ISAIAH 40:28–29 NLT

It's almost back-to-school time, and I'm already exhausted. How about you? Every year at this time, the girls and I go back-to-school shopping for clothes, school supplies, and other stuff. This, of course, is a several week process (several paychecks, too!).

Last year when we began this adventure, we could not find the right size of manila paper. It seemed that we drove all over the Lone Star State in search of this paper. I even called my friends in other states to see if they could find it and ship it. We finally found the paper at Staples, forty-five minutes from our home. We were tired, but we were victorious!

Being a mom requires that we take on many tiring adventures, but being worn out doesn't have to go along with the job description. God tells us in the above Scripture that He never tires and that He gives strength to the weak and worn out. So, if you're feeling a bit overloaded and tired today, ask God to supercharge your engine. He's even got enough strength to get us through this back-to-school season.

MOM TO MASTER
Lord, thanks for giving me strength and energy. Amen.

SURVIVING THE GOOD, THE BAD, AND THE UGLY

> *But no man can tame the tongue.*
> *It is a restless evil, full of deadly poison.*
>
> JAMES 3:8

Words can be lethal weapons. Did you know that? With our mouths, we can curse someone and do irreparable damage to that person. I was watching one of the daytime talk shows not long ago while I walked on the treadmill, and the title of the show was "You Ruined My Life." All of the guests who came onto that show shared heartbreaking stories of how someone had said horrible things to them, changing the entire course of their lives. Some of these guests had lived with the sting of these words for more than twenty years. Can you believe that?

The guests who were the most messed up had internalized damaging words from their parents. Wow. That show just put an exclamation mark at the end of what I already knew in my heart—we need to speak good things to our children! We should take every opportunity to tell our kids, "You can do it! You are well able to fulfill your destiny! You've got what it takes! No weapon formed against you is going to prosper! I love you, and God loves you!" So use your words wisely. They hold the power of life and death.

MOM TO MASTER
Lord, help me to speak only good things
to my children. Amen.

The mouth of the righteous man utters wisdom,
and his tongue speaks what is just.

PSALM 37:30

Do you ever feel like you've got a big *C* on your head, indicating your level of cluelessness? I am sure my *C* is visible from time to time. Growing up, I always thought that when I became a mom, I'd have all the answers. After all, my mom always had the answers. But, I've discovered being a mom doesn't necessarily come with the "Answer Key for Life."

Many times, I am clueless. Maybe you're clueless, too. But, thank the Lord, we don't have to remain clueless. Even if we don't have the answers, God does. And, here's the best part—He is more than willing to share that wisdom with us so that we can pass it onto our children.

It's perfectly okay to admit ignorance when you don't know the answer to a question that your kiddos come up with—really. Just tell them, "I don't know, but I'll find out. God has all the answers, and He is willing to share them with me." It's good for our children to see us vulnerable once in awhile. It's especially good for them to see us seeking God for His wisdom. So, go ahead, wipe that *C* off your head and seek God.

MOM TO MASTER

Lord, please fill me with Your wisdom
so that I can impart it to my children. Amen.

TAMING THE TONGUE

[Love] doesn't fly off the handle.

1 CORINTHIANS 13:5 MSG

How is your attitude today? Feeling kind of grouchy? There are mornings that I open my eyes, and I just feel grouchy. It's as if the devil was waiting for me to get up so he could use my mouth to say ugly things. Ever been there? On those days, I have to force myself to walk in love. Let's face it. If you haven't been sleeping enough, or if you're under quite a bit of stress, or if you're feeling ill, it's easier to be a grouch.

But moms aren't supposed to be grouches! Haven't you ever seen *Leave It to Beaver* on TV Land? Mrs. Cleaver is always joyful. And how about that Carol Brady on *The Brady Bunch*? She is so sweet, it's sickening!

In reality, no mom can be perfect all the time. We all lose our tempers. We all complain. We all act ugly. We all get grouchy. But God knew that when He created us. He knew our flesh would win out once in awhile. That's why He sent Jesus to save us from our sins, so we can repent for our grouchy attitudes and move forward in love. So, get those grouchies off and let love control you today.

MOM TO MASTER
Lord, flood me with Your love. Amen.

TAMING THE TONGUE

Every word they speak is a land mine.
PSALM 5:9 MSG

Have you ever wanted to say something so badly that you practically had to bite through your tongue not to say it?

Me, too.

There's a great exchange in the movie *You've Got Mail* that stars Meg Ryan and Tom Hanks. In this clip, she is frustrated that she can't ever say the exact thing she wants to say at the moment of confrontation. On the other hand, Tom Hanks's character is able to say cutting comebacks without any hesitation. She e-mails him that she wishes she had that talent. He tells her that he wishes he could give her his talent because it's dangerous, stating that saying exactly what you think, exactly when you think it, leads to guilt and regret. Later in the film when she is able to say the most hurtful comments on cue, she realizes the truth in her friend's e-mail. She felt badly for her hurtful words, but they had already been said.

That's the thing about spewing words without ever thinking about the consequences—you can't get those words back. They do damage immediately, and even when you say you're sorry, their sting remains. So, think before you speak. Do whatever it takes to keep the cutting comments from escaping your mouth. You may have a sore tongue, but your heart will feel good!

MOM TO MASTER
Lord, keep a rein on my mouth. Amen.

TAMING THE TONGUE

AUGUST 5

He traveled through that area,
speaking many words of
encouragement to the people.
ACTS 20:2

I think all moms were born to be cheerleaders and vice versa. That's one of the only qualifications I actually had when I became a mom. I had been a cheerleader from elementary school through college. Many times our children don't need correction; they just need encouragement.

School is tough today. So much is expected from our children. Due to funding issues, schools really push the children to do well on the yearly assessment tests. After months of preparation for these all-important tests, the testing week finally arrives. One of Abby's friends actually suffered with an ulcer last year due to the stress. School is really difficult today. When you add in all of the extracurricular activities and other stuff, it's no wonder why our children are stressed out!

So, it's our job to encourage our little ones. We need to tell them that they can do it! We need to tell them that they are special. We need to find creative ways to encourage them. For instance, leave little notes of encouragement in their lunchboxes. They need our approval and affirmation, so let's be quick to offer it. Get out those pom-poms and become a super encourager!

TAMING THE TONGUE

MOM TO MASTER
Father, help me to be an
encourager for my family. Amen.

Love never fails.
1 CORINTHIANS 13:8

Do you know that some children grow up without ever hearing "I love you" said to them by their parents? It's true. Maybe you're one of the people who grew up without ever hearing those three important words. If you are, then I'm sure you know how hurtful and devastating it is to never feel loved.

I have a friend who grew up in a home like that—where love was never communicated—and she has struggled in that area. Her father used to say, "I don't have to say it. My actions show that I love you." While that might be true, we still need to hear the words. As wives, we need to hear those three words from our husbands. And as moms, we need to communicate our love to our children.

There are many ways we can say "I love you." We can leave little love notes to our spouses and our children, sneaking them into briefcases and backpacks. We can verbally express our love every morning and every night. We can bake a big cookie cake and write "I Love You!" on it. Be as creative as you want, just make sure you take time to express your love every day. Be an ambassador of love in your home.

MOM TO MASTER
*Father, help me to better express my love
to my family. Amen.*

TAMING THE TONGUE

AUGUST 7

*"Therefore my heart is glad
and my tongue rejoices."*
ACTS 2:26

When I was in fourth grade, I went to church camp at Camp Wildwood in southern Indiana. One of my most vivid memories of attending that camp was singing "Rejoice in the Lord always, again I say rejoice" in a round on the bus. I've never forgotten that little chorus or the way I felt singing at the top of my lungs, surrounded by seventy other kids singing at the tops of their lungs. Let me tell you, we sang ourselves happy. It didn't matter that it was the hottest, stickiest, most humid day of the summer and we were riding on a bus without air-conditioning. We didn't care! We just praised the Lord anyway. Sometimes, I still sing that little chorus just to encourage myself. Do you ever do that? If not, you're missing out!

Praising the Lord is one of the best things you can do to encourage yourself. It's hard to be worried or depressed when you're singing, "Rejoice in the Lord always." Even if you're feeling down when you begin singing, before long, your heart will be glad. This Scripture says our tongues should rejoice, so let your tongue rejoice today. Let your kids see you rejoicing in the Lord, and before long, they'll join in. It's contagious!

MOM TO MASTER
Father, I praise You for being who You are! Amen.

TAMING THE TONGUE

For out of the overflow
of his heart his mouth speaks.
LUKE 6:45

"U-G-L-Y, you ain't got no alibi, you're ugly, Hey, hey, you're ugly. Whoo!" Did you ever do this cheer as a child? We used to say it to the opposing team when I was on the eighth-grade cheer squad. Nice, huh? And now this little chant has found its way into a song of the same name. (It's on the *Bring It On!* soundtrack.)

The kids love it. A group of girls recently performed this song in a local elementary talent show and brought the house down with laughter. It was really funny! One of the girls was dressed up like a big nerd, and the other cheerleaders chanted this song at her.

While that was funny in a talent show, it's not so funny on the playground or in the classroom. Unfortunately, children (tween girls especially) can be cruel to one another. They call each other fat, ugly, stupid, poor, and other terrible things such as "Loser!" As parents, we want our children to understand the power of their words and to choose them wisely. We want them to grow up to be kind and respectful of others' feelings. And they will if we continually remind them that saying ugly things indicates the presence of an ugly heart.

MOM TO MASTER
Father, help me to teach my children the power of their words and the importance of being kind to others. Amen.

TAMING THE TONGUE

AUGUST 9

*"My lips will not speak wickedness,
and my tongue will utter no deceit."*

JOB 27:4

"Ally, did you turn in your lunch money?"

"Yep," she answered, breezing past me in the hallway.

Fast forward to the next morning. As I'm cleaning out my daughter's closet, I discover the envelope with "Lunch Money" written on the outside. It had been ripped open, obviously to remove the money.

Can you say "BUSTED!"?

The school confirmed what I already knew—the lunch money had never made it to school. My little clever blond child had pocketed the cash. I confronted her when she arrived home from school that afternoon. She immediately began crying, asking for forgiveness for telling a huge lie. Of course we forgave her, but her lying resulted in punishment. She had to miss a party that weekend among other things.

It's easy to see that Ally's lie was wrong. But what about the little white lies that we encourage? You know, like when we ask our kids to tell the telemarketer that Mommy isn't at home right now. A lie is a lie is a lie. We need to be conscious of our words because our kids are paying attention. We're their role models. Let's make sure we're good ones.

MOM TO MASTER

*Lord, help me to be a good role model for my children,
and help us all to speak no deceit.*

*May the LORD cut off all flattering lips
and every boastful tongue.*

PSALM 12:3

Have you ever known anyone who always has to "one up" you? If you had twins, she had triplets. If you had a thirty-four-hour labor and delivery, she had a forty-five-hour trauma. If you share that you've lost four pounds, she's lost seven. Ahhh! It can drive you crazy! It's even more maddening when that person "one ups" you on your children's accomplishments.

You say, "My daughter just learned to do a back handspring."

And she says, "Really? My daughter can do a round off back handspring back tuck."

It's enough to make you want to join in the "one ups" game, too, but don't go there. The Bible tells us in 1 Corinthians 13 that love does not boast. So, if you join in the "one ups" game, your love walk will become more of a love crawl. It's not worth it.

The next time that someone tries to "one up" you, simply take a deep breath, smile sweetly, and move on. Give your frustration and irritation to God. He can give you a love for that person. He can help you see that person through His eyes of compassion, because someone who is always "one upping" everyone else is a person with self-esteem issues. That person needs your prayers, not your anger. So, take the high road and walk in love.

TAMING THE TONGUE

MOM TO MASTER
Lord, help me to walk in love no matter what. Amen.

*Go near and listen to all that
the LORD our God says.*

DEUTERONOMY 5:27

Do you talk too much? Listening has become sort of a lost art form in today's society. We are a generation of people who simply love to hear ourselves talk. But, you know, if we're constantly talking, we're missing out on a lot. This is especially true in our prayer lives.

When you pray, do you do all of the talking? From the time we're little children, we're taught to pray to God. We're taught to say the Lord's Prayer. We're taught to bring our praises and petitions unto Him. But very few of us are taught to wait upon the Lord and listen for His voice. It's a difficult thing, waiting and listening. It requires time on our part. It requires patience. It takes practice. God's voice doesn't come down from the sky and speak to us in a Charlton Heston-type voice. No, He speaks to us through that still, small voice—that inward knowing—the Holy Spirit. He also speaks to us through His Word.

So, quit doing all of the talking and take time to listen to Almighty God! He has much wisdom to share with us if we'll only be quiet long enough to receive it.

MOM TO MASTER
*Lord, I want to hear Your voice.
Help me to listen better. Amen.*

TAMING THE TONGUE

Your boasting is not good.
1 CORINTHIANS 5:6

Abby, my ten-year-old, has a very vivid imagination. In fact, I think she may become a writer and an illustrator when she grows up. But all of that creativity sometimes finds its way into her speech. Abby, like many children, has a tendency to exaggerate once in awhile. When she and Daddy go fishing, she always has an exciting "fish tale" to tell.

While this is kind of cute in our kids, it's not quite so cute and harmless when *we* do it. At times when I've been backed into a corner, I've resorted to exaggeration to justify myself. Maybe you've done the same thing. A few years ago, a colleague of mine said something condescending to me in front of other writers and editors. So, to defend myself, I exaggerated a bit on my financial situation. They were immediately impressed, and I was immediately depressed. I had exaggerated in self-defense, but no matter the reason, God isn't pleased when we stretch the truth—because "stretching the truth" simply means telling a lie.

If you have a tendency to exaggerate, ask God to help you. The Lord has helped me in this area. He reminded me that I don't have to prove myself to anyone. He is already pleased with me. He is pleased with you, too!

TAMING THE TONGUE

MOM TO MASTER
Lord, thank You for validating me with Your love.
Help me to stop exaggerating. Amen.

> *"If you have a message of encouragement*
> *for the people, please speak."*
>
> ACTS 13:15

"You go, girl!"

That has sort of become the expression of today's women, hasn't it? In the past, Helen Reddy's "I am woman, hear me roar" was the cry, but now it's simply an encouraging, "You go, girl!" We need to encourage each other. As moms, we should uplift one another in prayer, in word, and in deed.

I don't know what I would do without the gal pals in my life. There are days when I need to call and vent. There are times when I simply need my buddy to say, "You don't look fat." There are situations when I just need a hug and a simple, "You go, girl! You can do it!"

As moms, we are constantly speaking words of encouragement to our families. We're the cheerleaders! But we need a little cheering every so often, too. That's why it's so important to surround yourself with positive people. Find friends who are women of faith, and be there for one another. Pray for one another. Love one another. And encourage each other with a "You go, girl!" now and then. We're all in this motherhood experience together, so let's cheer each other on to victory!

MOM TO MASTER

Lord, thank You for the friends You've given me.
Help me to encourage them as You encourage me. Amen.

TAMING THE TONGUE

His mouth is full of curses and lies and threats;
trouble and evil are under his tongue.
PSALM 10:7

There's always one in every crowd—the troublemaker. The one who constantly speaks evil, taking great pleasure in stirring up strife. There's a little girl at Abby's and Allyson's school who fits this description. She is constantly in the middle of some dispute. She makes up lies about other children. She gossips and divides friends. She's a busy girl!

Maybe your children have had bouts with this kind of kid. It's tough to just stand by as a mom and watch another child destroy our children's reputations. I know; I've been there. But stepping into the middle of the situation and taking charge on your child's behalf isn't the best way. I know because I've tried that, too.

Do you know the best course of action? Prayer. Of course, that's the last thing you want to do when someone has hurt your child, but prayer is the only thing that will produce positive results. Pray that the troublemaker finds Jesus. Pray for wisdom to deal with the situation. And of course, pray for your child's protection. Confess together, "No weapon formed against me is going to prosper." The Word is powerful, and so is prayer. So, hit your knees and use your tongue in the right way. Prayer changes things every time!

MOM TO MASTER
Lord, I pray for my children's protection, and
I ask that this child who is causing so much hurt
will find You. Touch her, Lord. Amen.

My heart overflows with a beautiful thought!
I will recite a lovely poem to the king,
for my tongue is like the pen of a skillful poet.
PSALM 45:1 NLT

Do you want your tongue to be like the pen of a skillful poet? That's a lofty goal but one that is totally within our reach if we let God fill our hearts with His love. You see, the Word says that out of the heart the mouth speaks. So, if your heart is full of ugliness and trash, then your tongue will be writing ugly things.

As moms, we need to write very skillfully with our tongues because those "little poets" who call us Mom are taking notes all the time. They listen very carefully to everything we say—good or bad. We only have a short time to impact our kids for the Kingdom of God, so we need to make every word count.

Sure, we're going to miss it sometimes. We're only human. But, it should be our goal to be more like Jesus every day. If we become more Christlike, then our mouths will be like the pens of skillful poets, writing good things on the hearts of all we encounter.

TAMING THE TONGUE

MOM TO MASTER
Heavenly Father, help me to use my words wisely.
Fill my heart with Your love so that my mouth
might be filled with Your words. Amen.

*Timely advice is as lovely as
golden apples in a silver basket.*
PROVERBS 25:11 NLT

It's funny—as young children we thought our moms knew everything. As teens, we thought they knew nothing. As adults, we realize we were right in the first place—they do know everything. Moms are full of wisdom; however, when I became a mom, I didn't feel so wise. In fact, I didn't know the first thing about being a mother. As I've matured, I've learned a little about being a mom—mostly from my mom. Her advice is priceless.

We can learn much from the godly women in our lives. Maybe your mom hasn't been there for you, but God has placed other women in your life—an aunt, a grandmother, a close family friend, or your pastor's wife. Cherish their words of wisdom. God has placed them in your life for a purpose.

Just think, some day your children will look to you for wisdom—it's true! The Word says that they will rise up and call you blessed. So, make sure you have some wisdom to share. Treasure the advice that's been given to you, and more importantly, meditate on the Word of God. There's much wisdom waiting for you!

MOM TO MASTER
Heavenly Father, thank You for those special women in my life. Help me to honor them and You. Amen.

TAMING THE TONGUE

*"Take to heart all the words
I have given you today.
Pass them on as a command to
your children so they will obey
every word of this law."*

DEUTERONOMY 32:46 NLT

As parents, we have a mandate from the Lord to teach our children about God. We are to pass on our knowledge to our kids; however, that is difficult to do if we don't have any knowledge to pass on. Maybe you weren't raised in a Christian home. Maybe you are a new Christian. That's okay. God is great at giving crash courses in Christ. He longs to fill you full of His wisdom. He will enable you to memorize Scriptures. He will teach you about His character. He will help you pray. Just ask Him!

Even if you've been a Christian for as long as you can remember, there's still more to learn. Have you ever read a Scripture that you're very familiar with, but all of a sudden, it teaches you something totally new? That's the Lord teaching you. Isn't that exciting? God's Word is alive. It's there for you when you need it. It holds the answers you need. And it's never been more pertinent than it is right now.

Fall in love with God's Word. Listen to teaching tapes. Attend a Word-based church. Get wisdom so that you'll have wisdom to pass on to your kids.

MOM TO MASTER
Lord, teach me so that I may teach my kids. Amen.

TAMING THE TONGUE

In the morning, O LORD, you hear my voice;
in the morning I lay my requests before you
and wait in expectation.

PSALM 5:3

How do you start your mornings? Do you roll out of bed, grumbling and grumpy? Or, do you spring out of bed, praising the Lord with great expectation? If you're like me, you're not exactly chipper in the morning. But I'm learning to like those early hours a little better. Why? Because mornings are a great time to praise the Lord!

If you start your day giving praises to God, it's even more energizing than a shot of espresso. No matter how grumpy you feel, once you start praising God for His love and His goodness, you're bound to change your mood for the better. That's just the way it works!

So, why not use your mouth for something worthwhile like praising the Lord? Begin each day thanking God. It will take some practice, but you'll get the hang of it. The Holy Spirit will help you. Praise God for the many blessings in your life. Praise Him for another day to be alive. Praise Him just because He is God and deserving of our praise. Let your children see you praising the Lord, and encourage them to join in. If you do, the mornings around your house will be a lot brighter.

MOM TO MASTER
Lord, I praise You for who You are. Amen.

TAMING THE TONGUE

My brothers, can a fig tree bear olives,
or a grapevine bear figs?
Neither can a salt spring produce fresh water.

JAMES 3:12

We know from the Word of God that the tongue is hard to tame. Of course, I didn't need the Bible to tell me that fact. I am well aware that my mouth is hard to control. Maybe you have that same challenge. That's why this Scripture really brings conviction to me. If you're praising the Lord in church and hollering at your children on the way home, this Scripture probably hits home with you, too.

We need to continually ask the Lord to put a watch on our mouths. We need to ask for His help so that we might be good examples for our children. If they see us praising God one minute and hollering at them the next, they will be confused and disillusioned with the things of God.

James 3:9 says, "With the tongue we praise our Lord and Father, and with it we curse men, who have been made in God's likeness." We must be careful of our words because not only are our children listening, but God is also listening. And we'll be held accountable for our words—all of them.

MOM TO MASTER

Lord, please put a watch on my mouth that I
might only speak good things. Help me to be
a good example for my children. I love You. Amen.

TAMING THE TONGUE

*"Whoever would love life and see
good days must keep his tongue from
evil and his lips from deceitful speech."*
1 PETER 3:10

When I was a little girl, I lied to my father just once. When he found out, I received a few licks across my backside, but that didn't hurt nearly as much as what my dad said to me. He looked me in the eyes and uttered, "There's nothing I dislike more than a lie. I am disappointed in you."

Whoa! I could handle anything except my dad being disappointed in me. Today, as a mom of two little girls, I've been on the other side of that lying scenario a time or two. And I've discovered that I don't like being lied to any more than my father did.

It's not enough to just tell our children that lying is a sin. We need to take every opportunity to let them know that lying always has consequences. Once when I caught the girls in a lie, I told them that even if they got away with their lie, and I never found out about it, that God would always know. That got their attention. You see, they love God, and they didn't want to disappoint Him any more than I wanted to disappoint my earthly father. So, strive for honesty in your house. God will be pleased, and that's no lie!

MOM TO MASTER
Lord, help me to raise honest, godly children. Amen.

AUGUST 21

Dear children, let us not love with words
or tongue but with actions and in truth.

1 JOHN 3:18

Saying "I love you" to our children is very important. They need to hear those words on a daily basis. But, we also need to *show* that we love our children. Have you ever really thought about the common expression "Actions speak louder than words"? There's a lot of truth to that saying.

While it's easy to say "I love you," it's not so easy to show our love all the time. That's why another expression, "Talk is cheap," is used so often. As moms, we need to find ways to back up our "I love you's" every single day. In other words, walk the talk.

Make a conscious effort today to do something special for your children—something out of the ordinary. Leave them little love notes. Make them a special pancake breakfast and serve it by candlelight for added fun. Plan a family night out at one of their favorite places. Just find a unique way to show your kids how much you adore them. Ask God to help you in this area. He will. After all, the Bible says that God is love. He is the expert in showing love.

MOM TO MASTER
Heavenly Father, help me to show Your love
to my family on a daily basis. I love You. Amen.

TAMING THE TONGUE

Do not be anxious about anything,
but in everything, by prayer and petition,
with thanksgiving,
present your requests to God.

PHILIPPIANS 4:6

Do you pray for your children every day? I'll bet you do. Moms are prayer warriors. It's part of our job description. But, are your prayers effective, or are you canceling them out? Are you praying for God to give your children wisdom to do better in school, thanking Him for His intervention, and then canceling out your prayers by talking about Junior's inability to learn? You see, we can't be double-minded people. The Word speaks to that fact in James 1:8: "He is a double-minded man, unstable in all he does."

You see, a negative will always cancel out a positive. You can't pray about something and then talk against it, or your mouth has just cancelled out your prayers. That's why you must only speak words of faith. Our words are power containers. They shape our world, good or bad. So, be careful what you speak. Use your words to speak life to your children. Use your words to praise the Lord. Use your words to change your current situation. If you're in the habit of speaking negative things, just be still. It's better to be quiet than to speak against the Word. Get in the habit of speaking good things, and watch your world change!

MOM TO MASTER
Heavenly Father, help me to only speak words of faith.
Amen.

Nor should there be obscenity,
foolish talk or coarse joking,
which are out of place,
but rather thanksgiving.
EPHESIANS 5:4

Does your mouth filter ever quit working? You know, the filter that keeps you from saying the things you're thinking? Mine goes out from time to time. That's when I suffer from "foot in mouth" disease. That happened to me not long ago when I asked a lady when her baby was due and she informed me that she wasn't pregnant. Ouch! Okay, from now on, unless a woman is wearing a "Baby on Board" T-shirt, I'm never asking that question again!

Sometimes, we say things without thinking. We don't mean to say them; they just come out before we can retrieve them. Many times, those words can be hurtful. So, think before you speak. Run it through your Holy Spirit filter before uttering a single sylla-ble. Ask the Lord to help you say only uplifting, en-couraging, and wise words.

We need to help our children with this filtering process, too. Kids are notorious for saying inappro-priate things. We need to help them to be respectful of others—especially those who are different. Make sure your filter is turned on all the time, and help your children develop their filter, too.

MOM TO MASTER

Heavenly Father, help me to develop my Holy Spirit
filter, and help me to teach my children to watch their
words, too. Amen.

TAMING THE TONGUE

*"The good man brings good things
out of the good stored up in his heart,
and the evil man brings evil things
out of the evil stored up in his heart.
For out of the overflow of
his heart his mouth speaks."*

LUKE 6:45

Are you an angry person? In other words, do you have a short fuse? If you do, chances are your tongue betrays you all the time. Angry people typically retaliate with words—angry, hurtful words—at a moment's notice. They are quick to attack and slow to repent.

When we get angry, we often say things we don't mean. But, according to Luke 6:45, we actually speak what is in our hearts. That's a scary thought, isn't it? Who knew all of that yucky stuff was stored up in our hearts? I once heard it explained like this: If you squeeze a tube of toothpaste, toothpaste comes out. If you put pressure on a person who is full of ugliness and anger, ugly and angry words come out.

So, here's the key: We need to store up more of God in our hearts so that when the pressure is on, godly words will flow out of us. In other words, when our true colors are revealed, they will be the colors of Christ. Go ahead; fill up on God!

MOM TO MASTER
*Heavenly Father, I want more of You and less of me.
Please take away the angry part of me. Amen.*

AUGUST 25

My people are ruined because
they don't know what's right or true.

HOSEA 4:6 MSG

As moms, it's our awesome responsibility to tell our children about the things of God. That's what this verse communicates to me. If we don't tell them about salvation, they'll never know that Jesus died on the cross to save them from sin. If we don't tell them about His unconditional love, they won't run to Him in times of trouble. If we don't tell them about healing, they'll never know that God can heal their sicknesses. They need to know these important truths so that they won't perish for lack of knowledge.

Teaching our children God's Word and His ways are the two most important things we can give our kids, because if they have that knowledge, they have it all! As moms, we can't always be there for our children. But if we've equipped them with the Word of God, they will be all right without us.

It's like John Cougar Mellencamp says in one of his '80s tunes, "You've got to stand for something, or you're going to fall for anything." If our children stand on the Word of God, they won't be easily fooled or swayed. So, take the time to teach your children the Word. It's the most important investment you'll ever make.

MOM TO MASTER
Heavenly Father, help my children to love
Your Word and carry it with them always. Amen.

TAMING THE TONGUE

"So shall My word be that goes forth from My mouth;
It shall not return to Me void,
But it shall accomplish what I please."
ISAIAH 55:11 NKJV

I once heard Evangelist Kenneth Copeland say, "One word from God can change your life."

I wrote that phrase in my notebook and thought, *Wow, that is so true!*

It was certainly true for Lazarus when Jesus spoke, "Lazarus, come forth," and he got up and walked out of the tomb, grave clothes and all. It was also true for the little daughter of Jairus when Jesus said, "Little girl, arise," and she stood up after being dead.

The more I thought about it, the more I realized that if one word from God can change your life, then I should be speaking His words into my children at every opportunity. Of course, we can't shove it down their throats like we did those strained peas when they were babies, but we can spoon feed them the Word—a little each day.

And if your children are acting resistant to the Word, don't push. Just let your life show His love, and eventually they'll listen to what you have to say. They'll finally come around. God promises that His Word will not return void, so keep speaking it. That Word will finally take root in their hearts and produce some radical results.

TAMING THE TONGUE

MOM TO MASTER
Heavenly Father, help me to find creative ways
to teach Your Word to my children. Amen.

AUGUST 27

> *"Do to others as you would
> have them do to you."*
> LUKE 6:31

TAMING THE TONGUE

Remember those telephone company TV commercials that featured the slogan "Reach out and touch someone"? I always loved those commercials. . .the ones that were real tearjerkers. While that slogan has come and gone, its meaning is still very relevant. We can reach out and touch someone with our words every single day.

My father, who has suffered several strokes, can't get out and minister like he used to do, so he shares the love of Jesus to telemarketers when they call his home. They call hoping to sell him something, and he ends up telling them about the free gift of eternal life. That's what I call really reaching out and touching someone!

Others in my church call the shut-ins and those in the area hospitals and nursing homes weekly—just to let them know that someone cares. Still others take time to call all of the first-time visitors to the church, giving them a personal welcome. Through their words, they are reaching out with the love of Jesus. Maybe you've been feeling like you'd like to serve the Lord in some capacity but you didn't feel qualified in any area. Well, you can use the telephone, right? Ask God if this might be a way that He can use you, and begin reaching out today!

MOM TO MASTER
*Lord, help me to use my words to reach out
to others with Your love. Amen.*

"I know, my God,
that you test the heart
and are pleased with integrity."
1 CHRONICLES 29:17

My dad often talks about a time when a handshake and a man's word were the only things needed to seal a deal. There was no need for contracts. Everybody operated on trust and integrity. Can you imagine if the world were still like that today? Giving someone your word should be enough, but integrity—even among Christians—is hard to come by these days. After you've been burned a few times, it's easy to become jaded and start questioning everyone's integrity.

As Christians, and as mothers, we should walk in integrity. Of course, we know it's wrong to lie. That's a given. But there are other ways that we compromise our integrity. For instance, if you tell friends that you'll meet them at 10 A.M. and you don't show up until 10:20, that's a lack of integrity. The Lord convicted me of this just the other day because as anyone who knows me will testify, I am notoriously late.

It's our goal to set good examples for our children, right? So, let's determine today to be people of integrity in every area of our lives. Integrity is important to God, and it should be important to us.

MOM TO MASTER
Lord, mold me into a person of integrity, and help me to teach my children to walk in integrity, too. Amen.

He replied, "Because you have so little faith.
I tell you the truth,
if you have faith as small as a mustard seed,
you can say to this mountain,
'Move from here to there' and it will move.
Nothing will be impossible for you."

MATTHEW 17:20

We don't have many mountains in Texas, but I recently visited Colorado and was mesmerized by the magnificence of the Rockies. As I looked out over the landscape, this Scripture came to mind. I love this verse. I love knowing that if I have faith—and not even a lot of it—nothing is impossible. Isn't that good news?

But I want you to notice something else about this verse. It says that we have to *say* to the mountain, "Move." It doesn't say that we have to think it or write it or wonder about it. Those little utterances that roll off of our tongues make all of the difference.

So, don't just wish your life away—put some faith behind your words! If you want your kids to do better in school, begin praying that they have the mind of Christ. Speak it over them in the mornings. Teach them to make positive confessions over themselves. You've heard of the power of positive thinking, right? Well, the real power is in faith-filled words. Go ahead, fill the air with faith-filled words and watch God go to work.

TAMING THE TONGUE

MOM TO MASTER
Lord, please fill my mouth with faith-filled words.
Amen.

*"Now go; I will help you speak
and will teach you what to say."*
EXODUS 4:12

I love how God dealt with Moses. He was so kind and reassuring. Moses was full of self-doubt and unbelief. God told Moses what to say to Pharaoh, and Moses responded, "But what if he doesn't believe me?"

Later, after God gave Moses some additional instructions, Moses said, "But Lord, You know I am slow of speech. I can't do this."

But God said, "Moses, who made your mouth? Isn't it Me, Moses?" Still, God reassured Moses and let Aaron help him.

Maybe you feel overwhelmed today. Maybe you feel like you're losing the battle where your tongue is concerned. Maybe you are unsure of yourself as a mom. Maybe you are a little like Moses—full of self-doubt and unbelief. You don't have to stay that way! Just as God reminded Moses, I am reminding you. God made your mouth. God made your mind. God made you exactly the way you are. He knew you in your mother's womb. He knew that you'd someday be a mother. In fact, He knows the amount of hairs on your head. He has ordered your steps.

So, don't dwell in doubt—walk in faith. In the same way that God did mighty works through Moses, He can do the same through you.

MOM TO MASTER
Lord, I trust You. Teach me to trust You more. Amen.

TAMING THE TONGUE

He is our father in the sight of God,
in whom he believed—
the God who gives life to the dead and
calls things that are not as though they were.

ROMANS 4:17

"That's a good boy, Miller," Allyson said, petting our new dachshund puppy's head. "You are such a good boy."

At the time, Miller wasn't such a good boy. In fact, he was messing up my carpets on a daily basis. I wasn't sure he would ever be housebroken. I loved him, but I didn't like what he was doing to my house. Still, Allyson called Miller "a good boy." After several months of calling Miller "a good boy," he became one! Miller is the best dog we've ever had. He is loyal. He is smart. He is sweet. And, he is housebroken! I firmly believe that Allyson had much to do with Miller's transformation. She believed in him, called him good, and he became good.

This principle will work every time. Try it! Call things that are not as though they were—just like Romans 4:17 says. You know, God even changed Abram's name to Abraham, because Abraham means "the father of many nations" (Genesis 17). Every time someone said, "Hey, Abraham," that person was saying, "Hey, father of many nations." Call your children good names. Speak good things over them. Fill your home with positive words. It will make a difference.

MOM TO MASTER

Lord, help me to speak good things over my kids. Amen.

TAMING THE TONGUE

*The fear of the LORD is
the beginning of knowledge,
but fools despise wisdom and discipline.*
PROVERBS 1:7

Nobody likes to hear the word *no*—especially our children! We have a rule at our house that simply states, "No playtime until your homework is finished." Well. . .that's not always a popular rule. Maybe you have the same rule. If you do, I'll bet you occasionally get the same reaction I do—"Mom! Please! I don't have that much homework. I can finish it later. Let us ride our bikes now."

Yes, I have made exceptions to the rule for special outings and parties, but the rule stands most of the time. We have to think "future minded" for our kids because they live in "the now." I know that if they ride their bikes after school, they'll come in tired and grouchy and have no energy left to do their homework. And if they don't complete their homework, they'll make bad grades. And if they make bad grades, they'll have to be grounded. It's a whole chain reaction of negative circumstances, which is why we came up with the "homework first rule" in the first place.

So, don't be afraid to stand your ground. Don't cave in to the whining and begging. Your rules are for your children's own good—even if they don't see it that way.

MOM TO MASTER
Lord, give me the wisdom to make good rules and the authority to implement them and stick by them. Amen.

SEPTEMBER 2

Know then in your heart that
as a man disciplines his son,
so the LORD your God disciplines you.
DEUTERONOMY 8:5

When Allyson was in preschool, she adored the Disney movie *Mulan*. Her favorite scene featured Mulan cutting off her long ponytail so she could fool everyone into thinking she was a boy. Ally thought that might be fun, too, so she cut off her long, blond ponytail and hid her hair throughout our home. When I discovered the beautiful blond ponytail in my kitchen trashcan, I immediately confronted Allyson with the evidence. Her response? "Miller did it." Now, I'm not saying our long-haired dachshund isn't a smart doggie, but I was pretty sure he hadn't learned to use the scissors!

Ally was playing the blame game. Rather than just repent and move on, she decided it would be much easier to blame poor old Miller. As I dealt with Ally, the Lord dealt with me, pointing out the times that I had blamed other people and bad circumstances for my behavior.

I find that many times as I discipline my children, the Lord takes those opportunities to teach and discipline me, too. As it turns out, I struggle with many of the same challenges that my children do—imagine that? It pricks a bit when the Lord disciplines us, but we'll never mature if He doesn't correct. So, embrace correction.

MOM TO MASTER
Lord, help me to be quick to repent when You correct.
Amen.

My child, don't ignore it when
the LORD disciplines you,
and don't be discouraged when he corrects you.

PROVERBS 3:11 NLT

"Abby, you did number twelve wrong," I said, pointing to her homework.

"Did not!" she retaliated. "That's the way the teacher said to do it!"

"But it's wrong!" I explained.

"Is not," she argued.

Does this episode ever play out in your house?

Abby, my ten-year-old, tends to become very defensive and discouraged when she is corrected. Unfortunately, I think she's learned that from observing me. Let's face it—nobody enjoys correction. Even when correction comes wrapped in pretty words and encouraging insights, it still stings.

Maybe you also have difficulty receiving correction. It isn't much fun, but it's necessary if we ever want to mature and become more Christlike. This Scripture encourages me, and I hope it will encourage you, too. See, the Lord doesn't want us to be discouraged by His correction. He corrects us because He loves us. He knows all of our faults, and He wants us to get past them and grow up in Him. Don't argue with God or talk back to Him when He gently corrects you. Accept His criticism graciously and make the necessary adjustments. Just think, you're one step closer to being like Him!

MOM TO MASTER

Lord, help me to accept God's correction with
a good attitude. Amen.

DARING TO DISCIPLINE

SEPTEMBER 4

A refusal to correct is a refusal to love;
love your children by disciplining them.

PROVERBS 13:24 MSG

Have you ever spent any time with children who have never been disciplined? You know the kind—the ones who run all over a restaurant, scream when they don't get their way, and show disrespect to everyone. We spent some time with one of these children not long ago. This little girl was unbelievable! She broke toys. She intentionally hurt animals. She backtalked to her parents. And she disobeyed every direction. I desperately wanted to discipline her, but it wasn't my place. It was her parents' place. Unfortunately, the parents didn't believe in discipline. They apparently read some book about allowing a child to develop his or her own boundaries.

The only parenting book that's truly needed is God's Word. Proverbs 13:24 tells us that we show love by disciplining our children. In fact, that verse clearly states that it is actually a refusal to love if we don't correct our children. So, while Junior may not feel loved at the exact moment he is being punished, he is experiencing love.

Don't be fooled by the world's way of doing things. God's way is always the better choice. He knows a thing or two about parenting. After all, He is a parent. So, ask Him for wisdom and guidance when it comes to disciplining your children. He has all the answers.

MOM TO MASTER
Lord, teach me to be a better parent. Amen.

Get the truth and don't ever sell it;
also get wisdom, discipline,
and discernment.

PROVERBS 23:23 NLT

I grew up with a friend who definitely qualified as "Miss Perfect." I was always getting her into trouble. Let's just say that in the "Lucy and Ethel" scenario, I was always Lucy, dragging her into situations she would never have ventured into alone.

Much to my annoyance, my friend would tell on herself if she had misbehaved. Then, her mom would call my mom, and I'd be busted, too. She just couldn't stand to be dishonest, so she'd tell her mom and seek discipline. Sometimes, she would even suggest an appropriate punishment. It was amazing, really. Never once have my children come to me just begging to be punished. I might drop over from shock if that ever did happen! God probably feels the same way about us.

How often do you pray, "Lord, I am seeking your discipline today. Bring it on." I can honestly say that I've never prayed those words. I bet you haven't, either. However, it might be a good idea to pray that prayer once in awhile. If we'll be quick to repent and seek God's discipline, we can move on with Him. We won't have to go around that same mountain a hundred times. We'll learn the lesson and press on toward our dreams and victories. So, go ahead—ask God to bring it on!

MOM TO MASTER
Lord, help me to seek Your discipline more often. Amen.

DARING TO DISCIPLINE

SEPTEMBER 6

For these commands are a lamp,
this teaching is a light,
and the corrections of discipline
are the way to life.

PROVERBS 6:23

I guess I've never really thought of the corrections of discipline as a way of life, although looking back, I'd have to say I agree. I was sure that Abby would grow up thinking her name was "No, no" as many times as I said it to her during "the terrible twos." She was into everything! I had to tell her "No, no" to teach her safe from unsafe, right from wrong, and good from bad. I bet you had to do the same thing with your children.

Guess what? As our spiritual Father, God has to do the same with us. After all, we are His children. And I don't know about you, but my "terrible twos" went on a little more than two years in my spiritual development! There are some days when I revert to those terrible twos and throw a temper tantrum that's shameful. (C'mon, you do, too. Admit it!) That's when our heavenly Father steps in and disciplines us as only He can.

The corrections of discipline should be a way of life for us—not just on the giving side but also on the receiving end. Through God's disciplining, we can become the best version of ourselves.

MOM TO MASTER
Lord, thank You for Your discipline. Amen.

The rod of correction imparts wisdom,
but a child left to himself disgraces his mother.
PROVERBS 29:15

No matter where you stand on the spanking issue, this verse holds good meaning. You see, it's not so much about the spanking, it's about the wisdom that we impart when we discipline our children.

There are lots of differing opinions about how to discipline our children. Some experts say we should spank them with our hands. Others say we should spank, but only with a paddle. Still others say we should never spank, only punish by other means. It seems there is a new theory every year. So, what is the answer?

God is the only true answer. You must seek His face and ask His direction. He will teach you how to discipline your kids. He loves them even more than you do. He won't lead you astray. Just trust Him. Don't get caught up asking lots of people how you should discipline your kids. If you ask a hundred people, you'll get a hundred different perspectives. They don't know any more than you do. Go to the Source. He will impart wisdom to you so that you can impart wisdom to your children. You see, discipline and wisdom go hand in hand.

MOM TO MASTER
Lord, teach me the best way to discipline my children.
Amen.

A fool spurns his father's discipline,
but whoever heeds correction shows prudence.

PROVERBS 15:5

Did you know that parenting isn't a popularity contest? If it were, I would've lost a long time ago. How about you? No, as moms, we have to make some decisions that aren't very popular at times. We have to tell our children they can't go see some of the popular movies, even though all of their friends are going. We have to forbid them from attending certain parties, even though they don't understand why. It's all a part of what we do as moms.

It's the heartbreaking part of our job. I don't like having to say no to my girls. I want them to have fun. I want them to experience life. I want them to enjoy as much as possible. But, I also want to protect them and nurture them and teach them in the ways of the Lord. And sometimes those wants contradict one another.

Yes, I want my kids to think I'm cool. Yes, I want them to think of me as a friend. But more than anything else, I want to raise my girls to love God and walk in His ways. If that means making some unpopular decisions, then that's okay by me. God still thinks we're special. We'll always be popular to God.

MOM TO MASTER
Lord, help me to stand my ground
even when it's not the popular thing to do. Amen.

DARING TO DISCIPLINE

*But the lovingkindness of the LORD is
from everlasting to everlasting.*

PSALM 103:17 NASB

Did you grow up in a strict household? Was your father harsh to you? Did you obey the rules of the house
out of fear? Many people grow up in less than Brady-
Bunch-like households. Then, when they become parents, they sometimes carry on those negative parenting
skills. If you fit this mold, don't despair. God can heal
your hurts and help you parent with compassion and
mercy. See, even though you might not have had a
good role model growing up, God is the only role
model you need. He's here for you right now.

I'm so thankful that He is gentle, forgiving, and
merciful when He disciplines. He isn't harsh and scary.
He makes His children want to run to Him, not away
from Him. No matter how badly we mess up, He forgives and forgets.

So, if you are struggling with being too harsh with
your children, ask God to help you today. He will pour
His unconditional love into you so that you can pour
out that love on your children. You can break the cycle
of cold, harsh parenting. You can become the kind of
mother that God intended for you to be.

DARING TO DISCIPLINE

MOM TO MASTER

*Lord, fill me with Your love so that I can share
Your love with my children. Help me to be
more compassionate and caring. Amen.*

SEPTEMBER 10

> *For the LORD is good and his love endures forever;*
> *his faithfulness continues through all generations.*
>
> PSALM 100:5

God is so faithful. Can I get an "amen"? As a reporter for a daily newspaper, I was privileged to interview many wonderful people. Some of those stories stick with me today. I'll never forget interviewing a woman who was told she could never have children. She had a medical condition that prevented her from carrying a baby to term. Heartbroken, she cried out to God. She beseeched God for a miracle. This precious woman of God became pregnant and through an absolute miracle of God was able to give birth to a healthy baby girl. That little girl is in elementary school now—a living, breathing testimony to God's faithfulness.

God was faithful to her. No one will ever be able to convince her otherwise. She has experienced His faithfulness firsthand. Have you? Has God been there for you when no one else was around? Has He helped you make it through a difficult situation? Maybe you're in a tough place now and need His touch. Just reach out—He's right there.

No matter what your situation—He has the way out. If you're struggling with a disobedient child, He can help. If your marriage is falling apart, He can put it back together. If your children are in rebellion, God understands. He is able. He is willing. And He is faithful.

MOM TO MASTER
Lord, thank You for being faithful. Amen.

Do not boast about tomorrow,
for you do not know what
a day may bring forth.
PROVERBS 27:1

September 11 will forever mean something different since the tragedy that struck America in 2001. If 9-11 taught us anything as a country, it taught us to cherish our loved ones. As many found out that day, there's no promise of tomorrow. I've watched several news shows in which the family members of victims were interviewed, and almost every person said, "If only I'd had the chance to say good-bye. If only I could say 'I love you' just one more time. . ." Regrets lead down the road of guilt and condemnation. So, don't go there.

Instead, take time today to pray for the families who lost loved ones on that tragic day. Take time to pray for our nation and its leaders. And, take time to tell your family and friends just how much you love and appreciate them. Let God's love pour out of you and spill onto your children. Talk to your kids about the significance of 9-11-2001, and ask them to join with you in prayer. You might even make a donation to the American Red Cross or bake cookies for your local fire department. Whatever you do, make the most of every moment because we're not promised tomorrow.

MOM TO MASTER
Lord, help me not to take any day for granted.
I love You. Amen.

SEPTEMBER 12

If you are guided by the Spirit,
you won't obey your selfish desires.

GALATIANS 5:16 CEV

Did you know that we make approximately twenty-five hundred choices every single day of our lives? (No wonder I'm so exhausted at the end of the day!) So, if you aren't happy with your current life, you're probably making lousy decisions. The only way to make good, solid decisions is to turn off your reasoning mechanism and allow the Holy Spirit to guide you. Discernment and reasoning can't operate at the same time. Our minds reason, but our spirits discern. I don't know about you, but I don't trust my mind. I'd much rather rely on the leading of the Holy Spirit to make decisions—especially when it comes to disciplining my children.

With so many conflicting opinions in the media, I get easily confused. I don't want to be a tyrant, but I don't want to be a wimp, either. I want to raise good, godly kids, but I don't want to shove the Word down their throats.

There are no easy answers. What works for one parent/child relationship might not work for another. So, don't reason and worry your life away. Instead, ask for God's leading to help you make the best possible decisions. He will help you in the area of disciplining your kids. He has all of the answers.

MOM TO MASTER
Lord, I am asking for Your leading today.
Help me to do things Your way. Amen.

DARING TO DISCIPLINE

Before I formed you in the womb I knew
[and] approved of you
[as My chosen instrument].

JEREMIAH 1:5 AMP

Okay, I blew it again this week. In my efforts to be a good mother, teaching responsibility and other good morals to my girls, I went overboard. I actually went into the whole "Well, when I was your age. . ." Of course, that's an automatic disconnect for kids. As soon as you utter those words, their eyes glaze over.

Do you ever hear yourself saying something and think, "I've become my mother!" It's so funny, isn't it? One minute, you're hip and cool, and the next parental moment, you're giving your rendition of, "When I was a child, we had to walk through the snow, uphill both ways, barefoot to school. . . ."

On those days, when I feel like I'm losing this parental battle, it's nice to know that God has already approved me. Jeremiah 1:5 tells us that He knew us even before we were born and had already approved us. So, no matter how badly we mess up, God still loves us and sees us as great parents. He always has His faith eyes in focus. Ask Him to help you get your faith eyes in focus, too. See yourself as God sees you—approved!

MOM TO MASTER
Lord, thank You for approving me and
calling me to motherhood. I love You. Amen.

SEPTEMBER 14

Because the LORD disciplines those he loves,
as a father the son he delights in.

PROVERBS 3:12

My father rarely spanked me when I was a little girl. I deserved spankings much more frequently than I actually received them, but Dad was merciful. One time I lied to my father and he found out, and that was it! I knew I was going to get it. Mother sent me to my room to await Dad's visitation. When he came home from work, he said just one thing before he spanked me: "Honey, I'm doing this because I love you." Then, I got it—ouch!

Let me just share, I wasn't feeling the love at that exact moment. But, it really was true. Dad disciplined me because he wanted me to learn respect and obedience—because he loved me. We do the same for our kids, don't we? We correct and punish them because we love them. We know that if we don't teach them and discipline them, it will be detrimental to them in the long run.

God does the same thing for us. That's what this verse in Proverbs says to me—the Lord disciplines us because He loves us. He knows our potential, and if we'll let Him, He will mold us and make us into the moms He created us to be.

MOM TO MASTER
Lord, thank You for your discipline. I love You. Amen.

DARING TO DISCIPLINE

Come, children, listen closely;
I'll give you a lesson in GOD worship.
PSALM 34:11 MSG

If you could only teach your children ten things before you died, what would you share? Would you teach them to stand up for who they are in Christ Jesus? Would you teach them self-defense? Would you teach them good manners? Would you teach them to give to others? Would you teach them to treat others with respect? Would you teach them how to be a friend?

It's a tough call, isn't it? There are so many things we want to impart to our kids. We want to save them from making all of the stupid mistakes that we made. While we can't protect them from every mistake, we can put them on the road to success and happiness.

We can make the most of every opportunity to teach them about the nature of God—God the Healer, God the Provider, God the Savior, God the Deliverer, God the Great I Am! There are chances every day to share little lessons with our children. Ask the Lord to help you identify those opportunities so that you can take advantage of each one.

MOM TO MASTER
Lord, help me to share Your love with my children
each day. And, Lord, help me to take advantage of
every opportunity to teach my kids about You. Amen.

SEPTEMBER 16

> *Teach them to your children. Talk about them*
> *wherever you are, sitting at home or walking*
> *in the street; talk about them from the time you get*
> *up in the morning until you fall into bed at night.*
>
> DEUTERONOMY 11:19 MSG

Not long ago we were in a store where I overheard a conversation that really taught me something about parenting. A very attractive, professional-looking woman and her two preteen daughters were shopping together when they saw another girl they knew. She appeared to be in her teens. They visited briefly, and then the mother said to the teenager, "I just loved the muffins that you served the other night at the party. Could I get that recipe from you?"

This flippant teen said, "No, I don't share that recipe. It's a family secret. I may try to sell them someday."

After the teen left, the mother leaned in close to her daughters and whispered, "Girls, that is a good example of being selfish. Her attitude was wrong, and God probably won't bless her muffin endeavors because of her selfish attitude."

This mom saw an opportunity to teach a lesson and embraced it. See, as moms, we need to seize the moment and teach our children lessons as opportunities arise. God will provide the perfect situations, but we have to be "tuned in" to Him in order to take advantage of these precious opportunities. Tune in today!

MOM TO MASTER

Lord, help me to teach my children Your ways. Amen.

He will die for lack of discipline,
led astray by his own great folly.
PROVERBS 5:23

Obviously, this verse in Proverbs lets us know that discipline is an important part of our job as parents. No, it's not fun. No, it's not popular. But, it is very necessary. In fact, it's so necessary that if we don't correct our children and bring them up in the way of the Lord, they are sure to suffer.

None of us would intentionally hurt our kids. We love them. But sometimes we love them too much, meaning we don't discipline them for their wrong behavior. We let them get away with wrongdoing simply because we don't want to hurt their feelings or make a scene in front of their friends. But if we don't teach them right from wrong, they won't know how to make godly decisions. They'll make wrong choices, which will lead to heartache, ruin, and ultimately, destruction.

Our role is crucial. Ask the Lord to help you be firm yet loving as you discipline your kids. Ask Him for wisdom. You can do it. God has equipped you with everything you need to be a good parent.

MOM TO MASTER
Lord, I need Your divine intervention—help me
to discipline my children so that they will follow
You all the days of their lives. Amen.

DARING TO DISCIPLINE

> *"Declare what is to be."*
> ISAIAH 45:21

If you are going to live a victorious life, you must speak positive words of faith and say what God says about your situation. So, if your children are walking in rebellion today, you should speak what the Word says about your kids. Say, "As for me and my house, we will serve the Lord." If your children are struggling with their love walk and acting ugly all the time, you should declare, "Love is patient. Love is kind. My children will walk in God's love. My children will be patient and kind."

If you are unsure of your children's salvation, declare Psalm 103:17: "The LORD's love is with those who fear him, and his righteousness with their children's children."

Find Scriptures to stand on—Scriptures that fit your situation. Then, speak them out! Encourage yourself in the Lord. Pray according to His Word. Those are the kind of prayers that get results. Don't allow yourself to talk negatively about your children. Don't talk the problem—talk the solution. Trust the Lord to do what He says in His Word. His Word never returns void. It will accomplish its purpose. Get ready for victory—it's on its way!

MOM TO MASTER

Lord, lead me to the Scriptures in Your Word that will help me stand in faith for the salvation of my children. Help me to stand strong. I love You. Amen.

DARING TO DISCIPLINE

So do not throw away your confidence;
it will be richly rewarded.

HEBREWS 10:35

Are you focusing on the future, or are you having trouble seeing past the endless piles of dirty laundry that are in front of you right now? When today has so many worries, responsibilities, and obligations, it's difficult to be future minded. But we need to make a conscious effort. We need to let God stir up our faith. We need to start believing God for big things. We need to realize that even if the circumstances aren't so great today, God is bringing about a miracle in our future.

You see, no matter what you're dealing with today, God has a plan that will work things out better than you could ever imagine—if you'll just get your faith eyes in focus and become future minded. Ask God to help you change your focus.

The enemy doesn't want you to stand in faith for the fulfillment of your destiny. He doesn't want to see your children walking with God. He wants you to worry about all of the problems of today and forget about your future. Don't fall for the devil's plan. Focus on the future. See your children well and serving God. See your family happy and whole. See your dirty laundry washed, folded, and put away. Get a vision of victory today!

MOM TO MASTER
Lord, help me get my faith eyes in focus and
looking toward the future. Amen.

> *"But these things I plan won't happen right away.*
> *Slowly, steadily, surely, the time approaches*
> *when the vision will be fulfilled.*
> *If it seems slow, wait patiently,*
> *for it will surely take place.*
> *It will not be delayed."*
>
> HABAKKUK 2:3 NLT

Have you ever heard the phrase, "Rest and wait"? It's much easier said than done—especially when that waiting has to do with our children. Whether you're waiting for your kids to run back to God or simply waiting for them to be potty trained—resting and waiting is a good thing. Resting and waiting are meant to go hand in hand.

See, resting in God means trusting and not worrying. It means having so much of God on the inside of you that you can't do anything but rest. It's a place where you have absolutely no doubt that God is going to come through for you. It's a place where you no longer see the mountain, you only see a molehill. It's a place where all of us should dwell on a daily basis.

As moms, we need to rest and wait more than anyone else. If we're frazzled, we'll raise frazzled children. If we're impatient and worried, we'll raise impatient, worried children. So, here's your assignment—rest and wait! You'll have to discipline your flesh to do it, but God will help you.

DARING TO DISCIPLINE

MOM TO MASTER

Lord, help me to learn to rest and wait on You. Amen.

Therefore put on the full armor of God,
so that when the day of evil comes,
you may be able to stand your ground,
and after you have done everything, to stand.
EPHESIANS 6:13

We all face challenges in life. Some days we face more challenges than others. Let's face it, being a parent is a tough job. When you have children, there's no manual that comes with the job. Sure, there are lots of parenting books and magazines, but they all say conflicting things, giving opposing advice.

There's only one manual that covers it all. From disciplining your children to showing them unconditional love, the Word of God has got you covered. Need an answer for a specific situation? Don't rely on secondhand information. Go to the Source. Read the Word and let it come alive to you.

Stand strong as you face challenges. Don't bow down to them. Remain faithful. Fight that good fight of faith. Keep feeding on the Word and standing firm. If you'll stay in faith, God will promote you. He loves to bless His children. Make yourself a good candidate for His supernatural blessing flow. Keep standing. I don't care how bad it might look right now, stand strong. Go to the Manual. Your answers and your promotion are on the way. Hallelujah!

DARING TO DISCIPLINE

MOM TO MASTER
Father, help me to stand strong in the face of difficulty.
I love You. Amen.

SEPTEMBER 22

For these commands are a lamp,
this teaching is a light, and the corrections
of discipline are the way to life.

PROVERBS 6:23

Have you seen the recent infomercial that features the little stick-on lights? They are pretty cool. You simply take these round, flat lights and stick them wherever you need light. For instance, you can place them in your closet or post them down your driveway. I thought, *How neat! You can create a lighted pathway where there wasn't one before!*

Well, guess what? The Word of God is a lamp unto our feet and a light unto our paths, and you don't have to stick it anywhere! All you have to do is read it, and let God's promises and corrections fill you up.

Just think if we had an infomercial for the Word of God. Can you imagine? We could make claims like, "Guaranteed to produce results! Never gets old. Full of the wisdom of the ages! Works every time!" and they'd all be true! God's Word provides correction, keeping us on the straight and narrow path. It provides healing, prosperity, joy, and wisdom through its many promises. It is all we need to accomplish anything in this life. No matter what you need today, go to the Word. Let the Word of God come alive for you today.

MOM TO MASTER
Father, please light up my path today. Amen.

DARING TO DISCIPLINE

Have mercy on me, O God,
according to your unfailing love;
according to your great compassion
blot out my transgressions.

PSALM 51:1

Do your kids ever use "the puppy dog eyes" on you? Aren't those killers? As soon as they bring them out, my heart starts to melt. At that moment, no matter what they've done wrong, I am very forgiving. Of course, my children have learned this trick, so they use it often. Talk about manipulation! Ugh!

But you know, showing mercy to our children is a good thing. I don't mean that we should let them get away with horrible behavior, but we need to discipline in love and emulate our heavenly Father. Aren't you glad that we serve a merciful God? He is never harsh to us when we repent. He doesn't say, "I'm sorry. You've just made one too many mistakes. I'm not going to forgive you this time." Instead, He lovingly whispers, "That's okay. I love you, My child."

I want to be as tender and forgiving with my children as the Father is with me. If we aren't tender with our kids, they won't run to us when they make mistakes, they'll run away from us. We need to discipline them and teach them the ways of God, but we need to do so with love and mercy.

MOM TO MASTER

Father, help me to show mercy to my children
as You show mercy to me. Amen.

DARING TO DISCIPLINE

It's the child he loves that he disciplines.

HEBREWS 12:6 MSG

"You don't love me!"

Have you ever heard that response after disciplining your children? It's a difficult one to swallow. And it's a very inaccurate response. In fact, by disciplining our children, we're actually showing our love to them. Of course, no child is going to see it that way—especially in the heat of the moment. But, it never hurts to explain our reasons for disciplining our children, even if it seems they aren't listening.

Before you spank your child or ground him or her from attending a party, take a deep breath, count to ten, and explain what the Word says about the situation. This is working at our house. It's amazing! While Abby and Allyson have no problem arguing with me, they won't argue with the Word of God. They can't. They know God's Word is always right. So, if you can find a Scripture that pertains to the situation at hand, you have all the ammunition you need to lovingly enforce discipline. It takes the pressure off of us and puts it on the Word, and God's Word can handle the pressure. Many times when I tell the girls what God's Word says about their behavior or the choices they've made, it opens up a wonderful conversation. True, the dialogue typically begins with "You don't love me," but it rarely ends that way. Go ahead! Try it.

DARING TO DISCIPLINE

MOM TO MASTER

Father, help me use Your Word to combat strife in my house. Amen.

*Your obedience will give you a long life
on the soil that GOD promised to give
your ancestors and their children,
a land flowing with milk and honey.*

DEUTERONOMY 11:9 MSG

Have you ever really thought about the definition of obedience? Not long ago, I heard a preacher say that obedience is doing what you're supposed to do the first time you're asked. I love that definition! Immediately, I thought of how often I repeat myself in hopes that my girls will actually pick up their rooms. I begin with a cheerful, "Before you can go outside and ride your bikes, I want you to clean your rooms." An hour later, the girls are plopped in front of the TV, mesmerized by Cartoon Network. So, I say sternly, "I want you to turn off the TV and clean up your rooms right now." Thirty minutes later, as I walk past their rooms and see that they haven't been touched, I lose it and scream, "I want you to get in your rooms and stay in there until they are cleaned up! Do you understand me?"

We shouldn't have to ask our children numerous times in order to get their attention. We shouldn't have to get ugly with them in order to get obedience. Let's ask God to help us teach our children the true meaning of obedience today.

MOM TO MASTER

*Father, help me teach my children the true
meaning of obedience, and help me to immediately
obey You, too. Amen.*

SEPTEMBER 26

GOD is fair and just;
He corrects the misdirected,
Sends them in the right direction.

PSALM 25:8 MSG

Do you ever get lost? I am the queen of getting lost. My friends refer to me as "directionally challenged." In my defense, Texas is difficult for the directionally challenged because you can never come back the same way you went. Reversing directions doesn't work in the Dallas/Fort Worth Metroplex. It's the most aggravating thing! So, I spend most of my days aimlessly driving around, hoping to find a familiar street or shopping mall. Finally, when I've driven so much that I'm almost out of gas, I'll swallow my pride and call Jeff on my cell phone to ask for directions. With just a few corrections to my course, I'm once again headed in the right direction—toward home.

In the spiritual realm, God does the same thing with His children. He corrects our course, puts us back on the right road, and points us toward our heavenly home. Without His gentle correction, we might be headed in the wrong direction our entire lives. That's why the Word says that God corrects those He loves. If He didn't love us, He'd just let us wander around aimlessly. Taking correction is never an easy thing, but it's certainly a necessary one. So, thank the Lord today for His divine correction and direction.

MOM TO MASTER
Thank You, Lord, for Your correction. Amen.

DARING TO DISCIPLINE

Don't be afraid to correct your young ones;
a spanking won't kill them.

PROVERBS 23:13 MSG

My father only spanked me three times in my entire life. I probably had it coming a lot more than that, but he was a merciful father. (Besides, Mom made up the difference!) I'll never forget when Dad spanked me that last time. He came into my room where I was waiting for him, and he said, "This is going to hurt me much more than it will hurt you." A few minutes later, my stinging backside and I weren't too sure about the validity of his previous statement.

In all honesty, it pained my father to spank me. He loved me, and he didn't want to cause me any hurt. However, he knew that if he didn't discipline me, I'd grow up to be a bratty kid. So, he loved me enough to spank me. I feel the same way about my children. I wish I never had to discipline them. I wish they were perfect all the time. But since that's not the case, I have to take a disciplinarian stance from time to time. It's part of our job as mothers. We should never be afraid to discipline our children. We should be fearful if we don't.

MOM TO MASTER

Lord, help me not to be afraid of disciplining
my children. Amen.

DARING TO DISCIPLINE

> *"Not all people who sound religious*
> *are really godly. They may refer to me as*
> *'Lord,' but they still won't enter*
> *the Kingdom of Heaven. The decisive issue is*
> *whether they obey my Father in heaven."*
> MATTHEW 7:21 NLT

I was eavesdropping on my daughters and their friends not long ago, and I overheard the funniest conversation. One of the little girls said, "I obey my parents most of the time, but sometimes I just don't want to. I decide if the punishment is worth it, and then I go from there."

Wow! That was an eye opener for me. Obviously, obedience wasn't high on her priority list. Of course, I can understand that kind of thinking. I've acted the same way when it comes to serving God. You know—trying to get away with as much as possible, riding the fence. . . But this Scripture in Matthew is pretty clear—obeying the Father should be high on our priority list. And, it should be high on our children's priority list, too.

Obeying our heavenly Father shouldn't be a difficult thing. If we truly love God, we should want to obey Him. If you're having trouble obeying God, spend some quality time with Him. Make Him your first love, and obedience will soon follow.

MOM TO MASTER
Lord, help me to put You first and obey
Your commandments with a right attitude. Amen.

DARING TO DISCIPLINE

"You will be able to tell wonderful stories to your children and grandchildren about the marvelous things I am doing among the Egyptians to prove that I am the LORD."

EXODUS 10:2 NLT

Part of training up our children is sharing the miracles of God with them. Of course, we know to teach them the many mighty works that God performed in the Bible. We should tell them of God's miraculous deliverance of His people out of Pharaoh's hand. We should share the story of David and Goliath. We should tell them about Jonah and the whale. But, we should also tell them about the many mighty works that God has done personally in our families.

When I told Allyson how God had saved her life when she was only a few weeks old inside my tummy, her face lit up. She wanted to hear every detail. When I shared with Abby how God had protected us from a terrible car accident when she was only three, she hung on every word. Hearing those stories builds our children's faith, and it builds ours, too.

Spend time playing "Remember when God worked that miracle in our lives?". You'll soon discover that your children will love that game more than any other. Go ahead, have fun reminiscing. Recall the mighty acts of God and build your faith in the process. It's a game where everybody wins!

DARING TO DISCIPLINE

MOM TO MASTER

Lord, help me to tell my children of Your marvelous works. Amen.

These older women must train
the younger women to love
their husbands and their children.

TITUS 2:4 NLT

It was my first night home from the hospital. Baby Abby was sleeping peacefully in my arms. She was so precious. But as I looked down into her little face, I panicked. I thought to myself, *I have no idea how to raise this little girl. I have a hard enough time just taking care of Jeff and myself and our dog!* I remember praying for God to send me help. That prayer was answered by way of my mother. She was (and still is) a constant source of encouragement, strength, wisdom, and laughter.

I've learned so much from my mother. Not only has she taught me about being a mom, but she's taught me how to be a better wife. When my father suffered three strokes over a year's time, I watched in amazement as my mother took care of Daddy. She was so strong and in control, yet so tender toward him. I thought, *Now that's the kind of wife I want to be.*

There is much to be learned from our elders, isn't there? That's why I love Titus 2:4 so much. Maybe your mom isn't a person you turn to for advice—and that's okay. God will send other wise women to be part of your life. Ask Him to do that for you today.

MOM TO MASTER
Thank You, Lord, for placing wonderfully
wise women in my life. Amen.

DARING TO DISCIPLINE

"Give, and it will be given to you:
good measure, pressed down,
shaken together, and running over."
LUKE 6:38 NKJV

Did you know that God wants you to be happy? He desires for you to live life to its fullest. It doesn't matter that you might be elbow deep in diapers and carpools right now—you can still enjoy life!

One of the main ways you can guarantee joy in your life is by living to give. You see, true happiness comes when we give of ourselves to others—our spouses, our children, our extended family, our church, our community, and our friends. As moms, we're sort of trained to be givers. We give up our careers, many times, to become full-time moms. We give up a full night's sleep to feed our babies. We give up sports cars for minivans and SUVs to accommodate our families. In fact, we'd give our lives for our children.

But sometimes our attitudes are less than joyful in all of our giving, right? Well, rejoice today. God promises to multiply back to you everything that you give. When you step out in faith, you open a door for God to move on your behalf. It's the simple principle of sowing and reaping. And as mothers, we are super sowers. So, get ready for a super huge harvest!

MOM TO MASTER
Lord, help me to live to give with the right attitude.
I love You. Amen.

LIVING TO GIVE

OCTOBER 2

> *"In everything I did, I showed you that by this kind of hard work we must help the weak, remembering the words the Lord Jesus himself said: 'It is more blessed to give than to receive.'"*
>
> ACTS 20:35

As we approach the holiday season, the "gimmes" are in full swing at our house. With the onset of autumn, my daughters start marking the catalogs, making their Christmas lists, and dropping subtle "Buy me this!" hints. Maybe you encounter the same thing at your house.

I often worry about spoiling my girls. After all, we buy them a lot and so do their grandparents on both sides. There have been some Christmas mornings when they fell asleep before they could even open all of their gifts. That's why I was so blessed to see that their hearts are as big as their wish lists.

Not long ago, Abby and Allyson heard that a local ministry needed nice, gently used toys. Both girls sprang into action. By the end of the day, they had gathered seven bags worth of stuffed animals, board games, dress-up clothes, Barbie dolls, and more! As Abby was brushing a Barbie's hair, I asked, "Are you keeping her?"

She said, "No, I just wanted to make sure she looked nice when we dropped her off."

Now that's the right attitude! While my daughters love receiving, they also love giving. We should all give with such enthusiasm.

MOM TO MASTER
Lord, help me to be a cheerful giver. Amen.

*"So when you give to the needy,
do not announce it with trumpets."*
MATTHEW 6:2

There we were—Abby, Allyson, and I—hiding out inside our SUV, just waiting for the right moment. We were on a stakeout. Our mission? To deliver several Christmas presents without the receiver of the gifts ever finding out who delivered them.

"Now!" Abby said. "She's leaving. We can put them in her office."

As we watched her car pull out of the school parking lot, the three of us quickly grabbed the wrapped gifts and headed inside the school. Like the wind, we breezed into this single mom's office, left the gifts, and exited without anyone knowing we'd ever been there. The card simply read, "Merry Christmas! Love, Jesus." That was such an exciting time for us—getting to surprise this precious woman with gifts for her and her daughter. We had the best time choosing each gift, wrapping each one with pretty paper and bows, and sneaking inside her office to deliver them.

That Christmas, the girls and I learned that it truly is better to give than to receive. The girls will never forget that experience, and neither will I. We should constantly look for opportunities to give unto others.

MOM TO MASTER
*Lord, help me to take advantage of every opportunity
to give unto others. Amen.*

LIVING TO GIVE

OCTOBER 4

*Concentrate on doing your best for God,
work you won't be ashamed of.*

2 TIMOTHY 2:15 MSG

When it comes to being a mom, do you give it your all every day? Do you always do your best? Do you look for the easy way out, or do you go the extra mile? If you're like me, it just depends on the day. But according to this Scripture in 2 Timothy, we're supposed to concentrate on doing our best day in and day out. It doesn't say that we should just do our best when we feel like it or when the mood strikes us.

You see, serving God isn't about feelings—it's about faith. It's about stepping out in faith and doing your best on a daily basis. You don't have to feel like you can do it. You don't even have to feel good about it. You just have to put forth your best effort.

Ask the Lord to help you do your best on His behalf. He can help you do your best in every area of life—housework, raising kids, buying groceries, teaching Sunday school, volunteering for the PTA, etc. He expects your best because, after all, God gave His best for us. He gave His only Son to die on the cross for our sins. Give God your best today!

MOM TO MASTER
Lord, help me to always do my best for You. Amen.

LIVING TO GIVE

"You shall not give false testimony against your neighbor."
EXODUS 20:16

It's a good thing to live to give—as long as you're not giving false testimony against your neighbor. I realize that "neighbors" here doesn't necessarily mean those who live in close proximity, but it certainly includes those folks, too.

We've encountered a few neighborhood children who have chosen to give false testimony against Abby and Allyson, and those false testimonies were not very nice. In fact, they were downright cruel and, of course, not true. Maybe you've experienced the same situation in your neck of the woods.

As moms, it's tough to just stand by and let someone say hurtful untruths about our kids. I was so upset with those little boys who were making up stories. I wanted to call their mother and give her a piece of my mind. But the Holy Spirit instructed me to give something else—love. Ugh! That was the last thing I wanted to do. But, I was obedient.

You see, the Lord gave me something special as we walked through that ordeal. He gave me peace. He gave me love. And He gave me the ability to comfort Abby and Allyson. Life really is about giving—good or bad. Let's make a decision to give only good things today.

MOM TO MASTER
Lord, help me to give only good things.
Help me to be more like You. Amen.

OCTOBER 6

Have you ever heard the expression "Let go and let God"? It's easier said than done. We sing songs in church about giving our all to God, such as "All to Jesus, I surrender," when all the while, we're holding something back. I'm guilty, too. So many times I have gone before God and asked Him to take over every part of my life, and then later the Holy Spirit will point out an area of my heart that I didn't give to God.

It's silly, isn't it? I don't know why we'd ever want to hold out on God. He doesn't want us to give our all so that He can make us miserable. He wants us to give our all so that He can bless us beyond our wildest dreams. God isn't some big ogre in the sky, just waiting for us to give our all to Him so that He can control us like puppets. He simply wants us to give our all so that we can walk in the plan that He has for us. So, if you're struggling with giving your all today, ask God to help you. Go ahead—let go and let God. He will give you much more in return.

MOM TO MASTER
*Lord, I give my all to You today.
Help me to leave my life in Your hands. Amen.*

LIVING TO GIVE

*"Now I am giving him to the LORD,
and he will belong to the LORD his whole life."*
1 SAMUEL 1:28 NLT

Have you truly given your children to God? Sure, we all
say those words when our babies go through the dedication service at church, but how many of us truly mean
them? It's so easy to take back our kids. We trust God
with everything in our lives, but when it comes to our
children, *we* want to take care of them. We love them so
much that we are afraid to give them to God. What if
He calls them into the mission field in some unstable or
war-torn country? What if He asks them to move
across the country to begin a church? What if *His* plans
for your child conflict with *your* dreams for your baby?

It's scary, isn't it? But it shouldn't be. As moms, we
have to realize that God loves our children even more
than we do. If He calls them into a war-torn country
to serve Him, then that will be the place that holds
happiness and peace for them. After all, being in the
center of God's will is the safest place a person can be.
So, don't worry. Giving your kids to God is the best
thing you can do for them.

MOM TO MASTER
Lord, I give my children to You today. Amen.

> *"Whoever wants to be first among you must be your slave."*
>
> MATTHEW 20:27 MSG

Abby and Allyson both made Honor Choir this year. This, in itself, is a modern-day miracle because no one else on either side of the family can carry a tune. It's fun to hear the girls warm up. They go through this whole *"Mi. Mi. Mi. Mi. Mi."* routine. Well, that's okay if you're warming up your vocal chords, but if you're living with the *"Me. Me. Me. Me. Me."* mentality, that's no good. If it's all about you, then it can't be all about Him.

Have you given yourself to God—totally and completely? I find that I have to do that daily. If I don't, I get way off track. I follow the path that benefits my wants, my desires, my needs, and I neglect to check with God on major decisions. (Not to mention, I become a real self-centered jerk. It's not pretty.) Ever been there?

If you're singing the "Me. Me. Me. Me. Me." chorus today, don't worry. We all sing that tune from time to time. Just ask God to put a new song in your heart—He will. As soon as you get your eyes back on Him, you can move forward in your Christian walk. God has a good plan for your life—don't mess it up singing the wrong song.

MOM TO MASTER
Lord, I give myself to You today and every day. Amen.

LIVING TO GIVE

" 'These people honor me with their lips,
but their hearts are far away.' "
MATTHEW 15:8 NLT

Do you give a good witness for Jesus? Do you have a "Honk if you love Jesus" bumper sticker on your mini-van, yet you cut people off in traffic every chance you get? Do you wear "WWJD" jewelry, but you verbally attacked your kids in Wal-Mart, totally humiliating them? Does your T-shirt say "Radically saved and proud of it!" yet you just acted ugly to the store clerk because she wouldn't honor one of your coupons? Of course, we aren't going to be perfect. There are going to be days when we completely miss it, but our "miss it" days should be far fewer than our "get it right" days.

You don't have to be wearing "witness wear" in order to be a witness. Whether you are aware of it or not, you are constantly witnessing to those around you—especially your children. They are like little sponges, soaking up everything that you do and say. So, do and say things in accordance with the Bible. Let God's light shine big in you. Let your mouth speak good things. Let your actions mirror the Father's actions. Walk the talk—no matter what. Ask God to help you.

MOM TO MASTER
Lord, help me to be a good witness for You.
I love You. Amen.

LIVING TO GIVE

So now the L{ORD} says,
"Stop right where you are!
Look for the old, godly way,
and walk in it. Travel its path,
and you will find rest for your souls."

JEREMIAH 6:16 NLT

Do you ever have days when you just want to scream, "Give me a break!"

The laundry is piled high. The dishes are spilling out of the sink. There's a stack of newspapers in the kitchen that you haven't had time to read. Your toddler decided to express his creative side by coloring your dining room walls. And the puppy just shredded a roll of toilet paper throughout your house. Ahhh! Yes, on days like this we all want to scream, "Give me a break!"

While I can't whisk you away to a spa (although I think that's a great idea!), I can tell you how to get a break. And, no, it doesn't involve dropping off your children at the in-laws. Steal a few minutes today and retreat to the Word of God. If you're looking at that dusty old Bible sitting on your coffee table and wondering how an old book can give you rest, you've been missing out!

The Bible isn't just some ancient history book. It's alive! Just by reading it, you'll feel more energized and hopeful. You'll regain that vitality of life you had before having your children. God will restore you. Go ahead. Spend some time in His Word and find rest!

LIVING TO GIVE

MOM TO MASTER
Lord, help me to find time for Your Word. Amen.

"Give praise to the LORD your God!"
1 CHRONICLES 29:20 NLT

Have you ever worked with the preschoolers in your church? They are by far my most favorite group of people. Preschool children have no baggage or inhibitions. They are full of life and love and laughter. (I want to be like them when I grow up!) And, they absolutely love to praise the Lord! They'll lift up their hands. They'll shout to the Lord. They'll do all of the hand motions to match the words of the songs. They'll spin around and jump and dance before the Lord. They are professional praisers and worshippers! When it comes to making a joyful noise before the Lord, these kids have got it going on!

I can just see the Father smiling as He looks upon their pure and precious praise and worship. We should take lessons from preschoolers in this department. We should never be embarrassed or ashamed to worship our Father. And we shouldn't have to wait until Sunday morning to praise Him. Make praising the Lord a part of your daily life. Ask your children to join with you. Make it a family affair! Pretty soon, you'll be as proficient at giving God praise as the little ones.

MOM TO MASTER
*Lord, help me to praise You with the same
enthusiasm and vigor as little children. Amen.*

> *"Bring the whole tithe into the storehouse,*
> *that there may be food in my house. Test me in this,"*
> *says the Lord Almighty, "and see if I will not throw*
> *open the floodgates of heaven and pour out so much*
> *blessing that you will not have room enough for it."*
>
> MALACHI 3:10

Are you teaching your children to tithe? This has been an interesting aspect of learning at our house. When the girls were old enough to take on a few household chores, Jeff and I told them if they completed their tasks without a lot of griping, we would give them three dollars a week allowance. That three dollars seemed like a lot of money to a six-year-old and a seven-year-old.

Abby and Allyson could hardly wait until "pay day." Ally wanted to head straight for Wal-Mart's toy section. Her money burned a hole in her pocket. (Unfortunately, I think she inherited that "shopping gene" from me!) Abby, however, wanted to save her money. She immediately placed those dollars in her piggy bank.

On the way to church one Sunday, Jeff explained to the girls that ten percent of their money belonged to God. We helped them do the math, and both girls prepared their offering. Surprisingly, when the offering plate came around, they both put in way more than the required amount. And they were quite joyful about their giving! It seems they taught us more than we taught them.

LIVING TO GIVE

MOM TO MASTER
Lord, help me to be a cheerful giver. Amen.

" 'The LORD turn his face toward you
and give you peace.' "
NUMBERS 6:26

Have you ever asked the Lord to give you peace? I don't think that's one of those things we typically ask for as moms. But peace is available to us.

I'm not talking about that kind of temporal peace that a nice, long, hot bath brings. (Although, I'm not opposed to that, either!) I'm talking about the kind of peace that only the Father can give—the kind of peace that is present even in the midst of chaos. The Bible says it's a peace that surpasses all understanding. In other words, it's a kind of peace that people don't understand. It's hard to put into words.

I once interviewed a man and wife who understood this kind of peace. After having a premature baby who required three major surgeries during her first year of life, they got pregnant again. And again, the baby came early. This time the little baby only lived five and a half months. I asked them how they made it through that time, and they both said, "We had a supernatural peace." That's the kind of peace that I want to walk in every day—how about you? Let's ask God for it today.

MOM TO MASTER
Lord, please give me Your supernatural peace today,
and help me to walk in that peace every day. Amen.

LIVING TO GIVE

He gives strength to the weary
and increases the power of the weak.
ISAIAH 40:29

Do you ever feel like Mikey? You know, Mikey from the Life cereal commercials? I can still hear the older brother saying, "Give it to Mikey," as he pushed a bowl of Life in his little brother's direction. Sometimes, I know just how Mikey feels, only in my case it's "Let's give it to Missy (my nickname)." I think I've been on every school committee you can be on— from Room Mom to Talent Show Director to Carnival Co-Coordinator—I've done it all.

My mother gets very agitated with me for agreeing to do all of these things. She'll ask, "Why don't you just say no?" It's a good question. I don't know why I don't say no. I guess I'm afraid of hurting someone's feelings, so instead I say yes and become very overwhelmed, overworked, and weary. Ever been there?

Well, I've got good news for you. Even if you can't say no like me, you don't have to feel weary anymore. God says in Isaiah 40:29 that He will give strength to the weary and power to the weak. I don't know about you, but I qualify! The next time you're feeling overworked and overwhelmed, just call on the Name of the Lord. Ask Him to give you strength. He will do it every time!

MOM TO MASTER
Lord, please send down some
strength and power today. Amen.

LIVING TO GIVE

"A new command I give you:
Love one another.
As I have loved you,
so you must love one another."
JOHN 13:34

"C'mon, give me a little grin," Jeff and I would say in that goofy, new-parent voice.

We would say that to baby Abby over and over again just to see her cute little smile. Yes, we were annoying, but we were totally captivated by our firstborn. She was so amazing! If she yawned, we smiled. If she smiled, we laughed. If she made a mess in her pants, we called for Ma-maw. We gave Abby our undivided attention. We adored her!

After baby Allyson arrived, we gave Abby a little less attention because we had two little girls to amaze us. Just when we thought we couldn't love another human being as much as we loved Abby, we discovered that we could. We loved Ally with all of our hearts. God gave us more love to give our children. He literally increased our ability and capacity to love. I bet you experienced the same thing when you had your children.

It's like the song says, "Love is a funny thing." It is much more than an emotion—it's a state of being. And we should always be in love with the Father so that we can show His kind of love to our kids. Love your kids big today!

MOM TO MASTER
Lord, help me to give Your kind of love
to my children. Amen.

LIVING TO GIVE

> *"For I know the plans I have for you,"*
> *declares the LORD, "plans to prosper you*
> *and not to harm you,*
> *plans to give you hope and a future."*
>
> JEREMIAH 29:11

LIVING TO GIVE

Let's face it—life can throw you a curve once in awhile. When Abby was just two, she went through a "biting phase." Just when we thought we had it whipped, she sunk her teeth into the nursery director's son at church one morning. I was called out of the service to retrieve my troublesome kid—and I felt like the worst mother ever! It's not like Hallmark makes a card that says "Sorry my daughter bit your son on the arm." All I could do was smile, say I was sorry, and continue to discipline Abby for biting.

Eventually, Abby's biting phase passed, but the nursery director never seemed to care much for Abby or me after that one incident. I was elated when the woman relinquished her nursery director position the following year. Finally, Abby could return to the nursery, and I could attend services with the rest of the adults.

Isn't that life? You just can't plan for everything. But remember—while *you* can't plan for everything, God can. He has a plan for your life, so don't sweat the small stuff.

MOM TO MASTER
Lord, help me not to sweat the small stuff. Amen.

For everyone born of God overcomes the world.
This is the victory that has overcome the world,
even our faith.

1 JOHN 5:4

Are you feeling discouraged today? Are you about ready to throw in the towel? Have you given motherhood all that you've got, and you still don't feel like you're winning the race? We've all been there. And when I start feeling like that, I used to grab a Diet Coke and a chocolate bar and comfort myself. I'd dwell in the land of "Poor Pitiful Pearl" for awhile before I'd ever go to God. Somehow, feeding my face with chocolate made me feel better. (It cost me more miles on the treadmill, though.) But now I've learned that feeding my faith works much better to pull me out of discouragement than feeding my face!

The Bible says that faith comes by hearing the Word of God. As you hear the Word and store it in your heart, your faith grows stronger. So, listen to the Bible on tape while you do your housework or while you're on the treadmill. Then, the next time the enemy tries to make you feel worthless, discouraged, depressed, worried, or overwhelmed, you can put your faith to work by declaring the Word of God. Feed your faith, not your face. You'll feel much better!

MOM TO MASTER

Lord, I am feeling discouraged today. Please fill me up
with more of You. Amen.

*I will refuse to look at
anything vile and vulgar.*

PSALM 101:3 NLT

Have you ever heard a preacher say, "Give the devil no place in your life!" I always thought that was kind of an odd statement, because I would never *give* the devil a place in my life. But as it turns out, I was giving the devil a place in my life simply by allowing him in my thought life.

Did you know that what you think determines the direction and quality of your life? That's why the Bible tells us to think on things that are pure and lovely in Philippians 4:8. But in order to think on those things, we need to monitor what we allow into our hearts. That means we need to be careful about what we watch, read, and listen to. We need to fill our thoughts with the promises of God—promises of joy, peace, freedom, prosperity, and more!

We also need to monitor what we give our children to watch, read, and listen to. While spending the night at a friend's house, Abby recently saw a movie that she shouldn't have seen. Then she suffered with nightmares for weeks! Don't let fear and other negative material get into your children's hearts and minds. Be that filter for them. As a family, think on lovely things and give the devil no place in your home.

LIVING TO GIVE

MOM TO MASTER
*Lord, help me to feed on Your Word
and only think on lovely things. Amen.*

For wherever there is
jealousy and selfish ambition,
there you will find
disorder and every kind of evil.
JAMES 3:16 NLT

"Give it to me!" Abby shouted.

"NO, it's my CD player!" Allyson rebutted.

"You are such a loser!"

"No, *you* are the loser!"

Ahh. . .the sounds of loving sisters. Yes, my girls love each other, but there are days when I have to see that love by faith. Do your children fight? Are there days when you're sure they'll never be friends? Well, take heart. There is hope.

God put your family together, and He knew what He was doing. So, even though it may seem like the strife is there to stay, it's not. God is the answer. He can turn your kids into the best of friends in no time at all. Declare that your house is a household of faith. Declare that no weapon formed against your family will prosper. Declare that as for you and your house, you will serve the Lord.

Don't let strife take root in your home because you don't want to open up your household to every kind of evil as James 3:16 says. Instead, build your house on love. When your kids fight, nip it in the bud immediately. Pray for peace, and watch your family transform. You can have heaven on earth in your home. Start today!

LIVING TO GIVE

MOM TO MASTER
Lord, please help me to keep the strife
out of my household. I love You. Amen.

> *"See, I am doing a new thing!*
> *Now it springs up; do you not perceive it?"*
>
> ISAIAH 43:19

Are you an espresso junkie? C'mon, you can tell me. You know how you feel after a shot of espresso? It's like, *ZING!* Talk about a pick-me-up! Well, I have something even better. How about giving yourself a shot of victory today?

Okay, here's your victory shot: "God is doing a new thing in your life right now!" Doesn't that do something for your heart? Isaiah 43:19 doesn't say that God is going to do a new thing in a year or two. It doesn't say that He is doing a new thing next month. It says He is doing a new thing now! So, if you're in a faith rut, or if your kids are driving you crazy, or if you're fighting a weight problem, or if you're depressed—cheer up! God is doing a new thing for you. Isn't that good news?

God has a good plan for your life. He is working things out and lining things up for your life right now. He hasn't forgotten you. He wants you to develop a vision of victory so you can move forward and walk in the fullness of what He has for you. It's going to be so good—even better than espresso!

MOM TO MASTER
Lord, thank You for doing a new thing in my life
today. Amen.

LIVING TO GIVE

"There's hope for your children."
GOD's Decree.

Jeremiah 31:17 msg

Are your children away from God right now? Are they in a state of rebellion? If they are, I know that you're heartbroken. And even if you're not in this situation, I bet you know someone who is. It's tough. When we've raised our children to know the things of God and they still rebel, we immediately start blaming ourselves. We wonder where we went wrong. We wonder what we could have done differently. Well, stop wondering and start praising the Lord!

You may not feel like praising the Lord right now, but that's exactly what you must do. You see, the Word says that your children will return to the Lord. The Word says there is hope for your children. The Word says that if you have the faith of a mustard seed, you can move mountains. So, hey, bringing your children back to God is no biggie! God can do that in the twinkling of an eye!

But, you must praise God for the victory even before it takes place. He has commanded that we live in victory, so that means no matter how bad it looks right now, you can be encouraged. We already know how it ends—we win! We walk in victory, side by side with our children. Praise the Lord today! Your victory is on its way!

LIVING TO GIVE

MOM TO MASTER
Lord, I praise You for my children's salvation. Amen.

Gently encourage the stragglers,
and reach out for the exhausted,
pulling them to their feet.
Be patient with each person,
attentive to individual needs.

1 THESSALONIANS 5:14 MSG

When I was a college cheerleader, we did the whole, "Give me a *G!* Give me an *O!*" You get the idea. Yes, that was "a few" years ago, and my cheerleading uniform is faded and in storage, but that encouraging spirit still remains. I'm still the resident cheerleader of our house. That's what moms do, right? Don't you feel like a cheerleader most of the time?

Our children (and our spouses, too!) need our encouragement. They need to hear us say, "You can do it!" They need to hear us say, "You have got it going on!" They need our support and unconditional love on a daily basis. Of course, we cheerleaders need encouragement, too. In order to have encouragement to dish out, we have to fill ourselves up again. We do that by praising the Lord, praying to God, reading His Word, and taking care of ourselves by getting enough rest. Don't let yourself get empty and run-down or you'll be the grouchiest cheerleader in the history of the sport! Now, go forth and "Give me a GO! GO! GO!"

MOM TO MASTER

Lord, help me to be a constant source of
encouragement to my family. I praise You
for my children's salvation. Amen.

LIVING TO GIVE

*Let the Word of Christ—the Message—
have the run of the house.
Give it plenty of room in your lives.*
COLOSSIANS 3:16 MSG

Have you given the Word a prominent place in your life? This verse in Colossians says that we're supposed to give the Word plenty of room. That used to bother me. I'd think, "Doesn't God know how busy I am? How can He expect me to spend a lot of time in the Word and get all of this stuff done, too?" But you know what I've discovered? If I make time for God, He makes time for me. In other words, if I spend time with the Father—no matter how busy I am—He makes sure that I accomplish all that is on my plate. He supernaturally increases my time.

I once heard a well-known minister say that she had decided to read the gospels through five times in just a short amount of time. But it looked impossible! She had two little children. She and her husband had just moved into a new place, and there were boxes to unpack and closets to organize. In the natural, it seemed like an impossible goal. But do you know what? She not only met her goal but also was able to unpack every box, care for her children, and refinish a piece of furniture! Make time for God today. He will make time for you.

MOM TO MASTER
Lord, help me to make more time for You. Amen.

LIVING TO GIVE

OCTOBER 24

But those who wait for the Lord
[who expect, look for, and hope in Him]
shall change and renew their strength.

ISAIAH 40:31 AMP

Do you expect God's best for your life? Do you expect God's best for your children's lives? As moms, we sometimes put our dreams and desires on the back burner, and we forget to expect God for good things in our lives. Well, I am here to reawaken those dreams and desires today. I want you to grab a sheet of notebook paper and a pen and jot down your dreams. I want you to jot down the dreams you have for your children. Now, I want you to thank God in advance for bringing those things to be in your life. Believe God big time!

Don't let your lack of expectations set the limits for your life. If you never expect anything good, you're never going to receive anything good. If you don't expect things to change for the better, then nothing will ever get better. Start expecting to overcome every challenge in your life. Live every day filled with anticipation of what God is going to do in your life and your children's lives. He wants to bless you abundantly above all you can ask or think. So start expecting today!

MOM TO MASTER
Lord, I am relying on You for big things.
I praise You for working on my behalf today! Amen.

LIVING TO GIVE

Don't use foul or abusive language.

Ephesians 4:29 nlt

Do your children look for the best in people? Or, are you raising "Chris and Christina Critical"? Kids are brutally honest. Sometimes they are critical without even meaning to be.

Once when we were leaving a shopping mall in Indiana, we saw one of the largest men I've ever seen. He looked like one of those people you see on talk shows—the ones who are so large they can't leave their house. Anyway, it was hard not to stare at him. I was cringing inside, just knowing that my toddler, Abby, would say something. She was such a curious child. Well, sure enough, Abby said, "Mommy, look how BIG that man is!" (At least she didn't say fat!)

Being the diplomat, I said, "Yes, this is a BIG mall." I hoped the man hadn't heard her critical comment, but I'll never be sure.

As my kids have grown older, I've been amazed at how accepting they are of people. Sure, they have their faults, but making fun of others isn't one of them. In fact, they are usually pulling for the underdog in every situation. I'm thankful for that. If your children are critical, believe God that His love will fill them up and negate that critical spirit. Soon, they'll be "Polly and Peter Positive."

Living to Give

Mom to Master
Lord, help me to raise positive children—
kids who look for the best in everyone. Amen.

"Get wisdom, get understanding;
do not forget my words
or swerve from them."

PROVERBS 4:5

Could you use some more wisdom today? Me, too. This is especially true when it comes to parenting. You could ask ten people the best way to potty train a child, and you'd hear ten different theories. No matter what the topic, you'll find "experts" who hold opposing views, and each one will have data and research to back up the findings. One year, breast-feeding is better for babies. The next year, bottle-fed babies tend to be more well adjusted. Ahhh! It's all so confusing. We want to get it right, but it seems so hard to navigate the right path.

I'm so thankful that I can go to God for my answers. He is the ultimate expert. He doesn't have to consult with anyone to give you an answer—He *is* the answer!

No matter what you need today, you can go to God and seek His counsel. He wants you to! Proverbs 4:5 says to "Get wisdom! Get understanding!" He wants us to hunger and thirst after Him. He wants us to seek Him. He wants to share His wisdom with us. So, go ahead, take your questions and concerns to the Father. He's ready, willing, and able to answer.

MOM TO MASTER

Lord, I am seeking Your wisdom today. Thank You
for freely giving me all that I need. Amen.

LIVING TO GIVE

He will not allow your foot to be moved;
He who keeps you will not slumber.

PSALM 121:3 NKJV

I think the world needs more rocking chairs. We were at Cracker Barrel not long ago and had to wait for a table. So, we all went outside and plopped down in our own rocking chairs. I hadn't sat in a rocking chair since my girls were babies.

With each swaying movement, I was taken back to a precious memory of holding baby Abby and baby Ally in my arms. Now that they are older, they don't sit on my lap very often. They are far "too cool" for that. Sometimes, I long for those rocking chair days. Rocking chairs force you to slow down and enjoy the moment. It's almost impossible to be stressed out while rocking. Sitting in a rocking chair is like cozying up to a close, old friend. There's something very comforting and comfortable about spending time in a rocking chair.

You know, even if you don't have a rocking chair at your house, you can spend some quality rocking time in God's rocker. When I pray to the Father, I always picture Him sitting in a big, wooden rocking chair and beckoning me to sit on His lap. If you need to de-stress today, crawl into your heavenly Father's lap and rock awhile.

MOM TO MASTER

Lord, I need to spend some quality time just rocking with You today. Thanks for loving me. Amen.

*"I will dwell in them
And walk among them.
I will be their God,
And they shall be My people."*

2 CORINTHIANS 6:16 NKJV

Are your kids independent? As my girls approach middle school, they become more and more independent. I used to help them pick out their outfits, but now they want to choose their own clothes. I used to fix their hair each morning, but now they want to do it themselves. And they rarely want me to pack their lunches anymore. They are growing into very independent little girls.

My mom used to always say, "You're as independent as a hog on ice." I never really got that expression, but the visual was pretty funny! Well, now my girls are little piggies on ice, and I'm not too happy about it. I sometimes feel as if they no longer need me. Have you ever experienced those same feelings?

I bet that's how God feels whenever we try to do everything on our own without asking for His help or His intervention. You see, being independent isn't always a good thing. We should rely on God all the time. We should have our faith so far out there that we can't make it even one step without God. If you've become "a hog on ice" in the spiritual sense, come back to God. Ask for His help. He's happy to oblige.

MOM TO MASTER

Lord, help me to always depend on You. Amen.

LIVING TO GIVE

But the fruit of the Spirit is
love, joy, peace, patience,
kindness, goodness, faithfulness,
gentleness and self-control.
GALATIANS 5:22–23

Today I was in line at the grocery store, and I only had two items in the "20 items or less" lane. The man in front of me had the maximum amount of items, and he very kindly asked if I'd like to go ahead of him. That really made my day.

Wouldn't it be nice if all people in life were that kind, always thinking of others' needs above their own? Wouldn't it be nice if we could teach our children to be that kind? Well, we can! As Christians, we can have all of the fruit of the Spirit operating in our lives. We can claim that promise for ourselves and our children.

Put Galatians 5:22–23 in action today. Why not offer to carry someone's groceries? Why not send a card of appreciation to your pastors? Maybe you could bake some cookies for your neighbors. Or, perhaps you could offer to call on a few shut-ins in your community. Ask your kids to help you, and you can work on growing more fruit of the Spirit together.

LIVING TO GIVE

MOM TO MASTER
Lord, change my heart so that I might show kindness
to my family, my friends, and to strangers. Thank You
for always showing kindness to me. Amen.

OCTOBER 30

Doesn't it feel good to give? As moms, we're programmed to give. We give up our figures to carry babies in our bellies. We give up yoga classes for Baby and Me sessions. We give up golf for playgroup time. We give up sleep for nightly feedings. We give up a lot! But we also get so much in return.

In one of my favorite movies called *The Thrill of It All* starring Doris Day and James Garner, there's a great line describing motherhood. James Garner plays Dr. Boyer, an adorable obstetrician, and one of his patients says to him, "I don't know when I've been so happy. I guess there's nothing more fulfilling in life than having a baby."

I suppose that's true, although there are days when you haven't had a shower or any sleep that you might question that statement! Being a mother is a great honor and an awesome undertaking. It requires a great deal of giving—giving love, giving praise, giving encouragement, giving spankings, giving wisdom—giving it all! But we don't have to go it alone. On the days when we have nothing left to give, God does. He will supply all of our needs. He will give to us so that we can give to our families.

LIVING TO GIVE

MOM TO MASTER
Lord, help me to never grow weary of giving. Amen.

So we say with confidence,
"The Lord is my helper;
I will not be afraid."
HEBREWS 13:6

What's on your agenda today? Are you facing some big challenges? No matter what you're going to be up against today, God's got you covered. He says in Hebrews that He will be our helper. We don't have to be afraid.

I don't know about you, but I sometimes feel afraid. Sure, I put on a good outward appearance, but on the inside I feel insecure. I wonder if I'm doing a good enough job as a mom. Do you ever wonder if you're measuring up? I especially feel that way when I am around moms who are doing everything right. You know, the really cool mom who has a clean house, all of her laundry folded and put away, no dirty dishes in the sink *ever*, well-mannered children, and a perfect figure, too! I want to be a mom like that someday.

But until then, I am declaring that "I will not be afraid." God did not give us a spirit of fear, but of love and of power and of sound mind. We are up to any challenge. We can do all things through Him. We can be confident in Him today and every day.

MOM TO MASTER
Thank You, Lord, for helping me every single day
of the year. I couldn't do it without You.
I love You, God. Amen.

LIVING TO GIVE

NOVEMBER 1

> *"Then if my people who are called by my name will humble themselves and pray and seek my face and turn from their wicked ways, I will hear from heaven and will forgive their sins and heal their land."*
>
> 2 CHRONICLES 7:14 NLT

When terrorists attacked on September 11, 2001—it rocked the very foundation of America. I'll bet you remember exactly where you were when you first heard that the World Trade Center had been hit. For days, Americans were glued to CNN. And for days, we hugged our children a little tighter and prayed a little harder.

People all over the world hit their knees, seeking God's face, asking for wisdom, and praying for protection. Prayer became a priority from sea to shining sea. I know our family prayed longer and harder during those days following 9-11.

Now, several years since that fateful day in September 2001, the ribbons have come off the antennas on our vehicles and the patriotic clothing trend has died down, but the prayers are still going up on a regular basis. People have embraced this Bible verse and turned their faces toward heaven and prayed for this precious country. As Veteran's Day approaches, let's also pray for the men and women who have given their lives so that we might enjoy freedom. God bless America!

PRAYING MORE

MOM TO MASTER

Thank You, Lord, for America. Please direct and guide our leaders, and protect those men and women who protect us. Amen.

Our Father which art in heaven,
Hallowed be thy name. Thy kingdom come.
Thy will be done in earth, as it is in heaven.
Give us this day our daily bread.
And forgive us our debts, as we forgive our debtors.
And lead us not into temptation,
but deliver us from evil: For thine is the kingdom,
and the power, and the glory, for ever. Amen.

MATTHEW 6:9–13 KJV

Do you remember learning the Lord's Prayer when you were just a little girl? I remember sitting in a Sunday school classroom when I was only seven years old, reciting the words to the Lord's Prayer so that I could earn a Tootsie Roll pop. (Candy was a good motivator!) I am so thankful to that dear woman who gave up her time to teach our first-grade Sunday school class. It was the first time that anyone had really taught me to pray.

Once I learned the words to the Lord's Prayer, I was so excited! Sure, I was thrilled to earn the candy, but that wasn't the only reason I was excited. Just knowing that I could pray a prayer that Jesus once prayed seemed very cool to my seven-year-old mind. It still seems very cool to me more than twenty-five years later. If you haven't taught your children the words to the Lord's Prayer, why not begin today?

MOM TO MASTER
Thank You for the Lord's Prayer. Amen.

> *"Your Father knows exactly what you need*
> *even before you ask him!"*
>
> MATTHEW 6:8 NLT

Have you ever been so distraught that you didn't even know what to pray? I think we've all been there at some point in our lives. After my father had his first stroke and they didn't know if he would live through the night, I became numb. It was touch and go for several days, and all I did was drive to and from the hospital. On those forty-minute drives, I would try to pray, but all I could do was say the name of Jesus. Thankfully, that was enough.

In Matthew 6:8, the Word tells us that God knows what we need even before we ask Him. That's good to know, isn't it? Even when we can't pray what we want to pray, God knows our hearts. He knows what we need. If we simply call on the name of Jesus, He is right there beside us.

No matter how desperate you are today. No matter how hopeless you feel. No matter how far from God you think you are. . .God loves you. He wants to help you. He wants to help your children. He wants to bring you through this difficult time. Call on Him today.

MOM TO MASTER
Thank You, Lord, for knowing me so well
and hearing my heart. Amen.

Be joyful always; pray continually;
give thanks in all circumstances,
for this is God's will for you in Christ Jesus.
1 THESSALONIANS 5:16–18

There is a lot of good advice packed into the above Scripture. Think about it. If we're joyful always, pray continually, and give thanks in all circumstances, we're going to enjoy life no matter what!

One of the happiest people I've ever known was a man named Ivan Hunter. He taught children's church at the church that I attended as a little girl. Ivan loved to sing about Jesus. He loved to talk about the goodness of God. Even as a little girl, I sensed how deeply he loved the Lord. It wasn't until I became a grown woman that I learned that Ivan's life had been filled with much heartache. He and his wife had lost a child. He'd been in a serious accident and lost several fingers. And, he had battled cancer for years. Still, if you asked Ivan how he was doing, he'd praise the Lord and share how wonderful Jesus had been to him. He truly gave thanks in all circumstances.

I want to be more like Ivan. I want my children to be more like Ivan, too. Let's go into this Thanksgiving season with true gratefulness in our hearts. Let's look for opportunities to praise the Lord—like Ivan always did.

MOM TO MASTER
Lord, help me to have constant joy, pray continually,
and give thanks to You no matter what. Amen.

PRAYING MORE

NOVEMBER 5

Very early in the morning,
while it was still dark,
Jesus got up, left the house and
went off to a solitary place,
where he prayed.
MARK 1:35

Are you a list maker? If I don't have a to-do list for the day, I feel lost. It's sort of my map for each twenty-four-hour period. Of course, I rarely accomplish all of the things on my daily list, so I carry over the remaining items to the next day, thus beginning my new to-do list. It's an obsession, really. Maybe you can relate.

You know the problem with making lists? If I don't write it on my list, I don't do it. So, I've started adding "pray daily" to my list. Then, as I am checking off the things I've already accomplished such as "do two loads of laundry; work out; pick up dry cleaning; etc.," I see my "pray daily" entry. It's a great reminder.

You can pray all the time—continually—as it says in 1 Thessalonians, but you can also set a designated time for really intense, focused prayer. Mark 1:35 tells us that Jesus chose to do His praying in the very early morning, while it was still dark. Well, I'm not really a morning kind of gal, so I pray in the afternoon. Do whatever works for you, but just do it. Make prayer a priority in your life today.

MOM TO MASTER
Lord, help me to make time for prayer. Amen.

And he said: "I tell you the truth,
unless you change and become like little children,
you will never enter the kingdom of heaven."
MATTHEW 18:3

When Allyson was a preschooler, she loved to pray over our meals. She couldn't wait until that part of the day. I'd always ask, "Who wants to pray over our food?" Allyson would beam and shout, "ME! ME! ME!" And then she'd begin, "God bless Mommy, Daddy, Sister, Max (our dog), Ma-maw, Papaw, Nana, Granddad, Aunt Martie, Uncle Jan, Mandy, Autumn. . ." By the time Allyson finished her prayer, the food was totally cold. Still, there was something very sweet about her prayers. They were full of thanksgiving, humility, and genuineness.

I've learned a lot about prayer from my children. Both Abby and Allyson taught me to pray with enthusiasm, thanksgiving, and expectation. When Abby was only five, she prayed for her goldfish to live, and let me tell you, Bubbles was on his last fin. He was sort of swimming sideways in the bowl. He was fixing to go to the big fish bowl in the sky. But, Abby prayed and that little fish lived another two months. It was a miracle! She never had a doubt.

As moms, we need to have that same thankful heart and expectation when we pray to our heavenly Father. Learn from your little ones. They truly know how to pray.

PRAYING MORE

MOM TO MASTER
Lord, help me to pray like the little children. Amen.

Pray continually.
1 THESSALONIANS 5:16

I once read that Billy Graham said he prays without ceasing. In other words, he is in constant communication with God. He has a dialogue going with the Lord all day. I figured if Billy Graham thought that was a good idea, I'd do the same. After all, he is Billy Graham—one of the greatest men of God of all time!

So, I have endeavored to continually dialogue with God ever since that revelation. At first, it seemed a bit awkward. I struggled with it, wondering what to say. But after awhile, it became kind of second nature. I'd start praying without even realizing it.

Not long ago, we had one of those Texas "toadstranglers" come upon us on our way to gymnastics. I could hardly see to drive. The rain was intense. The sky was dark. And I was nervous. After a few moments, Abby asked, "Who are you talking to?" Her question made me realize that I'd been praying to the Lord, asking Him to make the rain subside, without even realizing I was praying. It had become my first instinct. Yay! I am making progress. I'm certainly no Billy Graham, but I am enjoying this continual conversation with God. If you haven't tried talking to God throughout your day, go for it! Talk to Him about everything. It's a wonderful way to live.

MOM TO MASTER
Lord, help me to pray all the time. Amen.

PRAYING MORE

"Again, I tell you that if two of you
on earth agree about anything you ask for,
it will be done for you by my Father in heaven."
MATTHEW 18:19

Did you know that you don't have to call a prayer line to get an answer to prayer? Growing up, my mother was on our "church hotline" phone list. Every other night, she'd get an urgent call from another lady on the prayer chain. Together, they'd go over an updated list of prayer concerns from people in our congregation. Sometimes, my mother would be on the phone for over an hour. Wow! That's a lot of prayer needs, isn't it?

From that experience, I grew up thinking that if I had a really urgent prayer request, I would need to call the local body of prayers or perhaps call a prayer line listed at the bottom of a Christian program I was watching. Somehow I thought they had a better chance of getting an answer than I did. Silly, isn't it?

According to this verse in Matthew, if *any* two agree on something and ask the Father, it will be done. Well, I've got good news—we qualify as any! So, the next time you have an urgent prayer request, grab your kids and ask them to agree with you as you lift up your request to heaven. Your family's prayers availeth much!

PRAYING MORE

MOM TO MASTER
Lord, help my family to establish
our own prayer hotline. Amen.

My help comes from the LORD,
the Maker of heaven and earth.
He will not let your foot slip—
he who watches over you will not slumber.

PSALM 121:2–3

Texas has terrible storms. Last summer, we had a really scary storm. The sky was dark and a tornado warning was in effect for much of the area. Normally, I don't panic when it storms, but Abby wasn't at home. She was with a friend at an amusement park. I tried calling her over and over again, but I couldn't reach her. By 9 P.M., I was hysterical. By 11 P.M., I was ready to drive through the torrential rain and search the entire Dallas/Fort Worth Metroplex for my little girl. I wanted to call several of my "prayer partners" from church, but it was too late to disturb them. It was so comforting to know that God wasn't asleep. He was waiting up with me. He heard every word that I prayed.

As it turns out, the phone service was out in much of the area, which is why Abby couldn't call me and I couldn't call her. She had been safe at her friend's house for hours. God answered my prayers. He will answer your prayers, too, no matter what time of day you pray. He is on call all the time!

MOM TO MASTER
Thank You, Lord, for always
listening to my prayers. Amen.

DRAWING MORE

*Devote yourselves to prayer
with an alert mind
and a thankful heart.*
COLOSSIANS 4:2 NLT

Do you ever fall asleep during your prayer sessions? Be honest. It's okay—I sometimes catch a few Zs during prayer time, too. I don't intentionally sleep, but I occasionally drift off into dreamland.

As moms (especially new moms), we get so few hours of sleep that once we're still for just a few moments, we tend to fall asleep. When my girls were both babies (and on different sleep schedules), I used to always fall asleep during my devotional time. But, I knew that God understood. He isn't some big ogre in the sky, just looking for a reason to bop us on the head. He knew I needed the rest, and He wasn't mad at me. If you have trouble staying awake during your prayer time, God isn't mad at you, either.

Ask God to help you be alert during your prayer periods, just like it says in Colossians 4:2. He will help you. And even if you still fall asleep, God will be waiting when you wake up. He's not offended. He's ready to talk to you whenever you're ready.

PRAYING MORE

MOM TO MASTER
Thank You, Lord, for understanding when I fall asleep during our conversations. Help me, God, to stay awake and be more alert when I pray. I love You. Amen.

Count yourself lucky,
how happy you must be—
you get a fresh start,
your slate's wiped clean.
PSALM 32:1 MSG

Whenever we play board games at our house, it turns out that my children hate to lose. Yes, they are poor sports. . .wonder where they get that? Okay, they inherited it from me—the biggest sore loser of them all. I am *way* too competitive for my own good! But, so are they. Here's how it usually goes down. If Jeff or I get too far ahead, the girls want to start over. They want to wipe the slate clean and start a new game. Typically, we won't start over because we want to instill good qualities in our children, building their character even when we're just having fun playing games. But sometimes, we'll go ahead and start over. We show mercy, just like God.

Isn't it nice that with God we always get to start over? No matter what we've done. No matter how badly we've acted. No matter how disappointed we are in ourselves, God still loves us and forgives us. And the best part is that we get to start over! We get to wipe the slate clean! All we have to do is repent, and then we get to move forward with our heavenly Father. With God, we always win!

MOM TO MASTER
Lord, thank You for always wiping my slate clean.
I love You. Amen.

O God, let me sing a new song to you.
PSALM 144:9 MSG

Is your prayer life in a rut? Do you pray the same words over and over, day after day, month after month, and year after year? If so, you're in a prayer rut. And the only way out of a prayer rut is to sing a new song. Praise the Lord with a new song, as it says in Psalm 144. Don't just ask God to bless everyone from your husband to your pet fish, Bubbles. Instead, spend some time just worshipping the Lord. Tell Him you love Him because He gave you wonderful children. Tell Him you adore Him for putting a roof over your head. Praise Him for the food He gives each day. Most of all, praise Him because He died on a cross so that you might live.

God is a good God. He is worthy of our praise. If you have trouble thinking of things to praise Him for during your prayer time, use the Bible to help. Quote Scriptures such as, "You are worthy of my praise for Your mercy and goodness endure forever." Praise Him from the bottom of your heart, and put that prayer rut behind you once and for all.

MOM TO MASTER
Lord, thank You for all of the blessings in my life,
but most of all, thank You for just being You. Amen.

What is faith?
It is the confident assurance that
what we hope for is going to happen.
HEBREWS 11:1 NLT

Prayer works. It doesn't just work once in awhile. It doesn't just work when you pray at a certain time of day. It doesn't just work when a minister prays for you. Prayer works all the time. There's only one requirement—have faith. If you're praying without any faith, then you might as well forget it. You have to believe in the Lord's ability to answer your prayers. You have to know that He is willing and able to meet your needs—no matter what they are. You have to know that He is all-powerful, all-knowing, and altogether merciful.

When Abby and Allyson were very little, I desperately wanted to work from home, but I couldn't see any way financially that we could make it without my source of income. We were living from paycheck to paycheck at the time. But God knew. I cried out to Him, and I told Him that I knew He was able to supply all of our needs. It wasn't long before several freelance writing opportunities fell into my lap, and I was able to quit my full-time job and see my children more. God heard and answered my prayers. He will do the same for you, if you'll only have faith.

MOM TO MASTER
Lord, help me to pray faith-filled prayers. Amen.

PRAYING MORE

Do not be anxious about anything,
but in everything, by prayer and petition,
with thanksgiving, present your requests to God.

PHILIPPIANS 4:6

I have a friend who prays for her children's future spouses every day. And her children are only four and six! I hadn't ever considered doing that, but the more I thought about it, the more it made sense to me. So, I've begun praying for my girls' future husbands on a regular basis. I pray that they are being raised in Christian homes, learning about the things of God, and growing up to be godly men. Of course, I wouldn't ever tell my daughters I am doing this because they would totally freak out. It's God's and my little secret. But someday when they get ready to walk down the aisle with the men of their dreams, I'll be able to share my secret prayers with them.

My friend who opened my eyes to praying for my children's future spouses has taught me many things about prayer. She prays about absolutely everything. She prays about things that I wouldn't think to bring before God. But she is seeing great results. She has challenged me to pray more—even about little things—and I'm excited to see God's manifestation in my girls' lives. I challenge you to pray more, too. Don't think it's too insignificant to bring before God. He wants to hear it all!

PRAYING MORE

MOM TO MASTER
Thank You, Lord, for caring about
every detail of my life. Amen.

> *Now when Daniel learned that the decree*
> *had been published, he went home to his*
> *upstairs room where the windows*
> *opened toward Jerusalem.*
> *Three times a day he got down*
> *on his knees and prayed,*
> *giving thanks to his God,*
> *just as he had done before.*
>
> DANIEL 6:10

Are you too busy to pray? Do you run 100 mph all day long? I am so there with you, sister! That's why we need to take a lesson from Daniel. Daniel was a wise man. He learned that in order to hear from God, he needed to slow down. As you can read here in the sixth chapter of Daniel, he stopped and dropped to his knees three times a day to pray to God. He knew that he needed to hear from God before continuing on. He knew that God was more than worth his time.

We should realize that same truth, too. No matter how busy we become with our motherly duties, we need to take time to pray. We need to seek His face on a regular basis. If we don't, we'll just be spinning our wheels. So, don't neglect your prayer time. Give time to God, and He will give time back to you. He isn't working against you, He is working *for* you. And together, the two of you can't lose!

MOM TO MASTER

Lord, help me to slow down
in order to hear from You. Amen.

PRAYING MORE

*Then Jesus told his disciples a parable
to show them that they should
always pray and not give up.*
LUKE 18:1

Are you waiting for God to answer a very important prayer request? Are you getting weary in praying about this matter? Do you ever feel like God has forgotten you and your request? Well, He hasn't. And He won't. He tells us in Luke 18 that we should always pray and not give up. So, keep praying! Don't give up! Your answer, your ultimate victory, may be right around the corner.

I once interviewed a woman who had always longed to meet her birth father. He left when she was just an infant, and she'd never been able to track him down. She had cried out to God many times to help her in her search. Then, finally, after more than forty years, everything fell into place, and she was reunited with her father. It was a glorious reunion. Immediately, they established the relationship that had been lost due to unfortunate circumstances. God brought them back together, and they are definitely making up for lost time.

This woman shared with me that she never gave up. Every year, she'd say, "This will be the year I'll find Daddy." What if she had quit believing that after only thirty-nine years? So, don't give up. Don't quit. Keep praying because God is still listening and working on your behalf.

PRAYING MORE

MOM TO MASTER
Lord, help me never to give up. Amen.

If we don't know how or what to pray,
it doesn't matter. He does our praying
in and for us, making prayer out of
our wordless sighs, our aching groans.

ROMANS 8:26 MSG

I once read this beautiful statement: "God hears more than words. He listens to the heart," and I've always remembered it. I love that thought. That means even if I can't communicate with words, God knows my heart. He hears my heart cries.

When my best friend had a stillborn baby a few years back, I couldn't get to her that night. I felt a million miles from her, and I wanted to be with her. I cried out to God, but I couldn't figure out what to pray. I was so heartbroken for her and her family. I couldn't believe that the baby we had been preparing for all of those months had already gone to heaven. I couldn't find the words, but the Holy Spirit prayed through me. After a few minutes of praying, I felt a sort of release. The heaviness left me, and I knew my friend was going to be okay. I knew her baby was sitting on the Father's lap and that someday we'd be able to hold that precious baby. If you're hurting today and having trouble knowing what to pray, just cry out to God. He understands.

MOM TO MASTER

Thank You, Lord, for hearing my heart. Amen.

"If you stand your ground,
knocking and waking all the neighbors,
he'll finally get up and
get you whatever you need."
LUKE 11:8 MSG

I really don't like having to ask for favors from my friends, because I never want to inconvenience them in any way. I don't want them to see my phone number on caller ID and think, "Oh, it's Michelle. I'd better not get that. She may want something." But sometimes we have to ask for help. Not long ago, I was stuck in Dallas traffic, and I knew I wouldn't be able to get to the school by 3 P.M. to pick up my girls. I was in a mess. I finally broke down and called my friend Karen. She usually lets her daughter ride the bus home, but after my call of desperation, she said she'd be happy to swing over to the school and pick up our girls. Whew!

As I was thanking her profusely, she said, "Michelle, it's no problem. I know you'd do the same for me." And that was it. She didn't feel put out or inconvenienced at all! I was so glad I had called her. She was a lifesaver that day.

Isn't it good to know that our prayers never inconvenience God? We can call on Him for help any time of day, for any reason at all. Let Him be your lifesaver today!

MOM TO MASTER
Thank You, Lord, for always being there for me. Amen.

*"That's why I urge you to pray
for absolutely everything,
ranging from small to large.
Include everything as you embrace this
God-life, and you'll get God's everything."*

MARK 11:24 MSG

Do you pray specifically or do you pray big, broad, general prayers? If you're praying general prayers, you're missing out. God wants us to pray specifically about small and large matters. He wants us to bring everything to Him, but not all at once. Think of it this way. It'd be like going into a department store and saying to your husband, "Buy me something pretty." You may be longing for a pretty ring, but he buys you a pretty scarf. You didn't get what you wanted because you didn't ask specifically for a pretty ring. It's the same way with God.

Instead of just praying for world peace, why not pray for peace in your home? Instead of only praying for the economy to turn around, why not pray for your family to become debt-free? Instead of praying for your children to be happy, why not pray for your children to walk in the plans that God has for them?

You have to give God something to work with. Be specific. Find Scriptures to stand on. Confess those daily. Praise God for the expected answers to your prayers and get ready for your miracles!

MOM TO MASTER

Thank You, Lord, for being concerned about the big and small things in my life. Amen.

PRAYING MORE

Then they brought him a demon-possessed man
who was blind and mute,
and Jesus healed him,
so that he could both talk and see.

MATTHEW 12:22

When people came to Jesus for healing, He didn't say, "Well, I'll be sure to put that on my prayer list." No, he acted then and there. Sometimes, He laid hands on them. Other times, He simply spoke words of healing to them. And one time He even spit in the dirt and made a mudlike substance and put it on a blind man's eyes.

You see, sometimes prayer is the best we can offer. But other times, we need to pray and *act*. When a missionary comes to your church in need of financial support, it's good to pray that his needs are met, but it's also good to drop a little money into the offering plate for him. Praying and acting will bless him more than just praying for him. In other words, don't use prayer as an excuse not to take action when you know that you should do something.

Follow the Holy Spirit's leading and act on His Word. Notice the Bible says, "Do unto others. . ." Doing means acting. Praying for someone is always a good thing, but don't stop there. Go that extra mile and be a part of the solution.

PRAYING MORE

MOM TO MASTER
Lord, help me to be compassionate enough to pray and act. Amen.

> *When you ask, you do not receive,*
> *because you ask with wrong motives.*
>
> JAMES 4:3

Sometimes our prayers aren't answered because it's not in God's timing. Other times, our prayers aren't answered because we haven't prayed in faith. Still other times, our prayers aren't answered because we're praying with the wrong motivation.

I have been guilty of this. A few years ago, I had been praying every day that my children's books would become New York Times bestsellers. That's every author's dream! I had confessed it in faith, and I just knew it was going to happen. Then one Sunday during praise and worship, the Holy Spirit asked me a question, "What's your motivation for publication?" No, I didn't hear a loud, booming voice. I simply heard that small, inner voice asking me over and over again, "What's your motivation for publication?" I had to repent. I knew my motivation had been wrong. Instead of praying that my children's books touch kids' hearts around the world, I'd been praying for New York Times bestsellers. I was ashamed.

It's easy to fall into the wrong thinking, which leads to the wrong kind of praying. So, if you're not seeing any answers to your prayers, check your motivation. That may be holding up your miracle.

PRAYING MORE

MOM TO MASTER

Lord, help me to always pray with a pure heart. Amen.

It is good to praise the LORD and
make music to your name, O Most High,
to proclaim your love in the morning
and your faithfulness at night.
PSALM 92:1–2

If you're like me, mornings always come too early. I am a night owl. I love the midnight hour when everyone in the house is asleep. At that time, it's just me, God, and my little dachshunds. The wee hours of the morning (which I consider late, late night) are perfectly wonderful for talking with God.

Whether you're a wee-hours-of-the-morning kind of gal or a first-thing-in-the-morning person, use that time to praise the Lord. Psalm 92 tells us that it's good to proclaim God's love in the morning. Spend those first few minutes of each day praising the Lord. If you can't think clearly enough to thank God for specific things He has done for you, simply read various psalms out loud. Tell God, "I praise You today because Your mercy endures forever and ever!" Sing a song of praise, such as, "I love You, Lord, and I lift my voice to worship You, Oh my soul rejoice. Take joy my King in what You hear. May it be a sweet, sweet sound in Your ear." Give God praise in the morning, and you'll have a much better day.

MOM TO MASTER
Lord, I praise You for who You are today!
I love You! Amen.

Is any one of you in trouble?
He should pray.
JAMES 5:13

When I learned that Allyson would have to have her tonsils out, I was less than thrilled—especially after I read through all of the bad things that could happen. It was quite scary. The more I thought about it, the more I worried. I asked my parents to pray that the surgery would go okay. I asked my friends to keep Ally in prayer. I put Ally on our church's prayer line. In fact, I did all of those things before I actually hit my own knees on behalf of my daughter. Isn't that pathetic?

Is prayer your first instinct? James 5:13 tells us that if we're in trouble, we should pray. It doesn't say to call your best friend and have her pray. It doesn't even say to call your pastor and have him pray. It says for *you* to pray. It's okay if we have others supporting us in prayer as long as we also pray.

If our children see us turning to prayer as our first line of defense, they'll do the same. They will hit their knees in prayer at the first sign of trouble. If we can teach them to do that, they'll forever be all right.

MOM TO MASTER
Lord, help my first instinct to be prayer. Amen.

PRAYING MORE

"When I fed them, they were satisfied;
when they were satisfied, they became proud;
then they forgot me."
Hosea 13:6

When you were pregnant, didn't you pray for that little baby growing inside of you every single day? When my first pregnancy became high-risk due to preterm labor, I prayed almost nonstop. But, guess what happened when Abby was born perfectly healthy and I had survived the ordeal? I quit praying so often. The scary crisis was over, so my prayers became fewer and far between. I was guilty of the common "run to God in bad times but ignore Him when things are good" syndrome.

Have you ever been guilty of that syndrome? We all have. Even the Israelites, God's chosen people, were guilty of this syndrome. They cried out to God when they needed freedom from Pharaoh, but after they were safe and sound and out of Pharaoh's reach, they started worshipping other gods. They built idols. They ignored the very One who had freed them in the first place.

Any way you look at it, that's lame. And here's something else to chew on—we need God in bad and good times. Even if we don't feel like we need God in the good times, we do. Keep in touch with Him all the time. It's the only way to live.

PRAYING MORE

Mom to Master
Lord, thank You for being there for me
in the good times and the bad times. Amen.

In him and through faith in him
we may approach God with
freedom and confidence.

EPHESIANS 3:12

Do you know what really gets on my very last nerve? Those automated telephone systems. Lately, Abby has been having a little trouble with her eyesight, indicating she's probably ready for a new eyeglass prescription. Since we're on a new insurance plan, I wasn't sure if eyeglasses were covered, so I called our insurance provider to ask a few questions. Of course, a recording answered and listed nine options, and the nightmare began. For twenty-five minutes, I was lost in a maze of numbers.

"Press 1 to talk to an insurance expert. Press 2 to talk to claims. Press 3 if you're a pharmacist." I was on the phone so long that my ear grew hot! Finally, I was transferred to my intended destination only to discover that the office was closed. I proceeded to yell into the phone, "It wasn't closed twenty-five minutes ago when I first called you!"

I'm so thankful that God doesn't have an automated answering system. Can you imagine if He did? "Press 1 to praise. Press 2 to submit a prayer request. Press 3 to repent. Press 4 for wisdom. Press 0 if this is a real emergency." Hallelujah, our heavenly Father is available 24-7! Call on Him today!

MOM TO MASTER

Lord, I am thankful that I can come into the throne
room at any time. I appreciate You. Amen.

Do not be anxious about anything,
but in everything, by prayer and petition,
with thanksgiving, present your requests to God.
And the peace of God, which transcends
all understanding, will guard your hearts
and your minds in Christ Jesus.

PHILIPPIANS 4:6–7

When you go into the throne room and enter the inner sanctum of God, do you crawl in on your belly, bawling and bellyaching, or do you walk in and kneel before the Father with thanksgiving in your heart? If you're like me, it would depend on the day. But, we should never crawl in and whine our way to Jesus. Philippians 4 tells us that we are to present our requests with thanksgiving.

I have a friend named Tracy who is a nurse, but she isn't just your typical nurse. She prays over all of her patients. Of course, she always asks permission first, but not one has refused her yet. She doesn't pray prayers of desperation or hopelessness. She prays with faith and thanksgiving, and her patients have a tremendous rate of recovery.

What kind of prayers are you praying? What kind of prayers are you teaching your children to pray? Begin praising the Lord for the victories that are on the way. Don't beg God to answer your prayers, present Him with Scripture to back up your requests. Like Tracy, pray faith-filled prayers, and you'll begin to see results!

MOM TO MASTER
Lord, I praise You that my answers are on the way. Amen.

NOVEMBER 27

And my God will meet all your needs
according to his glorious riches in Christ Jesus.

PHILIPPIANS 4:19

"Mom, can I have five bucks?"

"Mom, can I go to the movies with Macy?"

"Mom, can I ride my bike?"

"Mom, can you help me with my pioneer report?"

Are there days when you'd like to change your name from Mom to any other name? Be honest. There are days when you grow weary of hearing, "Mom. . ." hollered at you, right? I think every mom feels that way once in awhile. When I reach that point, I always answer, "Mommy is off duty. Please leave a message and find the father figure of the household. His shift just began." My children, of course, ignore my sarcasm and continue bombarding me with requests. But that's okay—it's all part of a mother's calling, right?

That's one of the reasons I am so thankful for God. He *never* tires of our requests. We can call on Him all the time, and He never gets sick of it! In fact, He wants us to bring all of our concerns to Him. It says in Philippians 4:19 that God will answer *all* of our needs, but He won't answer *all* if we don't bring all of them to Him. So, go ahead. Call on God right now!

MOM TO MASTER
Thank You, Lord,
for never tiring of my questions. Amen.

PRAYING MORE

Yes, you will lie down
and your sleep will be sweet.

PROVERBS 3:24 NKJV

Not long ago I read the cutest saying. It went something like this: "When you can't sleep, don't count sheep. Talk to the Shepherd instead." Isn't that great? I typically don't have trouble sleeping, but once in awhile, I have encountered sleepless nights. This is especially true when there's unrest in the household. When my children are sick, or they are struggling in school, or they are hurting inside from losing a friend. At those times, it's easy to trade in restful nights for sleepless ones.

As moms, we want to make everything all right for our children. It's what we do. But as hard as we try, we can't fix everything. And worrying about the things we can't fix doesn't help, either. It just causes us to lose sleep and require wood putty to cover our dark circles!

So, the next time you're up worrying, stop worrying and start praying. Call on the Good Shepherd. He's always awake and ready to respond. Give it to God and then go to sleep. Follow the wisdom that's in a song that Bing Crosby sings in the classic movie *White Christmas:* "When you're worried and you can't sleep, just count your blessings instead of sheep, and you'll go to sleep counting your blessings."

PRAYING MORE

MOM TO MASTER
Heavenly Father, I thank You for sweet sleep
and answered prayers. Amen.

NOVEMBER 29

"But when you pray, go into your room,
close the door and pray to your Father,
who is unseen. Then your Father,
who sees what is done in secret,
will reward you."

MATTHEW 6:6

Have you ever heard the expression, "Kneeling keeps you in good standing with the Father?" We need to find time to pray every day. That may take some planning on your part—especially if you still have little ones running around your house. When Abby and Allyson were toddlers, I used to retreat to the bathroom just to have a few moments alone with God. I didn't have a prayer closet—it was more like a prayer bathtub. Still, it worked for me. I was able to steal some time away with the Father in the sanctuary of our pink, ceramic tub.

If you're having trouble finding quality time to spend with God, get a plan! You may not be able to read the Word and pray first thing in the morning. The best time for you may be when the kids are down for their afternoon nap (assuming they all nap at the same time!). Or, maybe you can spend some time with God after you put them to bed each night. Find a time that works for you and stick to it. The Father is waiting. . . .

MOM TO MASTER
Heavenly Father, help me to take advantage
of every moment we can spend alone. I love You. Amen.

But Jesus Himself would often slip away
to the wilderness and pray.

<small>LUKE 5:16 NASB</small>

"Retreat and replenish." Remember that phrase? It's helped me a lot over the past few years. Every time I feel I have nothing left to give, Jesus reminds me that it's time to retreat and replenish. By spending time on my knees and in His Word, I am refilled with God's love, power, strength, joy, and energy. I give God all of my worries, sickness, concerns, tiredness, and grouchiness, and He gives me all the good stuff. What a deal, eh? Even Jesus recognized the need to retreat and replenish. After He had healed many people and driven out demons, He needed to retreat and replenish, too.

If you're feeling worn out today, turn to God. Let Him reenergize you. Let Him refuel you with His love so that you'll have love to give your children. As moms, we have to refuel so that we are ready to minister to our families.

As moms, we set the tone for the home. If we're stressed out and drained, our homes will be full of stress and confusion. So, do yourself and your family a favor and retreat and replenish. God is ready to fill you up!

MOM TO MASTER
Lord, fill me up with Your love and strength and joy.
I love You. Amen.

DECEMBER 1

If you'll take a good, hard look at my pain,
If you'll quit neglecting me and
go into action for me
By giving me a son,
I'll give him completely, unreservedly to you.
I'll set him apart for a life of holy discipline.
1 SAMUEL 1:11 MSG

Though I've never personally struggled with infertility, I have a very dear friend who has. She was able to get pregnant and have a baby ten years ago, but she hasn't been able to conceive again. She and her husband originally wanted a household of children, but they are content to have what God has given them. They thank God for their little girl every day. Infertility has been a difficult road to walk, but they haven't walked it alone.

God has been with this loving couple every step of the way. Through the medical dilemmas, the expensive infertility treatments, the ongoing disappointment, and the ultimate decision to quit trying to have another child—God has been there.

Infertility is a very common problem. Last year alone, there were more than two million infertile couples across the United States. Let's pray today for those who are experiencing infertility. God is still a miracle-working God. We stand with them for their miracle!

MOM TO MASTER

Thank You, Lord, for giving me children.
I pray for those who are still trying to conceive
or adopt. Please give them peace and patience
as they wait for their miracle. Amen.

Hannah did not go. She said to her husband,
"After the boy is weaned, I will take him and present
him before the LORD, and he will live there always."
1 SAMUEL 1:22

I love the story of Hannah. She so badly wanted to have children. She saw that her husband's other wife, Peninnah, was able to have many children, yet Hannah could not conceive. Can't you just imagine how painful it was for Hannah to see Peninnah pregnant over and over again? As if that wasn't hurtful enough, Peninnah taunted Hannah for being childless. Hannah cried out to God, and He heard her prayers, causing her to conceive.

Hannah had a son and named him Samuel. He was the answer to her earnest prayers. But now she had to give Samuel back to God because she had promised God that she would. Can you imagine how hard that would have been to do? But, she did. She gave Samuel to God, as she'd promised, to be raised in the synagogue. Later, God gave Hannah three more sons and two daughters. He honored her because she honored Him.

Are you honoring God today? Have you given your children to God? After all, He gave them to you. Giving your kids to God is the best thing you could ever do for your children. Give them to God today and every day.

MOM TO MASTER
Thank You, Lord, for my children.
Help me never to take them for granted. Amen.

GIVING YOUR KIDS TO GOD

DECEMBER 3

Glory in his holy name;
let the hearts of those who
seek the LORD rejoice.

1 CHRONICLES 16:10

My daughters are in the tween stage—in between being kids and being teens. It's an exciting age, full of adventure and fun. But it's also a difficult age. Maybe you have children who are tweens, too. If you do, then you are in the "uncool" club with me. Suddenly, everything I suggest or say is totally uncool.

I don't know how it happened, but I have become the embarrassing mom who picks out nerdy clothes for her daughters and comes up with lame party games. Just when I thought I was totally hip, the rug has been pulled out from under me. Sure, my girls still need me, but not as much as they used to. There are days when I feel totally useless and sorry for myself.

When I'm having one of those blue days, I run to God. In His presence, I feel complete and useful once again. He builds me up, giving me the joy and strength I need to move forward. He reminds me of His promises. He helps me to see a true picture of myself. He makes me feel loved again. So, if you're in a blue funk, go to God.

MOM TO MASTER
Thank You, God, for loving me
and building me up. Amen.

*If I give all I possess to the poor
and surrender my body to the flames,
but have not love, I gain nothing.*

1 CORINTHIANS 13:3

Have you read those wonderful children's books by Laura Numeroff? You know the ones—*If You Give a Moose a Muffin* and *If You Give a Pig a Pancake*. There's a lot of truth to those little books. Sometimes you give and give, and it never seems to be enough. If you're like me, you give until you get angry over your giving. Then, you give some more but in the wrong spirit. Ever been there?

Not long ago, we threw a Build-a-Bear party for Allyson's ninth birthday. We paid enough so that every child could get a $15 animal and one $5 outfit. One little girl who attended the party kept begging for more money. She *really* wanted the cheerleading out-fit for her $15 bear, but it was $15, too. She dropped hint after hint, and then she finally flat-out asked me for more money. I, of course, said no because it wouldn't have been fair to the other kids. Her un-grateful spirit really perturbed me.

It got me thinking, *I wonder if God ever feels that way toward us?* He gives and gives and gives, and then we say, "God, I *really* want the $15 cheerleading outfit for my bear. . .could You give some more?" No matter what, we should always keep a grateful heart. Greedi-ness is ugly, any way you look at it.

MOM TO MASTER
Thank You, God, for giving so much to me. Amen.

GIVING YOUR KIDS TO GOD

*"If you, then, though you are evil,
know how to give good gifts to your children,
how much more will your Father in heaven
give good gifts to those who ask him!"*

MATTHEW 7:11

Don't you love to give good gifts to your children? Moms are natural-born givers. We simply love to bless our kids. But, you know what I have discovered over the years? We can bless them in many more ways than simply giving them stuff that we buy. Some of the greatest gifts my parents gave me growing up didn't cost a thing, but I'll cherish them for a lifetime. For instance, my parents gave me an appreciation for Frank Sinatra music. I grew up singing along to "Fly Me to the Moon," "All of Me," and "New York, New York." My father taught me ballroom dancing to Mr. Sinatra's music. Today, I have an extensive collection of Frank Sinatra music and movies, and I'm educating my children in "Sinatra 101."

Giving me an appreciation for "Old Blue Eyes" is something I'll forever be thankful for, but of course, the greatest gift my parents gave me was a love for Jesus. I grew up in a Christian home, knowing who God is and what Jesus did for me. See, we don't have to have a lot of money to give good things to our children. If we teach them about Jesus, we've given them the greatest gift of all!

GIVING YOUR KIDS TO GOD

MOM TO MASTER

Lord, help me to teach my children about You so that they'll forever love You. Amen.

Those who know your name
will trust in you,
for you, LORD, have never forsaken
those who seek you.

PSALM 9:10

Do you trust God? Do you really trust Him? As Christians, we're supposed to trust God. It even says, "In God We Trust" on our money. Maybe you trust God in some areas of your life, but you have trouble trusting Him in other areas. That's where I am. I struggle a little bit when it comes to trusting Him with my children. I have to daily declare, "Lord, I trust You with my kids, and I thank You for taking such good care of them today."

It's not that I think I can do a better job than He can. That would be downright ridiculous. I just have trouble giving up control. You see, trusting means giving God your kids. It means giving God all of your worries and fears concerning your kids. And, it means giving God all of the dreams that you have for your children.

If you're having trouble trusting God with your children, get back in His Word. Read over all of the promises. Hold on to those promises. You can trust Him with everything—even your children.

MOM TO MASTER
Lord, I give my kids to You. I give You all of
my worries concerning my kids, and I give You
all of the dreams I have for my children. Amen.

GIVING YOUR KIDS TO GOD

DECEMBER 7

He who gives to the poor will lack nothing.

PROVERBS 28:27

It's almost Christmas. One step into the mall, and you'll know that it's Yuletide time. "Muzak" renditions of "Jingle Bells" and "White Christmas" play throughout the department stores, while shoppers hustle and bustle to finish their shopping. (In case you haven't finished buying for everyone on your list, this is for you: "Attention, Shoppers! Only eighteen days of Christmas shopping left!")

We are all in that gift-buying mode. It's fun! It's busy! It's tradition! And, it's not an activity that everyone can afford to do. The holidays aren't so happy for those who are needy. They aren't able to buy the latest toys for their children. They can't buy those designer sweatshirts and matching hair accessories for their little girls. They may not even have money to buy all the fixin's for a Christmas dinner.

If you know a family that fits this description, why not "adopt" that family this holiday season? Get your children involved in shopping for each adopted family member. Have your kids help you bake Christmas cookies for them. Make it a fun activity that your family can do together, bringing the true meaning of Christmas to the forefront of this holiday season. Give love this Christmas. It truly is the gift that keeps on giving.

GIVING YOUR KIDS TO GOD

MOM TO MASTER

Lord, help me to never lose sight of
the true meaning of Christmas. Amen.

*"For God so loved the world that
he gave his one and only Son,
that whoever believes in him shall not perish
but have eternal life."*

JOHN 3:16

Do you give God your best? Do you give Him your best praise? Do you give Him your best attention? Do you give Him your best effort? Do you give Him your best love?

If you don't, you're not alone. We all fail to give God the very best of ourselves. Instead of giving Him the best that we've got, we offer Him our leftovers.

Especially at this time of year, when giving is such an important part of the holiday season, we need to make sure we're giving God our best. We need for our children to see us giving God our best. Let them see you getting up thirty minutes early in the morning to spend time with God. Let them see you dropping more money into the offering plate. Let them see you praising the Lord at every given opportunity. Let them see you being kind to strangers. If they see you serving God wholeheartedly, they will want to do the same.

Give God your best today. After all, He gave us His very best when He sent Jesus more than two thousand years ago. He certainly deserves our best.

MOM TO MASTER

*Heavenly Father, help me to always give You
the best of me. Help me to put You first in
every situation. I love You. Amen.*

GIVING YOUR KIDS TO GOD

DECEMBER 9

*"So in everything,
do to others what you would
have them do to you."*

MATTHEW 7:12

Following September 11, 2001, my girls desperately wanted to do their part to heal America. They had heard on the radio that people could give blood at the American Red Cross in order to help, and both Abby and Allyson begged me to take them. I was touched by their enthusiasm, but I had to explain to them that they were too young to donate blood. Saddened that they couldn't help in that way, the girls came up with another plan. They set up a lemonade and cookie stand in front of our house. Ally held up the patriotic poster while Abby poured the pink lemonade. At the end of the day, they had collected a whole sock full of change that we could send to the American Red Cross.

Their enthusiasm to help really inspired me. I thought, *Wouldn't it be great if all of us lived every day like that. . .just looking for any way to help others?* It challenged me to think of others' needs before my own. I hope you'll be challenged to do the same. Let's not wait for another tragedy to bring out the best in us—let's start giving of ourselves today.

MOM TO MASTER

Lord, help me to live to give, and help me to teach my children to live to give, too. Amen.

"As for God, his way is perfect;
the word of the LORD is flawless.
He is a shield for all who take refuge in him."

2 SAMUEL 22:31

We do the best we can do as Christian moms. Like the Bible says, we train up our children in the ways of the Lord, and we pray for them on a regular basis. We take them to church. We offer words of wisdom whenever the opportunity arises. We try to set a good example for them. But in all of that doing, guess what? Our children will still make mistakes. They will still disappoint us. Why? Because they are only human. And though we like to think our little bundles of joy are perfect, they are far from it. They are no more perfect than we are. That's a scary thought, eh? There's only One who is perfect, and as long as we point our children toward Him, then we've done the very best that we can do.

And just as the Master forgives us when we stray, we need to do the same for our kids. We need to be merciful and loving like our heavenly Father. In fact, we need to emulate Jesus so that our kids will want to serve the Lord. So, do your best and let God do the rest!

MOM TO MASTER

Lord, help me to always point my children
toward You and Your Word. Amen.

GIVING YOUR KIDS TO GOD

DECEMBER 11

> *"It would be better for him if a millstone were hung around his neck, and he were thrown into the sea, than that he should offend one of these little ones."*
>
> LUKE 17:2 NKJV

How is your witness? Do you know that everywhere we go, we are witnessing? We are witnessing all the time—either glorifying God or portraying a poor reflection of Him. And, here's the kicker: Our children are taking it all in. They are like little sponges, absorbing everything we do and say, all the time. Wow! Have you ever thought about that reality? Our kids may be basing their view of Christianity on how we behave? Oh my!

I first realized that fact when Abby was just a toddler. She was a miniature parrot. She repeated absolutely everything I said—good or bad. Once I was on the phone with my mother, and I said that someone had acted like a horse's behind. Later that night when Allyson drooled on one of Abby's favorite dolls, Abby said, "You are a horse's behind!" While it was funny, it was sad, too. I knew exactly where she had heard the expression—from me!

So, like the song says, "Be careful little mouth what you say," and go forth and give a good witness. You have an attentive audience nearby.

MOM TO MASTER

Lord, help me to be a good reflection of you all the time. Help me to point my children toward you. Amen.

But Jesus said, "Let the little children come to Me,
and do not forbid them;
for of such is the kingdom of heaven."
MATTHEW 19:14 NKJV

Parents today are quite proactive. They have their un-
born babies on waiting lists for the top preschools in
the area. They have college funds established before
their children have ever spoken their first words. Parents today are really thinking and planning ahead.
That's a good thing; however, many parents are neglecting the most important part of their children's
lives—their salvation.

While it's wonderful to put so much thought into
the proper preschool for our little ones, it's much more
important to make sure we're attending a church that
will nurture and encourage our children's spiritual development. If you're in a church that doesn't have a
strong children's ministry, it may be time to seek God
for a new place of worship.

Ask the Lord to help you find the best church for
your children's sake. If you're attending a church that
simply entertains and baby-sits the kids, then start looking for another church. Let's face it, being a good dodge
ball player isn't going to help our children when they are
facing peer pressure. Let's be proactive about our children's spiritual lives. There's nothing more important.

MOM TO MASTER
Lord, please direct me to a church that will best minister
to my children. Amen.

GIVING YOUR KIDS TO GOD

> *"For the LORD does not see as man sees;*
> *for man looks at the outward appearance,*
> *but the LORD looks at the heart."*
>
> 1 SAMUEL 16:7 NKJV

How many times have you heard the phrase "heart of the matter" in your lifetime? Probably hundreds. But, have you ever considered its meaning when it comes to your spiritual life? If not, you should. It could totally change the way you pray and the results your prayers receive.

I used to pray for the Lord to make my daughters quit fussing all the time. I'd cry out, "God, they are driving me crazy! Please make them stop fighting and love one another." After months of praying this prayer, the Lord convicted me. In that still, small voice, He whispered, "Your heart is wrong. You're praying selfishly." I wanted God to cause my girls to stop fighting just so I could get a break—not for their benefit. My heart motivation was wrong, which caused my prayer to be useless.

Once the Lord pointed out the real "heart of the matter," I was able to pray more effectively and thus see results almost instantly. I had to get my heart right in order to get my prayers right. Maybe you need to do the same thing. If you're not seeing results in your prayer life, ask the Holy Spirit to do a heart check on you. Your motivation might be off!

MOM TO MASTER
Lord, help my heart to be pure before You. Amen.

As each one has received a gift,
minister it to one another.

1 Peter 4:10 NKJV

When I was a little girl, I used to love to go into our local five & dime store. Mom would give me a dollar, and I could shop forever. Today, the five & dime stores are pretty much a thing of the past, but we do have lots of dollar stores around. And I enjoy buying stuff in there, too. My children are especially amazed that the same stuff they find in other stores for three and four dollars costs only one dollar in the "Everything Is a Dollar!" store. In fact, they embarrass me sometimes by asking the clerk, "How much is this?" He just points to the large sign overhead that reads, "EVERYTHING is a dollar."

The girls are quickly learning the value of a dollar. Now that they earn an allowance, they realize how hard it is to make money and how easy it is to spend it. That's a valuable lesson. I want my girls to grow up and be wise shoppers. I take advantage of every opportunity to share shopping tricks with them.

As moms, we need to give our children little tidbits of truth every day. Maybe you can teach them how to shop more wisely. Maybe you can teach them to grow their own veggies. Give them your knowledge, and watch them grow. It's exciting!

Mom to Master
Lord, help me to recognize opportunities to teach. Amen.

Giving Your Kids to God

DECEMBER 15

We must pay more careful attention,
therefore, to what we have heard,
so that we do not drift away.

HEBREWS 2:1

When Allyson was born, Abby was already off the bottle. But guess what happened when Abby saw Allyson drinking juice from a bottle? That's right, Abby started crying for her "bah bah," too. "Where'd my bah bah go?" she'd ask, hands on her hips. If she didn't get the answer she wanted, she'd simply walk over, snatch Allyson's bottle, and be on her way.

It's a common occurrence for an older child to regress a bit when a new baby enters the picture. We certainly struggled with it, and maybe you did, too. You know, children aren't the only ones who struggle with this problem. As Christians, we sometimes go backward, too.

My father used to always say, "If you aren't moving closer to Jesus, then you're moving farther away because it's impossible to stay in the same place." He's right! If you get busy with the children and neglect your time with the Father, you won't stay the same; you'll drift away. Pretty soon, you'll be off the meat of the Word and back on the milk. Don't let that happen. Make time for God so that you will move forward with Him every day.

MOM TO MASTER
Lord, help me to move forward
with You every single day. Amen.

In the same way,
the Spirit helps us in our weakness.
ROMANS 8:26

When I was in eighth grade, I got my very first perm. Remember the '80s big hair? Oh yeah, I wanted that look. Well, the hairdresser rolled my hair on the really small rods, so you can imagine what happened. My hair came out looking like I'd stuck my finger into a light socket. It was so curly! As with all bad perms, it took many months to grow out. Once it finally grew out, I vowed never to get another one. Then, the summer of my freshman year in college, I let a friend talk me into getting another perm. We went together and both came out of the salon looking like pitiful poodles.

Why did I let myself get talked into something so stupid again? Call it perm peer pressure, but I let my buddy totally talk me into something that I knew wasn't good for me.

Guess what? Our children will fall for the same stuff if we don't give them a heads-up before it's too late. Today, it's not just perms—it's belly button piercings and tattoos. Before they grow up and want to pierce every body part, let's give them 101 reasons not to go there. And then, let's back it up with prayer.

GIVING YOUR KIDS TO GOD

MOM TO MASTER
Lord, help me to help my children be strong
in the face of peer pressure. Amen.

DECEMBER 17

*Jesus Christ is the same yesterday,
today, and forever.*

HEBREWS 13:8 NLT

Consistency. That's why athletes are so strong and perform so well—they train consistently. Unlike me, they don't run two miles one day and then skip four or five days until they can find time to work out again. It's a part of their daily schedule. Being consistent makes the difference between a casual jogger and an avid runner.

It's the same way in our parenting efforts. If we give unconditional love one day and yell and scream the next day, our kids become confused. If we enforce the rules in one situation and bend the rules the next time, we lose our kids' trust and confidence. If we say one thing and do another, we place doubts in our children's minds. We need consistency in every part of our lives.

Hebrews 13:8 tells us that Jesus Christ is the same yesterday, today, and forever, so He is the ultimate when it comes to consistency. Since we are commanded to be like Him, we have a right to ask God to help us in this area of consistency. The Holy Spirit will help you with this aspect of your parenting. It's not easy. It takes effort, but if you'll commit to being consistent in your parenting, your children will become consistently happier kids.

GIVING YOUR KIDS TO GOD

MOM TO MASTER
*Lord, please help me to be consistent as
I discipline and love my children. Amen.*

My son, pay attention to what I say;
listen closely to my words.
Do not let them out of your sight,
keep them within your heart.
PROVERBS 4:20–21

Have you ever been listening to the radio, and a song comes over the airwaves, and all of a sudden, you start singing every word, and you didn't even know that you'd ever heard that song before? Isn't that wild? That happened to me just the other day. A song called "Somebody's Watching Me" came on, and as soon as that first note came through the speakers, I remembered.

I've often thought I was a lot like Cliff on *Cheers*—full of tons of useless factoids and trivial information. Are you also a junior Cliff Claven? Well, don't feel too badly. That can actually be a good thing. If we can retain all of that useless information, that means we are also capable of retaining large amounts of the Word. We just have to program the Word into our system so that it's there when we need it.

If you're spending a great deal of time transporting your children to one practice after another, use that car time as Word time. Get yourself the Bible on CD, and start programming your mind with some useful information. C'mon, Cliff, you know you want to!

MOM TO MASTER
Lord, help me to retain the good stuff
and share it with others—especially my children. Amen.

GIVING YOUR KIDS TO GOD

That you do not become sluggish,
but imitate those who through faith
and patience inherit the promises.

HEBREWS 6:12 NKJV

Patience. Ugh! It's so hard to have patience, isn't it? As mothers, we are doers. Our motto is "Just do it!" We don't wait for somebody else to act on our behalf or take care of the situation. We just press forward and accomplish the task. But what happens when the situation is out of our hands? What happens when we can't solve the problem? That's where patience comes in.

Patience is power—did you know that? It gives us the strength to hold strong when our prayers aren't being answered immediately. Patience undergirds our faith until the miracle is manifested. Maybe you've been praying for your children to come back to God. Maybe you're standing in faith for your child's healing. Maybe you've been praying to conceive another child. Whatever it is, hold fast.

If you have been praying for something for quite some time, and the answer hasn't come, have patience. God hasn't forgotten you. He's heard your prayers. Stand your ground in faith, knowing that your answer is on its way in His perfect timing. Don't give up. Don't back down. Press on in patience.

MOM TO MASTER

Lord, help me to stand in patience until
the answer comes. I love You and trust You. Amen.

GIVING YOUR KIDS TO GOD

Do not throw away this confident trust in the Lord,
no matter what happens.
Remember the great reward it brings you!
Patient endurance is what you need now,
so you will continue to do God's will.
Then you will receive all that he has promised.

HEBREWS 10:35–36 NLT

Are you problem-centered or solution-centered? When you look at a glass that is half full of milk, do you see it as half empty or half full? In other words, are you a Polly Positive or a Nelly Negative? Well, if you're feeling more like Nelly than Polly today, let me encourage you with a few promises from the Word of God.

"You are strong, and the word of God lives in you, and you have overcome the evil one" (1 John 2:14).

"But thanks be to God! He gives us the victory through our Lord Jesus Christ" (1 Corinthians 15:57).

" 'What is impossible with men is possible with God' " (Luke 18:27).

You see, no matter what you're facing today, God has given you a promise to handle it. Don't dwell on the problem. Meditate on the Master. He has made you more than a conqueror and has already guaranteed your victory. So, don't fret. Rejoice! You have much to celebrate!

MOM TO MASTER

Father God, help me to become a more positive person.
Help me, Lord, to be Word-centered,
not problem-centered. Amen.

> *"I will prevent pests from devouring your crops,
> and the vines in your fields will not cast their fruit,"*
> *says the LORD Almighty.*
> *"Then all the nations will call you blessed,
> for yours will be a delightful land,"*
> *says the LORD Almighty.*
>
> MALACHI 3:11–12

Ch-ching! How is your bank account? Are your credit cards smoking from Christmas shopping? Are you in debt up to your eyeballs? If so, you're not alone. Almost one out of every hundred households will file for bankruptcy, and forty-three percent of all U.S. households will spend more money than they make this year. It's a sad fact, but it's a reality for many families.

Here's another reality for you: God is vitally interested in your finances. He wants to free you from debt and protect your finances, but you have to give Him that opening. The only way to open that door is through tithing. When you tithe, you give God the legal right to intervene in your financial situation. As it says in this passage in Malachi, God will prevent the pests from devouring your crops. In other words, when financial tragedy strikes, God will be there to rescue you. So, start giving today. Teach your kids to give ten percent to God, and secure their financial future, too!

GIVING YOUR KIDS TO GOD

MOM TO MASTER
*Heavenly Father, thank You for promising
to provide for me. I trust in You. Amen.*

*"Do not despise these small beginnings,
for the LORD rejoices to see the work begin."*
ZECHARIAH 4:10 NLT

I have discovered that I often don't give my children enough credit. Instead of expecting them to make the right choice or do the right thing, I often worry that they won't. Then, once in awhile, God will give me a glimpse of who they are in Christ Jesus, and I am truly humbled.

This happened just last week. Abby's good friend won a writing contest that Abby had hoped to win. Instead of acting ugly when her friend's name was announced, Abby jumped up from her seat and cheered for her buddy. There was no resentment or jealousy—just pure joy for her friend. I couldn't have been more proud of Abby even if she had won the contest. I am so glad that God gave me a glimpse of Abby's precious heart.

Sometimes, we get caught up in the parenting and forget how precious our kids are. We need to give them more credit because they are awesome creatures. Even when they are having "off days," we need to see them through our eyes of faith. Ask the Lord to help you see your children as He sees them. They are precious in His sight!

MOM TO MASTER
*Heavenly Father, thank You for my precious children.
Help me to always see them as You see them. Amen.*

GIVING YOUR KIDS TO GOD

DECEMBER 23

Because of that, we have even greater confidence
in the message proclaimed by the prophets.
Pay close attention to what they wrote,
for their words are like a light
shining in a dark place—
until the day Christ appears and
his brilliant light shines in your hearts.

2 PETER 1:19 NLT

When my girls were little, they would only sleep in their rooms if the nightlights were plugged in and shining brightly. If the lights wouldn't work, or if I forgot to plug them in, the girls were quick to point out the lack of light in their bedrooms. They would not stay in a room that was without light.

We are people of light. We like light. We're sort of like moths—if a light is on, we're drawn to it. That's a good thing. We should want to head for the light. Of course, Jesus is known as the Light of the World. And, Psalm 119:130 says that the entrance of God's Word into our hearts brings the insight we need. In other words, the Word sheds light on every situation we could ever have.

If you're struggling with something today, head for the light! God's Word will shed light on your situation and drive out the darkness of confusion. C'mon, step into the light today.

MOM TO MASTER
Heavenly Father, thank You for
the light of Your Word. Help me to turn
to Your Word in every situation. Amen.

*"You will be able to tell wonderful stories
to your children and grandchildren about
the marvelous things I am doing."*
EXODUS 10:2 NLT

It's all about family this time of year, isn't it? I'll bet your family has wonderful holiday traditions. Every Christmas Eve, we head to my parents' house and spend the night there. We play games and eat lots of fattening stuff, and we allow every person to open just one gift. (Okay, sometimes we talk my mom into letting us open two gifts on Christmas Eve, but usually she's a real stickler on the "one gift rule.")

It's my most favorite night of the year. It's not because of the board games or the yummy sweets or even the gifts. It's my favorite time of year because we're all together. After everything settles down and the kids are not so "sugared up," my father always reads the Christmas story. And even though we've heard it a thousand times, it's just as exciting every year. And, sometimes, we'll have a spontaneous testimony service where every person shares something he or she is most thankful for that year. It's very special.

Whatever your traditions, I hope you'll include Jesus as part of them. Don't let Santa and his reindeer take center stage. Give your children the true meaning of Christmas this year. Jesus is the reason for the season.

MOM TO MASTER
*Heavenly Father, thank You for sending Jesus
as a baby some two thousand years ago. Amen.*

GIVING YOUR KIDS TO GOD

DECEMBER 25

Then Peter came to Jesus and asked,
"Lord, how many times shall I forgive my brother
when he sins against me? Up to seven times?"
Jesus answered, "I tell you,
not seven times, but seventy-seven times."

MATTHEW 18:21–22

Christmas is the time of year when we give lots of presents. It's also a time when family members get together—maybe the only time of year when everyone is together. If you've been harboring unforgiveness against someone in your family—maybe a sibling or a cousin or a parent—give the gift of forgiveness this year.

Maybe you thought you'd forgiven that family member, but every time you think of that person, a little tinge of "ickiness" fills your heart. Get rid of those icky feelings today. Forgive that person.

You might say, "Michelle, that person isn't even sorry!" That's okay. That person doesn't have to be sorry in order for you to forgive. Ask God to help your heart to forgive and your head to forget so that you can start the next year free from any baggage.

Give the gift of forgiveness, and you'll receive gifts, too—freedom, love, joy, and more! It's time to forgive and forget. Let Jesus fill your heart today so that there's no room for any hurt. And, have a merry Christmas!

MOM TO MASTER
Lord, thank You for forgiving me.
Help me to forgive others. Amen.

"I am the vine; you are the branches.
If a man remains in me and I in him,
he will bear much fruit."
JOHN 15:5

The presents are all unwrapped. The Christmas programs are over. The carolers are hoarse. The children are already bored with their new toys, and you're pretty sure you put on five pounds in the last two weeks. I'm there with you, sister! I feel like singing a rendition of "The Party's Over." The excitement of Christmas shopping, wrapping presents, and baking cookies is over, but there are always the after-Christmas sales to hit! Oh, yeah!

Seriously, aren't you glad that Christmas is about so much more than presents, carols, cookies, and Santa? If it weren't, we'd be so let down on the day after Christmas. But we can celebrate Christmas all year long because Jesus lives inside of us! We can look forward to getting out of bed each day just to see what He has in store for us.

If you know someone who is depressed this time of year, why not share Jesus with that person? Get your children involved. Go witnessing as a family. Give the gift of Jesus—the gift who truly keeps on giving.

GIVING YOUR KIDS TO GOD

MOM TO MASTER
Lord, thank You for giving me a reason to celebrate
every day of the year. I love You. Amen.

*But the fruit of the Spirit is
love, joy, peace, patience, kindness, goodness,
faithfulness, gentleness and self-control.*
GALATIANS 5:22–23

Recently, I was at a local department store, and the cashier behind the counter was totally stressed. I thought she was going to throttle the woman in front of me. They had ugly words with one another, which didn't help this cashier's mood.

Oh great, I thought, *and I've got an exchange. She's going to love dealing with me.*

"Do you have your receipt?" she barked.

"No, it was a gift," I said perkily.

"You didn't get a gift receipt?" she snapped.

"Uh. . .no."

"Well, I'll have to give you the sale price then," she explained, which was practically nothing.

"Fine," I said. "I understand."

Then I proceeded to ask her about her holidays. I complimented her beautiful rings, and we had a pleasant conversation. She just needed someone to be nice to her. See, I had a choice to make. I could've become ugly over the sale price refund, but I chose to let Jesus shine through. (Now, I don't always make the right choice—trust me.) Every day, we have opportunities to share joy or share ugliness. Choose joy. Our joyful spirits will win others for Jesus. They'll want whatever it is we've got! So, go forth and be joyful today!

GIVING YOUR KIDS TO GOD

MOM TO MASTER
Lord, help me to share joy with others. Amen.

I will be glad and rejoice in you;
I will sing praise to your name,
O Most High.

PSALM 9:2

As the year draws to an end, you're probably reflecting on the past twelve months. It's a good time of year for reminiscing and reflecting, as long as those mind activities don't lead you down the paths of regret and guilt. Hey, we've all made mistakes this year. Yes, even Christian moms occasionally do things that displease the Lord. But, don't let those mistakes haunt your holidays. If you've repented for those misdeeds, God has already forgiven them and forgotten them. So, you need to do the same. God says in His Word that He has removed your sin as far as the east is from the west— and that's a long way!

Instead of feeling guilty or regretful over past mistakes, take this time to think on the good things that God did through you and in you and for you this year. Think on all of the miracles He performed on behalf of your family.

If you keep a journal, take a few minutes to read through it, and like the song says, "Look what the Lord has done!" Praise God for the victories—both big and small. Let Him know that you appreciate Him today. Give Him praise today! That's the way to close out one year and begin another—praising God!

MOM TO MASTER
Lord, I praise You for all that You've done
and all that You're going to do. Amen.

GIVING YOUR KIDS TO GOD

DECEMBER 29

I can do everything through him
who gives me strength.

PHILIPPIANS 4:13

Is there something you've been putting off? Have you been neglecting your time with God because you're too busy? Have you been putting off starting that diet and exercise program because you're afraid of failing again? Have you been putting off organizing your house because you just don't think it's possible to have closets that don't explode when you open them? Have you been putting off having a family devotional time, even though you know that your kids need it?

Whatever you've been putting off, it's time to get to it! And here's the best part—you don't have to do it alone. God is right there beside you, ready, willing, and more than able to help you. The task may seem big, but nothing is too big for God. Just call on His expertise. If it's willpower you need to stay on a healthy eating program, ask God to change your taste buds to crave only healthy food. If you need more time to accommodate a family devotional time, ask the Lord to help you better organize your day. He will help you. All you have to do is ask.

MOM TO MASTER

Lord, I need Your help today. Help me to accomplish
_____ that I've been putting off for too long. I
can't do it alone, but I know You will help me. Amen.

*"Submit to God and
be at peace with him."*
JOB 22:21

This time of year, you hear a lot of talk about peace. People send out holiday greeting cards that say "Peace to your family." All of the networks run season's greetings commercials proclaiming "Peace on earth." Peace is very popular during the holidays, but as Christians, we can enjoy peace throughout the year. And, as moms, we need peace in the worst way, because if we aren't peaceful, our homes won't be peaceful. We set the tone for our homes. We need to let peace rule our hearts, our homes, and our children.

If we let God in and give Him total control of our lives, we are guaranteed peace. He is the giver of true peace. God's kind of peace isn't a temporal thing. It isn't affected by the outside world. It's a peace that passes all understanding. When God takes control of your circumstances, your challenges, your situations, and your messes, He brings peace on the scene. Jesus wasn't just called "the Prince of Peace," He *is* the Prince of Peace. Turn to Him today. Give peace priority in your life.

GIVING YOUR KIDS TO GOD

MOM TO MASTER
*Thank You, God, for bringing peace to my heart
and my life. Help me to walk in that peace
every single day of the year. I love You. Amen.*

> *But the fruit of the Spirit is love,*
> *joy, peace, patience, kindness, goodness,*
> *faithfulness, gentleness and self-control.*
> GALATIANS 5:22–23

Did you get a fruit basket this year for Christmas? How about a fruitcake—did you get one of those? (If not, I'll send you one of the fruitcakes that I received—yuck! I am not a fan of fruitcake.) But, maybe you like fruitcake. Or maybe you enjoy giving fruit baskets to your friends and family members at Christmastime.

Let me tell you what's even better than giving a fruit basket or a fruitcake—giving the fruit of the Spirit. And we don't have to just give love, joy, peace, patience, kindness, goodness, faithfulness, gentleness, and self-control during the holidays—we can radiate those qualities year round!

Our children need to see us walking in these qualities. They need to feel that love, joy, peace, patience, kindness, goodness, faithfulness, gentleness, and self-control operating in our homes. Sure, we're going to miss it once in awhile, but as long as we're growing in those things, that's all that counts. God isn't keeping score on how many times we lose self-control; rather, He is celebrating with us as we grow in every fruit. So, go on. Radiate good fruit today, and if you must, send out a fruitcake or two!

GIVING YOUR KIDS TO GOD

MOM TO MASTER
Thank You, God, for the fruit of the Spirit.
Help me to grow in each fruit this coming year
so that I'll become more like You. Amen.

SCRIPTURE INDEX

Inspirational Library

Beautiful purse/pocket-size editions of Christian classics bound in flexible leatherette. These books make thoughtful gifts for everyone on your list, including yourself!

When I'm on My Knees   The highly popular collection of devotional thoughts on prayer, especially for women.
    Flexible Leatherette. $4.97

The Bible Promise Book   Over 1,000 promises from God's Word arranged by topic. What does God promise about matters like: Anger, Illness, Jealousy, Love, Money, Old Age, and Mercy? Find out in this book!
    Flexible Leatherette. $3.97

Daily Wisdom for Women   A daily devotional for women seeking biblical wisdom to apply to their lives. Scripture taken from the New American Standard Version of the Bible.
    Flexible Leatherette. $4.97

A Gentle Spirit   With an emphasis on personal spiritual development, this daily devotional for women draws from the best writings of Christian female authors.
    Flexible Leatherette. $4.97

Available wherever books are sold.
Or order from:

Barbour Publishing, Inc.
P.O. Box 719
Uhrichsville, OH 44683
www.barbourbooks.com

If you order by mail, add $2.00 to your order for shipping.
Prices are subject to change without notice.